When in Maui

By Colleen Nye

TATE PUBLISHING
AND ENTERPRISES, LLC

Published by Tate Publishing & Enterprises, LLC
127 E. Trade Center Terrace | Mustang, Oklahoma 73064 USA
1.888.361.9473 | www.tatepublishing.com

Tate Publishing is committed to excellence in the publishing industry. The company reflects the philosophy established by the founders, based on Psalm 68:11,
"The Lord gave the word and great was the company of those who published it."

Published in the United States of America

ISBN: 978-1-62854-002-4
1. Fiction / General
2. Fiction / Contemporary Women
13.10.30

To Carrie Peterson
Without your dream, your faith in me and your brutal
honesty, I might not have started this story.
Without your unique personality, I might not have had
such an inspiration for Alice.
And without our friendship, I might not have had such
an awesome story.

To Stephanie and Linda
Thank you both for your help, your editing and your
praise. Your proofreading and always asking for more
kept me writing to keep up with you.

To Morgan and Isabelle
-My girls-
I hope this book will inspire you to always work
towards your dream.

Chapter One

The Invite

"Come to Maui with us, please..." she pleaded with a slight tone of mischievousness to her words.

Having her beg me to go was always hard. She'd been planning this trip for six months and I so wanted to go, to get away to a far-off fantasy land. It's not as if life was exactly all romance and fairytales as it stood here. To be honest, every time she brought it up my mind instantly slid off to those exotic sandy beaches and beautiful island breezes.

I imagined myself walking down a white, sandy beach in a light and flowing sundress, a soft breeze rolling off the water. The scent of fragrant, wild island flowers and salt water would bring my steps to a pause. I would turn and gaze out over the ocean, wondering how any place could be so beautiful and exciting at the same time.

I was fairly certain that she could see it in my eyes every time.

"No."

I muttered with disdain at having to say it. The bite of a cold Michigan breeze brought me back to a reality I didn't want to come back to.

Alice grabbed my shoulder with her hand, shaking me playfully.

"Oh, come on, Viv, sandy beaches, Mai Tai's and hot cabana boys. It's just two weeks of getting away from everything. Something you need more than I do. Well, maybe not more than I do, but you do really need to get away."

She wasn't wrong about that. I did need to get away. Alice always knew what to say to hit home. I never quite understood that dynamic between us. We were nothing alike in thoughts or wants, but we always seemed to *know* each other. It was that dynamic that people seemed to pick up on when we would start talking--just about everyone asked us if we were sisters or long time roommates.

Actually, we had never lived together. Come to think about it, we had never spent long periods of time together. Sure, we've steadily hung out for a few months here and there, and we've known each other for fifteen years by now. It's just that there was always a close friendship there. No matter how much time we could go without speaking, or how long we'd spend day and night together, the bond was always the same. If I had to describe it, I'd say she was my soul sister. Cheesy, I know.

Thinking about this made me chuckle softly.

"What?" she asked, looking at me, hoping I was going to change my mind about going to Maui.

"Nothing, just thinking." That wasn't a lie.

"You know that I can't leave my kids for two weeks to go away to Maui no matter how much I'd love to.

Tim wouldn't be able to handle them on his own, even if I did set up sitters. Plus, you know how he's gotten."

Her face turned sharply angered.

"I don't know why you've stayed with him this long. I actually never understood why you married him in the first place. It's not like you've ever had great luck in your choices of men, but come on, Viv. You've done better, and that's saying a lot!"

I never had much to say about that. She wasn't exactly wrong. Plus, when I tried to argue, she would always go off on a tirade about Tim's shortcomings and the way she (and most everyone else) hated how he treated me.

"You know you want to. I can see it in your face every time I've brought it up or you've gone shopping with me."

This was true. I hated the shopping trips. And that was saying a lot for this shopping addict. It was just painful. She and I had worked so hard on getting back in shape and had planned on going on a vacation to show off that hard work, and now she was going without me.

Why couldn't I have a plethora of sitters? I thought to myself, wishing I had her luck finding someone to help with my kids as she did hers.

Alice had dragged me from department store to department store, looking for what she called 'the perfect Maui wardrobe.' I was pretty sure she did it more than necessary to rub it in. Her way of twisting things around so I would change my mind.

I remember one shopping day at Macy's where she dragged me around for a good three hours. We were standing in the dressing room. I was usually appointed the 'extra opinion.'

Normally, this would have been fun. We'd both be trying things on, walking out of our dressing rooms to show each other and complimenting the clothes or laughing. However, I didn't take much pleasure this time. Her trip was only a few days away, and I wished I were going, too. The clothing parade was just making it worse.

Alice stepped out of her dressing room in a rather cute little sundress. White with dusty rose floral designs on it. It complemented her coloring. Her long, curly, red hair wouldn't have to be pulled back to wear this dress and it would still be classy yet casual. Plus, being 5' 6" with long legs, this dress would only assure that she would turn heads.

"Very nice… and very you," I complimented.

"Thanks, I think this one's my favorite." She went back into her dressing room, admiring herself in the mirrors as she passed through.

I sighed. *Where was my adventurous spirit? I had always taken a chance to have fun! What was holding me back?* I screamed silently to myself. Not that it helped at all.

I stood in front of the mirror, holding up one of the dresses she had decided against. I was pleased that I had gotten back in shape. Just barely over 5', I was finally back to a nice trim figure. My hair had grown back out to a rather cute chin-length, spiky, pixie-looking style. I was coloring it a deep wine color with larger chunks of a brassy blonde through it. I wasn't pleased about having shorter hair, but it was a product of a bad haircut.

At least my hair grows quickly.

I didn't exactly find myself gorgeous. I never quite felt as beautiful as Alice. However, I was aware of the fact that I didn't usually have trouble finding attention. My favorite feature was my eyes. They were a rich green, but the lower half of my left eye was a dark brown. This feature usually made me feel a bit above ordinary, and I liked that.

I resigned myself to the fact that I seemed to have lost my edge when I had children. This thought was almost more crushing than missing the chance to go to Maui, but I had to look as if I were planted in my decision to stay. I had to smile and see them off.

"Have fun and bring me back a cute island boy." I said with an unmistakable sadness in my words.

"All right, but it's your loss. I was totally planning on getting you drunk on one glass of wine, since you're such a lightweight, and getting you to cliff dive... naked." Her eyes were taunting. She knew I loved a challenge.

"Yeah well, I've already done that, so ha." I was amused at her look of shock. It still amazed me that she was surprised by my past, and I was pretty sure it surprised her at her own surprise.

"I should have known."

Alice left then to go back to work. I usually visited her at work. It was kind of a getaway, I'm not sure why. It was just a chain restaurant in the small town where we lived. I usually didn't see many people to talk to and she always came and talked to me, dragging some coworker with her for us to tell some story about our past. She was always up for shocking a new acquaintance with our crazy youth. I loved to see the surprise on their faces too.

I sat there wondering why I was so reluctant to go as badly as I wanted to be there. She had saved enough to take me with her; I would just need enough money for food and entertainment. I usually never turned down an adventure. This time felt different.

That weekend, I went with Alice and four of her friends to the airport. They were all chatting excitedly about the things they wanted to do while in Maui... and the fantasies they hoped would happen while they were there. It was quite amusing to listen. Well, until I noticed that Alice wasn't chatting. She was glancing at me every now and then, thinking intently. I knew she was trying to figure out a way to convince me to go, too.

"No, but thanks." I muttered, catching her as she glanced over again, surprised I had said anything.

"Fine," she scoffed, "but it's your loss. I'll call you and rub it in every day."

"I figured as much."

After the plane took off, I walked back to my minivan with mixed emotions. I was glad I wasn't going to have to deal with her begging me to go anymore. I was dreading the phone calls at all hours, telling me how much fun she was having. I was bored at the thought of going back home to my drab life.

Suddenly, I had a feeling I hadn't noticed before... I knew something was going to happen, and I was going to be involved, and I was excited for it.

That thought puzzled me. I continued walking. It was drowning out all the other thoughts. Why would I be feeling that? I chalked it up to the restlessness in my current life and my sadness over missing this adventure. It was a silly wish rather than a sense of things to come. My mind trailed off to the 'what ifs' that could happen.

I was engrossed in my little fantasies when I realized I had been sitting in my minivan for a while, cold, hungry and very late getting home to let the sitter go. I raced out of the parking lot, my mind still dwelling on the 'what ifs.'

Snow had begun to fall softly on the parking lot. It wasn't sticking, thank goodness. March in Michigan was pretty hit and miss on the weather front. You could have a nice, sunny, 60-degree day and snow the next.

If you don't like the weather, just wait five minutes. I thought about the old saying for a moment. It was true. The thing about Michigan seasons is there are only two … winter and road construction. I scoffed.

I was pretty much over winter, as I usually was this time of the year. This fact only made me more upset at myself for not going with Alice.

I drove home in time for Tim to leave for work. He was his usual "perky" self… sarcasm intended. Adding insult to injury, I had just seen my best friend off on our vacation, without me, and I get to come home to this. Wonderful.

He was usually distant and snippy, but he seemed a little more so than usual. He didn't really look at me as he went by me to the front door. As he passed by, he shoved a small bag at me.

"Alice came by earlier and said to give this to you today," he snorted. "I don't know why she had to bother me about this when you took her to the airport, but whatever."

They never could stand each other. Come to think of it, none of the guys I'd been with got along with her. I guess it was the wonderful and charming way she always told them they were never good enough for me.

"Thanks," I said quickly, grabbing the bag and heading for the kitchen. "Have a good night."

"Sure, later," he said in his usual irritated tone.

I went into the kitchen, wondering why she felt the need to sneak over here. I knew it had to be good considering she despised talking to Tim and would avoid it if possible. Her reasoning was that if I weren't there when he was, she'd say things that would speed the divorce process. I thanked her for keeping her distance, but I never really understood why. As I got to the counter, I set the bag down, slowly pulling out the tissue paper. A small note fell onto the counter that read:

Just in case you change your mind, I know that there's a hot cabana boy who would LOVE this on you.

My stomach rolled over just thinking about all of the possibilities that might be in the bag. I reached in and felt a string, not much thicker than dental floss. I pulled out what seemed to be part of a bathing suit. I blushed.

"Thanks, babe, but I am not sure I would have been daring enough to wear this even in my pre-children days," I said to myself, shoving the bikini back into the bag and tossing it into the laundry room.

I turned to go into the living room, returning to my thoughts on the 'what ifs.' It was a long evening.

Chapter Two

Missing Out

"If that's her calling again to tell me about some 'pretty flower' or 'hot cabana boy', I am going to go to Maui today and smash her phone!" I muttered as I walked over to silence the ringing.

Alice had not let up on her calls. They had involved some form of her still trying to get me to come. Telling me she had more than enough money to fly me to the island, especially considering what happened with her hotel rooms when they got there.

That was what kept me amused with her phone calls. As much fun as they were all having, she was infuriated at some guy. She assumed he was a celebrity or at least extremely rich because he was given anything he wanted. That included one other hotel room, a table at a nice restaurant they had reserved and a tour around the island they had waited for hours to take.

She would just ramble on and on about how much she hated him and his kind. What was he thinking? How smug was he? Whoever he was, she hated him. It was a nice distraction from her play-by-play accounts of her day and begging me to come.

"That's it!" she shouted as I answered the phone, "I don't care who he is. I'm going to wring his neck!"

I couldn't help but laugh. "What happened now?"

"Sarah and I went to get spa treatments this morning. We had to book them before we even came!" I could hear the anger in her voice, fuming.

"We got there, and who do you think was walking into the room in front of us? Huh? Huh? Him!" She let out a growl.

"So? I am sure he could have made an appointment, too." I knew this would set her off. I prided myself on knowing how to push her buttons.

"No!" She shouted. "Oh, no. The receptionist walked up to us after they closed the door behind him and told us that he was a high priority client, and they couldn't refuse him. They couldn't refuse him?! Who the hell is this guy? I just let Sarah take the other spot, and I'm down on the beach, pacing."

"Well, maybe you should change hotels or something."

"We can't! Everything is booked," It almost sounded like defeat in her voice. "There's some sort of big to-do going on this time of the year... go figure."

"I don't know what to say, Alice." That was the truth. "Try confronting him, then."

I tried to envision that happening. I guess the one thing Alice and I shared was temper. She hated confrontation, and I didn't mind it if it got a situation resolved quickly, but when either of us did confront someone, it usually wasn't very pleasant. We've both made football jocks take a couple steps back with a couple words and angry looks.

"Oh, don't think I won't," she snapped. "I'm going to make him feel about as big as an ant. I don't know who this guy is, but there's no one *that* special that they can ruin my vacation. He deserves a piece of my mind, and I'm going to give it to him right now."

I laughed. I couldn't help it. Now, I wished I could be there for that. That was for sure. Leave it to Alice to find drama on a vacation. She's a magnet for it.

"All right," she continued after a couple deep breaths. "I'm going to go slap him around. Tell my kids I love them and miss them when you take your kids over to play tomorrow."

"I will. What? No usual barrage of reasons to get me to come out? No nagging? No telling me that I'm missing out?" I joked.

"Well, well, well, Vivianne. If I didn't know better, I'd think that you were thinking about it after all."

I could hear the pride in her voice at the thought that she might have bent my will to her way. A task not easily accomplished by most, not even her. So she took great pride and every opportunity to rub in my face when she did.

"No, I just had gotten used to it," I lied.

She laughed and hung up the phone. I knew it wouldn't be long before I'd get a call back. When she set her mind to something, she usually went for it. I just wasn't expecting a call that quickly... fifteen minutes later, the phone rang again.

"So?" I asked, anxiously. "What did he have to say for himself?"

She was silent.

"Hello? Are you there? What happened?"

"Ummm… Viv." She paused, and I was getting more anxious. She was never at a loss for words. "You really need to come out here."

"Alice!" I snapped. "Please tell me that you didn't call me just to bug me about coming…" She cut me off then.

"No, I just figured out who he is." She paused again.

"And?" I asked eagerly.

"I went to the spa to see if he was still there. I had every intention of laying into him!" She seemed to cringe when she said that. "I was ready to go off on him. I had it all worked out in my head and was thinking about telling him he was being rude and pompous and arrogant. I wanted to ask him if he thought he sweated gold."

"And?!" I asked impatiently.

She sighed, "I told him how rude and inconsiderate he was and he couldn't be a real man if it took flashing money around to get his way. I said these horrible things to him when it clicked in my mind who he was. I was mortified. I just walked away mid-sentence. He's Ryan Perry. "

I could just see it. Alice fuming with rage and ready to tear into Ryan Perry. Marching up to the spa building, fists clenched, teeth grinding and stomping her feet with every step. Then, out comes this man that infuriated her so much.

She opened her mouth and started the flow of words that would have surely insulted him and put him in his place when her eyes took him in. 6' 1", thin yet muscular, with dark brown, shaggy hair, and eyes that seemed to pierce through you. And those full lips. All of her anger flew out of her lungs with a gasp, and she was at a loss for words.

"Can you die of embarrassment?" She asked me.

After a moment of silence, I started screaming, "What?! Ryan Perry?! *The* Ryan Perry?"

Ryan Perry was not just a celebrity to us. He played a role in a movie that Alice and I were in love with. Then again, thousands of women were in love with his fictional character. The movie was based off a book series that had engrossed us both. And for it to be put on screen, seeing the character come to life, was incredible. So, meeting him was like coming face to face with the object of your fantasies. Of course, we knew he wasn't actually that character, but, well, you know. Even if he wasn't, there was some element he gave the character that enthralled so many people, and made him much more appealing.

I shouted, "Get me an autograph!"

"Oh, yeah, that'll work out well," she said sarcastically. "How do I start that? 'Excuse me, I am sorry for bothering you, and this doesn't change the fact that I hate you for ruining my vacation, but my friend, Vivianne, would like an autograph.'"

I was about to say something when I heard her gasp and a man's voice near her say, "That'll be a start." His British accent was as thick as his voice was deep.

I am sure I could see the shades of embarrassment run over her face. I heard a slight crack of plastic when I realized that she had clenched down on her phone. I couldn't help but burst into laughter.

"Shut up," she hissed through her teeth.

"OH! No, this is too rich!" I laughed.

"Hello, my name is Ryan," the man said, very politely, I might add. "I am truly sorry for all of the confusion. I truly didn't know that I was taking anything that had been promised to someone else. If I had known..."

"Sure, whatever," Alice snapped. "You probably get everything you want wherever you go. What's it to you if you stomp on someone else's plans?"

"I would never do something like that on purpose," he said coolly. "Listen, let me take you to dinner to make up for it."

Another burst of laughter shot out of me as I envisioned the shock that would have rolled across her face at that moment.

"Shut up, Viv," she snapped, and turned her attention to Ryan. "And what makes you think I would want to go to dinner with you?"

"Your friend's autograph," Was the reply, with a certain calm and confidence.

"Fine."

I was laughing again as she snapped the phone closed. I quickly sent her a text.

Enjoy! Call me as soon as you can! And DON'T forget my autograph!

I could hardly stand sitting and waiting for her to call me and tell me everything. I occupied my time by shuffling around the clutter that was my house and watching the movie we loved. I paced every so often. And I have to admit I was torn between jealousy and being happy for her.

21

That's one thing about Alice and me, we were never jealous over each other when it came to friends, clothes or guys. We were always happy for each other, even if one wanted what the other had. This small bit of jealousy was a very unwelcome feeling. I knew it was just because of the role he played in the movie and what that character meant to me. So, I put it out of my mind and returned to my anxious feelings of needing to know what was going on.

Two hours later, my phone rang.

"What's going on?" I yelled into the phone before she could even realize that I had answered the phone. "Tell me everything!"

"I'm still out with him," she whispered into the phone. "I snuck off to the restroom to call you."

"So?" I was impatient for her to tell me anything. "What's going on?!"

"Well, I have your autograph." She knew how I hated being held at arm's length for information, even though she loved torturing me by doing it.

Oh, some great friend she is, I thought to myself, *holding back on one of the most exciting things she's ever gone through.*

"And?" I started asking with urgency. "What...?" I was cut off before I could ask.

"I'm leaving it at having your autograph that you begged for, and now I have to get back to my dinner. I'll call you when I'm done being embarrassed," she said quickly, and the phone went silent.

I was beside myself with curiosity, let alone the fierce agitation I felt for her at this point. I could hardly stand the suspense any longer. I got up from my chair with every intention of going straight to the airport. Then, I stopped myself. That's exactly what she wanted me to do. For all I knew, she was making this whole thing up just to get me to come out there.

I fumed, opened a bottle of wine, poured myself a glass and settled down to a book. I never got truly into that book that night. My mind was back and forth between anxious curiosity about her supposed evening and wanting to strangle her.

I fell asleep with the book in hand.

Morning came after what seemed like eternity. I awoke to my phone ringing.

"Ow!" I forgot about the wine. I never really drank, but when I did, it was only a glass, maybe two. Not the four I put down the night before, trying to slow my racing brain.

It took a couple rings before I realized that it was my phone ringing, not some unholy, evil being from the depths of hell trying to burst my head open with its wailing. Ok, melodramatic, maybe, but hey. It had been ages since my last hangover, and I thought at that moment that it needed to be ages before my next one.

"Hello?" I answered, my voice rather harsh.

"Good morning, sunshine!" Alice's voice rang through the phone all happy and high pitched, very odd for her.

I wanted to slap the glee out of her. "I hate you," I muttered. "So? What happened?"

"Oh, nothing," she answered. I could envision the smug smirk she had on her face. She wore that smirk every time she knew something that I didn't.

Bitch, I thought to myself.

"Nothing? Nothing? You've got to be kidding me!" I yelled into the phone. Well, as much as I could stand to yell. "Come on, Alice. I can hear it in your voice that you're happy."

"Ok, fine. Nothing like *that* happened. We just hung out, talked, ate, drank and walked the beach. He told me that he hadn't known the room and the table were mine. He even asked me to use the spare bed in his room so I wasn't sleeping on a couch. So, I got some good sleep last night. Then we got up and got some..."

I stopped her shortly, "What?! You slept in his bed?!"

"No!" She said. "You're not listening as usual and jumping ahead to fantasy-land. I said I slept in his spare bed. There are two beds in his room. Nothing happened. We just hung out. You sound horrible!"

"Um, yeah." I didn't want to tell her, but who was I kidding? She already knew. "I opened a bottle of wine. Four glasses later... well, you get the picture."

"Ouch." I heard that smirk in her reply again.

"Anyway, what's the plan for today?"

"You know? I don't know." She pondered for a moment. "He's at some meeting right now. Maybe I'll try to make my escape and save the embarrassment for later."

"Alice, I swear, if you sneak out and not hang out with him again this trip, I'll never forgive you!"

"Forgive me?" Defense rang in her voice. "Forgive me for what?"

"This guy seems into you. He's hot. He's rich. He's got manners. He's worth getting past whatever insecurities you have to spend time with him. At the

24

very least, wouldn't it be cool to have a famous friend to go hang out with from time to time?" I hoped she had seen rational thought ringing in my argument.

"Fine," she snapped. "For you, I'll humiliate myself."

"You're a true friend," I said rather smugly.

We got off the phone at that point. I knew that she was scared of letting any guy close, but I had a feeling about this. Besides, it would, at the very least, make a great story to tell people.

Chapter Three

Trouble with the Husband

It was a pretty normal day for the small town we lived in. Slow. I had grown so bored here, but hey, family, friends... better than being alone raising two kids. However boredom bothered me, it was the constant barrage of arguments Tim would fling at me that made the days go from tedious to horrible.

Another petty argument about something so inconsequential that I just wanted to slap him in the face, grab my kids and run until I collapsed.

Hmmm...I thought to myself, *I'm living the American Housewife's life. Me? I never would have thought it in a million years.*

Crying, I grabbed my phone to call Alice. I hesitated for a moment. I knew that she and Ryan had been enjoying their time together the last five days. I knew because she called and told me everything. I just wished she would wake up and see that he had feelings for her, and that she shared those feelings for him. Yet, I needed my best friend.

"Vivianne, I'm so glad you called! Ryan and I were just..." She trailed off when she realized she could hear my sobs.

My stupid sobs telling her things were not all good on the Western front.

"What did he do this time?" Her voice became rigid.

"Same old, same old." I mustered up some words instead of sobbing. "You know, he did something stupid, I tried to talk to him about it, he got mad, called me names and got loud. Same thing I've been working on getting away from for how long?"

"A couple of years," she added.

"I know," I cried. "It just doesn't make it any easier to handle no matter how close the end looks."

Her tone had turned from blissfully happy to very serious and concerned. I felt horrible. I had ruined her great day. I needed her shoulder right then. We talked for quite a while. Ryan had checked on her in the beginning. He sounded genuinely worried about her serious tone and the sobs and yelling from my end of the phone. He didn't keep intruding though. He gave us our privacy. For that I was grateful.

After about an hour, I apologized for ruining her day. She assured me that I hadn't and said she'd call me later.

When she called back, I knew *I* was not the one who had ruined her day. I had to admit, I was a bit relieved, even though I still felt badly that I had dumped on her. However, my thoughts turned to amusement at her rather embarrassing developments.

"Hello?" I answered, confused, not recognizing the number on the caller ID.

"Hey, Vivianne." A weary voice came across the line.

"What? Were your ears ringing? I was just thinking about you."

"You're always thinking about me. What's new?" she said sarcastically.

"What's up? You sound… well… disturbed."

"Oh, my God!" She gasped.

"Are you going to make it there, punchy?" I asked.

"If only you knew! Today has gone from happy and fun to the most embarrassing day of my life!" She could have crawled into a hole and died, by the sound of her voice.

"Ok?" I asked.

"So, now I am holed up in Ryan's bathroom, dying of embarrassment… oh yeah, revisiting that faithful question, 'Can you die of embarrassment?' Well, at least I am hoping for it to be swift." There was no amusement in her voice.

"What happened, Alice? Are you ok?" I actually got a little concerned at this point.

"Yeah, I'm fine. My phone isn't. My new dress isn't. My new heels aren't. Come to think of it… NO! I'm NOT okay! I just fell in the damn ocean!" She screamed.

I couldn't help but laugh. Rolling off my chair, onto the floor, I listened to her recount the events that led to her refreshing swim in the ocean.

"We were walking down the pier. Everything was going fine. We were just talking, and of course, as my luck would have it, I caught my heel into the only crack on the pier, and stumbled into the railing. It gave way, letting me fall oh-so-not-gracefully into the ocean." Stiffness came across in her words. I knew she was about to call it a day.

28

"Wow, Alice. I don't know what to say other than..." I paused for a moment to gather myself, a laugh right behind my words. "That sucks."

"Thanks," she said coldly. "I'm going to go take a shower now. I hope it snows in Michigan. Enjoy the cold. Buh bye."

She hung up the phone. Normally, I would have been offended, but considering I did nothing to help the mood, I could accept her frustrations with me. I knew she'd call back.

I set the phone down to go start dinner for the kids when it rang again.

"I am so sorry, Alice." I realized she probably needed me to console her if she was calling back already. "Is it that bad?"

"Is what that bad?" A man's voice rang from the other end.

"Hello?" I asked, confused. "Who would this be?"

"Vivianne?" the voice asked.

"No, I'm Vivianne. You don't sound like a Vivianne. Who... are ... you?" I thought if I asked the question slowly, it just might click.

"No, I was asking if you were Vivianne. This is Ryan."

"Ryan?" I asked meekly. "Um.... hi?"

I was at a loss. Why was he calling me? Was he so mortified at whatever Alice had done that he wanted a way out? Surely not. He wouldn't let her best friend in on ditching her. There had to be another reason.

"Hey, listen, I don't mean to be a bother, but I need some help," he said. "I, as you know, have been spending a great deal of time with Alice, and I'm very fond of the time we've spent together. However, she seems reluctant to even notice that I am interested in her."

I gasped, and then was a bit embarrassed at that. "Ok? And what can I do?"

"Fly out here and help me?" he asked unexpectedly. I actually think he was taken aback by his own request. "We've been having a lot of fun, but since this afternoon's events, she won't look at me."

"You want me to fly out there?" I was shocked at his request. "You obviously don't know Alice. If she's barricaded herself into your bathroom, keep listening for the hammer and nails. She's not coming out until you leave. What happened? She told me a little of it, but I don't get it, did you laugh at her? She hates that, I know."

"Um… I think I might have let out a little chuckle," he said hesitantly. "But I tried to help her out. She threw down her purse and phone, threw her shoes halfway to the mainland and said, 'Don't touch me, I've got this.' I didn't know what to do."

"Oh, she likes you," I said, betraying my friend. "Put the phone on speaker and set it next to the door. I'll see if I can talk to her. She won't talk to me unless you leave the room."

"Ok, thanks," he said. I could almost hear a sigh of worry after he clicked the speaker button.

He did as I asked, at least I think he did. I heard another door shut before I started talking. "Alice? Listen, I've seen you do far more embarrassing things, and he sounds like he thinks it wasn't anything other than mildly humorous. So, what do you say about opening the door and letting it go?"

"Nope," she said sharply. "I am mortified. I took out a railing. Who takes out a railing? I do, that's who, and what's worse, I did it while I was with Ryan Perry. Yup, that's me. I might as well have left my skirt tucked into my underwear after going to the bathroom."

I, once again being the great friend that I am, chuckled at her mishaps. "I'm so sorry, Alice." I heard the door open, and the line went silent.

I wasn't sure what to expect, but I knew it wasn't going to be pleasant. She was very upset, and I just made it worse. I still couldn't help but laugh some more. I called back a couple times with no response. So, I gave up.

She'll call me when she's ready to talk. I just hope that she doesn't wait too long to talk to him. I'd hate for her to ruin her chances, I thought. I knew by his words, though, she hadn't.

As embarrassed as she was about the entire thing, I got the impression that this mishap was more endearing for him than off-putting.

I went about my task of making dinner. I tried to distract myself with the mundane daily duties of motherhood, but I couldn't escape the visions of Alice falling into the water. I also couldn't help but feel badly for her. She obviously had feelings for him, and that was as clear to me as his feelings for her were. It just wouldn't have been for those who didn't know her as I do.

I was one of the rare people who understood her exterior personality and how it was usually masking something on the interior that was far more penetrable and soft. This was a fact she didn't like to admit to... not even to me. When I'd tease her about it, I usually ended up with a bruise on my shoulder.

I failed in my attempt to revert my attention to other tasks and was lost in the thoughts of past events. Alice and I were pretty well known for embarrassing yet funny moments that we liked to recount--usually one of us telling the other person's story, against her will.

The phone rang. "Alice or Ryan?" I answered.

"Ryan," he said.

"Is she out yet?"

"Yeah, she went for a walk." I heard genuine concern for her in his voice. "So? How about that flight out?"

"Are you serious?" I asked. Why did he think he stood a chance at getting me out there when my best friend failed miserably?

"Well... yes. I am serious. She told me that if you could have gotten a sitter, you would have come."

"Well, there's more than just that," I said sheepishly. "My husband and I aren't exactly getting along, and he wasn't too fond of the idea of my going."

"Then we tell him that she needs you, and I'll pay for a professional nanny while you're gone. There, that settles that," he said smugly. "The next flight leaves in the morning, and I will call you a car service."

"A car service?" I laughed at the idea of one in this town. "Do you have any idea where we live?"

"Sure, but with the right amount of money, one can get a car service to anywhere. Let me take care of the details. You just get yourself out here, ok? The nanny will be there at five in the morning, and so will the car to take you to the airport. So, be ready. Your flight takes off from Lansing at eight. That'll put you here at about eleven since it's a non-stop flight."

Well, I guess it was settled then. He had the name and numbers for a sitter already, the flight booked and the car service waiting. I was going to Maui!

Excitement overcame apprehension.

"Wow, I guess you're prepared then. Fine, I'll start packing. I have what, 11 hours before they are here to pick me up? I had better get moving, especially if I'm going to get any sleep tonight."

"We'll see you in the morning... and thank you." He hung up then.

I cleaned up the dinner dishes, told the kids about my trip and put them to bed. It was never easy to go someplace without the kids, but I could not shake the feeling that I needed to go. I remembered the feeling I had the day I took Alice to the airport. I knew I was going to go, and that something would happen. Well? Here it is, and that something is Alice meeting Ryan.

I was not looking forward to telling Tim, but I was pretty tired of being pushed around, and considering everything was all planned and set up, he wouldn't have a reason to tell me no.

I didn't want to think about that conversation. So, I plugged my iPhone into its kicker speakers, clicked to play a compilation playlist and set it to random.

"Another Way to Die" by Alicia Keys and Jack Black started first. A great way to set the mood, I thought to myself, a rather spunky song. Kind of "Mission Impossible".

I went through the house, picking things up, cleaning, and then started packing. I sang the songs I knew the words to and tried to figure out what I should do to get through to Alice. She was a tough person to crack. However, it sounded like she needed to let him in. He sounded genuine, and I had a good feeling about him.

I finished packing my clothes, toiletries, shoes, etc. *Typical woman, overpacking, I'm sure.* I laughed at myself. Then, I went to the kitchen and reluctantly picked up the bag with the dental floss bikini Alice gave me, carrying it to the suitcase and shoving it into the front pocket. Just because I'm taking it doesn't mean I'll have to wear it.

After circling the house a few times, making sure things were in order, everything I would need was packed and my clothes and carry-on were all set, I set my alarm and settled down into bed. I wanted to fall asleep before Tim got home from work. I got back up, thinking I could write him a note.

Dear Tim,

I am going to join Alice in Maui. I know you don't want me to go, but she needs me. Something has happened, and I am the only one who can help. Things are all set. There's been a professional nanny hired, and a car will be here in the morning to take me to the airport. I'll let you know when I know more. I'll be back soon.

--Vivianne

I settled back into bed, knowing that he was going to wake me, angry, when he got home. I just hoped he wasn't drinking too much while at the bar so it would just be a small battle rather than a huge fight.

I changed the playlist to Michael Buble and drifted off to sleep. I didn't sleep well. A combination of dreading the conversation with Tim, fear of leaving my girls for that long and excitement of going to Maui. Oh, and meeting Ryan frickin' Perry. How cool was this?! I dozed off here and there, anxiously waiting for the morning.

The argument with Tim was quick, much to my surprise. I really didn't let him say much. I sat up when he came into the room, note in hand. He was about to say something, but I interrupted, telling him there wasn't a choice. Things were set up, and I was going. I told him about the nanny and made sure he had phone numbers for my family just in case he needed anything. He looked furious, but I told him I needed to sleep and lay back down. To my surprise, he didn't say anything other than, "Whatever, it looks like your mind is made up. Just make sure you call me and tell me when you're coming back. And tell the nanny to stay out of my way."

By morning, it didn't feel as if I had slept at all. Oh well, I could sleep on the plane. I turned off my alarm, jumped up and started shuffling my stuff to the front door and getting myself ready.

The nanny was a nice, younger woman. She was a college student with a very pleasant disposition. I briefed her on everything, left emergency numbers and showed her to the spare room. The girls woke up as I was finishing getting ready. They took to her right away. That brought a huge amount of relief.

Before I knew it, the car was there to take me to the airport. I kissed the girls goodbye and got into the car. Maui!

Chapter Four

Coming Together

My flight was an easy one since I pretty much slept through it. Ryan and I had concocted a plan. He wasn't going to tell Alice that I was coming. He was just going to ask her to come along to the airport to pick up a friend of his. Considering that she had started talking to him again, he didn't think it would be too difficult to convince her to go along, especially if he bribed her with a helicopter tour of the island later in the week.

"Well, well, well," she exclaimed as she saw me getting off the plane. "What? Come to revel in my embarrassment?"

"Sure, what are friends for?" I asked with a sly grin, "Besides, when a man like Ryan Perry asks you to come join him in Maui, how do you say no?"

I saw the lines of frustration on her forehead thin out as she stood there contemplating where the nearest exit was. Then she walked over to me and whispered in my ear, "Thanks, hon."

I grinned and winked at Ryan over her shoulder. His smile said it all ... hope.

I turned to Alice, "Not a problem. Besides, maybe if you embarrass yourself enough, I'll have a chance." I looked at Ryan again. This time, he blushed.

She slugged me in the shoulder.

"Ryan, this is Vivianne, as I am sure you already know," Alice said with a slight bit of disdain for our plotting. "Vivianne, this is your partner in crime, Ryan Perry."

I stepped forward to shake his hand. "Nice to meet you in person, Ryan."

"Nice to meet you, too, Vivianne. How was your flight?"

"Not bad, not bad at all. Now, how about I use the restroom and steal Little Miss Chipper away with me for a bit?" I suggested with a grin.

"Not a problem. Take your time." He smiled.

I grabbed hold of Alice's arm and basically shoved her in the direction of the bathroom. I knew what I had to say. Ryan and I had talked quite a bit over the night while Alice was asleep. He told me the things that he had noticed about her that made her endearing and how even her little mishaps made him smile.

"Listen," I started once we were safely in the bathroom. "I don't know what you're on, but you better start to dish, and by dish, I mean telling me some good reason why you're letting him slip through your fingers."

"Slip through my fingers?" Alice said with a wince. "As if he is looking for anything more than an island fling. I'm just having fun making a friend and enjoying my vacation."

"Oh, yeah, that's a good one. Because all celebrity 'friends' fly an island fling's best friend to join them just to get a little." I felt the ice drip from my words.

"So, you seem to have some delusional thoughts that this very smart, very successful and totally sexy

38

man would ever be interested in a small town divorcee with two kids... oh, and don't forget, clumsy, breaks railings and falls into oceans. Sure, I can see the appeal in that." She rolled her eyes.

"Well, I can see your logic," I agreed. "However, the fact still remains that this, quote, 'very smart, very successful and totally sexy' man has flown me halfway across the world just to have an ally to get through to you that he likes you. Hmmm... small town and clumsy or not, you seemed to have made an impression." I gloated at the victory of fact over logic.

"Whatever." She tried to pass it off. "All I know is that I've got a cool guy as a good friend. If he is interested in anything more, it'll be down the road. I'm not going to deal with ending up being an island fling because I like this guy."

"Fair enough, I can understand that." I was stewing in the anger of losing this debate with her. How quickly it turned--normally I kept an upper hand in our debates.

I figured there could be no way out if I presented a strong front with Ryan, but I could see her reasoning behind not wanting to make a move or accept an advance from him in fear that she'd give in and never hear from him after they parted.

She was guarded like that, and I understood why. Neither of us had ever had great luck in the love department. The last thing she needed at this point in her life was to fall for someone and have that person use her. If he was going to win her over, he was going to need some patience. It was not going to happen here.

However, I knew I had to find out what she thought. "So? Aside from thinking he's hot, which you obviously do, what do you think of him?"

"I really don't think it matters," she said, smugly.

I pushed her shoulder and smirked. "Just humor me."

"Fine." She rolled her eyes. "He's 'hot.' He's smart. He's funny, generous, has good manners, isn't full of himself, well-off, talented and all-around perfect."

"So why the fight to stay just friends?"

"I can't handle getting hurt right now, and I cannot believe that he feels for me what he says he does when he can have any woman he wants. It's like a fairytale, and, as you know, my life is not a fairytale." Her eyes took on a look of melancholy.

"Well, there's no reason for it to not turn out like one," I said with a wink. "Maybe your fairytale just started a little later than others."

I turned to walk away with a smirk on my face.

She grabbed my arm. "Don't you dare do anything to embarrass me!"

"Oh no, hon, I don't have to do that. You're doing a good enough job of that on your own." I pulled my arm away. "I just have to wait for you to stop burying your head in the sand and see that you have a great thing being presented to you in the form of a great man. Until then, I'll be here encouraging him and smacking you upside your head, trying desperately to wake you up and bring you to your senses."

I pushed through the door with a bit of confidence that I might have cracked her wall of abstinence. She followed right behind me, starting to protest my obvious show of not backing down, when we were greeted with an anxious smile from Ryan, waiting right outside.

"Are you two done talking about me?" You could see the hope in his eyes.

"Nope, but it's a good time to break," I said with a smile. "I am famished. Let's go eat."

I gave him a look that he understood to mean I would tell him about our conversation later. I wasn't looking forward to the talk, but he seemed reasonable. It's not that she didn't want something to happen between them. It was that she was a tough nut to crack, and he would have to work at it for a while before she would trust him.

I just hoped he would understand, but I was sure I could help him. I couldn't resist a good challenge, and why wait? If they both felt this way, there shouldn't be a delay. They should go for it. I would just have to make sure I set it up right.

When we got back to the hotel, Alice's friends grilled me for information. It seems she had been keeping them in the dark. That's Alice, never wanting the spotlight but being drawn to the drama. She had pretty much all but abandoned them, but it's not as if they cared much. They were off doing their own thing, happy that Alice seemed to be enjoying herself. They each expressed that she had needed this for a long time.

"He's nice," Sarah said. "She hasn't talked much about him, but then again, she hasn't been around much either. I suppose we might have cared if we were not all occupied with other things."

I was glad that Sarah and the girls were not upset at Alice. I know she felt a little like she was ditching them. Talking to Sarah made me sure they were far happier for her then slighted that she hadn't been around. That would ease Alice's mind when I told her.

"I am glad you guys are so understanding," I said. "Alice is scared out of her wits about the whole thing. I just hope I can slap some sense into her before she lets him get away."

"I agree," Sarah said.

We all took island tours, swam in the ocean, went to luaus and all the stuff any normal sight-seeing group would do. It was a blast. Still, I couldn't get Alice to open up to Ryan. I'm pretty sure that's when Ryan and I bonded, since we again had to plot together.

It was our last full day on the island. The sun was bright, the breezes were soft, and the thought of leaving this fantasy made the reality of the next day unbearable. I'd be trading the soft caresses of sweetly blossoming wildflowers and the soothing sounds of crashing waves on the shore for frigid temperatures and brown landscapes.

I knew I was in need of distraction from those thoughts. So, I shook my head, trying to diffuse those horrid thoughts to something a bit more pressing… plotting the match-making of Alice and Ryan. This was, no doubt, a very daunting task.

Alice and I woke up early that morning, and decided to go down and take in an early swim at the hotel's gorgeous private beach. After that, we took in one last tour of a nearby island favorite and ate a filling lunch of *lomilomi* and long rice at a local diner. It was already a full day by early afternoon.

As any normal women would, we concluded we had not done enough shopping. This was perfect. There was a nearby little town filled with shops that would easily distract Alice. Walking through the streets and shops, filled with exotic handmade jewelry and traditional Hawaiian clothing, I could hang back at Ryan's side and talk to him about that evening, for which I had concocted a plan.

"All right, Ryan, let's get the two of you alone," I said, getting frustrated at her reluctance.

Alice was, as I had anticipated, preoccupied with the many trinkets and souvenirs that were dazzling and tempting her thoroughly. She was having what I fondly referred to as one of her 'Oooo, shiny' moments. I took great advantage of it.

Ryan and I wandered over to a drink stand and ordered fruit smoothies, a nice complement to the warm weather. I was thinking how happy I was that I had been able to eat healthy with an array of fresh foods. If only I could take this place home with me... or make this place my home. I sighed.

"But she's avoided that since you got here." He had a look of defeat. "She goes right to bed when you're not in the room with us. She always has an excuse to go with you when you leave the room. I don't know what else to do. Maybe she's not interested."

I laughed. I realized they had to be together, as absurd as they both were.

"No, hon, she likes you. That's why she's avoiding alone time. That's one thing about Alice. She's

43

backwards. If she didn't like you, she would give you all the time in the world just so she could shoot you down and get it over with."

A wave of confusion washed across his face. I let out a little giggle at this, knowing it meant he had a lot to learn about Alice.

"So? What do we do?" he asked.

"Ok, we're leaving the island tomorrow. So, tonight, we walk the beach."

Once again, a wave of confusion washed across his face. "But isn't she going to just have excuse after excuse to avoid this?"

I walked past a rack where a beautiful, abstractly decorated cotton dress hung, letting my hand run over the material as I walked past. I tried hard to look nonchalant, not wanting him to see the frustration in my eyes. I was afraid it might scare him off. I was trying to make him think that I knew what I was doing, and that she just needed a tiny nudge.

"I know it's hard, knowing that she returns the feelings, but you have to understand," I pleaded. "She is scared that you're going to get what you want and forget about her when we leave the island. So, you have to find a way to get her to trust in you; she needs to understand that you actually care about her."

"No, I'm falling for her, Vivianne." His eyes brightened. I could see the emotion in them. "I don't want to lose her."

"Then don't do too much. Just make it known how you feel, establish that first connection and leave a lot for the future. She'll come around. I know she will." I had no doubt in that. I was just concerned about how long she'd draw this out. She's stubborn like that.

"Have you ever just known something? I mean, really *knew* it was right?" His eyes looked unfocused as if thinking of something far off.

"Yes, but not in love," I whispered. "I've known about places to live or certain situations in my life, but I've never been certain about spending the rest of my life with someone."

"But you're married."

"I know." My thoughts trailed back to Tim's proposal and our wedding day. "I wanted to spend the rest of my life with Tim, but I was never certain of anything with him. There were signs from the beginning. I just chose to ignore them. I hoped far more than I knew. Now look."

"Not going so great?" His voice was full of sympathy, "Alice hasn't told me much more than she can't stand him. That she barely tolerates him just to make you happy."

"Yup, that's Alice," I said. "And no. It's not going great. I am pretty sure a divorce is pending in the very near future… if my taking off to Maui hasn't set it entirely in motion. Needless to say, I am not looking forward to going home."

We walked out into the courtyard to sit, motioning to Alice that we were taking a break, but that she could continue shopping. She smiled and waved, eager to get on to the next shop.

We sat down on a wooden bench that overlooked a public beach, lining a section of the main drag.

"I know you're nervous, and I'm not saying it's not going to be work getting Alice to come around." I tossed my empty smoothie cup into the nearest trash can. "But if you truly do care for her, you'll keep trying. So many guys have taken a liking to her, but they give up so easily. She's got a lot of baggage, especially from her ex-husband. She's afraid to get hurt again, and I don't blame her."

"Yeah, she's talked a little bit about her ex. Something about him being an alcoholic. That he was never home, and their kids thought the bar was where he lived. He drank away the kids' savings and sometimes the bill money. It sounds like it really destroyed her."

"She did love him, but their relationship was more along the lines of security and being good friends, more than an "in love" situation. When that all went away because of him being at the bar, things got bad. Then there was the cheating."

"Cheating?" His eyes narrowed with concern.

"Yeah." I shook my head. "He pretty much started treating her like a maid, babysitter and an occasional lover. I know he's not a bad guy, he just did some crappy things to her, and it tore her apart."

"I don't doubt that."

"Anyway." I wanted to get back into talking about that coming evening. "Let's go to the beach this evening. I'll start to jog away and say something about needing to grab a juice when we get near the beach-side bar. You grab her hand and keep walking."

Ryan shook his head. "She'll just follow you."

"Not if I point out some cute native boy or hot tourist that I spy up the beach," I said with a smirk. "One thing about our friendship, we will put ourselves out if it means giving the other a chance at happiness. I know her, she won't interfere if I tell her I'm going to go flirt, especially since she wants me away from Tim so badly."

"And what if she sees that you don't go talk to anyone?"

"Well, it's your job to distract her." I winked. "I'll just find some random guy as a decoy. I am sure someone will help me out. Then, you stop and sit her down, alone, and talk to her. She melts around you. She'll at least give you a sign of hope... I hope."

"Oh, very encouraging." he winced. "Thanks."

"Well, this is Alice. It's going to be a lot of extra effort before she lets her guard down and lets you in."

Just then, Alice came sauntering back, holding up a very cute little wrap skirt outfit. Its pattern was large hibiscus flowers in red and salmon and large palm leaves with a cream colored background. The coloring was great for her skin. "Isn't it perfect for our last night here? What are we going to do?"

"I think we should go down to the beach." I elbowed Ryan. "There are going to be some luaus tonight, and the weather is perfect for a walk."

"Ok." She shrugged. "As long as I get to wear this." She shoved the outfit into one of her bags.

"Let's go back to that smoothie shop." I was thirsty again, and another strawberry smoothie seemed exactly what I was craving.

On the way back down the walk, I almost teared up thinking about going back home and dealing with Tim. I missed my girls terribly. Elizabeth, five years old, and Victoria, three years old, were my whole life, and it was truly difficult to be away from them this long. However, dealing with Tim these days had proven to be a daunting task that I spent most days avoiding.

I knew that he would be stewing over me going to Maui, let alone over the way I gave him no choice. I had been telling Alice that I wasn't going to join her on the Maui trip because of lack of sitters. It was more along the lines that Tim wasn't going to allow me to go.

Sure, I probably could have put my foot down, but I tried to pick my battles carefully, and a trip to Maui wasn't a battle I had been willing to charge into. There were other places I wanted to go and other situations that needed my attention more.

Funny how things worked out, I thought. Well, I'd just enjoy the last night. It would be a situation at home with him no matter what. No sense in letting it ruin a good time.

I bought another strawberry smoothie, and we walked back to the hotel. Alice unpacked her day's findings, laying out the new outfit so she could change into it. It was perfect for her last night. She looked great. This was not going to help the situation of not encouraging Ryan... at all.

Dinner was pretty average. The weather was very comfortable, of course. It was Hawaii, after all. We chose a little place that was a favorite of the locals. Places like these usually had better food, quieter atmospheres and less chance of Ryan being recognized.

It made for a rather hectic dinner, usually resulting in an unfinished meal, when we were in a place where people knew who he was.

For dinner, I had huli-huli chicken for the main course and haupia for dessert. As I ate, Adele played softly in the background. I trailed off in thought, comparing the foods to food from other cultures I had experienced. I had always prided myself on having a decent amount of food knowledge, especially compared to those who lived around me. However, it occurred to me at that moment that I had never experienced Hawaiian foods. *How odd.* I thought. Especially considering how much I had been enjoying the foods on the island.

I was trying to keep myself out of the conversations by looking around the room, acting totally engulfed in my dish or scrolling through my phone. If she wasn't going to take time to be alone with him, I was going to give him the chance to talk to her without my being part of the conversation. I had to give it to her, though. She's a lot tougher than I thought she was. I knew she liked him, but she was resisting with amazing force.

Stubborn girl.

"You ready, Viv?" Alice nudged my shoulder. I guess I had trailed off for a moment, a little too disengaged. She had been trying to get my attention.

"Oh, um, yeah," I said, a bit dazed.

We paid for dinner and headed down toward the beach. You could see the waves crashing on the nearby rocks and softly rolling onto the beach. The moon reflected on the water, making the already bright moonlight that much brighter, giving everything a glowing quality.

The sand was still warm from the sunny day. We walked for a while, getting closer to the private beach of our hotel. I continued to stray from the conversation, only answering when spoken to.

I took my sandals off, flung them over my shoulder by the ribbon straps. I loved those shoes. They were a chocolate brown, matching very nicely with my simple baby doll-style dress of the same color with a smaller flower design. They had long, silky ribbons that I would wrap around my ankles a few times and tie in a bow in the back. They had a simple design with an elegant touch.

I scanned the beach for an escape. Just a little way up, I saw a resort where the outdoor bar had a decent crowd but wasn't too full.

"Hey guys." I touched Alice's arm. "I'm going to go up to the bar and get us some drinks."

"I'll go with you," she said without missing a beat, still trying to avoid alone time with Ryan.

"Um... no." I looked for the perfect distraction. "You see that guy sitting at the table on the left? He's been looking at me as we've been walking. He's kind of hot. I think I might just go talk to him." I hoped she hadn't picked up on my making that up as I went along.

"Really?" Her eyes widened in amused shock. "Ok, then. Have fun."

That was easy. I started up the beach, walking as seductively as I could muster in order to look like I was actually intending to look good for this guy.

Feeling a little foolish, I walked up to the attractive stranger and explained my situation and wondered if he would mind if I joined him to continue my charade. He was amused and completely obliging, letting me take a seat that faced Ryan and Alice, who were seated on a cluster of rocks near the water.

I ordered some fruity drink by my new companion's suggestion and watched the couple, hoping that she would give way to her feelings. We made idle conversation, but my attention was more into what was happening on the beach. The moonlight, the warm breeze and the much-awaited time alone made for the perfect setting.

They sat, just talking, for quite a while. Then, I saw Ryan slide his hand over the rock surface, slowly, to test her resistance, gliding his fingers over hers where they rested on the rock beside her. She didn't move. He entwined his fingers with hers, pulling her hand up to his chest as he turned towards her.

They talked for a moment or two, her face never turning to meet his. He reached up, placing his strong hand on her cheek, gently turning her to face him. Without hesitation, as her eyes lifted to meet his gaze, he leaned in, hand still on her cheek.

There was such a sense of gentle passion in that kiss. Any woman would have melted with its heat. I melted, even sitting as far away as I was, making me long for that kind of connection again.

Just then, Alice jumped up, her hands at her mouth, shaking her head. I thanked my attractive stranger and ran down the beach.

"I am sorry, I just can't do this right now," I heard Alice cry as I got closer.

"But why not?" Ryan pleaded. "I am falling for you. I want to get to know you better. I want to be with you, and I don't mean for just one night. I mean it all. I've never met anyone like you in my life, and I will not let you just walk away."

"I just can't." She took off running down the beach towards the hotel.

I caught up with Ryan. I could see the look of destitution in his eyes. I put my hand on his shoulder. "I'll go talk to her."

"I'm not giving up," he sighed, staring at the sand beneath his feet.

"Good." I took off towards Alice.

I found her sitting under a palm tree on our hotel's private beach, arms wrapped around her legs, pulling them tight up to her chest, her head bowed... crying.

"I just don't understand why I can't give in and let myself fall for him," she said plaintively as I walked up to her.

"I do. I just wish that you could get past it all." I knelt next to her and wrapped my arms around her shoulders.

She cried for quite some time. I saw Ryan pass us after a bit with a look of concern in his eyes that said all he wanted to do was come over and comfort her. But he knew she needed him to just keep walking.

"I really do like him." Her eyes were all puffy. "I just can't get past this fear that he's going to get what he wants and leave me. I can't take another chance. Not right now."

"I know." I soothed her. "Then you just stay friends for now. See how things pan out later. Maybe you'll come around if you give him some time to show you that he's not giving up on you."

"Maybe." She stared off over the water.

We stood up and walked towards the hotel, grabbing a drink along the way. I wasn't sure how I was going to salvage the night. We had been staying in Ryan's suite, and he was waiting for our return to make sure he hadn't ruined any chance with Alice. Yet, this was our last night on the island, and I was determined for us to enjoy it.

Chapter Five

Payback

We got back to the room. "Why don't you get changed?" I told Alice. "I saw a really cute dress you bought earlier that would be perfect for going to the club. I think dancing is what we need to celebrate our last night. I'll call the girls and tell them where we're going. I'm sure they'd love to join us."

"All right." Alice ducked past Ryan and into the bathroom to get changed.

"Listen," I said to Ryan, putting my hand on his. "She doesn't want you to give up on her. She's angry that she can't give in to you. I told you she was going to be a lot of work. She has a lot of baggage, but if you truly do feel the way you've told me you do, you'll stick around and give her time."

"As long as she doesn't tell me to leave her alone, I'm still going to be around, hoping she'll give me a chance." His determination was sweet.

"I'm going to go change. We're going to the club."

He sat back into his chair. "Okay."

"You had better change, too. I doubt that outfit is very comfortable for a night of dancing."

"You sure she will want me to go after that?"

"Ummm… Yeah. You would be a fool not to go. Plus, you'll get to hang out with her friends." I playfully slapped his shoulder and skipped off to join Alice in getting ready.

I called Sarah and the girls to see what they were up to. They were in town, trying to figure out what they were going to do with their evening. I told them nothing about what happened between Alice and Ryan except that there was a strong "tension" between them, and I needed to get them out to have some fun. Sarah seemed to pick up on what I meant and said it sounded like a good time. She was sure the others would love to go along. So, I told her which club and said we'd be there within the hour.

I sifted through my wardrobe to find something suitable to wear and headed into the bathroom, setting up next to Alice at the vanity. Her demeanor had changed. She had an obvious look of excitement about her. She had already changed into another outfit and was reapplying her makeup.

"I called and talked to Sarah, and she said they were game to meet us there." I smiled.

"Very cool." Her eyes stayed focused on her hair as she worked on taming her curls into an up-do. "I haven't hung out with them as much as I should have while we've been here. This should be fun."

"Yeah. I'm ready to shake it!" We laughed.

We finished primping and headed out into the main room. Ryan was waiting, standing at the balcony doors, sipping a double of Glenfiddich, looking dapper in a white linen suit, hair done with his usual messy style and a slight smile of approval as we walked into the room. "You ladies look amazing."

"Thank you very much, sir." I curtsied, and winked at him.

"Alice, I…" Ryan started.

"Ryan, let's just enjoy tonight. It's ok. There's nothing you did wrong. I am just a stupid woman. Let's just let it go for now," she interrupted.

It was obvious she wanted to say more, but I barged up to them, taking them both by the hands, and dragged them towards the door. I know there was a lot to be said, but I wasn't going to let this potentially awkward situation drag down the evening. They could talk in the morning. Tonight, we were going dancing.

The club was close enough to walk to, so we took advantage of the gorgeous weather and walked the main roads to the club. Sarah and the girls were waiting for us outside. It was amusing to see that his celebrity status still got a couple of the ladies awestruck. Tammy, Charity and Sophie seemed to be speechless whenever he was around. This amused us greatly. Ryan still wasn't used to his fame and his reaction had a shy and embarrassed quality. There was more than one upside, though--we headed into the club without having to stand in line. I made a beeline straight for the dance floor, dragging Sarah with me. The others scattered, and Ryan guided Alice to a booth toward the back of the room.

I watched for a moment to make sure Alice was okay with being alone with him. As much as I wanted them to have time alone, I knew that after this evening's events, she might not trust herself. I watched for a signal to come and get her until I was satisfied they were doing well. I started getting into the music.

Sarah and I danced for quite a while, occasionally chatting about the atmosphere of the club or glancing up to see what the others were doing. After a few songs, Sarah wandered off to find Tammy, Charity and Sophie, wanting to do a couple shots in celebration of the trip.

This gave me the chance to really get into dancing. Before having kids, I was a bit of a vagabond. I traveled around to different cities, staying with whatever new friends I found or whoever asked me to come stay. When I would get to a new place, I would, inevitably, find a good club or three and become a regular. Many clubs actually would hire me as an "inspirational dancer." I was depended on to come early and dance throughout the night, encouraging others to get on the dance floor.

This was never a problem for me. To this day, a part of me wishes I could still be doing that. Dancing is like therapy for me; to get so into a song--music being such a pure and thorough form of expression--to let your body just flow and move with the tune and the lyrics. Your mind forms its own impression of the meaning, making it personal and bringing it out through movements and body language.

Dancing gave me a simultaneous escape and a way to let my subconscious mind take over the things I needed to work out and work through them without the distractions of my conscious mind. It never ceased to amaze me how, after a night of dancing, I could more easily come to conclusions about the situations that were plaguing me at the time. Most days, if I wasn't spending quality time with my daughters, I wanted to be on a dance floor.

A few songs passed, I was sure, when Alice came down to the dance floor. She touched my shoulder for a moment to let me know she was there. She knew that if I was into a song, it was hard for me to stop. I pretty much saw it as rude for someone to interrupt me, and she knew that. After the song was over, I turned to her. "Everything golden?"

"Oh yeah, things are all good." She smiled.

"Okay. So? Did you two talk at all or just avoid the whole situation?"

"We talked." She was nonchalant about it. "I told him that it wasn't for a lack of feelings for him, and I loved that he had feelings for me. I am just scared. We talked about some of the things in my past a bit more. He said he understood, and as long as I didn't tell him to go away, he'd be here for me, waiting for me to be ready."

"That's awesome!" I beamed.

"Yeah, so I hope you're happy," she said smugly. "I told him that I have feelings, and he's going to keep trying. Great, just what I need... a man in my life. I thought I was avoiding them for the rest of my life unless I needed some heavy lifting."

I laughed, considering this is what she actually told me the day her divorce was finalized, right before she asked where the bottle of tequila was. "Well, you know, he's not just any man, and it's not like either of us have ever been very good at sticking to the rules, let alone our own, right?"

"Right." She grinned. "Anyway, we were watching you dance, and…"

"Wait! You were watching me dance?!" I am sure I turned seven shades of red. "Why the hell would you do that?!"

"Oh come on, it's not like you don't know you're an awesome dancer, but he's never seen you dance."

"Oh Lord, I don't care how many people have seen me dance, I never get used to people watching. Plus, I'm so out of practice."

"Well, you wouldn't know it by watching you. You looked great, and Ryan was impressed. He said that if you ever come out to London, he's taking you to the clubs there. He says you have a great style that's all your own."

"I guess I can't do anything like the masses," I joked.

"He's impressed. That's cool, right?" she asked.

"Sure, but I can't really take him for his opinion, now can I?" I looked at her out of the corner of my eye.

"Why not?" She was a bit confused. "Who wouldn't want Ryan Perry complimenting them on anything?"

"Well, he's falling for you. He can't have great taste." I laughed out loud and nudged her with my elbow.

"Oh, very nice." She gave me one of her signature punches to the shoulder.

"Ouch!" I grimaced. "Thanks."

"No problem." A proud smirk came over her face. "I'm going to go get a drink. Don't forget to drink something. You know how you get about forgetting to take a break. I don't want to have to drag your passed-out little behind back to the hotel. I'll leave you to them." She pointed to a group of five guys, standing just off the dance floor, staring in our direction.

"Oh, great, just get their attention while you're at it." I scowled. "I really don't need to get myself into trouble on my last night."

"But you didn't seem to mind talking to a cute boy earlier," she said with a wink. I knew the gig was up. She was aware it was a ploy to get them alone.

Alice flipped her hair and swaggered back toward the booth to Ryan, ordering a drink from a passing waitress on her way.

I was really going to get it. I just wasn't sure what she was going to do. What I did know was that it wasn't going to be pleasant.

I danced pretty much the whole time until it was time to leave, taking breaks just to get a water a couple times. Alice rounded all of us up just after last call. As we walked back to the hotel, you could see an obvious closeness between Alice and Ryan, though it obviously wasn't quite to the giving-in point for her. I was just happy that she was at least admitting her feelings. It meant there was hope for her yet.

I let everyone walk ahead of me. I wanted time to finish sorting through the thoughts that were swirling around my head about my own life. I knew things were not great at home, and I had been both working on them and preparing myself for becoming a single mom. This thought scared me more than I liked to admit to.

Alice had been divorced for a couple years, and her kids were older. Tina was eleven and Cameron was eight. She was going back to school for summer courses, and she had a job at the restaurant and worked weekend nights as a CNA at a local nursing home.

Me? I didn't think I had what it took, I guess. I was afraid that I would fall flat on my face, taking my kids down with me. However, I knew my situation was not healthy either. I had been working on getting out. I had started to build my career again; I picked up freelance positions with a couple of newspapers and had a regular column for the paper in my town. It wasn't great money, but it was enough.

That did not change the fact that such a huge change was scary. I had never stayed put for any long period of time, yet I had been in this house, with Tim, for four years at this point. There was a lot of our lives and property intertwined. When I thought about it, it felt like a huge knot that would be horribly difficult to untangle.

I knew I had to, though. I needed to be me again, and I needed to get out. My girls didn't deserve to grow up watching our dynamic. It would taint their views on relationships, and that thought crushed me.

"Viv!" Alice shouted.

I had gotten so deep in thought, once again, that I wandered past the doors to the hotel. "Oh, sorry. I must be really tired."

Ryan laughed and turned to go to the room, but Alice knew that wasn't the case. She took me by the arm and leaned in and whispered, "We'll talk on the plane ride home."

"It's been a pivotal point in our lives, for both of us. Hasn't it?" I teared up.

"Yes, it has." She smiled an appreciative smile, "Thank you for being a part of mine. You always seem to be the one that's there to walk with me through the major turning points of my life."

"Isn't that what friends are for?"

"Friends or enemies. That depends on if you consider this a good thing or not." She nudged me and smiled. "Friends," she said, giving me a hug.

I collapsed into bed as soon as we got into the room, club clothes and all. There was no way around the sheer exhaustion from a good night of dancing.

I have to leave him. Sad as it is, it's the best thing for me and my girls. I trailed off to sleep with that thought, a strange sense of relief and anticipation came over me.

I slept soundly that night.

I was happy to find a note on the bedside table, when I woke, that said she and Ryan had gone to breakfast... alone. She made sure to point that out. I giggled. I knew that her walls were crumbling. This was a good sign.

I started a playlist on my iPhone and went about the room getting ready for the day. With The Tossers playing loudly, I shuffled around, packing up anything I wouldn't need for the day. Our plane wasn't taking off until that evening. So, we had the whole day to play and say goodbye to the warmth.

It was a bittersweet feeling, looking out the window at the beautiful sandy beach, the blue water and green foliage that seemed to have a personality of its own. I wasn't ready to let it all go, but I had a new sense of intent. I wanted to get back to start moving into my new life… without Tim.

I threw on a pair of plaid Bermuda shorts and a tank top. The most relaxed outfit I'd worn since I got there. I ran a brush through my hair, making sure it wasn't standing on end, and put a small amount of makeup on. I didn't want to get done-up, but I also didn't want to look as haggard as I felt.

I headed down to the hotel's outdoor restaurant to get a bite of breakfast. I was in the mood for some loco moco and fresh fruit. I took a seat at a table by myself in the outer part of the dining area closest to the beach, so I could eat and watch the waves on the water.

I was completely engulfed in enjoying my breakfast and the serenity of the landscape when I heard something drop on my table. I swallowed hard, having a feeling that I was not going to want to look.

"Let's get changed, chick." Alice's voice had an amused harshness to it.

Oh crap, I knew she was going to make me pay, but I hadn't thought to hide the bikini. "Do I have to?"

"Do you need to ask?" She pulled me up, shoved the bag with the bikini at me and dragged me to the nearest bathroom.

"But I need to pay," I pleaded, trying to give myself time to think of a way out.

"Oh no, Ryan has it covered."

"That traitor!" I scowled. "He's supposed to be working with me. He's not getting away with this."

Once in the bathroom, I changed into the bikini, completely self-conscious, thinking of how I hadn't even worn something this skimpy before my kids came along. I didn't want to think about how horrid I looked right then. I didn't know what she had planned, but I was scared. However, I owed it to her. I put her on the spot, so turn-around was fair play, right?

"Let's go for a walk on the beach," she said, and then took off her sundress. She was wearing an awesome little one-piece bathing suit. It was green with diagonal peach and cream stripes across the midsection, fitting her just right in all the right places.

"Wow, Alice." My jaw dropped. "You look awesome! I guess as long as you look like that, maybe no one will notice how awful I look."

Alice scowled, "Look in the mirror," she pointed.

I turned to face the mirror with a feeling of dread. I knew I had been working hard at getting back in shape, but there's no way I could pull off a tiny bikini like this. It was a deep red string bikini. Very skimpy and revealing. The kind of thing you would see on beer commercials.

My eyes met my face in the mirror and paused before scanning down. I hesitated for a moment. Not horrible on the top. I didn't want to look any further, but I did. Okay, it's not a horror movie. "I still don't know about going out in public like this."

"Well, you don't have much of a choice. You came to Maui, and we're going to get you to live it to the fullest." She gathered our things and yanked me out of the bathroom and down to the beach.

As embarrassing as it was, I have to admit, the look on Ryan's face as we walked out of that bathroom was worth it. I got a smile and nod of approval, which thoroughly surprised me, but I am guessing that he

64

didn't anticipate Alice participating in the whole bathing suit show-off. His jaw dropped. His eyes widened. I took it he hadn't seen her in anything this revealing before this point.

He was so obviously speechless that we had time to make it a few feet past him before he could say anything. "Wow, Alice. You look great."

"Thank you." She flipped her hair and added a little extra weave to her walk.

Once on the beach, I noticed Sarah and the others. Sarah popped up and waved us over to the umbrella they had reserved for our group. Then, she paused and slapped Sophie on the shoulder, leaning in to say something to her. The others stood and turned in our direction.

"Don't... say... anything," I warned them.

"Why not? You don't like compliments?" Sophie giggled.

"Yeah, the two of you look ridiculously hot!" Tammy fanned herself with the magazine she had been reading.

"Doesn't she?" Alice beamed. She seemed proud of what she was making me do.

"All right, when do I get a cover-up?" I rolled my eyes and started for the bag on the mat.

"Oh, no." Alice grabbed my arm. "You're going to stay in this. It's part payback, part 'I bought this and you're going to get use out of it' and part that you need an ego boost. Check out all the guys checking you out," she motioned to a few different guys that were staring in our direction.

"They could be looking at you."

"Well, then you'll just have to go walk out to the water and see their eyes follow you," she said, shoving me out toward the water.

Why did I have to open my big mouth?

"You hate me," I said.

Ryan caught up with us right then, shaking his head with a smile.

"Be careful, I'm sure there are a lot of guys on the beach just hoping for a wardrobe malfunction."

"Oh great, I was just nervous about looking horrible in this thing, now I have to worry about it staying on? I hadn't thought about that. Thanks." Disdain was dripping from my words. "Let's get this over with."

I started for the water, which was about fifty feet from our spot. Everyone in the group started whistling and shouting. I can only imagine how badly I blushed. In all my dancing days, I had never felt so on stage as I did at that moment.

I turned to look at them about halfway down, when their shouting had quieted. Alice pointed at a few guys around the beach. Well, maybe she was right. I noticed I was being checked out. Guys were staring and commenting to each other, and the looks they were giving me were good, not mocking like I had expected.

I wandered the rest of the way down to the water and dove in. I did have a moment I wasn't sure if I was going to be able to keep my top on, but I caught it just before anything was revealed and retied it, quickly.

After a few minutes, I walked out of the water, tossing my head back to shake the excess water from my hair and strutted back up to Alice. Sarah and the girls had gone down to swim, but Alice was waiting for me to come back up to gloat.

"That wasn't so bad, was it?" she teased.

"Whatever." I tried to play it off.

I had a kind of realization that I had lost a bit of myself in the few years that I had been with Tim. I had been letting his words and actions affect how I viewed myself, and that was something I was very angry at myself about. I had sworn to myself that I would never let anyone change how I viewed myself.

This little stunt of Alice's had brought to light that I still had it as far as looks, and considering that I still made friends easily, I knew right then that my old self wasn't buried too deeply. I just had to get her out of the dark.

I knew I had to apply this revelation in not only my daily life, but I also had to be sure to hang on to this revived sense of self-assurance to getting my life back on track. However, at that moment, another realization had struck… It was time to go to the room and pack to go home.

"Let's go and get a bite to eat and get packing." My eyes almost welled up just thinking about it. "I am not exactly ready to go, but I miss my girls. So, I don't want to miss the plane." This was true. I did miss them terribly.

"Yeah, I was just thinking about packing." Alice started picking up our towels and beach bag. She motioned to Sarah and the others that we were going to head up the beach. "We're going to go get a bite to eat and then head over to pack. You guys want to join us?"

Sarah looked over at the girls, who were lined up, sunbathing, "Nah, I am pretty sure they are comfortable, and I am going to head down for a quick swim. Have fun. We'll see you at the airport," she said with a wink.

"Well, in case I don't see you in the terminal, it was very nice meeting you ladies." Ryan shook Sarah's hand.

"Thanks," she replied with a blush. "Nice meeting you, too."

The three of us turned and headed up to the hotel. I made a mental note of the way the warm sand of the beach melded with my toes with every step, the way the sun seemed to gently kiss my skin with warmth. I filed away pictures of the entire landscape, knowing that this would be my "happy place" when back in Michigan.

A quick sandwich at the hotel restaurant later, we started packing. Ryan wasn't leaving until the next day. So, he just hung out while we wandered through the room, reluctantly taking our items from the dressers and vanity and placing them into our suitcases.

"Do you think we are going to fit everything into our bags, or are we going to need to buy another suitcase?" I joked.

Laughing, Alice said, "Oh, I already thought about that," as she pulled a large duffel-style suitcase, still in the plastic, out from under the bed.

"Well, thank goodness one of us thinks of everything," I said, laughing.

"If you need, either of you, I can send any of your things to you that you can 't fit in your bags," Ryan offered.

"Thanks, Ryan." I shuddered at the thought that we might have spent enough to have to have things sent to us. "Let's just hope it hasn't come to that."

We all laughed for a moment, but you could feel the sadness in the air. Each of us having our own reason... reasons, rather... for not wanting to leave. Yet, we all knew this was going to happen. There were responsibilities, children, houses, jobs, families, etc. to go back to. However, I am sure we all also shared the feeling that this was not a goodbye.

After packing, we headed out for dinner and one last walk through the area, taking more pictures of each other and the town. We had a couple hours to kill with this. So, I was sure that we'd have some great photos. That made me smile.

Our plane was taking off at 8 p.m., putting us in Detroit at about 11 a.m. We would be home no later than 2 p.m. Ryan had gotten me on the flight with them, and we had decided to just rent a van or SUV for the ride home considering that I had taken them to the airport a couple weeks prior.

I called both Tim and the nanny to give them a heads up. The nanny had been telling me that the girls missed me, and they were little angels. She hadn't had any problems. This made me happy. She and Tim had even gotten along, providing she stayed out of his way and didn't attempt to say any more than she needed to him, she said.

Tim was very quiet and short with his words. I had no false hopes of a warm welcome from him. He was stewing pretty well, and having a timeline of my arrival just fueled his need to vent on me. Strangely, it didn't seem to affect me the way it would have in the past. That thought made me smile.

At the airport, we checked our baggage and found seats in the terminal. There was a little time to spare, and I knew Alice and Ryan would want some time to talk. Well, Ryan would want some time to talk to Alice. So, I pulled out my book and acted like I wasn't interested in their conversation.

"It's going to be odd with you not around." Alice hung her head and started fidgeting with her fingers.

"I'll visit whenever I can, and I'll keep in touch any way I can." He reached over to hold her hand but hesitated for a moment and just put his arm around her shoulders.

The airport was pretty busy. People were bustling around and rushing to their flights. The voice that came over the speakers was loud and booming. It almost shook my attention from Ryan and Alice.

There was such a tension between them that it filled the air, and I wanted to scream at them to just kiss and get it over with already!

"When do you go back to work?" she asked, attempting idle chit-chat.

A look of melancholy washed over his eyes. You could see he wanted to talk to her about their relationship, but he was trying very hard to not dwell on it. "Well, I go back to London for a few weeks to get some affairs in order. Then, I'll go back on set to wrap up filming. I'll stop in Michigan on my way through, though, to see you, if you'd like."

"Yeah, that'll be nice." You could see a sparkle in Alice's eyes.

"Then, I can show you around where I'm from, and you can meet my kids. They're such great kids, and my daughter loves you." She trailed off on a tangent for a moment, completely focused on the two little people that were her whole life. They were what kept her going through some of the worst parts of the last few years, and I knew how she felt, because my kids were the same for me.

She continued, "I miss them so much. As much as I want to stay, I can't wait to get back and have them around again. So yeah, you should come and visit. Besides, I'm sure Viv would love that, too." She nudged me with her elbow.

I tried to act like I hadn't been listening to every word. "What? Huh? Oh, yeah. That'll rock."

The booming voice came over the speakers, telling us it was time to board. We got up, gathering our carry-ons.

"It was really nice to meet you, Ryan." I hugged him. "I'm sure I'll be seeing you soon… and often if I have anything to do with it." I slapped Alice on the shoulder.

He gave me another hug. "Yes, it was very nice meeting you, too. And yes, if I have a choice, I'll be around a lot." His eyes flashed over to Alice and winked. She blushed.

I headed for the walkway to the plane.

"I'll talk to you really soon." He turned his head as they hugged so his cheek was pressed against hers and held her there for a long moment.

She gathered herself and caught up with me. We walked to our seats on the plane in silence. The others were already seated, staring at us, obviously waiting for some gossip. I shook my head, letting them know she didn't want to talk.

I honestly didn't know what to say to her. I wanted to hit her upside the head and tell her to run as fast as she could to him. Tell him that she loves him. Tell him anything so as to not leave it this way.

I also had thoughts of him running onto the plane, finding us and kissing her like in the movies; the kind of kiss that melts everything in the room and convinces the emotionally stunted one in the relationship into giving in to their feelings. Walking up to her and telling her that he couldn't let her go. That he loves her and can 't bear to see her just walk away with things so unresolved.

I was deeply frustrated with them both, but I knew how intense and how quickly their emotions had developed, and how guarded she was. She needed time to come around, and he needed to be around when she did. I knew they would, though, and that was what I reminded myself of. My best friend would be happy one day. She'd come around, and a good man would be there waiting for her.

As we taxied away from the airport, we waved at Ryan. I listened as the girls, who were seated behind us, giggled and chattered about who all they were going to tell about their adventures. Alice leaned her head back and let out a sigh. I saw a tear run down her cheek.

I reached over and held her hand, leaning my head back, too. Nothing had to be said. I knew she was tortured over her own stubborn reluctance. I couldn't be mad at her, though. I understood. I'd seen her go through so much with the men in her life. She was right. She couldn't go through another bad ending right now. The last one almost broke her. She knew she had to get into a better place before attempting to go after love again.

I was also jealous that my fairytale hadn't come along yet. I was flying home to my own personal nightmare. At least I'd found my own emotional weapons of defense, though. My renewed sense of self esteem would come in handy. I knew that for sure.

The ground gave way to the ocean, and things suddenly seemed so uncertain, yet finally going forward. I had a feeling of impending change. It was oddly comforting. We sat there, holding hands as if it was the true connection of our friendship and both drifted off to sleep. I was thinking about what the future might hold for us.

Chapter Six

Michigan... So the Weather Isn't the Only Thing Changing?

Well, if he was anything, Ryan was thorough... and connected. When we got off the plane, there was a message for us at the counter in the terminal.

Dear Ladies,

It was so nice to meet each of you. I hope that your flight was pleasant. My last few days in Maui will not be the same without you here... nor as much fun. Thank you for making my holiday one to remember. When I come through town in a couple weeks, I hope we can all get together.

Alice--I miss you already. I know that we talked and decided to keep it friends, and I respect that. However, you never said I couldn't flatter you. You are such a wonderful woman, and I am not giving up. I am merely going to be here for you as you go through what you need to go through to be ready. Then, I'll show you what a true man is like in a true relationship.

I'll call you as soon as I get back to London.

Vivianne--You are like a sister to me now. Thank you so much for coming out, compromising your home life, to help me... to help Alice. You are truly a best friend, and I hope that you enjoyed the trip despite it all.

Take care of Alice, as I am sure that you already do. Well, I can see it's a mutual thing for you two. I'll call you, too, when I get back home to plan my trip there.

I hate the idea of you ladies renting some beat-up, used, gas guzzling auto. So, I took the liberty of arranging a ride for you all. There will be a driver in the baggage area waiting for you. They will have a sign with Alice's name on it. Enjoy.

My sincerest regards,
Ryan Perry

"That was so sweet!" exclaimed Charity.

"Yeah." Alice's eyes welled up again.

"Okay," I said, trying to distract everyone. "Let's get going. I am dying to be home with my girls again."

We started for the luggage pick-up area, and Alice leaned in towards me. "Why did he have to do that?"

"Do what?" I asked.

"Embarrass me like that," she said. "The letter started off to everyone. Now, with everything he said, none of the girls are going to let up. They're going to be pushing me to get together with him more than you are. At least you understand why I'm being a moron. Plus, I am thinking that this isn't just a van or SUV. They are never going to let this slide."

I laughed. She was right. "Yeah, but you know they just mean the best." I patted her on the back, "They can only wish they could have a chance with someone like

Ryan. I wish I had a chance with someone like Ryan. Give it time. Either they'll let up or you'll come to your senses."

She glared at me out of the corner of her eye and stomped ahead of me. I just smirked.

We got to the luggage area, and sure enough, there was a man, in a suit, holding a sign with Alice's name on it. He couldn't have been any older than 35, shorter, dark hair and mustache. He was really quiet when he introduced himself. We gathered our luggage and wheeled it out to our ride… our stretch limo.

"Nice." Alice put her hands to her forehead.

"Wow!" Sophie and Charity said in unison.

"So?" I tried to ease the excitement. "What? It's a limo? To be honest, he probably just wanted to help out with a ride but couldn't think of anything large enough for six women and all their luggage."

Alice excused herself to the restroom.

"Hey, guys." I grabbed Sarah and Charity by the arms. "Let's not push Alice too hard or even mention Ryan at all. I know she's being foolish, but so does she, and she is very torn. You'll just make her pissy or cry. So please tell the others not to mention him, ok?"

"Ok, we'll try," Charity said hesitantly.

"Thanks." I motioned for everyone to get in. When Alice came back, she and I climbed into the back seat. The others had taken seats, scattered through the car, playing with the different switches and gadgets.

As we pulled away from the terminal, people were staring. Some people were even pointing. It was an unusual amount of attention just for six women getting into a limo, but we disregarded it for the most part.

Actually, Sophie and Tammy took advantage, rolling the windows down and waving at the people as we drove away. They were blowing kisses and everything. I was amused, but Alice just stared out the window, head in hand. She was obviously in deep thought, glancing over at me from time to time.

I chatted with the girls for a while. I was surprised and very thankful that they were being so awesome and not mentioning Ryan. They even stayed away from talking about our outings with him. They mainly talked about cute guys they met, how beautiful the island was, the things they bought and how they were not looking forward to going back to everyday life.

After a while, I sat back and leaned my head back on the headrest, letting out a sigh. The conversation had turned to life back home, and that wasn't something I wanted to think about at that moment. I let my thoughts drift back to the conversations of Maui, even hanging out with Ryan. Alice couldn't fault me for missing my new friend.

"So, I noticed a change in you the last day or so." She looked over at me, waiting.

"Um... yeah." I knew what she was getting at. "I know. I've been pulling away from him, and you, along with everyone else, think that I've just been delaying leaving him. Your little stunt with the bikini made me a little more confident again, and now I'm ready. I am just trying to figure out how to do it on my own."

This thought is what kept me up some nights. It wasn't that I thought I couldn't raise my kids on my own. It's that I didn't know how I'd be able to provide for them on my own. Plus, the thought of daycare was truly scary to me. I hated the thought of paying someone to raise my kids.

"Well, I was thinking about that, a lot." Her look was careful. "I am going back to school and working the two jobs. You want to go back to school and need more writing gigs. What if we get a place for both of us and our kids? Then, we can help each other and maybe avoid childcare all together."

"Wow." I was shocked. "I hadn't thought about that. We will have to look into this. It just might work."

Having someplace to go and someone who understands my situation was a comforting thought, let alone having that person actually willing to work with me... It was a bit frightening considering that I hadn't been in the workforce for several years other than my freelance jobs, and to be honest, I wasn't thrilled to go back to bosses and time clocks. I had a lead on a work-from-home job in case I couldn't dredge up more writing jobs, but it was commission-based, so I was unsure about it. But, I knew a move had to be made. One or the other had to happen. As far as school went, I had to think about what I would even want to go for.

One thing at a time, Vivianne, I thought to myself.

"It wouldn't be a permanent thing, of course," she said. "Just until we are both on our feet."

"Of course," I said with a smile. Her attempt at acting indifferent was amusing.

"I called my sister while we were in Maui to have her start looking for places with four or more bedrooms for rent." She sipped a glass of champagne that the girls had passed her. "She said she found a couple. So, we can go look at them in the next week or so and start getting things in order if you want."

"Wow." My head was spinning. "This is going so fast. I just decided that I was going to make the move to leave him. I need to let my head settle into that before I can start making the move."

She turned her head with an impatient look. "Listen, you've been going at a snail's pace with this for far too long. It's time, and I'm going to help you. Besides, I need your help. So, it's not just all about you." She looked back at her glass.

"Oh, yeah," I said sarcastically. "I forgot the world doesn't revolve around me. Wait... did you just ask for help? Can I get that in writing?" I laughed.

She was not amused.

The rest of the ride was pretty relaxing. We bounced between silence, singing to the radio and chatting about this and that. The drab scenery of Michigan's early spring was flying by. I occasionally stared out the window wishing I was seeing the sandy beaches and green foliage of the island.

We dropped the girls off at Sarah's house where they had left their cars. We all hugged and made a plan to organize a lunch outing in the very near future. They gathered their bags and scattered to their own vehicles and Sarah headed into her house.

We left Sarah's to take me home pretty much in silence. Alice called Ryan to tell him we landed in Michigan and thanked him for the car. She got his voicemail. Her message was brief, as I figured it would be. Aside from that, we both just enjoyed the silence.

As we pulled up to my house, a mixed feeling of excitement to see my babies and dread of dealing with Tim washed over me. The driver put the car in park, but I stayed in my seat, contemplating the different ways my return might go. I knew I would probably have a few minutes of settling in before he attacked me. The nanny was there, and I had to run through things with her before letting her go.

"You going to be okay?" Alice was obviously concerned. She knew Tim's temper. "Do you want me to come in with you?"

"No, I'm fine," I lied. "I am sure I'll be calling you later, though." That part was not a lie.

"Ok, I'll keep my phone with me." She hugged me as I got out.

I gathered my bags from the trunk. "Thanks. I had a lot of fun! I'll talk to you later. Wish me luck."

"Good luck." Her smile was as obviously concerned as her words.

I gathered as much composure as I could, hugged Alice and headed up the walkway to my front door. I turned and waved, giving a half-hearted smile that let out a revealing sigh with it, giving my uneasiness away as they pulled away.

I walked into the house and set my bags down against a wall.

"Girls?" I called for them.

"Mommy!" I heard both of them come running towards the living room.

I picked both of them up in my arms, hugging them and twirling around. I was home, and the best part of my life was clinging to me as if I'd been gone for years.

80

They babbled about all the things they had done while I was gone, asked me where I had been and went on and on about Ms. Tiffany, the nanny, and how much they loved her.

Tiffany walked into the room with a friendly smile. "Hello, Mrs. Cook. How was your trip?"

"Too short, but I missed these two something fierce!" I smiled.

"Yeah, I can imagine," she said.

I set the girls down and started for the kitchen. "So? How was everything?"

"Oh! They were great!" she said excitedly. "We played, read, took walks, everything. They ate great at most meals. They went to bed when told to. They cleaned up after themselves--well, Elizabeth did more than Victoria, but Victoria helped. They were great!"

"Very cool." I had no doubt. "I am glad things went so smoothly. What about Tim? Did you two get along? He can be temperamental from time to time."

"No, we got along just fine." She shook her head. "I didn't see him much, and when I did, he pretty much kept to himself. He's actually downstairs in his rec room," she said carefully.

"Well, good." I turned towards her, leaning against the counter. "Anything to report? Do I owe you anything? When are you available? If I need someone, I can get in touch with you if you want."

"Any time!" She was excited, writing her information down on a pad of paper I keep on the counter. "Here's my information just in case you don't still have it, and Mr. Perry took care of me, so you don't owe me anything." Tiffany started getting her coat on, and her bags were already packed.

"Okay, then, I guess that's all," I said, walking her to the door.

She hugged the girls, telling them she would miss them, and ducked out the door, thanking me. The girls were waving and yelling that they didn't want her to go, and they wanted her to come back soon.

After she pulled away, we turned, the girls hanging on tight to a leg each. I closed the door and walked towards the couch. I sat down and sighed. I hated that couch. Not long after Tim and I got together, we went to buy one. I had picked out a nice, fashionable, functional couch. He whined and moaned until I gave in and bought this pee-yellow monstrosity of a pillow couch. It was micro-suede, which did not weather well with kids. The back and sides were these huge pillows that, once smashed down, didn't ever come back into a comfortable position. Then there were the seat cushions. Needless to say, they were severely lacking in comfort.

I sat down and pulled my girls in tight. I was trying very hard to let my feelings of happiness that I was holding my girls again override my desire to run away from this house, screaming and never looking back. I knew I had to do the right thing, and that meant setting things up so my girls could still have a good life with just one parent in the household. That's when Tim walked into the room.

I swallowed hard. "Hey, what's up?"

"Well, well. Look what the cat dragged in." He had such a way with cheesy put-downs. "Did you send Tiffany away?"

"I let her go home," I corrected him.

"Too bad, I wouldn't have minded her staying. She was a better mother and housekeeper than you are." He wouldn't even look at me, but turned around and went to the kitchen to get a beer.

I told the girls to go to their rooms and stomped into the kitchen. "Excuse me?" I started. "I knew that you were going to be mad that I went, but there's no reason to be immature about it or try to hurt me."

"I'm not being immature, and I'm not saying anything that isn't true," he snapped.

"True?" I was truly hurt. That was true. "So, you're saying that you would trade me in for some girl that you claim is a better mother to those children then I am? That I am a bad mother?"

"Well, if you can just take off and abandon them to go vacation in Maui? Yes!" He turned and stared at me.

"Why don't you just admit it." I glared at him. "Admit that you're just mad because you feel like you can't control me. I went and did something even though you didn't want me to, and you hate it. You don't even care why I went or what I did."

He slammed his fist on the counter. "No! I don't care why you went. For all I know, you went to go off with some guy. Personally, I don't care. Your place is here, in this house, cooking, cleaning and taking care of these kids!"

I was appalled at his thought process. Who thought like this anymore? Wasn't this the 21st century? Were we not past this line of thought? I was having trouble wrapping my head around his completely sexist way of thinking. What a controlling mess! What did I ever see in the ass?!

He slammed the rest of his beer and got another out of the fridge before I could speak again. He grabbed me by the arm and got right up in my face. "If you have any thoughts of keeping me, you'll start realizing your place in this family and start acting like you give a damn about those kids and about me." The stench of beer and cigarettes on him turned my stomach.

"Thoughts of keeping you?" I said, calmly. "Huh, ok. I see. So, I'm a bad mom, a bad housekeeper and a bad wife?"

"Well, if the shoe fits," he said coldly, staring right into my eyes.

It was odd, really. I wasn't angry. I wasn't scared. I wasn't... anything. Except for decided. I turned away from him and started for the bedrooms, taking the suitcases out of the closet on my way.

"What the hell do you think you're doing?" He grabbed my arm again as we entered the bedroom.

"Get your hands off of me," I said with a stern voice.

He didn't let go and instead gave a yank. "Don't you dare think you're going anywhere after the stunt you just pulled."

"I am going to take the girls and go away for a while." I really didn't know what I was doing other than not putting up with him anymore.

He let out a chuckle. "Ha! And where do you think you're going? You aren't worth anything, and you need me. I don't know what you're thinking. Like anyone else will give you a second glance, and that stupid dream of being a big-time writer? Ridiculous!"

This just put the nail in the coffin. I pulled out of his grip, picked up the phone and called the police. He struggled with me for the phone, trying to get it out of my hands. I dialed 911, telling the operator that I was trying to leave my husband, but he was trying to keep me there and was showing signs of violence.

He managed to get the phone out of my hands and hung it up, slapping me across the face. I paused for a minute and held my hand to my cheek. I am sure he was waiting for me to come at him. Actually, I think that's what he was hoping for. Instead, I regained my composure and went back to packing. I couldn't stop now, even if I did want to grab the nearest blunt object and hit him in the head with it. It was now or never, I had to get out now; if not for myself, for my girls. They didn't need to be subjected to this, and I couldn't let it get out of hand and allow him to go this far with them.

He started following my every step and yelling at me. When I was done packing my own things, I started packing my girls' things. He came at me again, yelling, "You're not taking my kids!"

I told the girls to go put on their coats and shoes and sit on the couch. Once they left the room, I got right back up in his face and said without even a quiver in my voice, "I am not leaving them here with you. A court will let us know when you're allowed to see them."

I finished packing everything and placed the bags next to the front door, all the while ignoring him yelling at me. I picked up where I left off. "Until then, you're not going to be alone with them, and I don't want to have anything to do with you unless it's about visitation with them or getting more of our things."

He threw a small, glass figurine across the room just as a police car pulled up in front of the house. I saw his face change. He knew he was defeated. I actually felt sorry for him, but it didn't change my direction. I knew we had to leave.

The officer stood over Tim while I got our bags and the girls loaded up into the van. I expected to feel some sort of sorrow about leaving, but I didn't. I was filled with a sense of relief. Almost more like a newfound sense of freedom. Instead of thinking of what we'd gone through, I was preoccupied with thoughts of the future.

I drove straight over to Alice's apartment. Once there, I just walked the girls up to the front door. She answered, a puzzled look on her face. "Hi?"

"Um, yeah…" I paused and started with a really bad urban accent. "I just looked at him and said, 'Don't be gettin' all up in my puddin'. You don't know what flavor it is'," with a head shake and all.

She couldn't help but laugh at me. "I take it you left him and need to come in?"

"Can we?" I asked.

"I guess," she said, opening the door wider, scooping the girls up and hugging them.

Tina and Cameron came running out and swiftly shuffled the girls off to Tina's bedroom to play and watch movies. Alice took my arm and guided me over to the couch. I sat down and put my head in my hands, trying very hard not to break down. It was futile, though. As soon as Alice sat down next to me and put her arm around me, I lost it. The waterworks were in full effect.

I tried to talk through my sobs, but it ended up sounding incoherent. I took in a deep breath and wiped my tears. "I don't really know why I'm crying. I should be celebrating." I let out something between a whimper and a laugh.

"Well, then, let's celebrate." She got up and went into the kitchen, returning a moment later with a couple of white wine glasses, a wine key and a bottle of Leelanau Cellars Select Harvest Riesling.

"Oh! My favorite!" I took the bottle and the wine key, uncorked the bottle and filled our glasses. "Thanks!"

"No. Thank you." She sipped her wine. "Well, let's figure out how we're going to set things up here. We can start looking for a bigger place tomorrow. I'll call my sister in the morning and get information on what she found."

"Sounds good." I finished my glass and poured myself another. "I brought the girls' air mattress beds. So, we can put them in Tina's room. I can just sleep on the couch, if that's fine with you."

"That'll work for the girls. If you want the couch, you're welcome to it, or you can sleep on my camping air mattress in my room. Then, if the kids get up before you, they won't wake you up."

"That might not be a bad idea. I could use the rest, that vacation wore me out." I gave her a tired smile.

"So, do you want to tell me what happened?" she asked.

I hadn't realized that I hadn't. "I went through things with Tiffany to make sure everything went smooth. He was hiding in his rec room. After she left, he came waltzing into the room, swagger and all. He started telling me that he wished she'd stay. That she was a better mother and housewife than I am."

"Oh my god!" she gasped.

"Oh no, it gets better." I motioned for a refill. "He proceeded to tell me that a woman's place was to take care of the kids, cook, clean and all. Oh, and that I basically sucked at it."

"Huh." I could see that she wanted to go right over and slap him. "I see."

"Yup, that's when I started packing. He tried to grab me. So, I called 911." I took in a breath. She took my hand. "I told them I was leaving my husband, and he was scaring me. That's when he took the phone and smacked me."

"I'm going to kill him." She started to get up. "I hope you hit him with something so hard that he's not getting back up."

"No, I did worse, I ignored him for the most part." I smiled. "He can't stand it when I don't respond. He was looking for a confrontation. I told the girls to get ready to leave, finish packing, and load us up just in time for the cops to get there basically. I came right here."

"So you're completely done then, huh?" She sounded hopeful. "I mean I figured so when you showed up on my front stoop, but I just want to make sure. He hit you. He should be in jail."

"That's not going to help in getting him to give me as peaceful of a divorce as I can get. You know how he

88

gets, and I don't expect this to be easy." I knew it was going to be a battle. I just didn't want to cause any waves. "Yes, though, I am done."

"On that note," she said, going to the kitchen and coming back carrying a new bottle. "Cheers!"

"Did we finish the other one already?" I looked for the bottle, realizing that I was a bit tipsy. "I can't do too much more. Let me go get the girls down to bed. One more glass. We've got a lot to do tomorrow."

We put our kids to bed, sat back down in the living room, enjoyed a couple more glasses and talked about the changes to come. Life had changed so much for both of us. She had a new man in her life (even though she was avoiding her feelings for him), and I was ridding myself of the one in my life.

She went and set up the air mattress in her room. So, we moved in there to finish off our glasses. It was funny. It felt a little like a high school slumber party. At some point in our chatting she fell asleep.

I laid my head back onto my pillow. The best part is, we are back in charge of our lives, and we have each other. I am not sure either of us could go through this without the other. I drifted off to sleep.

Chapter Seven

You Did What In Maui?!

The next day, Alice had to go to work. I figured it would be nice for the kids to all go up there for dinner. "Hey Alice, I'll give you a ride up to work. That way, I can take the kids all to dinner. They've been good all day."

"Ok, I am sure that Lisa can give me a ride home." She finished getting ready as I got the kids together and set to go.

Once we got there, Alice went back to the kitchen area to clock in. I had just gotten the kids situated when I heard a squeal from the back of the restaurant. "You and Ryan Perry?!"

Alice came storming out of the kitchen area straight towards me. "How dare you?!" She was fuming.

"Me? You know better than that," I pleaded.

"Who else knows?" She searched the dining area for any of the others that had gone with her to Maui.

Just then, Lisa came up with a copy of Celebrity Magazine in hand, and showed it to Alice. "You're all over all of the magazines. You're famous!"

"No!" Alice screamed. Everyone in the dining area turned and looked. She looked at me. "How did they get these photos? I didn't notice anyone taking pictures while we were there!" She shoved the magazine into my hands.

The kids all leaned over. Cameron jumped up, shouting, "Mom! It's you!"

Sure enough, right on the cover of the magazine, there was a picture of Alice and Ryan walking on the beach, holding hands. The title read 'Has Ryan found love or just a fling?' Inside, there was an entire spread. There were pictures of all three of us in town and on the beach. There was even a picture of Ryan and Alice and their kiss. I could see that Alice was embarrassed beyond belief. She was generally a private person, and this was not private.

"I don't know what to say, Alice." I was at a loss for words. All I could think was that I needed to smooth this over before it made her run from him more.

She put her head in her hands. "This is yet another thing that I didn't want to deal with. I've got to get to work. Can you just take the kids home? I really don't need them subjected to this if people are going to make comments. Here's $20, pick something up on the way home." She handed me some cash.

"Ok, let me know if you need a ride later." I gathered the kids and headed home.

I thought about calling Ryan, but her talking to him at this point was not a good idea. She was angry, and she'd make this all his fault. If I gave it a few days, she'd calm down and be able to think it through better. Plus, if she was going to get a lot of publicity over this, she'd be a bit more used to it by then.

Several days later, things had calmed down a bit. Alice and Ryan had played phone tag a few times, and people were not asking as many questions as they had the first few days. Alice and I were packing boxes in both of our places. She had found us a cute, five-bedroom house in the country. It was a decent sized house on about two acres. It was brick, had a full front porch, two-car attached garage and a back patio. It was older, but it definitely had charm. The land around it was all woods. So, that was really nice for privacy.

Even though I don't care for living in the country, I knew there were several good points to this one. So, I made a list.

1. We lived in a small town. So, the country wasn't a large leap.

2. Since it was in the country, the rent was a lot less. So, we could afford something with enough bedrooms for all of us.

3. If Ryan were to visit, there would be some sort of privacy.

4. There was enough of a yard so the kids could run and play.

5. We have a home, and it's not with Tim.

We had about a week left to stay in her apartment. She had finished out her two-year lease a while back and had been on a month-to-month lease since then. So there wasn't a problem telling her landlord she was moving.

We had done a lot of preparation while looking for a place, but it seemed like there was still so much to do. However, the thought of getting into a place big enough for all of us was definitely a driving force. It had been less than a week, but with two adults and four kids in a small, two-bedroom apartment, it was a tight squeeze.

After spending the morning cleaning up the apartment, I headed over to get some packing done at

Tim's house. This was a task I did not look forward to. I tried to see him as little as possible. Being successful thus far, I dreaded each trip, worrying that this trip would be the time he'd come home while I was there.

I was getting a few things organized and packed, fairly unmotivated, when my phone rang. Ryan! "Hello?"

"Hello, Vivianne," he replied.

It was awesome to hear his voice. Like it made Maui real. Things had been so chaotic since we got home that it felt like Maui was a dream.

"How are you? I understand that you're back in London?" I asked eagerly.

I don't know why, but I wanted to babble at him. I wanted to tell him everything that had happened. I wanted to tell him that he needed to be there with us to help keep Alice together and motivated since I was such a mess. Plus, I needed my brother.

"Yes. I got home a couple of days ago." His voice sounded apologetic. "I am sorry I did not call. There was a lot to take care of when I got home, and they want me back on set as soon as I can get there."

"No, that's ok. Alice said you have been playing phone tag. Does that mean you're not coming to visit?" I was disappointed.

"No!" He sounded surprised I asked. "That's actually why I am calling. Well, one of the reasons. I wanted to make sure that you both wanted me to come visit."

I laughed. "Like you even have to ask? Of course!"

"Ok, then I can be there next Friday if that'll work for you both. That's just over a week away, and I can stay a couple of days."

Funny how that'll work, we might only have some boxes unpacked, but at least we'll be moved, I thought to myself. "Sure, sounds good."

"Where do you want to meet? I can come to either of your places."

"Oh," I returned to the feeling that I wanted to spill it all out right then. "Alice and I got a place just outside of town with our kids."

"What?" There was concern in his voice. "I take it there have been some developments since you've both gotten home?"

"Oh yeah," I said with a laugh. "You can say that. I'll tell you more when you get here. We both will, I am sure. I can't wait!"

"Why didn't you call me?" The concern in his voice was stronger.

I was shocked that he expected a call, "I didn't know you would have wanted us to, and Alice has been torn. She misses you like crazy, but she feels that calling you will just make her miss you more." I knew that would have been saying too much in her eyes, but he needed some encouragement to stick around.

"I miss her, too." He sighed. "Ok, tell me if anything more happens, and just call me. I want to be sure you both are ok."

"Will do, sir," I joked.

He laughed. "All right, I'll book a flight and make some calls. I'll give you the details later today."

"Do you want me to tell Alice or keep it as a secret?"

"No, tell her, but not until I give you the details. That way she can't try to discourage me or anything. It'll all be set. I'll call you later."

"All right, thanks for calling. Later." I didn't want to let him go. I didn't realize how much I missed chatting with him until then.

"Goodbye." He hung up.

That gave me a new motivation. I whisked through the house, packing and sorting. The thought of having him to hang out with for even just a day and to see that look in Alice's eyes again lifted my mood.

After a couple more hours of packing, I cleaned up the stray boxes and packing supplies, piled up all the packed boxes and looked around. I was glad that the girls were not there. This was so hard, and I needed a moment to let it sink in.

I wandered through the house again, looking into each room as I passed them. When I reached the front door, I turned and looked around. I knew that I still needed to come back and finish getting our stuff, but this time felt like a goodbye. I knew I would officially be a former resident of the house.

I had been in that house for six years, and so much had happened in those years. I had brought both of my girls back from the hospital to this home. Tim and I were married while living here. I had built a life here, and despite Tim's problems, it was a pretty good life.

Now, everything was changing. I was torn between feeling sad that this life was ending, but I was so excited to start anew. I was getting a chance to get back out there. It felt like I had hit the reset button, yet I got to take my girls with me.

I am going to miss this house. As I thought this, I knew it was only a half-truth. I walked out the door and drove to go find something familiar to distract me. I called Alice and told her I had left the house, but that I was going to stop by the store on the way home.

I didn't want her to worry about me, and I knew she would if I told her I just wanted to be alone, not in Tim's house. I also didn't want to be at the apartment when Ryan called back.

I headed into downtown. There was a coffee shop there I liked to go to when I wanted to sit and be alone. It usually wasn't busy at all. So, it was nice. Once there, I bought an Orange Crush and a chocolate chip scone, took a seat at a corner table, plugged my ear buds into my iPhone, turned on Blue October's album "Foiled for the Last Time" and started writing on my laptop.

I didn't have anything in particular to write. I was more just wasting time, not even really focusing on what I was writing most of the time. After an hour or so, I leaned back in my chair and drifted into the music. The album had changed a couple times, and I was listening to Massive Attack 's "Mezzanine." I jumped when the song was interrupted by a call coming in. It was Ryan. "Hey!" I squealed.

"Hey, Vivianne." He sounded upbeat, especially for as late as it was in London.

"I was wondering if you were going to call. It's got to be what? Half past midnight there?" I asked.

"Yeah, sorry. I wanted to make sure everything was set before I called," he replied. "I'll be there in the evening next Friday. I have a car reserved and a room at the Sheridan the next city over. I hope it's not too far of a drive."

"No," I said. "It's only about fifteen minutes away. The Sheridan is a lot nicer than the motels here in town. I'd say to stay at one of the bed-and-breakfasts considering they're pretty nice, but people talk a lot in this town, and you'll never get any privacy."

"Yeah, that wouldn't work. As much as I am used to it, I am sure that Alice wouldn't appreciate it."

"No," I paused. "She's having a hard enough time adjusting to the magazine articles and entertainment program spots and all of the attention that's gotten her."

"Oh, no." I heard that same concern in his voice. "I didn't realize. Tell her I am so sorry."

"I'm just going to leave it alone. She's finally calmed down, and the attention has died down a lot. You can talk to her when you get here. You honestly didn't know?" I asked.

I heard him take in a deep breath, "I saw one magazine here, but I didn't even think about it being a big thing in America. I should have known."

"Oh, yeah." I chuckled. "It's been all over. Pictures of you two kissing, all three of us walking around, you two holding hands. It's been a media circus around here."

"I am so sorry, Vivianne," he apologized.

"It's ok," I lied. "It's to be expected, even if there wasn't anything between the two of you. They still would have made that assumption for one of us with you, right?"

"True," he replied. "Thanks for being so cool about this. Well, I have to get some sleep. I have a pretty busy several days. I just hope it goes fast. I am looking forward to seeing where you ladies live."

"Ok, keep in touch," I urged. "We will see you soon."

"Yes. Good night."

"Good night."

I gathered my things and started for home. I wasn't exactly sure how Alice was going to take Ryan's visit. I know she wanted him to come, but she also was frustrated with the attention, and it's not like she could hide him the whole time he was here. He said to tell her, though. So, I figured the best thing to do was to just come out with it like it was nothing.

I pulled up to the apartment complex and parked, sitting in my car for a few minutes to finish the song I was listening to. When I walked into the apartment, Alice was cleaning up the dinner dishes while the kids were getting ready for bed.

I set my stuff down on the couch and walked into the kitchen. "Hey, lady, thanks for letting me have some time to myself tonight. Do you need any help?"

"Nope," she said with a smile. "I've got it. Did you enjoy it?"

"Yeah. Well, as much as one can when this sort of thing happens." I looked at her to read her mood. When I was sure she was in a fair mood, I continued. "Ryan called. He's going to be here to visit next Friday for a couple of days."

She stopped what she was doing for a moment, looking down at the counter. I was a bit nervous that she was going to yell at me, but she started working on the dishes again. "Cool. It'll be nice to see him again."

"Really?" I was shocked.

"Um, yeah." She looked confused. "Why wouldn't it be?"

"You know, it should be. I was just half expecting you to be upset considering all of the attention the magazine articles and stuff have brought."

"Yeah, well, I miss him. Are you happy?" She flashed me a dirty look. She put down the dish she was washing and picked up a hand towel to dry her hands, leaning back on the counter.

"I just don't know what to do," she continued, her eyes welling up with tears. "I miss him so much. Every part of me is crying out to tell him that I love him, and that I want to be with him except for that little part of me that is so scared and keeps me pulling away. What do I do?" She sat down on the floor, pulled her knees up tight to her chest and put her face in her hands.

"I hate seeing you like this, Alice." I kneeled down next to her, wrapped my arms around her shoulders and laid my head on her shoulder. "Take it slow. There's no reason to rush anything. He'll be here waiting for you when you're ready."

"How do you know that?" she asked. "How do you know I'm not screwing this up? Like I said in Maui, he can have any woman he wants. Why would he wait around for me?"

I sat up and looked at her. "Because he loves you," I replied.

She looked up at me, hope in her eyes. "You think?"

"I know," I assured her. "Give him time to prove it while you're taking time to let him in. It'll work out."

We got up and finished cleaning the kitchen. At least she was excited about seeing him. I didn't want to have to force her. I laughed to myself.

After the kitchen was clean, she and I settled in for a movie and talked about getting moved and preparing for Ryan's visit. Alice called the landlord to see if we could start moving boxes in the next day. He said that would be fine. He would be available for us to come get the keys in the morning. Yet another thing that was going in our favor... thank goodness. The house might be unpacked and presentable enough when Ryan came to visit.

We spent the next week packing boxes, moving boxes and unpacking boxes. I had picked up two regular column jobs at two papers. One was our local paper, and the other was from a city down by Detroit. So, it was nice to have more of an income.

I had filed for divorce and was about three weeks away from our first hearing in front of a judge. My lawyer was a friend of mine that I went to high school with. So, he wasn't charging much. That helped a lot. He was sure I had a good chance that it would go my way, especially since I wasn't asking for the house. I had also gotten primary custody of the kids, pending the formal hearing, and had worked out visitation weekends with Tim to coincide with Alice's free weekends so we were without kids at the same time.

Alice was registered for school and was pulling in extra shifts at both jobs. She was trying to save up as much money as she could for when she started taking classes. She would have to cut back at work in order to attend her classes and log flight hours, considering she was going to school to be a pilot.

Things were looking up, and it felt good. The kids were adjusting to living together. Our first time taking the kids to the new place was our first night living there. They ran around the house and the yard, staking claim on rooms. Cameron and Tina had their own rooms, and Elizabeth and Victoria were sharing a room. They were only a couple of years apart, so it worked out great. There was also a playroom area in the basement. That made the kids really happy.

We all seemed to settle into the new house. Plus, with me working from home on my writing, her work and school schedule and the kids' school schedules blended nicely. There wasn't going to be any problems as far as needing daycare other than if we wanted to go out together for a night without kids. Then, we'd just hire one of the local teenagers to come over. Not a problem.

Alice had taken the weekend off so she could spend time with Ryan. We had talked about how we were going to plan the weekend. Friday evening, I was going to cook dinner, and we would stay in for the most part. This way, he could meet the kids and just relax.

Saturday, we would all do breakfast and maybe a movie or something. Then, I would take the kids home while they went out to dinner and spent some time alone. Sunday was up in the air. We didn't know when he was leaving for sure. He said he'd be able to stay for a couple of days, but I wasn't sure exactly how long or even if he had anything in mind that he wanted to do.

When Friday morning arrived, I woke up at about eight. Alice was already awake. I heard her moving things around in the other room. Well, rooms, I should say. I got up and wandered into the living room. She was frantically unpacking, decorating and cleaning the house. I laughed when I saw her setting up a small ladder in the dining room to hang a piece of art.

"What are you laughing at?" she snapped.

"You." I laughed harder. "You're doing your usual '*I'm stressed*' cleaning thing. It's funny. Are you a bit nervous about Ryan coming to visit?"

"Um, ya think?" she said sarcastically. "I don't want him seeing this place in boxes. He's rich and classy. I'm insecure enough without feeling like he's seeing this place a mess."

"True. I grant you that." I picked up the cleaner and a cleaning towel. "Let's get to work. He'll be here in a mere ten hours." I laughed.

She threw a dirty paper towel at me. "Shut up and start making yourself useful."

We spent the day cleaning and unpacking. When the kids got up, we even put them to work unpacking their rooms and the play room. By lunchtime, it was looking like a home rather than a storage unit. So, that felt good.

We kept the kids home from school that day. It was a combination of the kids being very anxious to meet Ryan and us needing their help to get things unpacked. One day couldn't hurt, and it was nice seeing everyone so busy and hard at work.

I could see Alice's stress slowly changing into motivation. She was great at stress cleaning, which was something I wished I could pick up. Normally, when I get stressed, I just write or go dancing. I have always admired her for that quality. It was helpful to be around her when I was stressed, though. She usually got me into that frame of mind, and I got more accomplished. I hope I can make this a habit.

Right about four in the evening, we stopped cleaning and started getting ourselves ready by showering, changing clothes and getting ourselves presentable. We chose to go casual but nice considering we were just going to be hanging out at the house. Just regular, nice clothes. That decision helped Alice feel a bit calmer. She wasn't big on dressing up. When she had in the past, it seemed to make her that much more nervous.

I finished getting dressed first and made sure the kids were presentable before starting dinner. I didn't want it to be ready the moment he walked through the door. I was sure he'd want to relax and look around first. So, I waited to start until about 5:30.

About 5:45, Alice emerged from her bedroom. She was wearing a sleeveless, satin top in light blue. The straps criss-crossed in the back, and the bottom of the top floated away from the body. She had picked it up while in Maui but hadn't worn it. It looked great with her jeans, ankle-height boots and a very simple silver necklace with the sapphire pendant she had inherited from her grandmother.

Her make-up and hair looked the best I'd seen in years. Yup, she had worked for this. I watched as she waltzed through the room, tossing a royal blue cardigan over the back of the lazy boy in the living room. You could see the tension flow off of her as she was trying so hard to look calm and put together.

"Hey, woman, you ok?" I asked.

"Yeah," she said, fidgeting with setting the dinner dishes on the table. She walked into the kitchen, trying to avoid looking at me. Finally, she snapped, "Fine! I'm nervous. Shut it. I just haven't talked to him since Maui. Now, he's coming here."

"Yeah, that's got to suck." I grinned.

"Thanks." She slugged my shoulder. "What a good friend you are."

"I know," I said, slyly. "Listen, it's going to be a good night. The kids look fine. I look fine. The house looks fine. You look amazing. He will be impressed. He doesn't expect a mansion and chandeliers. He knows our situation, and he's not coming for our money. He's coming for your booty."

"Oh, thanks." She left the kitchen to go check and make sure the kids were still presentable.

I had just gotten the chicken in the oven and finished chopping the veggies for the salad when the doorbell rang. It was just about six o'clock. *How punctual*, I thought.

"You answer it," I yelled from the kitchen. "I've still got the rice and rolls to make."

"Great," I heard her mutter. Then she yelled down the hallway, "Kids, get in the living room, please!"

The kids all came running; Tina was the leader of the line. They all took seats on the couch as Alice answered the door. "Ryan! It's great to see you," Alice said nervously.

104

Ryan stepped into the house and gave her a hug. "It's really nice to see you again. I take it these are the little ones I've heard so much about?" he said, motioning to the kids.

I made sure I was at a good stopping point, grabbed a hand towel and headed into the living room. "Ryan!" I ran over and gave him a hug.

"Vivianne, I'm so glad that you helped organize this. Thanks!"

He hugged me back.

"I'm so glad that you made it. These are the kids," I motioned for them to stand. "The two youngest, Elizabeth and Victoria, are mine. The two eldest, Tina and Cameron, are Alice's."

He walked over and shook each of their hands, telling them it was nice to meet them. I thought Tina was going to faint. She answered politely and ran off to her room, dialing her cell phone on the way.

Ryan laughed. "I get that a lot."

"Oh, so we don't look silly then?" Alice asked.

"Oh no, you do," he smiled at her. "But that's ok. I like your kind of silly."

I went back into the kitchen and got a bottle of white wine out of the fridge, a wine key and three glasses and took them into the living room,

"Dinner is going to be about forty-five minutes. So, I cleaned up the back patio and chilled a bottle of wine."

I passed the glasses to Alice and Ryan, handing my glass to Alice as I opened the bottle. Ryan took the bottle before I could get started, handing me back my glass. "Allow me," he said. He opened the bottle and poured us each a glass. I put the cork back in the bottle and put it in the fridge.

"Hey, Alice, why don't you show him around, and I'll meet you both on the back patio in a few?"

"Ok." She led Ryan down the hall and started giving him the tour.

I finished preparing the rest so all we had to do was wait for the chicken to finish baking. As I basted it again, I heard the two of them chatting and laughing on the patio. The kids had gone down to the basement playroom. Well, except for Tina, who was in her room gossiping to her friends.

I wiped the counter down, grabbed my glass and headed out to the patio, "Hey, guys, have I missed anything?"

"Just the tour of your very nice home," Ryan complimented. "I am impressed at how much you both have done with the house in such a short period of time. It looks great!"

"Thanks." I was honored. "See, Alice? He's impressed." She glared at me.

"How are you holding up, Vivianne?" Ryan hadn't asked about my pending divorce yet.

I put my hand on his arm and tilted my head a little, trying to give an impression of amused candor.

"I am doing great. It's a new life with new freedom. I couldn't be better, and the girls are adjusting better than I thought they would. Thanks for asking." I looked at Alice. "We're doing great."

"Yes, we're all doing a lot better." Alice backed me up. "It's odd how things are falling into place."

Alice and Ryan made idle chitchat for a while. I was pretty content to just sit back and stare at the stars. I really didn't have a lot to say. Well, nothing I really wanted to say out loud to anyone present, anyway.

I heard my timer go off and excused myself to go in and get dinner on the table. I told the kids to get their hands washed and take their seats at the dinner table. Then, I informed Alice and Ryan that dinner was pretty much ready.

They came into the room, still chatting about Ryan's new movie that he was filming and what all of the traveling was like. I couldn't believe that Alice was actually interested. I wasn't sure why, but it struck me as odd.

Alice went over to the wine rack and selected a bottle of red wine for dinner. I was pleased with her selection. It was a light red with a floral tone to it. It wasn't too heavy for a chicken dinner, and yet it was robust enough to take the stage on its own. I was teaching her well, it seemed. A good knowledge of wine can only help a person in high society settings. I could also see she was proud of herself when Ryan and I approved of her selection.

I took the wine glasses and rinsed them out, setting them at our places at the table. The kids had taken their seats, as did Alice and Ryan. I set the rest of the serving dishes on the table and took my place, serving up the chicken to the kids and myself as everyone started passing the other dishes around.

"Does everyone have what they need?" I asked, noticing everyone had already started eating.

I settled into eating. It was funny how things were quiet for several minutes. I had to take that as a compliment.

After a while, Ryan looked up from his dish and said, "This is great, Vivianne. Very well done. Thank you."

"No. Thank you, Ryan." It was nice to be complimented by someone that was surely used to eating gourmet meals by professional chefs.

He turned to the kids, and asked, "How are all of you enjoying the new house?"

All of the kids started talking at once. Then, Tina spoke up. "We all love the house. Cameron and I like having a yard, and the girls love having a big brother and big sister around."

"That's got to be nice for you all to be so close already," Ryan observed.

Alice spoke up. "They've been close since Vivianne had them. Actually, I think Tina and Cameron, especially, bonded with the girls when they were in Vivianne's belly."

"You know," I interjected. "I think you're right. They used to always feel my belly and lay their heads on there, trying to hear the baby. They even talked to them all of the time."

"That's very cool." Ryan looked over at the kids. "I can see how people think you two are sisters."

Alice and I looked at each other and smiled.

"So, how long are you planning on staying, Ryan?" Alice asked.

Ryan smiled. "I fly out Monday. I have to be on set and ready to get back to work by Tuesday."

"On set?" Tina asked, excitedly.

"Yes." He looked at Alice out of the corner of his eye. "I have been filming a new movie but decided to take a vacation while they finished some scenes they didn't need me there for. Now, I have to go back to finish my scenes."

"What movie?" Tina was hoping to have some sort of gossip for her friends.

He looked right at her this time. "It's the sequel to your Mom and Aunt Vivianne's favorite movie of mine." He turned to smile at both of us.

Tina's eyes got huge. "Wow! I didn't know they were making a part two! My friends are going to freak!"

Ryan, Alice and I laughed.

Tina scarfed down a few more bites and asked, "Mom, can I be excused?"

Alice laughed. "Sure, Tina. Just don't be too loud."

"Mom!" She was embarrassed and rushed off to her room.

"She's beautiful, Alice," Ryan commented. "All of the kids are beautiful and very well behaved." He looked at Cameron. "Well, the girls are. You, Cameron, are a very handsome young man."

"Thank you," I said, jumping in. "Yes, the kids are great. We are truly blessed."

Through the rest of dinner, everyone chatted. My girls even started opening up. They were usually shy when they first met someone, and they hadn't really said much to Ryan since he had arrived.

It was a very nice and relaxing dinner. Alice and Ryan's exchanges were always so genuine and easy. It wasn't hard to see how well they fit together. I saw through the meal how they would get so close together while talking. Their hands would move so they would be just barely out of reach. I kept hoping one of them would make that move to reach out, but it never happened.

After dinner was over, I told the kids to go get ready for bed and told Ryan and Alice to head out to the patio, handing them the bottle of wine. They tried to protest, but I assured them that it would be much more efficient with just one person whipping through it. So, they reluctantly headed out.

I worked slower than I normally would to give them more time. It was nice to hear her laugh and flirt. This was truly a turning point. I could see it in her eyes. His meeting and getting along with her kids was a huge point in her eyes. Plus, how he didn't judge her or our house even though he comes from so much more money was a major selling point, too. She had been judged by so many people in her past, and so many of them had no real reason or ground to stand on in their judgments.

After the table was cleared and the dishes were loaded into the dishwasher, I made sure the kids were all tucked into bed and headed out to the patio to join them. Alice topped my glass off, and we sat back and chatted for a couple more hours. I tried to give them privacy a couple of times, but each time, Alice would tell me that she didn't want me to leave. So, I stayed.

Around midnight, Ryan left for his hotel. He hugged us both and kissed Alice on the hand. We made plans to come to the hotel with the kids and have breakfast at the hotel restaurant.

After he drove out of the driveway, I latched onto Alice's arm and guided her to sit on the couch with me. "So? I know there's something you need to tell me."

"I don't know what you're talking about." Her attempt at being coy was almost annoying.

"Listen, lady, spill it." I yanked her arm.

"Fine." She poured the last of the bottle into her glass. "He gets along with the kids. He didn't look at us like trash even though we clearly have less than him. Talking to him is easy. And yes, I am very attracted to him."

"Ha!" I snapped. "I had a feeling that tonight was a turning point for you."

"Oh, don't get me wrong." She cut me off. "I'm not just going to jump into anything. I still don't want anything physical yet. I need to take this slow."

"I understand." I hadn't expected a complete turnaround. "At least you're open to it now. That's a huge step."

"True." She looked down at her glass. "He's wonderful. It's just hard to let go and give in."

"Yeah." I knew it was going to take time. "I am sure you'll come together in time. I've never seen you so at ease with someone even with your feelings of apprehension."

"I know!" She looked up at me. "He scares me to death, but I can't help but feel so relaxed and comfortable with him. It's very strange."

"It's very cool." I nudged her shoulder and smiled.

We both leaned our heads back and sat quietly for a while. I was sure her mind was on Ryan. I thought about that a little, but mostly, I thought about me getting involved with anyone else. My marriage had ended. I was single again. Would I be like Alice if I was presented with someone new?

I used to jump into relationships so quickly, and I usually tried not to carry baggage from one failed relationship into my view on the next relationship. However, I wasn't sure that I wouldn't react like Alice the next time. Actually, the way I felt, I wasn't even sure there would be a next time. That thought scared me.

I pondered that for a moment. What if there wasn't a next time? What if I had become so jaded that I wouldn't be able to see anyone in that light anymore? What if I let someone really good for me pass me by because I couldn't get past the thought that they could hurt me? What if I never have anyone come my way who is what I want and need? Could I spend the rest of my life without another half?

The answer that came to mind surprised me. Not just because it was a 'yes' but because of how quickly it came to me. I could spend the rest of my life without a partner. I just didn't want to. I wanted that passion, dedication, loyalty and love. I wanted someone to stand by me, protect me, support me, walk with me, guide me, hear me and embrace me. I wanted someone that would be there with me through everything. For me, for them and for my kids.

I loved what Ryan was working towards with Alice. I wanted my own version of Ryan. I just wasn't sure it was going to happen.

I got up from the couch and put in my Afghan Whigs CD, "Black Love," and selected track number eight, "Night by Candlelight." I returned to my place on the couch. There wasn't much to be said. I had witnessed the evening, and what needed to be said had already been said.

After the song was over, I got up and loaded a few CDs into the CD changer and hit shuffle. Music always helped me think through things. It was a good visit.

I knew we would enjoy the rest of the weekend. Tonight, however, we needed to just sit back and think about the situations we were going through. If she wanted to talk, she would. I didn't want to burden her with what was on my mind. She had enough going through hers.

Come morning, I once again found Alice already up and around. It was seven in the morning. We were supposed to be at the hotel by nine. She was already showered, dressed and sitting on the couch drinking a cup of coffee.

"You are making me look like a slacker, you know," I teased.

"I didn't sleep well," she mumbled.

"Are you ok?" I saw a bit of worry had returned to her face.

She shook her head. "Yeah. I'm fine. Just dwelling on silly things. I'm just thinking about tonight."

"Ah." I put a hand on her shoulder. "You'll be fine."

"Oh, I know," she assured me. "I am just going back and forth about how to handle any moves he might make."

"I would say to just let things happen that happen." I walked towards the kitchen to make a cup of tea. "I mean, decide when and if a situation arises. I know you're feeling more and more for him, but you're not going to be ready until you're in a situation and feel it. So, don't worry about it. Don't stress yourself out. If he makes a move tonight, you'll only know at that moment if you're ready to give in."

"True." She finished her coffee and joined me in the kitchen. "He was great last night, wasn't he?"

"Yup." We sat at the table. "You suck."

She laughed. "I suck? Why?"

"Oh, you don't want me to answer," I said with a smirk.

"Why not? You know me. I always want to hear what you have to say, even if you're wrong… as usual."

"Oh, is that how you're going to be?" I threw my napkin at her. "Well, then, you have one of the best guys in the world after you, and you are hesitating." I smiled. "I want a Ryan."

"I knew it!" she howled. "You want Ryan!"

"No!" I was embarrassed. I was hoping she wouldn't take it that way, but I knew she would. "I want my own version of Ryan. He's cute and nice and everything. He's just not quite my type."

"Oh, yeah, right. How could Prince Charming not be your type?" She threw the napkin back at me. "Then what's wrong with him?"

"Nothing is wrong with him." I fidgeted with the napkin. "He's great. However, one of the things that has allowed us to be friends is that we can see why we are interested in guys, but we don't usually get interested in the same guys. I can totally see why you're interested in Ryan. Like I said, he's great. I would just tweak a few things for my own version."

"Oh?" She looked at me intently. "Like what?"

"Well, I'm not sure." I was a bit puzzled at my inability to describe it, to be honest. "I am not sure if it's that Ryan isn't really my type or if it's because he's basically with you, but I am not into him like that. The things I would change? Well, someone that's not into you or who you're into, number one. Aside from that? I guess a little more like me. Ryan complements you very nicely. He's quiet and stands back to let you have control. I like control, but I need someone that will take control when he knows what I want. As far as looks go? I won't deny, Ryan is very good-looking, but he's got a roughness to his look. It's not for me. You like that."

"Yeah, I can see both points." She nodded. "You're right. He's not right up your alley. I'm sorry for thinking that. I never thought you'd try anything, but, you know."

"Oh, I do." I got up, refilled my cup and leaned on the counter. "I have what I want in my mind, but I am not sure if I am ever going to find it. I don't want to keep trying guys that only have part of what I want. I want what I want. It scares me to think that my mother is right. I'm afraid that guy doesn't exist. If that's true, then I'd rather just stay single than deal with the same failures over and over."

115

"I guess I can see your point." She stared out the back sliding door into the woods. "I just don't want to see you alone for the rest of your life."

"Hey, it's me." I laughed sarcastically. "I will be fine. At the very least, I'll be happier than with some jerk."

"True, very true." She got up, rinsed her mug out and put it in the dishwasher. "Well, let's get the kids going. It's seven-thirty, and I still have to get all pretty yet." We laughed.

She walked down the hallway, knocking on the kids' bedroom doors to wake them. "Get up, kids! Let's get ready to go have breakfast with Ryan."

I could hear Tina jump out of bed and start rifling through her closet. The other kids were moving a bit more slowly, coming into the kitchen to get breakfast. I reminded them that's what we were going to go do with Ryan. They mumbled as they returned to their rooms to start getting dressed.

On the way to the hotel, Alice sat in the passenger seat, staring out the window and fidgeting with her purse strap. I couldn't believe how easily she got lost in thought these days.

The kids were playing and chattering in the back of the van. Tina was texting away. I laughed out loud at the thought of what she could be telling her friends. Was she happy for her mom or completely jealous? I laughed again.

Alice's demeanor didn't change the entire way there. She pretty much stayed quiet through most of breakfast, but it was a good time. We all chatted; the kids behaved; the food was great. Plus, they sat us in a closed area in the back. The privacy was nice and allowed us to relax and have a good time.

After breakfast, we took the kids to Impression 5 Children's Science Museum. The kids loved going there. I suggested it because I wanted her to see him in a light that was focused on the kids.

I was not surprised at how well they all got along with Ryan. He was great with the kids, and I knew it could only help her view of him. Plus, he seemed to be able to easily switch from a formal setting to playing with kids. So, why not? Right?

After the museum, I took the kids back home so Alice and Ryan could hang out without any distractions. The kids each hugged Ryan and told him they wished he was coming with us. He said he'd see them soon.

He then hugged me and whispered in my ear, "Thank you, Vivianne."

"No problem," I responded. "You'll bring her home?"

"Yes," he assured.

"Good, I'll have a bottle of wine or three chilled."

He smiled as I took the kids to leave. We headed back home, stopping by the corner store to grab soda, snacks and the wine. Then home to bide our time until they got home.

Alice sent me texts off and on. I was anxiously waiting between messages to hear what was going on. I knew that after we left the hotel, they were heading downtown to Riverwalk to walk and talk for a while, then to dinner. They were not sure after that.

I was getting texts ranging from silly little comments like "He's so sweet" or "He's so wonderful" to "Why am I being so stupid?" It was amusing, almost like being inside her head on a first date sort of thing. I even got a description of the meal they ate. I shook my head as I read that. She wasn't very adventurous when it came to eating new things. Yet another thing I hoped he might be able to break her of and show her there's so much more out there.

After dinner, they opted to come back to the house and hang out. I was not surprised. Her texts had been getting more and more endearing. So I was sure that she was ready to have me around as a buffer for her emotions and a distraction for them both. I wished that she would have stayed out with him, but then that wouldn't have been Alice.

It was a relaxing evening, though. The kids went to bed on time, and we mainly sat at the dining table, playing cards and chatting. We talked about where each of us came from and how we were raised. How Alice and I met and became friends. He told us about his childhood and how life in London is.

Overall, it was a getting-to-know-you kind of evening. It was nice to be past the ice-breaking stage and finally back to being friends. I had missed this from when we were in Maui.

I had moments when I felt like a third wheel, however. I wanted to excuse myself, but I knew they both were enjoying the group conversation, even if Ryan did want more time alone with her.

The rest of Ryan's stay in Michigan was fun. He would come and hang out at our house. We took the kids to the hotel to go swimming. We all went out to see a movie. We kept pretty busy. On his last day, the kids were all outside playing, and I was working on organizing the kitchen some more when I saw them sitting next to each other on the couch.

They both looked really into whatever they were talking about and were leaned in to face each other. There were serious moments, lots of smiles, staring into each other's eyes and occasional laughing. They were leaning in toward each other little by little, each with a hand placed on the couch close to each other. By all the signs, this would have been the moment that someone should have held the other's hand or even leaned in for a kiss.

They had inched in a little further every time I peeked around the corner. I was acting busy in the kitchen, even though I had been finished for a while. If I went into the living room now, it would only stop any chances of something happening.

Finally, they both leaned in for a long hug. Well, it's better than nothing. As they pulled back, he kissed her on the cheek. She leaned into it, and you could see his hold on her get slightly tighter and a smile come to his lips.

They stood up and came into the kitchen. He came up to give me a hug. "It's been truly great to see you again, Vivianne, and meet your kids. I hope to see you all soon, and I'll call when I can."

"Sounds great." I gave him another hug. "We'll miss you."

Alice called the kids in to say goodbye. They all hugged him and said they hoped he was coming back soon. After their goodbyes were done, they scattered back to playing. Tina was obviously upset at his leaving, but Alice and I could see it wasn't that whole "he's a celebrity" thing anymore. She really liked him for her mother, and she didn't want to see him go.

He headed out to the rental car. I stood on the porch as Alice walked him out. They stood there talking for a few minutes and then hugged for quite a while. He pulled back after a moment and held her arms in his hands, looking into her eyes. She reached up with her hands and held his forearms.

They talked for a moment standing like that. Then, he leaned in and kissed her on the forehead. I was sure he was going for a kiss on the lips, but she pulled her face down as he leaned in.

Give it time, she'll come around, I thought.

Ryan got into his rental car and left. Alice came walking up to the porch and shook her head at me as she came closer. She knew I had seen what happened and that I wanted to talk about it, but she didn't, as usual.

However, to my surprise, she came right up to me and hugged me. I had rarely, if ever, seen a display of emotions come from her. She had started crying as she walked up. I was at a loss for words for a moment. Usually she didn't want me to say anything, but I had a feeling that this time, she wanted to hear that it was going to be all right.

"I can't possibly know exactly how you are feeling. I know your emotions are basically waging war with each other, but I know that you'll get this sorted out, and Ryan will be here waiting for you when you do.

You guys are too perfect for each other for this to not work out," I consoled her.

"Thanks." She wiped her eyes.

"Now, how about that last bottle of wine?" I smiled.

Chapter Eight

A Long and Busy Summer

I think we both would agree that that summer was both very long and very busy. Alice had cut some of her hours back on her serving job to make room for classes and flight time. She was doing about the same on the weekends except for when she had to log flight hours or something for a class. It was the first of five semesters for her training. She was excited to finally be on track with her plans.

I was pretty busy myself. I still had some freelance writing jobs and both of those columns I had gotten when we first got back from Maui. The column was a mom's advice column. I was giving tips about everything from the various household uses for vinegar to ways to cope with feeding a child with food allergies.

Then, my writing had started getting recognized. That column was picked up by four other papers in nearby, larger cities. Another local paper asked me to do a column about local events and staple places to go for kids and families. I was thrilled to be doing that sort of thing. I knew the area inside and out. So, it was a pretty easy column, but I knew it would help out others that were searching for good places to go.

It was nice that things were still going the way they were planned. To be honest, things were better than that. They were falling into place, nicely. Alice was going to school to be what she always wanted to be. She had two jobs that worked with her on her schooling whenever she needed. The kids had adjusted well to the house, and we were on a regular workout schedule

My writing was taking off. The girls loved having Alice and the kids around. The working out kept me motivated when I needed to sit for a few hours and write. The divorce was pretty much over. The last thing to do was to split a few last material items and finalize visitations and child support. Tim had cooperated much more than I anticipated, which made things smooth when we would have to go to court and deal with a judge.

Ryan made a few more stops. He was out our way for a few days about once a month. Each visit was too short, it seemed. We would have a great time, almost as if he hadn't been gone for a while. Then, he'd be off again.

It was nice that he made time like he did, though. A couple of the visits were while he was shooting his latest film. He actually had to rearrange some schedules to make them happen. I think Alice noticed that effort and appreciated it.

I could see them growing closer and closer each time he came. They would actually have time alone by her suggestion. Usually, it was just sitting out on the back patio or taking a walk through the woods or something, but time alone was time alone.

On his August visit, they had wandered off to take a walk after dinner. I had time to clean up the dishes, put the kids to bed and watch almost all of "Boondock

Saints" before I saw them walking back up the drive... holding hands!

I wanted to jump up and burst through the door. I wanted to run over to them and ask if they had finally made a move toward getting together as a couple. I knew, though, that if I were to go running out, it would probably make things awkward. So, I stayed sitting on the couch, tapping my foot.

They lingered outside for a while on the porch, just chatting. Chatting? They're just chatting?! If they have moved into holding hands, why are they not in here sharing the news of this new stage in their relationship with me? Have they no decency to know that I must have seen them at some point and that I would be overly anxious to know what's going on?! I stomped off to the kitchen to occupy myself with the menial task of cleaning out the fridge.

I was knee deep in leftovers and pretty much had the contents of the fridge emptied onto the counter and the floor, cleaner and paper towel in hand, when they came waltzing into the kitchen.

Alice half gasped and half laughed. "What are you doing?"

"Oh, I don't know," I said, sharp sarcasm in my voice. "Maybe trying not to come running outside and interrupting your visit to find out what's going on."

"What are you talking about?" She tried to play coy.

I stood up, almost knocking over a few bottles of dressing. "Don't even act like you two lovebirds were not just walking around holding hands. I saw you."

"Oh, that?" She laughed.

"Yes, that." I stared her right in the eyes, trying not to burst out in laughter.

Ryan was laughing. "You two are hilarious."

"Hilarious or not, spill it, you two. I have not worked so hard and had so much patience for something like that, as trivial as it may seem, to happen and you not tell me what's going on." I shook my finger at them.

Alice turned to leave the room. "I'll tell you later."

"Oh, you're going to play like that?" I was astounded that I would be left out of the loop so easily. "Fine. I see how you are. I'm going to bed."

I shoved everything back into the fridge and stomped off. I couldn't help but laugh. If anything, this would encourage Alice to keep up the level she'd reached with Ryan. Yet, I couldn't help but think that they had a hidden agenda. I dismissed it as their unwillingness to let me in on what changed and brought them closer. I changed for bed, put in a movie and laid down to sleep.

Before Ryan left that night, he peeked into my room, knocking first. "Vivianne?"

"Yes?" I was half asleep, watching "Pride & Prejudice."

"Are you really upset with us?" he asked.

I laughed. "No, I was just playing around. I figured it would be easier to get out of the way if I made a spectacle of myself. If I just said I was going to bed without a reason or anything, Alice might have tried to convince me to stay and hang out. When I saw that you two were holding hands, I wanted to make sure I stayed out of the way tonight."

"Oh." He let out a breath. "Okay, I was worried for a moment. Thanks. I did miss your company tonight, though. I'm leaving tomorrow, but I'll call you soon. I'm going to need a favor."

"Oh?" I was curious. "What kind of favor?"

"Let me make sure it's going to be able to pan out first, and I'll call you then." He winked.

"Sure." I smiled. "I am sure whatever it is, it'll be no problem."

"Again, thanks, Vivianne. You're a great friend." He closed the door.

The rest of August passed with us staying even busier than the last few months. The kids had gone back to school, and all that that entailed kept our free time pretty scarce. We were a couple of weeks into September before we knew it.

It was a nice day out. Victoria was playing on the back patio, and I had decided to work on that week's mom column from my laptop on the patio table. A warm breeze was blowing, and the sound of Beethoven's Symphony No. 9 was coming from the living room stereo system. All in all, a peaceful day.

I was typing away, trying to tie up the end of the piece when my phone rang. I didn't even look at the caller ID before answering. "Hello?"

"Hello, Vivianne, how are you?" A familiar voice rang from the other end of the line. "I am so sorry I haven't called before now. I have been trying to get things in order."

"No, not a problem," I replied, happy to hear his voice. "Things have been crazy around here, and Alice has told me that you two have been in contact. So, I know you're not blowing us off."

He laughed. "I wouldn't ever. So, I have some time free next week, but I wanted to talk to you before I made arrangements for this visit."

He only ever talked to me about visits when he had a surprise. "Okay? What's up?"

"Well, it's actually for all of you, but I want to surprise her with it if you think it's a good thing." He sounded nervous.

It was for all of us, so proposing is out of the question, I joked to myself.

"What about both you and Alice bring your kids to London over Christmas and New Year's? I am having a party for both holidays, and I'd truly love it if you all were there."

"Wow, Ryan." I was amazed at his request. "I am game. I think that would be great. I am not sure how Alice will respond, but it's worth a shot to ask."

"I also want to take Alice to a charity benefit I am going to in New York next month."

"That sounds awesome!" I was happy for her and jealous at the same time. I love those kinds of events, and she saw the whole dressing up thing as frivolous.

"I will hire a nanny for while you are with me in London, but I was wondering if you could watch her kids when--well, if--she joins me in New York next month," he requested.

"Like you have to ask." I was surprised he was so apprehensive to ask. "I'll be more than happy. Besides, depending on the weekend, they might be at their dad's that weekend. So, even less of a worry."

"Good, I am glad. I didn't want you to think that I was leaving you out," he clarified.

"Nope, I don't expect you guys to have me tagging along for everything. I'm not down for three-way relationships." I laughed. "I like you, Ryan, just not like that."

He laughed with me. "Oh, I see. You're too good for me?"

"Yes," I joked. "Besides, you like my best friend. That just makes you uckie."

"Now I'm uckie?" he joked back.

"Yup, uckie. So, uckie is off limits. Be as cute and charming as you want to be. Once my best friend is into someone, I can never see them in that light," I explained.

"Well, I am glad we have that cleared up," he said. "So, I'll be there next Wednesday, but it'll only be for one night. I am doing an interview Wednesday morning on the Today Show and will fly there right after. Then, I have to be in London Friday morning for a family thing with my mother and father."

"I believe Alice is working that evening, but she is usually out and home by nine. So, we can work around that, right?" I was trying to scan over my online calendar I kept for the household in my head. "You can come to the house whenever you get in town and hang out with the kids and me. We can set up a nice, relaxing atmosphere for when she gets there, and you can let her in on the plans then."

He paused. "Yeah. I was thinking about taking her out, but you're probably right. It'll be less pressure, and she won't have everyone staring. That would not be good. She might turn down the invitation just because of that."

"Yes. She doesn't do very well when there's a lot of attention on her. The best place to ask her is here, at home." I thought for a moment. "If you two want to go out after she says yes to going, I can stay here with the kids."

"Sounds like a plan. Besides, she might be too tired from school and working to go out anywhere. She might just want to stay in for the night and relax. I'll just call her and tell her that I'll be there for one night, but I won't tell her anything else. I don't want her thinking it's anything more than a regular visit." He was getting even more nervous. I could hear it in his voice.

"We'll just have to play the going out thing by ear, and I won't tell her anything either. I'll let her tell me about your visit as usual. If I tell her that I know you're coming, she'll know something is up," I suggested.

"Not a problem. I had better get going. They're calling me to finish up the scenes, and no one likes an actor too busy to work. I'll talk to you next week?"

"Next week," I echoed. "I can't wait to see the look on her face. I am sure she'll love the idea. Well, later."

"Let's hope so. Goodbye." he hung up the phone.

I went back to wrapping up my column piece and played with Victoria for a while. I think I was nervous about Alice saying no, too. It would be foolish of her to not take him up on either offer, let alone both. Now, I just had to contain my excitement so she didn't know something was up.

This proved to be a fairly difficult task over the next few days. When she told me about his visit, I had to act like I was really into cooking what I was making for dinner so I didn't give anything away.

Finally, Wednesday morning rolled around. He also told her that he was doing the Today Show interview. So, we both got up early to watch. As usual, there was a huge line-up of topics and people. We watched all about some new supposed discovery to cure stretch marks. There was a specialist on the newest all natural make-up line. Rachael Ray was doing her latest recipes, etc., etc. Finally, Ryan came on.

Alice sat in the recliner, sipping her coffee, staring at the TV. I was amused at how she watched like it was breaking news on a cure for cancer. I didn't tease her, though. She was nervous. When we first returned from Maui, there were so many people who wouldn't leave her alone because she spent time with Ryan Perry. She convinced most of them that it was just a vacation friend thing, and we had not been real public when he came to visit.

This interview would be watched by so many of the women in our community. Whatever he said would be known by all of these women, and they had plenty of other women on speed dial. I guess I was a bit nervous, too, if I was honest about it. I mean, I had gotten a bit of attention from people for hanging out with him, too. So, whatever he said could affect both of us.

There were two major differences, though. One was the fact that he and I were just friends. She would get far more publicity if he mentioned her than I would. The second thing was that I could handle and even sometimes liked the attention. She, however, did not in the least. She was a social butterfly, for sure, but when it came to her personal life, she was very private.

I found myself sitting on the edge of my seat as the first words were being spoken. Alice and I were completely silent, just watching and waiting to see how it was going to go.

"Good morning, Ryan," Kathie Lee greeted him.

"Good morning." He smiled.

"We're very glad you could join us today. I know that you're very busy these days with multiple projects as far as producing, acting and composing. Thanks." She touched his hand.

"Not a problem." He pulled his hand away and took a drink of his water. "I enjoy doing these interviews. For most of us, our fans are a major reason that we do what we do, and interviews give fans an insight they wouldn't otherwise get."

"This is very true. So? How is filming going? Any exciting news for us?" She prodded.

"Filming is going very smoothly. I am working with a great cast and crew, and they're very understanding of my schedule. I couldn't have asked for a better film to work on," he said.

Picking up on a way into the question she had wanted to ask him, "Well, let's just jump right into the question that's on the mind of all of your female fans. You were spotted spending time in Maui with a very beautiful woman. Actually, two beautiful women, but one who seemed closer to you. What's going on there? Has our perpetually single man of mystery finally been snagged?" Her eyes were fixed on him.

He tilted his head and looked out at the crowd. Looking back at Kathie Lee, he answered, "I went to Maui as a getaway. While I was there, I met two very wonderful, and yes, beautiful, women." He looked a little nervous. "I made life-long friends, and I am truly happy that I met them."

She paused for a moment, searching for a way to get more details. "Friends?" She laughed. "There are pictures circulating of you and one of those women in an intimate kiss on the beach. Has anything come of that friendship?"

"She is very special to me, yes." He glanced at the camera for a moment, down at his hands, and then up at Kathie Lee confidently. "What we have is private. Am I with her? No, not at this time. However, I am considering myself off the market at this point. That's all I have to say about it right now."

Alice jumped up, grabbed the remote and hit the mute button. I was waiting for a scream, squeal or anything, but she just stood there, gripping the remote tightly and staring at the TV. The interview continued. I wanted to hear what else he was saying, but I knew better than to go anywhere near her at this point.

After a minute, she put the remote down on the coffee table slowly and walked to the kitchen. I didn't know what to say. I didn't know what was going through her mind, so what could I say?

"Alice?" I crept around the corner into the kitchen, carefully.

She was refilling her coffee mug. "Yes?" Her voice was eerily calm.

"Are you ok?" I inquired.

132

"Yup," she replied shortly.

"Ok?" I didn't want to pry too hard, but I knew she was thinking about what he said. I walked over to the counter and started fixing myself a cup of tea.

"Fine." She slammed her mug down on the counter. Coffee splashed out onto the counter and her hand. I noticed her wince from the heat, but she didn't stop to clean it up. "So many people saw that interview, and he basically said that he's waiting for me. The comments and looks are going to start up all over again." She sighed. "I just don't like to deal with all of this!"

"But you're not going to run this time, are you?" I handed her a damp towel.

She wiped her hand off and started cleaning off the counter. "No. I'm in too deep now."

"Good." I smirked.

"Good?" She glared at me. "What do you mean by good?"

"Listen." I grabbed her hand from the other side of the counter. "I know that you hate the publicity and everything, but he's good for you. You will get used to that in time, and it'll fade. I just don't want to see you let him go over something that can be dealt with."

"Yeah, I know you're right." She pulled her hand away and took the towel to the sink to rinse it out.

"It doesn't make it any easier. I guess I'm going to have to call him and tell him that he has a purpose behind his visit today, and it's that he needs to come and help me cope with the mess this is going to cause." She smiled slyly.

"That's not a bad idea," I said, smiling back, knowing that he was going to be there that night and what he was planning. "You do that."

She looked at me, a bit curious. "Ok? I will. I'll call him on my way to work. Speaking of, I should go get ready."

I knew she knew that something was up, and I probably should have kept my mouth shut, but it was not always a good thing to spring something on Alice. So, hinting that something was up wasn't a bad idea at all. However, she wasn't going to get anything more than that.

She went about getting ready for work as I got the kids up and to their buses. After they all left, and it was just Victoria and me, I got the house cleaned up, spent some time working on her preschool lessons and settled in at my desk to work on that week's columns. Alice sent me texts a couple of times to tell me about the people who were asking all about her and Ryan and if he ever visited her. Before I knew it, he was knocking on the front door.

Wow, the day just flew by, I thought as I walked to the door. "Ryan! I'm glad you made it."

"Well, how can I turn down a request from Alice to come help buffer the direct attention on her?" He smiled and gave me a hug.

I took a step back. "And just how do you propose to do that?"

He smiled a very sly smile that told me he was up to something. "After the kids all get home, let's go see her at work."

"Oh, that'll keep people from gossiping," I said sarcastically.

"Oh. I know people will talk, but it'll clear up all the 'Is it true?' questions, and most will be too star struck or embarrassed to ask questions after seeing me here. I don't mean to sound all egotistical, but if they're gossiping, then they're interested. If they're interested, then they'll divert their attention from her to me while I'm here."

"But aren't you concerned about people knowing that you come here to visit?" I questioned.

"It's bound to happen eventually." He was confident in that. "I've never been big on secrecy. Usually when the public wants to know something about where I go or who I am with, I just tell them. It's better than trying to sneak around. They search harder for the information and make our lives more miserable. Sooner or later, they'll figure out who you both are and where you live, and they'll show up here to see if you'll give them answers. Let's just get it out there. I know I opened a can of worms in the interview today, and I'd rather them come here while I'm here than bother you both while I am gone."

"Wow, it's all very dramatic." I laughed. "I guess I can see your point though. So, let's get this done then."

The kids came home and were very excited to see Ryan as usual.

Tina had been calming down when it came to being star struck. She had gossiped with her friends a lot in the beginning, but was growing more and more used to having him around. So, when he was at the house when they got home, it had become hugs and "happy to see you" comments rather than the in-awe reactions they had in the beginning.

They threw their backpacks in the closet, and started to scatter about the house for their usual evening agendas. I let them know that we would be leaving soon to go to Alice's workplace for dinner. She was working a double that day, as she did most days she didn't have class.

"If we are going to do this, it's better that we do it before they get busy and you cause a riot." I smiled at him.

Ryan laughed and walked to the living room. "Fair enough. Then let's get the kids and get going."

I couldn't believe we were going to do this. Ryan Perry in a public place in this small town when we were already getting flack for some supposed pictures. I just hope that Alice doesn't lose it. However, I did see his point. Let's just get it over with and out in the open. People can get their questions out and then get used to him being around. The longer we kept the whole thing a secret, the more elaborate people will make the story, and they'll never tire of the intrigue. You wouldn't believe a few of the questions we've gotten.

The kids came out and started getting ready. They were usually pretty excited when it came to going places with Ryan. They found him so much fun to be around, and it was always exciting to be in public with him with all of the attention he drew. I knew that he would make a great father figure for Alice's kids, and my kids saw him as the fun uncle type.

We headed up to the restaurant and walked in like everyday people. Just as I suspected, people started

136

whispering and pointing. A younger woman squealed and came running up to get his autograph.

Alice came towards us quickly, an angry look on her face. "What are you doing? Are you trying to get me fired?" She grabbed Ryan and me by the arm and took us all to the back corner area of tables. "I can't believe this! Now people are really going to talk!"

Ryan put one hand on each of her arms. "I know you hate all of this attention, but as long as we are spending time together, even as friends, people are going to talk. So, we might as well let people know I'm here, we're friends, and let them talk. They'll get used to the idea soon enough, and will stop seeing it as such a bloody event. Then, we won't have to worry about it any more."

"Well, it's not like I can erase all of their memories of seeing you here, so I have no choice, now, do I?" She flashed me a dirty look as if to say "How dare you?"

"Hey, while we're here, if someone asks you a question, point them in his direction." I figured that would only be right since it was his idea. "I am sure he'll field all questions. Wouldn't you, Ryan?"

"Absolutely." He smiled. "We will have a long dinner, and you can just tell anyone who has questions to just come and talk to me. I'll keep some of the heat off of you while we're here."

"Whatever." She stomped off, flipping her hair and rolling her eyes.

"Well, that went better than I expected." I laughed nervously.

"Why's that?" he asked.

"I thought she'd kick us out the moment she saw us walk in."

"No, as much as she hates this, she knows I am right. Let's just get it out there and over with."

Sure enough, people started coming up to our table, asking for his autograph and asking why he was in town (among other questions). For the most part, Alice kept busy with work. She refused to talk about why Ryan was in town. I think the manager had more to say, and maybe even enjoyed getting involved.

Girls, teenagers and grown women all came up to say hello. It was actually kind of fun for us. I don't mind dealing with publicity, and Tina loved it when someone she knew came over. I was sure this was only going to help her as far as popularity went. Ryan was taking the whole thing in stride.

After we ate, we just hung out for a while chatting with each other and anyone that came up. Alice would come over and sit every once in a while. I was glad for that. It could only mean that she was getting used to it. Otherwise, she would have been hiding in the kitchen as much as possible.

"Well, we've caused enough commotion." I noticed it was about time for dinner rush. "Like I said, no riots for you, Ryan."

He laughed. "True. I'd hate to make more of a scene than necessary."

"Aw, but Aunt Vivianne," Tina whined. "I'm having so much fun!"

"I know, but this is your mother's job, and if we make it hard for her to work, especially during a dinner rush, she might get in trouble." I drank the last of my milk and started gathering the girls' things. "I am sure we'll have plenty of public appearances with Ryan in the future."

"True," she said reluctantly. "All right."

We started for the front door when Alice came out and was standing by the bar waiting for an order. Ryan detoured and walked right up to her, wrapped his arms around her and kissed her forehead. She scowled at him, pushing him away lightly, as he laughed.

"I'll see you in a few hours?" He smiled and took her hand.

She yanked away from him, noticing all the people that were watching them. "I'll be going to my house when I get out later." She whipped away to escape as quickly as possible.

Her manager came right up and put a hand on Ryan's shoulder. "I will have her out of here as early as I can spare her."

"Thanks," he said, looking her right in the eyes and smiled that smile he gave the camera.

He joined us at the front door to leave. Of course, a few people stopped us along the way. Finally, we made it to the van and headed back to the house.

"I had so much fun!" Tina was beaming as we walked into the house. "Thanks so much, Ryan!" She jumped up and gave him a hug.

"No problem, Tina. I am glad that you did." He looked at me, a little shocked.

"Yeah, Alice has always said that Tina is my child and Elizabeth is hers by the way they act."

"You know, the more I spend around them, the more I can see that," he said with a laugh.

139

Ryan and I took a seat on the back patio to bide our time until Alice got home. I sat on our comfortable reclining lawn chair. It was a nice evening out. Warm, sunny, a mild breeze and the quiet of the country. It was relaxing. However, as we sat there in silence, letting our minds drift, I thought about how much I missed living in a big city.

It was nice to be able to get a fresh start with the back-up of my best friend by my side. Plus, in getting to know Ryan, it had been convenient that we were secluded. Then again, not as many people would have been fazed in the right city. The bottom line was that I missed the city.

I had talked to Alice a few months prior about what we planned to do with our lives. I was writing more and more, and it didn't seem to matter where I lived. So, I could go where I wanted. Living with her was giving me an ample chance to save up some money. So, when it was time to move on, I would have a nice nest egg saved up.

Alice was going to school, and with her pilot's license, she was looking at a job with the U.S. Border Patrol. That could take her to many locations, but she was hoping for the South. She had to do about a year and a half to two years of schooling. I had promised her that because she had taken us in when we needed her, I'd stick by her and help while she finished her degree. I would just have to be satisfied with visiting larger cities for a while.

I noticed it was getting darker out and the time was about right for the kids to be getting into bed. Alice would be home soon enough. I don't think either of us knew what to expect. You know, sitting there thinking about it, that was part of what a person loved about her. She surely was not predictable.

I got up and got the kids into bed and returned to the back patio. Ryan had set a tablecloth on the patio table and already had the strawberries and other fun foods I had picked out set about. He even had the wine poured.

"Alice sent a text to your phone saying she was on her way while you were putting the kids to bed," he said shyly. "I wasn't prying. The message just popped on your screen automatically."

"No, not a problem." I took a sip of the wine. "Thanks for getting everything all ready."

"Do you want to start off with the tickets or wait and try to bring her around to the idea first?" he asked.

I didn't have to think about the answer. "Oh, bring it up shortly after she gets settled. I know she'll know something is up. So, the longer we delay bringing it up, the more time she'll have to prepare herself to get on the defense."

"True. I hadn't thought about that." He nodded. "Thinking of it in that light, we'll need the entire evening to convince her to not throw the tickets back at me."

I burst into laughter. "That is a very strong possibility."

Alice came walking back to the back patio. She looked exhausted and a bit confused. "Hello? What's going on?"

"Alice!" I called to her. "Come sit and have a drink with us."

"Okay, let me just go get changed and out of these dirty work clothes." After a minute, she came back, in more comfortable clothes and refreshed. "So, what's the occasion?"

"Ryan is here visiting." I tried to play coy.

Ryan looked at me and back to Alice. "Actually, there is a reason for my visit."

"And I suppose this is aside from me asking you to come here and help me deal with the mess you caused with your interview this morning?" She scowled at him.

"Yes," he said hesitantly. "I had already planned on coming in for the night, but it wasn't just for a simple visit. I wanted to give you these." He slid a manila envelope across the table to her.

"What's this?" She looked at the envelope curiously.

"Open it, Captain Questions," I urged.

She took the envelope and opened it, glancing back and forth from Ryan to the envelope to me. Once she had it open, she sat there for a moment, clutching it in her hands and staring at the table. You could see thoughts racing through her mind. She had no clue what he was giving her, and that was scaring her to death. I am sure she was contemplating not even looking at what was in the envelope.

As she pulled the contents out, her eyes grew wider. She held three airline tickets for a moment and turned toward Ryan, waving them at him. "What are these?"

"Those are airline tickets," he replied sarcastically.

She tossed them onto the table. "I realize that, but what for?" She picked them back up to read them over. "London? Christmas time? What's this all about?" She searched for answers in our faces.

"Well, to put it simply, three tickets to London at Christmas time," I said.

Ryan burst into laughter. Regaining himself, he explained, "I have made arrangements for you, Vivianne and all of your kids to come to London from a couple days before Christmas until a couple days after New Year's Eve. I have a nanny hired and everything."

"What for?" She searched for more explanation.

"Well, for starters, I am having both a Christmas and a New Year's Eve party, and I would love for you all to be there." He looked her right in the eyes. "Second? I want to show you around where I am from. Third, I want to spend the holidays with you. Are any of those a good enough reason?"

"Wow, Ryan. I don't know what to say?" She stared at the tickets, flipping them end over end a few times. "I don't know if I can accept this. I also don't know if I can get that kind of time away."

Ryan shook his head and smiled. "Listen, the tickets are non-refundable, the nanny is hired, and Vivianne and her kids are coming regardless. So you might as bloody well, too. You will be on break from school, and if you will let me help with costs while you're gone..."

"No way," she interrupted.

He looked down at the table and back to her. "Then this gives you ample time to save up a little extra so you can join me."

She sat there for a moment, looking between the tickets and Ryan. "This sounds too good to be true. As much as the stubborn side of me wants to turn you down, I know there's no real reason to. So..." She looked at me. "Okay, let's do it. Let's spend the holidays in London." She started laughing and got up, hugging Ryan. "Thank you so much! It's too much!"

"Not at all." You could see the bliss in his smile. "But, there's more."

"More?" She looked leery.

"Yes, I also have this for you." He handed her another envelope.

"Ryan, I don't know…"

"Just look at it and hear me out," he interrupted.

She opened the envelope and pulled out another single airline ticket. "New York next month? What's this for?"

"I have an event I am attending, and I'd like for you to join me, as my date, for the evening."

"An event in New York? Your date? Wow. I don't know what to say." She looked at me.

I reached out and grabbed the ticket. "Say you'll go! I am totally jealous, and I want to live vicariously through you. I will keep the kids with me for the weekend. Just go live it up, and I want details!"

She snatched the ticket back. "Fine, but you're helping me pick something to wear."

"Ok," I said.

"Are we really going to London?" she asked me.

"Why, yes, we are. Ryan has already given me the money to pay for expedited passports so we can make sure that we have them in time." I patted his shoulder.

"No, I can't let you do that," she pleaded to Ryan.

He shook his head. "Too late. I've already given it to Vivianne."

"Give it back, Viv," she demanded.

144

"Why? Can you afford to get us all passports, expedited at that? It's expensive, and I want to use what extra cash I have to play while I'm out there." I tried to make that sound plausible.

Mainly, I just thought Ryan should be allowed to help with something other than the plane tickets. He wanted so badly to pay for everything, but she never let him. This was my way of helping him help her without her being able to say no, and he knew that was my intention, too.

I looked at Ryan, and he winked at me. We both smiled.

Chapter Nine

Taking the Leap. I Mean, Trip

The December holidays were approaching quickly, but we were ready. The arrangements were all set, and our families had been notified we would be gone. So, they scheduled get-togethers on other dates so we could still go to them.

Alice had gone to the charity event in New York with Ryan. She said she had a lot of fun and would do something like that again. I was very happy to hear that, considering I could see them getting closer, and that sort of thing went along with his career. She was a little strange when she came back, though.

When I asked what her look was all about, she said, "Oh, nothing," and went to her bedroom to unpack.

I let her be for a little while and made dinner. After the kids talked all through dinner about their Halloween costumes and had gone to bed, I cornered her at the dining room table

"Ok, spill it," I demanded.

"Spill what? I don't know what you're talking about." She seemed amused and distracted.

"Oh, don't play innocent with me." I threw Elizabeth's unused dinner napkin at her. "Did you and Ryan... you know?" I tilted my head inquisitively.

"Oh, no!" She seemed surprised that I would even ask that. "No, I had a great time. The first night, we went to a really nice restaurant and a show. Then, Saturday, we went to the event. It was amazing! It was elegant and beautifully decorated. You would have loved it."

"I bet." I was sure she was right, since she knew I loved that sort of thing, but I couldn't shake the feeling that there was something that she wasn't telling me. "Yeah, yeah, yeah. So it was beautiful, classy and fun. All things that I would love. There's something you're not telling me, and I'm not going to rest until you tell me what it is."

"Then you had better rethink quitting caffeine," she said with a smirk. "I had fun. Ryan was a complete gentleman. The party was elegant. Thank you for going shopping with me, by the way. That dress worked perfectly. Other than that, there's nothing more I am going to share with you."

"Nothing more you're going to share with me?" I was starting to get frustrated. "So, there's more, and you're not going to tell me?"

"Oh, don't get me wrong," she said, laughing. "I'll tell you. When it's time."

"Oh, no, you don't," I said. "You can't pull something behind my back. I'm the one in charge of surprises."

"It's not my idea. Ryan started the talking. I just think it's awesome!" She smiled. "Listen, don't worry about it. It's nothing big. It'll just be fun to see how you react."

"How I react?" I rolled my eyes. "Thanks. Now I'm going to be your amusement. Nice."

She laughed as she got up. "Yes, and you will love me for it."

I thought back on that conversation as I started packing things for me and my girls to get ready for our trip to London. I was so anxious for the trip that it was the only way for me to keep from going stir crazy beforehand. So, I packed all the things I knew we wouldn't need before then.

It was a week before the trip, but there was also a lot to do that week. When I wasn't running errands, writing a couple of extra columns just in case I didn't have time while I was gone, getting together with friends and family, participating in Elizabeth's school parties and functions, or making preparations for the house to be vacant for two weeks, I was packing random things and trying to keep my mind off of the trip. I felt like my excitement could just jump out of my skin and run around all on its own, without the necessity of my body.

Alice would just look at me and laugh when I'd go off, babbling about everything that needed to be done, what I had gotten done that day or what I wanted to do while gone. I usually responded with a half-irritated "It's easy for you when you work outside the house and have classes to keep you busy." She would roll her eyes and laugh again, going about her relaxing evening.

That week was so long and yet so fun. I love getting prepared for a trip, even though I usually look like a complete mess. I got everything done on my list and tried to help Alice out as much as I could so she could focus on her finals and things with her kids.

When it was time, we finished packing the important last-minute items, locked up the house and headed for the airport in a car Ryan provided. He said we didn't need to leave our cars in an airport parking lot to be broken into and have to pay for parking. He added that he thought a limo to the airport would be fun for the kids.

Amazingly enough, Alice didn't put up a fight. She had been going along with things more and more over the last few months. I actually was seeing a little excitement at his generosity and sweet gestures. The day he sent flowers to her at work, I was sure she was going to freak out, but she smiled, moved them to the break room until bringing them home and carried the note card in her apron her whole shift. Terri, one of her co-workers, even said she would look at it every once in a while, smiling.

I knew she wasn't letting Ryan in on her little secret, but she would flash looks and say little things that let me know. I also knew she wasn't ready to talk about it. So, she let me arrange our seating on the flight so the three eldest kids were sitting next to each other, and Victoria was sitting with us. This way, we could talk.

We checked our bags and played travel games in the terminal until our flight was called. As we filed onto the plane, Alice caught my hand in hers. "I'm nervous," she said. She didn't even look at me, and I doubt it was loud enough for anyone else to hear her.

"Me too, but I'm sure it's not for the same thing." I tried to lighten the moment before getting into the serious question. "Listen, I have been picking up on the fact that you are coming around to the thought of a 'you

149

and Ryan' thing. I don't expect that when we get there, you're going to be running and jumping into his arms or anything, but what's going on in your head?"

"I don't know." She shook her head as we took our seats, giving me a look to tell me to wait until we had taken off and the kids were distracted.

The plane taxied down the runway. The kids started pulling out their hand held games and various things to keep their attention. It was going to be a long flight, and they had been briefed beforehand to make sure they brought enough things to keep them occupied.

As soon as we were in the air, she started talking. "I am starting to like all the little things he does for me. Plus, I've always had feelings for him, and I'm starting to not hate them. I'm still scared, but I was just thinking that if this vacation goes well, for the kids as well as for us, I might give it a chance." She looked me right in the eye. "I might give him a chance."

"Really?" I was shocked to hear those words from her mouth. "You mean to tell me that you are beginning to soften?"

"Oh, don't make a big deal out of it," she said, rolling her eyes.

"But it is a big deal, Alice! Ryan is a big deal, and he has been since the beginning. You're the only one that's refused to see this." I was getting frustrated with the blinders that she put on herself about this whole thing.

"You're the only one to get a chance like this. Things like this just don't happen to people, and you're being given a fairytale on a silver platter. I understand why you're apprehensive and all, but if you want to give in to your feelings, then also give in to knowing how huge this is."

"Fine, it's a big deal, but you know me. I don't know if I can ever completely let down my walls." She looked down at the magazine in her hands. "So, shush about the whole feelings thing. Like I said, I'm waiting to see how things go. I might decide it's not a good idea after all."

"Ok, ok. Whatever," I said exasperatedly. "I think you're going to be disappointed, though."

"And why is that?"

"Because you want him to let you down. You don't want to have to face your feelings for him, and you think it'll be easier for you if he were to mess up so you can walk away without dealing with the whole love thing."

"What are you talking about?" She was annoyed.

"Oh, don't act cavalier," I scolded. "You know exactly what I'm talking about."

"Well, soon enough, you won't care how Ryan and I are doing." She flipped her hair and smirked at me.

"Somehow, I doubt that. So don't try to change the subject. Why would you even think that?" I was confused.

"Oh, no reason."

"Alice," I said, turning to lean in toward her a little. "What are you trying to not say?"

"Oh, nothing. I'll just say that if you keep quiet about my feelings and let me deal with them as they come, then I won't torture you with what I know."

I realized she was trying to blackmail me into leaving her alone so she didn't have to think about how she felt for Ryan.

"Fine," I said reluctantly. "For now." I leaned my head back, even more frustrated with the whole thing. As if it wasn't bad enough that I was watching my best friend gamble with her love life because she was afraid of it, now I had to be tormented with this knowledge that there was something she knew that I didn't. Yet, I was a part of it, if not the center of it. That bothered me.

The flight attendant started the first in-air movie while another started taking drink orders and bringing around dinner. I tried, but I couldn't keep my mind from reeling. I thought about Ryan and Alice, the "surprise" she had for me, actually getting to go to London, if I brought enough, if I was going to be able to find the gifts the kids wanted there, and so on.

I half watched the movie and picked at my dinner, surprised that it was actually good. I had only taken flights a couple hours or shorter over the last several years. The last time I had been on a flight long enough to warrant a meal was as a child. I did not remember the food being even a fraction this good. I made a mental note of this and took it as a sign of a good beginning to a great trip.

There wasn't any more serious talk the rest of the trip. The kids played and enjoyed the movies until they fell asleep. Once, Alice sighed and squeezed my hand for just a moment. They had all fallen asleep for part of the trip but were awake and anxious by the time we touched down in London.

I had nodded off for a few moments, but for the most part stayed awake. I couldn't miss my favorite part of the flight--seeing the approaching land and looking at London from overhead as we flew over the buildings and streets I had been longing to see my whole life, and would soon be walking through. That made me smile.

At the airport, we filed into the terminal, stretching and chattering about our excitement. We filed down to the luggage area, looking for a person with a sign to take us to our car. There was no sign, but we found a person.

"Ryan!" Elizabeth squealed. She ran over to him, wrapping her arms around him as he kept his eyes on Alice.

"Hey, everyone!" He managed to look away, sweeping all of us with his gaze, but looking right back at her. "I am glad you all can make it."

I interrupted with a "Hey!" He turned to me and gave me a hug. "Well, Ryan, let's go see your homeland."

He smiled, walked to Alice's side, took her by the arm. "Hello there, did you have a good flight?"

"Yes, it was peaceful." She shot me a look.

"I am happy to hear it." He glanced at the rest of us again. "I arranged a place for you all to stay close by me, just a few blocks away. It's what you Americans call a duplex. I rented both sections for the holidays for friends. You all get the larger apartment. We can stop by there to drop off your luggage. I'll let you get settled in and freshen up and will send a car for you in about an hour? I hope you're all hungry. I have a meal being prepared back at my house."

"If it's only a few blocks, maybe we can walk it," I said, hoping the others wouldn't mind.

The kids grumbled at that, and Alice protested, "I'm really hungry, and it seems the kids are, too."

"Oh, I was just hoping to walk to see more than we would in a car." I was a little disappointed. "But I guess we do have two weeks."

"Yes, and the nanny, Tiffany," he said, smiling, "should be at the apartment when you get there."

"Tiffany? The same nanny from when we were in Maui?" I asked.

"The very same." He smiled at my girls as they cheered. "She arrived two days ago to get settled in and briefed on what's expected of her while here. She's excited to see the girls again and meet the other kids."

"Thanks, Ryan. I figured your judgment as far as a nanny would be good, but I was a bit nervous. I always am when it comes to my kids," I said.

"As any good mom should be," he said. "Well, let's get going."

Once in the car, I looked around in wonder and amazement. *I am actually in London! I can't believe it! It's so beautiful!* I took in as much of the architecture and general feel of the city as I could.

It was so much more than I expected, and I was anxious to get out and wander the streets in detail. The richness of its history seemed to seep into me. I knew I hadn't been wrong that I had always felt the need to visit there. The drive seemed to go too quickly, but like I had said earlier, I did have two weeks.

At the "apartment"--which was far more like a huge house nestled into a line of huge houses all connected and entwined through a few of London's city streets-- my girls rushed in to find Tiffany. They cheered and shared stories of playing and having fun with Cameron and Tina as she whisked them off to show them their rooms and get them ready to go to Ryan's.

Ryan walked us to the doorway and told us he would be sending the car back and was looking forward to seeing us a little later. He said we would have roasted chicken, herbed boiled potatoes and a vegetable medley. Oh, and chocolate soufflés for dessert. We complimented him on the menu and said our "see you soons."

Alice and I wandered through the rooms, impressed at the well-balanced mixture of contemporary and classic interior design. After walking through the main rooms of the house, taking note of the tiny details of color balance throughout and warmed hand towels in the bathroom, we found our bedrooms.

I unpacked my things and changed into fresh clothes. Alice met me in the foyer, where the kids and Tiffany were already waiting, playing a game of I Spy. The phone rang. Alice answered. It was a short call. She hung up and told us the car was waiting for us whenever we were ready. We all got our coats on and filed outside.

The car took us just a few blocks away. From the street, the house looked similar to the one where we were staying. Upon going inside though, there was a noticeable difference. It was large and filled with art, luxurious furniture and decorations that told guests the owner had very fine taste, but was still young and current.

Dinner was very nice. Actually, the next couple of days were very nice. We had arrived on a Thursday evening and spent Friday seeing a few sights and shopping. Ryan had Tiffany keep the kids for a while and insisted Alice and I go with a professional shopper to get dresses and accessories for his Christmas party the next day.

"Something between a cocktail dress and a formal gown. This is for the Christmas party, tomorrow. Next week, you can shop for the New Year's Eve party, on me," he told us. There was such anticipation in his voice when he instructed us, almost as if he couldn't wait to see what we picked out. "Please get all new things, dresses, shoes, jewelry, everything. I know you're going to feel like you're taking advantage, Alice, considering how well I know both of you, but it's what I want. I want to treat you both."

I have to admit, Alice and I took to that task with such enthusiasm you could have mistaken us for teenagers given the keys to the family car for the first time. We both jumped up and down, squealing and hugging Ryan. He laughed so hard and told us he'd never expected to see that side of us, ever. I don't know which was stronger, his surprise or his happiness that we were excited.

He said he had some sort of interview to do that day. Considering Alice didn't want to think about interviews yet, we rushed off to the stores. He had directed us to the first shop which was close by his place, so we could walk like I had wanted. The personal shopper was waiting for us there.

Rifling through racks and boutiques, trying on combination after combination, we were having a blast! Some of the shops were just like Ryan's neighborhood, old shops that had been there for generations, laden with history and old world charm. Some of the shops were newer and contemporary, hip and chic. To be honest, I hadn't quite expected to find places like those shops in London. I guess it makes sense, but I'd always just thought about the older and classic parts, I hadn't even considered the newer parts.

We settled on outfits after a mere four hours. I almost wasn't ready to be done. Alice, of course, had picked one out three shops and an hour and a half earlier than I had.

She had chosen a nice, contemporary Marc Jacobs number. It was a teal satin, and form fitting. The fitted part stopped at the knee with a sharp flare about six inches long that quickly flitted away from the leg upon walking or when caught by a breeze. The top of the dress had a deep V but held its shape nicely despite its single, loose strap.

She had picked a matching ruched clutch with silver fittings and teardrop-shaped crystals that lined the top of both sides, dangling to catch the light and the eye of everyone passing by. Her shoes were also Marc Jacobs. They were classic three-inch, patent leather heels in black. There was a teal stripe that started at the arch and wrapped up around the top of the back and landed on the center of the outside of the foot. Very sleek and very in tune with her dress.

Her jewelry went just as well as her shoes did. The earrings were a crystal stud that held a single teardrop crystal, matching the clutch. The bracelet was a single lined, crystal tennis bracelet. Her necklace, well, it gave the whole combination its character. It was a black, patent leather choker about an inch wide. From the center, a larger teardrop crystal was suspended from a four-inch silver chain, holding it just at the center of her breast bone in the middle of the V of her dress.

How she found all of those pieces that fit so well together in different shops was beyond me. I had seen her get them one item at a time, but when she found that last piece, she tried them all on together. I was astounded and jealous, to be honest. She was chic and beautiful. She would be making heads turn the whole night.

My outfit? Well, I chose to go a much more classic route. Not that it's surprising. Alice had always been more contemporary and I have been more classic in my tastes, anyway. I found myself more enthralled at the smaller, owner-operated shops.

I finally found exactly what I needed. It was a simple, black cotton, A-line dress with a very 1960s cut to it, including a crinoline under the skirt. The skirt fell just below the knee, and the neckline was a wide, straight across cut on the chest. The dress fitted closely up my ribcage and had three-quarter length sleeves.

There were V-shaped sections on the front and the back of the bodice that were filled, symmetrically, with midnight blue polka dots. The polka dots also encircled the hem of the sleeves and the hem of the skirt.

Since the skirt was full, I had a seamstress put pockets in it. This way, I didn't need to carry a clutch around everywhere or have some monstrosity of a purse disrupting the fairytale we would be living for a night.

I focused on jewelry next. I chose Tahitian pearls for everything. The necklace stopped an inch above the front of the dress in a single strand. The bracelet was a triple strand, and both used oversized black, satin bows to fasten. I chose not to wear earrings, as usual, keeping the focus on the rest.

For shoes, I went for a pair of Versace black satin four-inch heels. The toe was pointed and simple. The heel was silver and sleek. The back had a simple cover in satin that gave way to sturdy straps that wrapped around the ankle across the front with an oversized bow on the back. The inside and arch of the foot were exposed.

I was satisfied with the outfit after trying it on in front of a couple of sales clerks and the tailor, who were all too happy to compliment me on my selections. They assured me that I would fit in well in London's society and not look too American. Alice also liked the outfit, but she had to make note that she would never wear it herself, of course.

When we went back to our apartment to meet up with everyone, but before we could show Ryan what we had gotten, he had the kids file out, showing off their new ensembles. We were floored. Tiffany, upon instruction, had taken the kids out and gotten them new outfits, too. They were perfect.

He then turned to us and our bags and said he didn't want to see our dresses until the party. I thought that was really cool of him, but Alice was a little frustrated. As much in love with her outfit as she was, she wanted his approval before showing it to all of his friends, and possibly--probably--his family.

We took our new finds to our rooms and Ryan took us out to a nice restaurant for dinner, and we talked about our trips, shopping and how much fun we all had. We all shared some of the stories of horrible and ridiculous outfits we had come across. Everyone laughed and had a great time.

I asked Ryan if there was anything we could do the next day to help get ready for the party. He assured us that he had everything under control. His mother and two sisters were coming in tonight and were going to be staying with him and getting up early to help set up anything he didn't already have hired out.

Alice leaned in to me and said quietly, "Mother and sisters? How many other family members are going to be there?"

"I am sure most of his family will be there," I answered, trying to jokingly scare her. "What? It's not like you two are a couple or anything." I jabbed her in the ribs with my elbow.

"No, but I am sure they know all about the interview where he said he was off the market and know me as the woman keeping him on a string." She looked a little bitter at the thought.

"Listen, if I've learned anything about Ryan, it's that he is generous. So, I am sure he was generous in explaining the situation, and they probably understand." I tried to console her.

I could see her look fade to worry. "Maybe you're right."

"You two all right over there?" Ryan had been trying to ignore our obvious gossiping while talking with the kids about their days.

"Yeah, just talking about our outfits and how I am going to have to go about keeping you from attacking Alice at the sight of her." She slapped my shoulder.

Ryan winked at Alice. "I am sure I'll control myself, even if it does take your bodyguard here tossing drinks at me." He smiled at me.

"Besides, I am sure we'll be distracted with our little plan anyway, right, Alice?"

Her eyes grew wide with amusement. "Oh yeah! That's right."

"What?" I was a little angry that they were both taunting me with this "plan." "You're both in on it? I mean, I figured and all, but come on! I hate being left in the dark, especially when it comes to something for or about me. Pleeeeeease?" I drew out the word with a whine.

"Tell me, tell me, tell me!" I pleaded like a child asking for cookies.

"No," they chimed in unison.

"Fine then. Well, don't think I won't antagonize the both of you then, the rest of the night and tomorrow. This is war," I snorted, half laughing.

We all laughed and went about our meals. Occasionally, the three of us would snap a glare at the other as if we were detectives, sizing up the suspect across the table.

The next day, Alice and I followed orders again and went out to get our hair and nails done. This time, we were accompanied by Ryan's two sisters, Giselle and

Emma. Both of who were beautiful and rather obviously English women. We had just been told to be ready to be pampered and a car would pick us up. So, when they were sitting in the car as we climbed in, and introduced themselves, we were a bit taken aback.

Emma was the youngest of the three siblings and had been married to a man named Reginald for four years, yielding a set of four-year-old twins, Nathaniel and Natalie. Reggie, as they called him, was a banker, and Emma was a homemaker.

Giselle was a model and part-time actress, mostly in French movies. She was gorgeous and statuesque. She had the grace and charm of royalty with an edge of bitterness to her. All in all though, she was still really nice and warm to us both. They both were.

They picked us up from our apartment about four in the afternoon, talking about how great Ryan's place looked and how much fun we were going to have. Emma said she and Ryan had gotten up very early to get started, while Giselle and Mary, their mother, got up shortly after. Then, the rest of the family; father, aunts, uncles, cousins and grandmother, started arriving for their traditional holiday lunch. Most people were out and about, getting ready for tonight, but some had stayed to give Ryan and his hired help a few extra sets of hands.

We enjoyed lattes and pastries while getting pampered as the sisters chatted about Ryan's childhood and how wonderful a man he had grown up to be. They also asked us so many questions. How did we meet Ryan? What did we think of London? They even asked why Alice was holding back.

It seemed they really liked Alice and were hoping that there was a simple explanation that they could help solve to get them together. She managed to blow it off like it was nothing, giving the sort of answer that led them to believe that she and Ryan were just taking their time. I was sure she just didn't think they needed to hear all of the melodrama going on in her head.

Even though they asked so many questions, it seemed to be a pretty casual outing. I didn't even see Alice squirm that much as they talked about her meeting so much of the family. It was nice, and we all had fun.

I did see some texts between Alice and Ryan right after the drive to the salon though. It was amusing to see their usual bantering dynamic, and he seemed to have the upper hand in this. I just felt for Alice considering I know how she is when it comes to meeting someone's family.

Alice: *Your entire family is going to be there tonight?! Cousins three times removed and all?*

Ryan: *No, just my closest family members. Plus, a whole lot of friends. Is that a problem?*

Alice: *Not a problem per se. I just hadn't realized I was going to meet so much of your family so soon.*

Ryan: *Well, it isn't as if we are a couple, though. Now is it? There shouldn't be any pressure with that in mind.*

Alice: *Ouch! I just got pimp slapped via text. Give me some slack. I'm here, aren't I?*

Ryan: *Yes, and I do understand what you're on about.*

Alice: *It's just that, by the sounds of it, they all know more than I thought they did about us. Never mind.*

Ryan: *Don't worry about it, love. Just relax, have fun and blow it off. It's a party night, and they'll be more distracted with that than worried about us.*

Alice: *Whatever. I'll see you at the party. Oh, thank you for dropping your sister bomb on my head today. I wasn't expecting that.*

Ryan: *You're welcome. See you later.*

She really hadn't said anything about the texts other than handing me her phone so I could read them. Other than that, she did what he asked of her, though it was so unlike her character, and tried to relax and have fun.

Emma and Giselle dropped us off back at the apartment about seven to get dressed and said they'd send the car back for all of us about eight. The plan was for all of us to go at eight and Tiffany would bring the kids back to the apartment about ten.

I could feel the excitement grow in me over that hour. We were bustling around, getting ready to head out. I just kept thinking about the little plan they were concocting for me. It was Christmas time. So, who knows? We had all made a deal not to exchange presents that night and had planned to do that Christmas day. So, I was not sure.

I had gotten all ready and made sure the girls were ready to go. I stared out the front window, waiting for the car, thinking, *Well, I guess I'll know soon enough.*

164

The car pulled up, and we started for the door. I noticed Alice had gotten fidgety, so I held her back and let the rest go ahead. "What's up? You look nervous."

"Of course I'm nervous. I'm meeting his family all at once, and they all are wondering what's going on," she snapped.

"They will all love you just like his sisters do," I said.

"And they are all wondering why we're not a couple." She looked at the ground.

I knew she needed consoling, but I was having trouble finding the words. "Well, things will come around. You've even said you're not freaking out like you once were."

"Ah yes, but we're not a couple, as everyone likes to point out lately, and they are all going to wonder if I'm just taking advantage of him. It's just a lot of pressure, and I feel that if I don't give in soon, they'll hold this against me forever." Her eyes met mine, pleading for a best friend's comfort.

"You know," I said, putting an arm around her shoulders. "Somehow, I don't think they're that kind of people. Plus, they're a close and open family, and they probably trust his judgment."

"Let's hope so." She took a deep breath as we got in the car.

We talked about how we all looked very nice, even Tiffany. Ryan had told her to treat herself to a nice outfit, too. She chose a linen suit and muted accessories. It was comfortable enough to wear while watching the children.

It was such a short drive, and yet it seemed like a different world as we rounded the corner to his street. There were valet attendants, fancy cars lining the street, beautifully elegant people casually strolling into his house, kissing each other's cheeks and shaking hands.

As we walked up to the house, I took in the newly decorated front stoop with tiny lights and fresh garland. Inside, I understood just how correct Emma and Giselle were. It was beautiful. There were more tiny white lights that covered archways, mantles, banisters, pillars and a huge and finely decorated tree that dominated the living room in off-white and burgundy decorations.

The food spread was gourmet to say the least. It was a buffet in the dining room that had a wide range of foods to appeal to every taste. The kids headed straight for the food, filling plates with each of their favorite foods from the dishes arranged with great detail and appeal.

In the living room, across from the tree, there was a pianist and a few musicians playing stringed instruments. They were playing classical music, and a few people were gathered around, chatting and listening to the small orchestra.

Tiffany assured us that she had the kids taken care of, and Ryan had one of his spare rooms set up with games and movies for any children that were going to be visiting that evening. She scooted Alice and I off in the direction of the bar with a smile.

As Alice and I were waiting for our turn to order a drink, Emma and Giselle came up to us with an enthusiastic welcome, flagging down the bartender. Alice ordered a fuzzy navel, and I ordered a simple glass of white wine. I was surprised to hear the range of selections. So, I went for a Piesporter to start the evening off with. Once our glasses were in hand, the sisters rushed us off to Ryan's side.

He turned towards us as we were about halfway across the room. The look in his eyes was better than the look on his face when Alice and I came out to the beach in those bathing suits in Maui. It was deeper. He smiled at me and at his sisters, but he stared at Alice. She had to have noticed, at least subconsciously, because her walk became more seductive and gentle.

"Wow, ladies." Ryan scanned over all four of us and fixated on Alice. "You look gorgeous."

"Thank you." Alice blushed.

He set his hand, lightly, on Alice's arm. "No, you are stunning."

"Really? You like this outfit? I thought it was a little over the top, but I fell in love with it and couldn't pass it up."

"The outfit is great, and you look beautiful in it," he complimented.

Ryan wasn't exactly lacking in the attractive and well-dressed department himself. His black tuxedo with a white shirt was very contemporary with no tie, vest or cummerbund. The top two buttons were left undone. His shoes were black patent leather without designs, very sleek. His hair was his usual messy style. There was a little something that was a different. His cuff links were a simple, single crystal. I thought about how well his ensemble went with Alice's.

"Well? What do you think?" He waved his hand, slowly, through the air as if presenting his house to us.

Alice was so enthralled with him and nervous about being there that she simply replied, "Um, yeah, I'd hit it twice and holler back later."

He turned beet red and choked on the sip he just took. "Wow, I meant the house, but thank you, darling."

Alice's face was mortified for a moment. She downed her drink and mumbled, "Note to mouth, check with brain first." She looked up at Ryan and said meekly, "It's beautiful, excuse me for a moment," and rushed off towards the bar.

We stood there for an awkward moment, when Emma burst into laughter. "Wow! She really can embarrass herself. Come on, Giselle, let's go see if she's ok."

Ryan and I started idle chit chat to relieve the awkwardness. We drifted into a conversation about pizza, and I chose to shift the focus of embarrassment onto myself and shared my cheesy pick-up line with him, "Want to go back to my place to have sex and pizza?" When he looked sufficiently confused, I finished, "What? You don't like pizza?"

We were laughing and sharing other pick-up lines as they returned. Alice's face had gone back to her usual color, and she asked what we were laughing about. We told her nothing, and Ryan asked again what she thought about the house.

We all commented on how beautiful it was and how much work it must have taken to get that much done so quickly. Alice told him how much we loved the tree and the color scheme. He told us his mother decorated the tree by herself. I guess she did this every year, no matter where they held their gathering.

168

So many people were there. There were actors and musicians from local to famous. There were artists, business people, so much of his family and just ordinary people from London and other places all over. I was amazed at how many people could comfortably fit in his house. Then, there was the fact that they all looked so beautiful and well dressed. Everyone there had great manners on top of looking great, which impressed me.

I wandered about for a while, occasionally stopping to chat with someone or check in on Ryan and Alice, who barely left each other's sides. I went to the kids' makeshift playroom for a while to make sure they were having fun and pulled Tina and Elizabeth out to mingle and meet a few of the people they would appreciate meeting. I thought that would make for a great story to take back to their friends in the States, especially for Tina to meet three of the four members of her favorite boy band, The Crushes.

As the kids wrapped up to head back to the apartment, I walked them out to the car. Alice was going to walk them out, but I had gotten increasingly fidgety, so I told her I would just go. We had been there for two hours and still no big surprise yet. It made me nervous that they seemed to be waiting until after the kids left.

So, when they were tucked, half asleep, into the car and were down the road, out of sight, I walked back up to the front door, slowly. As I walked through the door, handing the doorman my coat, Alice came up and took me by the arm, leading me over to Ryan.

"Come join us!" she beamed.

"Are you enjoying yourself, Vivianne?" Ryan casually inquired.

"Actually, I am," I replied just as casually.

"Good. I would like you to meet my parents." He motioned to the couple standing with them.

I was shocked that Alice was being so casual, but now I understood why she was eager for me to join them.

Ryan did the introductions. "Mom, Dad, this is Alice's best friend, Vivianne. Vivianne, these are my parents, Mary and Henry Perry."

We exchanged the usual nice-to-meet-yous and struck up a casual conversation. I could see that I was right; they were a very open and closeknit family. Plus, it was apparent that Alice did not, in fact, need to worry about their approval. They seemed extremely accepting of her and eager to get to know her.

After about a half hour of chatting with his parents and then mingling by their sides, I went to go get another glass of wine and wander through the rooms of interesting and social people.

I had drifted into the living room, admiring the tree, when I, per my usual luck with the guys, was approached by one that had a few too many buttons undone, a little too much chest hair and a truly receding hairline. I could hear him using the phrase, "Why have just a six pack when you can have the whole keg?" while patting his belly.

As it turns out, he was a throwback lawyer from the 80s, struggling to gain clients from the entertainment business. He said he usually crashes these types of parties, looking for potential clients. Oh, and the horridly creepy pick up lines? Wow.

"Baby, you're like a prize-winnin' bass. I don't know if I want to mount ya or eat ya," he said, sliding his hand over his slicked-back hair and winking.

I couldn't help but think about my conversation about cheesy pick-up lines with Ryan earlier. Maybe this was payback.

I was truly astounded by this guy's ability to make every word that came out of his mouth sound like it was dripping with slime. I kept trying to walk away from him. I was trying to be polite and say I needed a refill or to go to the bathroom, but he'd grab my arm and just keep talking.

I looked around while he was talking, hoping to find Alice to get her to come save me. Finally, I spotted her in a group of people, just in the next room. To my relief, she glanced over at me. She waved and gave me an "Oh! There you are!" look.

I tilted my head toward the man, trying to motion that I needed help. She just laughed, tugged at Ryan's sleeve and whispered to him, obviously to look at what I had gotten myself into. He looked amused, too, and they both turned around and continued their conversation. I think I even saw them motioning to me to share their amusement with whomever they were chatting with.

I tried a couple more attempts at walking away from him, but to no avail. Finally, I lied and told him that I had a boyfriend. He continued to try a few more times, telling me that he didn't mind and handing out more cheesy compliments.

I was growing more and more irritated. I kept trying to get Alice's attention, but she wasn't looking my way for more than a glance at a time. So, I insisted that my "boyfriend" wouldn't approve.

He put his hands on my shoulders. "What your boyfriend doesn't know won't hurt him."

"But what he overheard will hurt you," I heard a man's voice from behind me.

This mystery man put a hand on my waist and stepped around so I could see him. I wasn't sure if I was more stunned by someone I didn't know stepping up to rescue me, or by how gorgeous he was. He continued, "I am kindly asking you to leave now. On behalf of my girlfriend and the host." He put his arm around my shoulders and pulled me in. I just kept staring at him.

The sleaze's voice shook me from my reverie. "Listen, I am sorry. I didn't think she was with anyone," he pleaded.

"It doesn't matter. She asked you to leave her alone, and you didn't. Ryan has asked me to tell you to leave. Now, don't make this difficult. Just know that you're not welcome and take yourself out the door." His voice was stern with a hint of amusement.

"Fine." The sleaze turned to look at me. "I didn't mean to offend you, hon."

I just blinked, stunned by the developments. He smiled and held his hand out to the mystery man. After a moment, he realized that the gesture was not going to be returned. He lowered his hand and sighed. "You are a very lucky man. She's not only beautiful but kind and generous. Take good care of her."

The mystery man squeezed me and just nodded at the sleaze. We stood there for a moment and the mystery man motioned, with a nod, towards the door and then nodded at Alice and Ryan. The man sulked out of the house.

The mystery man stepped around to face me and put a hand on my shoulder, asking, "Are you ok?"

"Um, uh," was all I could muster.

"Need a drink?" he asked with a smile.

I could only nod a yes, and he disappeared into the crowd toward the bar as I watched him walk away. He was about five foot nine, slender but obviously in great shape. Dark, wavy hair that fell a little lower than chin length in the front and was a bit longer in the back. He had large, green eyes and full lips. I couldn't help but be taken aback by how he was surprisingly comfortable to be near despite his intimidating good looks. Oh, and his voice? His voice was like that favorite song that you get chills from every time you hear it, and you just can't seem to get enough of.

He was in a black suit. The jacket was a longer jacket with a vest over a long-sleeved, button down shirt. There was no tie, the vest was undone, and the shirt was untucked. Despite that, no one could mistake his fashionable look for unruly or messy. Plus, I am sure his confident swagger as he walked through a room helped a lot. Women turned to look at him on his way both to and from the bar.

When I saw him reappear through the crowd, carrying two wine glasses, my heart skipped a beat. He smiled a smile so warm that I couldn't help but smile back. He had a crooked smile. The kind where one corner of his mouth comes up more than the other, making him look just as amused as happy.

I was embarrassed and sure that he could see just how enamored with him I was. I knew I couldn't hide it without making myself more transparent. I smiled even bigger as he approached.

He handed me my glass and asked, "Piesporter, right?"

It took everything I had to answer more than an "um" or an "uh," but I swallowed a decent drink of the wine and smiled meekly. "Yes, thank you very much. How did you know?"

He tilted his glass towards Alice. I looked up as she held her glass up in our direction and smiled. "Alice and Ryan said you looked like you needed help, and if I were to get you something to drink, this is what you would like."

"Oh." I blushed. "I should have figured."

He held his hand out and took mine in his, kissing it gently. "My name is Justin. It's very nice to meet you, Vivianne." He added a little bow to his introduction, face angled down and peering up at me through his long lashes.

I thought that I couldn't get redder… I was wrong. I giggled. Then, I cleared my throat and regained my composure.

"Thank you so much for what you did. I had been trying everything to get away from that guy. My next move was to yell "Fire!" and start running for an exit."

He laughed and said, "I doubt that would have even scared him off. He seemed rather persistent. I can see why, though."

174

Ok, this whole turning more and more red thing was getting impossible, but he seemed to keep finding a way to get me to blush more. "Oh, well, thank you." I looked down at my glass and started to swirl it.

He gently laughed and shook his head. "Anyway," he said, clearing his throat. "How are you enjoying London so far?"

"Oh." I paused for a moment, surprised that he started up idle conversation. "Um, we've only just arrived Thursday, but what I've seen, I love. I've always wanted to come to London but had never had the chance."

"It's beautiful. I love it here," he said.

"You are not from here, though. Right? I mean, you don't have an English accent. You sound American, maybe even a little Southwestern American," I pried.

"You're very observant," he complimented, "Yes, I am American. I live in California, and I've spent a great deal of time in the Southwest. Texas, mainly. However, my family has taken me to many places, and London is one of my favorites."

"I don't blame you. For me, it feels something like home. Not like "I live here" home, but more like that I can feel so many of my ancestors came from here home. It's just that... I... am... babbling, and I'll stop now." I took another drink of my wine.

"You are so cute." He took my hand in his. "Shall we go join Alice and Ryan?"

"Yes, please. Before I make a fool of myself." I felt like a schoolgirl.

"I doubt you could." He smiled, looking me right in the eyes.

175

He led me over to where Alice and Ryan were talking with three others; two men and one woman. The woman was very beautiful and elegant. I recognized one of the men as Tom Scalova, a famous sculptor.

"Hey, you two," Alice greeted us as we approached.

Justin shook hands with the other two men and greeted the group. "Well, Alice, I see you were right about our damsel in distress... on both accounts."

"Wait," I demanded. "Both accounts?"

"Nothing." Alice tried to avoid the question. "I merely mentioned that you needed help with your admirer."

"Sure." I sneered at her. "Well, thank you anyway."

"No problem," she said, looking delighted. "So, you've met Justin Ronin. This is Tom, Caleb and Jane." She nodded to the others in the group. "This is my best friend, Vivianne."

"Nice to meet you all," I said as I shook their hands, though I still had hold of Justin's.

They all replied in greeting, but I found myself completely distracted as my mind wrapped around the knowledge dawning on me that Justin wasn't just a mystery man who came to help me out of a jam. He was *Justin Ronin*. The Justin Ronin that I knew as one of the up-and-coming actors of the day and co-star of that film series of Ryan's that Alice and I love. I can't say I wasn't a little star struck.

I was floored that not only hadn't I recognized him, but I was standing there, holding his hand as if he was just any normal man. Then I realized that he was also not letting go of my hand.

176

I let go of his hand and took a step back. "Justin Ronin?" I asked, puzzled.

"Yes, that's my name," he replied, flashing that crooked smile.

I shook my head. "I didn't recognize you. Wow, I can't believe I didn't. I love your work."

"Well, thank you." he blushed a bit at my compliment. "So, Vivianne Cook, shall we?" He gestured towards a couple of seats at one of the bar tops.

"Yes, thank you," I started for the seats as I felt his hand on my lower back, guiding me.

"We're going to have a seat," he told Alice and Ryan.

"All right," Alice replied. "We'll join you two in a minute."

We sat at the bar top talking for a while. Basically, getting to know each other. He asked about where I was from, where I've been, and about my girls. I asked him about the places he's traveled, about acting and why he lives in California.

I had almost forgotten we were at a party. You know how they say that when you're with someone that hits your heart, the whole world just seems to disappear? I always thought that was just a saying.

I figured out that night it wasn't.

As we chatted, I took note of the little brushes of his fingers over mine and the way he would just stare into my eyes during the serious parts of the conversation. He was so captivating. Knowing myself, I should have been intimidated by him, but I wasn't. I found myself so in awe, yes, but I was so comfortable around him. There was such an ease to our conversation.

I have no clue how much time had passed before Alice and Ryan came to join us. It seemed like both an eternity and as if it wasn't enough time. Alice's face showed an expression of pride and happiness. They stood by us, talking about a couple of the guests Alice had asked about.

Just as Justin finished his sentence, Ryan and Alice approached. Alice put her arm around my shoulders. "So? How are you two doing? Hitting it off, I assume?"

"We're doing fine," I answered casually.

"I would have to say, we're doing better than fine. Thank you, Alice," Justin reiterated. "This is a great party, Ryan."

"Yes, I would have to agree," Ryan replied. "It's nice to see everyone."

"Yeah." Justin looked over the room. "I see you got most of the cast here."

"Oh, yeah. Have you gotten a chance to talk to anyone?"

"No," he said, turning to look at me. "I've been a bit captivated since I got here." He smiled gently.

I could have melted. The looks he gave me were too sweet and warm. "I don't want to keep you. If you have people to see, by all means."

"No, I am great just where I am. If I don't get to see them tonight, I'll see them later." He waved at a small group of people across the room. I recognized a few of the supporting actors of the series they had been doing together, "That is, unless you would like to get rid of me."

"No!" My reply came out with such startling force that Alice laughed at it. I grinned and blushed, clearing my throat. "I mean, no, I am enjoying talking to you. It's not every day that you get a chance to meet one of your celebrity crushes." I could have died right then and there. I looked at Alice. "Did I just say that out loud? Ok, I am going to go curl up and die of embarrassment."

I have always had a tendency to say things I think I have enough courage to say and then feeling their weight afterwards. This was one of my worst examples so far. I was scrambling through my mind for something to say to recover, but I was at a loss.

"Why, yes, you did," Alice said, amused.

"Great." I could feel my face flush.

"Turn about is fair play?" she said.

Justin put his hand on mine. "I am sure that my enthusiasm in meeting you is just as strong," he said with a chuckle. "I've got an idea, let's refresh our drinks and go socialize." We handed our glasses to the bartender.

"Are you sure I'm not going to embarrass you as much as I have myself?" I took my glass from the bartender, filled.

"I am sure that I will adore anything you do." He took his glass, setting a tip on the bar. He reached his hand out to take mine, helping me off my stool and guiding me over to some of the other actors we had just spotted.

The rest of the night at the party was a bit of a blur. We didn't leave each other's sides except for brief moments or bathroom breaks the rest of the night. I met so many people. We drifted through the crowds and occasionally resumed our private conversation to get to know each other.

It was funny and rather awkward whenever someone told us what a cute couple we were or asked if we were together. I would just giggle as he would graciously tell them no, that we had just met that evening. I don't think there was a single person who inquired that wasn't a bit shocked at this. Some even told us they wouldn't have ever guessed that. I can't say this didn't make me smile each time.

It was getting late, about two in the morning, when most of the guests had gone. Ryan's family members that were staying with him had all retired except for his sisters. Alice came over to me with them both in tow and asked Justin if they could steal me away.

"Bring her back soon," he said. He smiled at Alice and turned to chat with Ryan and a couple of other guys.

"Well, he sure has taken a liking to you," Emma noted as we walked away.

"I guess," I shrugged, trying not to believe it. I was afraid to put too much meaning into his actions. I didn't want to get my hopes up.

"You guess?" Alice snapped. She grabbed my arm and swept around, facing me with both Emma and Giselle flanking her sides. "He hasn't let you out of his sight all night."

"Yeah, you guys look like a happy couple," Giselle added.

"Ryan and Justin are close friends," Emma said. "I've seen him over the last few years with and without girls. He's never had this look on his face."

"What look?" I asked.

"Bliss," she answered quickly.

"So?" Alice interjected. "What do you think? Is he great or what?"

"Um…" I was at a loss for words again.

"Um?" Alice teased. She looked at the sisters. "Oh, she's smitten."

They all laughed. Giselle put her arm around my shoulder. "You know that you're making a lot of women very jealous, including me."

"I'm sorry," I apologized.

"Sorry? You silly girl. You should be rubbing it in. He's such a great catch, and he's never been taken with anyone like he seems to be with you. You should be standing on the balcony singing *nah nah nah nah nah nah* at every woman." They laughed again.

"Listen, I just know that we're hanging out. That's it. It's not like he's kissed me or anything. For all I know, he just thinks I'm a cool girl to talk to or doing Ryan a favor to keep me preoccupied so he can have Alice all to himself." I forcefully motioned at Alice with a shake of my hand. "I am not banking that I would ever have a chance with someone like him."

Alice shook her head in frustration. "She does this all the time."

Emma blinked at me in disbelief. "Are you trying to tell me that you don't think you're worthy of his attention?"

"Look at him!" I glanced over at him, so dapper and so attractive. "He's so... so... He's just so gorgeous and awesome!"

Alice slapped me on the back of my head. I yelped. "Ouch! What was that for?"

"That's for the airport bathroom in Maui. Besides, someone needed to." She scowled at me before laughing.

"Did that put some sense in your head?" Giselle asked. "Vivianne, you are so cool and such a great woman. Plus, you're beautiful! You are one of the best looking women here. We've each had a few men ask about you tonight. We had to fend them off so Justin could get to you first."

"What do you mean, 'so Justin could get to me first'?" I picked up on that odd wording.

Alice flashed her a look, and Giselle tried to cover her tracks. "Nothing. We just had to tell several guys that you were off limits. That's all."

"Wait. I've been picking up on some odd comments and odd looks. What's going on?" I was starting to get really suspicious.

"I don't know what you're talking about. Do you, ladies?" Alice had a hint of sarcasm to her reply.

"Nope," both Emma and Giselle said with smiles on their faces.

"So, now we know that you're into him, and he's obviously into you. You can go back to him," Emma said as she turned me and gently pushed me in his direction. "It's the end of the night for us. We'll see you tomorrow for brunch and the outing."

"Have a good night," Giselle called after me.

"Good night, you two." Alice waved as she walked me back to the guys.

We walked up to Ryan and Justin's sides as they were saying good night to the last of the guests. Alice took my glass. "I'll take these to the bar and be right back."

"The car is ready whenever you are. I'm going to ride with you all to make sure you get back all right," Ryan said, putting his arm around Alice as she walked back up to us.

"I'm ready," she chimed in.

"Yeah, I guess I am, too. Especially considering we have to be presentable for brunch and an outing tomorrow." I yawned as I finished my statement.

The guys walked to the front closet and returned in their coats with ours in hand. They held them out for us like true gentlemen as we slid our arms into the sleeves.

"This was a great party," I told Ryan.

"Thank you, Vivianne. I am so glad that you both were able to come."

"Me, too," Alice added.

We headed out to the car and started out to the apartments. I began wondering about the next day's event. I had been told there was something going on, but I hadn't really gotten the details. I just knew about brunch and some outing. I didn't even know who was going.

Curiosity got the better of me, and I interrupted the idle talk about the food from the evening. "Who all is going to be there?" I asked Ryan and then looked over to Justin, hoping he would say he was.

Ryan spoke up. "Most of my family, a bunch of local friends and pretty much everyone that's here from out of town for tonight's party. So, I've reserved a banquet room for brunch at 40/30. Then we're all going to split up and go on a tour of London's best holiday decorated places. I thought that would be fun for all ages."

"That sounds like fun," I said. "Are you going to be here through tomorrow?" I asked Justin.

"Oh, yeah." He smiled. "I am staying at one of the apartments Ryan reserved through New Year's, and I'll be there tomorrow."

I couldn't help but smile at the thought of seeing him even once more. "Very cool. So, I'll see you around?"

"I hope so." He took my hand in his again.

We pulled up in front of the apartment--and all got out, to my surprise. Justin pointed at the door next to ours. "This is me, too."

"Oh, you're staying next to us?" I asked, nervously. "When did you get here?"

"I just arrived earlier today. I saw you when you came back with Alice and Ryan's sisters, but I didn't know that was you. I mean, I recognized Alice, Emma and Giselle, but I hadn't seen a picture of you or anything."

"What do you mean you 'hadn't seen a picture'?" I snapped.

"Oh, well?" There was a question in his voice as he looked at Alice and Ryan.

"Well! I am going to go in to bed," Alice stammered. "Good night, Ryan. Thank you for a lovely party. I'll see you in the morning?" She kissed Ryan on the cheek, gave him a hug and started for the front door.

She turned and pointed at Justin. "Oh, and you! You're off my Christmas card list. Remind me not to tell you where Jimmy Hoffa is buried. Thanks for ratting me out." She shot through the door.

"Uh, yes. I'll have the car here at ten. I'd better get going, too. I'll see you all in the morning." He quickly got back in the car and waved goodbye.

"Wait, you both need to explain!" I yelled, but they both took off. I put my hands on my hips and looked Justin in the eyes. "Explain."

"Crap. I take it she hadn't told you about meeting me in New York a couple of months ago?" he asked.

"Um. No. Is this a set up?"

"Well, sort of, I guess."

"What do you mean, sort of?"

"When Ryan took Alice out to New York for that benefit, he had asked me to come to meet her. I am sure you know how much she means to him." He paused.

"Yeah, go on," I urged.

"While we were all talking, you would come up in conversation. Things from how awesome you were for helping out with the trip and watching her kids to your interests. She really doesn't stop talking about you." He smiled. "Not that I minded. The more you were brought up, the more intrigued I was."

"Intrigued?" I didn't know why he would be intrigued in someone like me.

"Yeah. I can't explain it." He scrunched his eyebrows up in stern frustration and shook his head slightly. "I just knew that I needed to meet you. I started

185

asking Alice questions. It seemed the more I asked, the more she offered. Then, she said what I was too nervous to ask. She asked if I wanted to meet you. I told her yes, of course, and we started planning. Ryan mentioned his annual holiday parties. So, we figured it would work out great."

"Wow. Now I feel even more pressure than I have all night," I confessed.

"Pressure? Why would you feel pressure?" he asked with a confused look.

I was trying to walk toward the door, waiting for him to tell me something like how he had made me out to be this wonderful and gorgeous woman in his mind, but I was not what he was thinking, though he'd like to be friends or something.

"I mean, look at you. You're handsome, sexy, smart, funny and famous. It's a lot for a girl to compete with, especially when you're someone like me. I'm not saying I'm ugly and stupid, but I am not Giselle, and I am far more sarcastic and bitter than the average female."

He reached out to take my hand. Just then, I hadn't realized how close to the three-step stairway to my door I had gotten, and tripped over the bottom stair. I stumbled a couple of steps and started to go down as he caught me. He pulled me up.

Completely embarrassed, I just kept my face down. "Now I know how Alice felt in Maui."

"Yeah, I heard about that story." He laughed, put the fingers of his right hand under my chin, lifted my face and brushed my hair out of my eyes with his left hand.

186

I pulled back from his touch, startled by the rush of emotions it caused. "I am so sorry. I should go in."

"Vivianne, you are so much more than I expected." He reached out to touch my face again.

I grabbed his hand with both of mine and put all three on his chest. "You... are... well? I never get speechless, yet I can't seem to formulate constructive sentences when you're around or even when it comes to talking about you. So I am going to go inside, to sleep and try to get a better rein on my schoolgirl side."

"I find it endearing." He pulled my hands up to his face and kissed them. "I will see you in the morning?"

"I guess that's the plan." I tried to hide the melting look in my eyes.

"I can't wait." He let go of my hands and headed towards his apartment. "Good night."

"Good night." I watched him walk to his door, speechless.

He walked into his place, turning to flash me a smile as I walked through my door at the same time. I hadn't even noticed that I hadn't been the one to open it. Alice was holding it open with a look of triumph on her face.

She shut the door, and I snapped out of it. "Oh, you little..."

She held her hands up. "Are you honestly going to get after me for doing the same thing you did? Plus, look at him! He thinks you're sexier than socks on a rooster!"

We both started rolling with laughter. She always had a way to lighten a situation, keeping me from getting too melodramatic. We both did that for each

187

other. However, I couldn't escape my fears of being faced with another possible heartbreak.

"But it's so scary to think about getting involved with someone and get crushed again," I slumped into the overstuffed chair in the living room and wrapped up in a throw blanket, trying to cocoon myself from the feelings. Maybe I was trying to cocoon myself with them to keep them as long as they would last. I didn't know.

"Now you know what I have been saying." She touched my shoulder as she walked over to the couch and sat down. "It's that, right there, why I've been holding back from Ryan."

"I know. The thing is, though? I am not going to. As afraid as I am of being hurt, I am going to see where this goes." I stared off to the other side of the room.

"Really?" She sounded shocked. "Why do that so freely when I can see it's obvious you're scared out of your wits?"

I snapped out of my thoughts and looked at her. "A couple of reasons. First, I am sure I'm going to get hurt. Well, at least, my bitter side automatically is assuming it, but this feels different. He's different. Second, I see what you're doing and how you are gambling with the love of a man that loves you more than any other man has. I don't want to give up a chance for love and happiness."

"Ok?" She got stern. "So, as usual, you're going to jump into something just because of that thump in your chest that quickens when he's around. You know that thump has been what's gotten you hurt in the past. It's misleading."

"I know." I twisted the corner of the throw blanket around my finger. "But that's where the third reason comes in. You, Emma and Giselle were right. There is something to the way he looks at me and is around me. It was instantaneous for both of us. I've never felt the way I do for him for anyone before, especially right off the bat. Plus, I've never had anyone look at me the way he did all night. It wasn't just a fleeting feeling or like I was a conquest. There was so much more in his eyes."

"That's true. We all saw it. Actually, we all saw it so much that most people that knew him commented on it." She laughed.

"Really?" I felt like my response was that schoolgirl rushing back in. "Who?"

"Ryan and his sisters, for sure, but there were some of the other cast members and some random people that know him, must be friends, that all asked who you were and how long that had been going on."

"Well? As hard as it all is to believe, I am going to find out where this is going. I have to, and tomorrow's outing will tell a lot." I heard hope in my words.

Alice sat up and leaned towards me. "I'll tell you what I think when you're with him tomorrow."

"I would appreciate that. Let me know if it's in my head or it was just the romance part of a scene."

"Exactly," she smiled.

"Now, what about you, Miss Holding-back-for-so-long?" I winked at her. "You and Ryan didn't leave each other's sides all evening. What's going on? It there anything you should be telling me?"

"Fine, he's wonderful, handsome, sexy, funny, smart and great to me."

189

"Great for you, don't you mean? Plus, let's just hope he's just plain good, too." I smirked.

"That, too." I saw her mind trail off momentarily. "I should give in, I know. I am getting there. He's proving himself to be in it for the long haul. So, it's getting me to quit being a coward." She rolled her eyes.

"Well, at least you can admit it." I smiled. "Well? Now that we're both sufficiently open in a raw emotional sense, let me tell you this, your underhanded, sneaky, and I-know-what's-best stunt of not telling me that you talked to him and tried setting me up?" I tried to look angry. "Thank you," I laughed.

She got up and flipped her hair. "I knew you'd see it my way."

"Whatever, let's get some sleep." I stomped past her and went to my room, stopping halfway through my door. "Thanks."

"You're welcome," she whispered as she went into her room. "Good night."

"Good night," I whispered back.

I got changed, carefully hanging up the dress and laying out an outfit and accessories for the next day. I finished getting ready for bed and climbed in, wrapping my arms in the covers and pulling them up to my chin.

I heard a knock on my door, "Yeah?"

Alice poked her head through the door. "Oh, by the way, did you have a nice trip?"

I shot her a dirty look. "Ha ha. Very funny."

"Well? At least it wasn't into an ocean, and he had better reflexes to catch you."

"Goodnight," she smiled and closed the door.

I laid my head down and let thoughts of the evening filter through my mind as I analyzed his looks and gestures. Then, I reminded myself that he was right next door. He could be right on the other side of the wall that my headboard was resting against. I had the urge to knock on it, but I didn't because of the thought that he might be asleep, or it might not even be the right wall. However, the thought of him possibly being right on the other side of that wall, laying in bed, maybe even thinking of me, made my heart skip a beat.

He does that a lot to me, makes my heart skip a beat. I thought to myself.

I drifted off to sleep thinking about that evening. I couldn't wait for morning to come but I was so scared at the same time. I was worried that he would rethink things or being around the girls would change his mind.

My hopes were already firmly in place. There was no going back now. I was already head over heels.

Chapter Ten

Falling and Giving In

Morning came, and I woke up with a start, sitting straight up as my eyes came open. I threw on my robe and bolted over to Alice's room. She was still asleep.

How can she be sleeping at a time like this?

I sat down on the side of her bed, bouncing a little before settling still. She stirred a bit, moaning something about me going away. So, I shook her shoulder and whispered her name.

She just moaned louder, peeked at the clock and tried to push me off the bed. "It's only seven in the morning. What are you on?"

"I can't sleep any more. You have to get up! I don't know how you can sleep at a time like this." I bounced on the bed as the words came out.

"Very happily. I've only had four hours of sleep, and it's going to be a long day. Let me be," she grumbled, rolling away from me, pushing me off the bed with her feet.

I slumped onto the ground, huffed and stomped out of her room like a child. As I started to shut the door, I said, "Fine, but I'll be back for you soon. I'm going crazy here."

"Whatever." She threw a pillow at me, just barely missing me as I closed the door all the way.

I wandered into the kitchen, checking on the kids along the way. Everyone was asleep. I think that thought made me even more anxious. I didn't have anyone to be all giddy with.

I remembered there was a little café across the street, on the corner. Knowing that Alice wouldn't be any use to me until she had her caffeine, it was the perfect place to get her something she would like, to perk her up.

I figured since it was so early on a Sunday morning, I could get away with not primping. I washed my face, brushed my teeth, pulled the top half of my hair back and threw on a pair of jogging pants, a T-shirt and tennis shoes.

I pulled on my coat, grabbed my purse and the book I was reading and headed out the door. It was brisk out, but the café was just a few doors down, so I pulled the collar of my coat up as far as I could, huddled into myself and hurried across the street.

Once there, I burst through the door, aided by the strength of the wind behind me. The door made a crashing sound as it slammed into the doorstop. As if that wasn't embarrassing enough, I instantly spotted Justin sitting at a table by the window, sipping a cappuccino and reading a Dean Koontz book.

Could he be any more perfect?

He looked relaxed yet confident and aware of his surroundings as he looked up in the direction of the lunatic bursting through the door. I had thought about turning around instantly to run away, but it was too late. He looked right at me.

193

Of course, my heart skipped a beat. I smiled at him as his lips formed the crooked smile I had taken note of the night before. He wasn't dressed at all like the night before, but he wasn't any less attractive. He was wearing a blue short-sleeved T-shirt over a white long-sleeved thermal shirt. His jeans were well worn but not tattered, and he had on a pair of black and white Converse All-Star low tops.

I nodded as I tried to get to the counter quickly. I thought that if I could brace myself on the counter with my back to him, I could try to collect myself. The counter attendant was waiting for me and asked what I would like. I knew I had a drink in mind when I left the apartment, but it was gone now. I searched the chalkboard menu hanging on the wall for something that might sound good, settling on a simple hot chocolate without whipped cream.

The teenager quickly set out to get my order. At first, I thought the service was prompt, but there was another employee waiting by the back room door for my attendant. They gathered together and were mumbling about Justin being there and how awesome it was. I listened in as the two teenage girls talked about his movies and some of the rag magazine gossip going on about him.

After a few moments and lots of gossip, I cleared my throat to remind them that I was still waiting. My attendant looked up at me, and it was obvious that she had almost forgotten what she was doing. She finished up my hot chocolate and cashed out my order. The teenager thanked me and returned to her gossip partner's side and resumed their conversation, as they began daring each other to approach him.

I took a deep breath, calmed my nerves as much as I could and turned to face the room. There were two other tables with one person each at them. Then, next to the window, was Justin, not nearly as into his book as he was when I first stormed in. He looked up at me and motioned me to join him. I giggled to myself as I heard the teenage employees moan in disappointment.

I got about halfway to the table when all of a sudden, I was mortified. It dawned on me how I must have looked. I knew I had brushed my teeth and brushed my hair, but I had pulled my hair back and didn't put any make-up on. I had barely taken off what I had worn the night before. Besides, my outfit? Well, it was, by far, not the classiest, nor the most stylish outfit in my wardrobe. I could only imagine what he was thinking, seeing me like this.

As I sat down in the chair across from him, he leaned in and said, "Well, don't you look cute in the morning?"

I was floored. What did he mean, 'I looked cute?' I looked like a hobo. "Thank you, I guess. What are you doing up so early?"

"I couldn't sleep." He put his bookmark in his book. "I had a really good night last night. I laid in bed thinking about today and couldn't get back to sleep."

"Oh? Me, too." I blushed. At that moment, I thought if they could power a house with the energy a person's blushing generated, I could power a country when he was around me. "Actually, I laid in bed thinking for quite a while last night and finally fell

195

asleep, but I woke up wide awake this morning. I had to get out before I woke everyone else up shuffling around the kitchen."

He smiled at me and looked at the book in my hand. "Another Dean Koontz fan, I gather?"

"Yeah." I held it out to look at the cover. "He's my favorite author."

"Mine, too. What's your favorite book by him?"

"Oh, Night Chills, by far." I pointed at his book. "But Phenomenon is really good, too."

"This is my fourth time through this one. I do like Night Chills, though." We exchanged smiles.

We talked more about Dean Koontz and then moved onto other authors and hobbies. He asked me what I did for a living, and I told him I was a columnist but felt inspired to write a book one day when life calms down. He was actually impressed by what I did.

Finally, I checked my phone for the time, realizing it was eight. I jumped up. "Oh no! It's eight. Two hours isn't going to be enough time for Alice to get up and be ready to go by ten if I don't get her some caffeine. I need to go order something for her."

"I'll walk you back, if you don't mind." He started gathering his things.

"Sure." I grabbed my book. "That would be nice."

I went up to the counter and ordered Alice her favorite, a white chocolate chai latte. The attendants whispered to each other as one made the drink. When she brought it up to me to cash me out, the other teenage girl was in tow. They asked me about six questions all at once.

After a moment, they narrowed it down to start by asking if that was really Justin Ronin. To which, I assured them it was. She then asked me if I was his girlfriend. I smiled, paid for Alice's latte and turned to go back to Justin. A couple of steps away from the counter, I looked at Justin waiting by the door for me and turned back to look at the teenagers. They were whispering wildly but stopped and looked at me like they were waiting to find out if I had the answer to life.

"Here's to lasting connections." I winked, whipped back around and went to Justin's side.

As he held the door for me, and we walked through, I heard one of the girls squeal, "She's so lucky!"

I didn't notice the cold and wind nearly as much this time. I curled one arm around my book and held Alice's latte under my chin, taking in the hot steam with each breath. Despite the cold, we walked fairly slowly; chatting more about books and then about that day's plans. Our eyes would meet intermittently. My free hand hung by my side, and I noticed it brushing against his here and there.

As we approached the apartment doors, he wound his fingers around mine and pulled us to face each other. I couldn't look up at him. I just stared at the buttons of his coat.

"I am glad that we had the same thought this morning, and you came over to the café." His voice was gentle. "See you in a couple of hours?"

"Yeah." I was struggling for words. I pulled my hand away and started for my door. "I'd better get this in to Alice. I'll see you in a little while."

I rushed through the door, shutting it quickly and leaning against it; head turned up and slumped to the floor. I let out a sigh and pulled my knees up to my chest, set down my book and the latte and rested my head on my knees. After a moment, I could feel eyes on me. Looking up, I saw Alice standing over me with her hands on her hips.

"Isn't it a little early for melodrama?" She snickered as she grabbed the latte. "I take it this is for me?"

"Yes." I set my head back on my knees.

"I also take it you had a run-in with a certain fluster-invoking hottie?" She smirked.

"Yes."

"Well? What happened?" She reached down and lifted my hand to help me up.

I grabbed my book and stood, pulling off my coat. "I went to get you coffee since I couldn't sleep. He was there, and I looked like this."

"Oooo, ouch," she winced.

"But he said I looked cute, and we chatted about books and stuff. He walked me back and grabbed my hand at the door. I just pulled away and ran inside." I was embarrassed.

"Wow, hon, you really do like him, don't you?" She led me to the chairs at the dining room table.

I tossed myself into a chair, letting out a quick sigh. "Yes."

"Well? You're beyond help now." She sipped her latte. "But this latte is fantastic."

"Great, thanks. Shouldn't we be getting ready?" I sneered.

198

I got up and went to get the kids awake. I greeted Tiffany as I passed her in the hallway and noticed the kids were already getting ready. She said she was going to go make a small breakfast for them since we were going to brunch.

Alice and I stood at her closet for about fifteen minutes, discussing what she should wear and talking about her and Ryan. It was nice to take the focus off of me, and it was especially nice to hear her talk about Ryan in such an endearing way. She really was giving in to love as I was falling into it. Well, not that I knew it then, but I would soon enough.

She settled on a silk blouse and knee-length skirt with a pair of heels. She said she would have the accessory thing under control, so I went to my room and threw on the outfit I had picked out the night before. I had chosen a long-sleeved, black sweater with an argyle design on the front in red, white and grey. It paired nicely with my black slacks and a pair of black heels with white trim. I kept my accessories simple, a necklace; an opera length strand of different black, red and silver beads that I wound around twice to hang at three lengths. Other than that, just my watch and the rings I always wore unless I was dressing up.

We finished our make-up and hair just in time to get our coats when Ryan pulled up. We walked to the foyer and helped the kids with their coats. They were going on about how excited they were to see the holiday decorations.

Alice walked up next to me and leaned in. "I see you're tempting fate by wearing heels again," she said. "Didn't you get enough embarrassment last night?"

"Very funny," I snorted.

The doorbell rang, and the kids ran out the door to the car with Tiffany in tow. Ryan stepped through the door after them and walked up to Alice.

"You look very nice," he complimented, taking her by the hand. "Shall we?"

They walked out the door as I stood there for a moment, breath held, waiting to see Justin. I walked through the doorway and didn't spot him. I felt my heart sink. Maybe he decided not to come? That thought was dreadful.

Then I spotted him. He was locking his door and walking up to me. His gaze didn't fall from my face, and he had that beautiful crooked smile and a sparkle in his eyes.

"Good morning, again." He held his arm out for me to take. "Shall we?"

As we walked to the car, he asked about the kids. I told them their ages and names and who belonged to who.

Settling in, we all took off our coats. The kids were playing with Tiffany in the front of the long seating area. They loved riding in a limo. Alice was leaning in to Ryan and telling him about my encounter from that morning. Then, Justin took his coat off.

His attire was, as usual, not disappointing. He was wearing a suit, as was Ryan, but Ryan's was fairly standard. Justin, however, had turned his three-button black suit into something beyond that. He wore a deep red turtleneck sweater under the jacket and had a long, white linen scarf tucked under the jacket collar that fell down to the waist at both sides.

He had a black fedora hat with red pinstripes that he took off in the car, allowing his thick hair to tousle around his face. He was wearing a silver watch and black and white wing-tip shoes. I heard Alice and Ryan take note of us matching.

"So? Did you two plan this?" Ryan nudged Justin with his foot.

"No, actually, but I guess we do match, don't we?" He looked at me. "You look beautiful."

"Thanks." I scanned his outfit again. "You are, as usual it seems, very stylish."

"Thank you." He looked at Ryan, "It's not like the two of you clashed."

I noticed that Ryan's suit was grey with a white button-down shirt and the only color in his outfit was a peach handkerchief in the breast pocket. This matched her outfit nicely. Her silk blouse had a geometrical pattern to it that was rose reds, pale yellows, off white, greys and peaches. Her pencil skirt was a grey wool, and her heels were that same peach.

"So, did you two plan that?" I laughed.

Alice's face turned red. "No," she snapped and then burst out in laughter.

"This is getting all too weird," I announced.

"What?" Ryan asked.

"Us. All of us. You two are perfect for each other. I've never met anyone that complemented Alice in so many ways. I mean look, you guys even complement each other's outfits without planning." I waved my hand at them dismissively.

"And what about you two?" Alice asked accusingly.

I glanced at Justin. "Our color scheme is pretty common. Anyone could have chosen these colors," I tried to underplay my thoughts that he and I could be as well-fitted as they were.

Justin looked me in the eye. "I don't think it's any less noteworthy. You have to admit; we do seem pretty well matched." He searched my eyes for a sign that I agreed.

I lowered the volume of my words to say, "I know."

He just smiled.

The rest of the drive consisted of chat about the party the night before and talking to the kids. The kids, especially Elizabeth, had lots of questions about the buildings and scenery on the way. Ryan seemed all too happy to explain some of the history and humor them with jokes and funny stories as Justin added in here and there.

I was surprised when Justin would jump in and join the conversations. It was nice to see men that could converse with kids and not make it seem forced. Actually, Alice, Giselle and I all talked about how awesome the guys were with the kids and how the kids took to them so comfortably.

We had all seen our kids with Ryan, but it wasn't any different with Justin. They hadn't met him before, but they were asking him questions, laughing at his jokes and playing around with him just as they did with Ryan when they first met him. Even Tina was chatting with him, occasionally turning to us when he wasn't looking, dropping her jaw in awe and pointing at him. We were amused.

The guys showed them what each button did in the limo and continued sharing stories about things as we passed them. Sometimes they talked about the history of some place. Sometimes it was a funny story or that some famous person lived or had lived there. The kids were enthralled.

Where else can you get a first hand history lesson intermixed with stand-up comedy?

As we pulled up to 40/30, Justin leaned in and whispered, "They're beautiful, Vivianne."

I just looked at the girls for a moment. "Yeah, I have been blessed."

The car stopped, and the kids rushed to the back, where we were, ready to get out and see what new and exciting place Ryan had brought us to. We filed out, just barely escaping being trampled by them.

40/30 was impressive and very upscale. The room he had reserved had already started filling with people. I recognized quite a few people from the night before. Many of them hadn't met the kids, so they would stop us and ask about them, greeting them warmly with hand shakes and hugs.

The kids, Tiffany and the four of us all sat together at a larger table at the head of the room. The food was delicious, and the people gathered were all mingling and having fun. It was a calmer and smaller version of the night before.

After brunch, Ryan and his parents broke the party into groups and gave them details on where we were all going. There was about forty of us in total. So, it wouldn't work for us to all be at the same place at the same time.

Tiffany, Emma and a couple of Ryan's female cousins took the six kids in one car. Ryan, Alice, Justin and I took Giselle and three of Ryan's friends from out of town with us--one of which Giselle had taken a liking to the night before, so that made her happy.

The rest broke up into three groups and headed out. Every car had Ryan's twenty sights planned. Four of them were places to get out and go through for the inside decorations. Three were places that were outside mini tours. The rest were places that we drove past and saw the huge displays.

They were all breathtakingly beautiful. It was a perfect holiday outing, and Ryan was right. It was suitable for all ages. He couldn't have planned something more fitting for a Sunday afternoon right before Christmas.

While driving around, we all started talking about going shopping and what we had left to get as far as gifts go. I knew that Alice and I brought some gifts, but there were more to get, especially since we had met so many people that had become important to our lives.

Alice looked at Ryan at one point. "What do you want for Christmas? I've been racking my brain, but I can't seem to come up with anything."

"Just you," he smiled.

"You're infuriating," she argued.

He chuckled. "Well, hon. Now you know how I feel."

She slapped his shoulder and huffed back into her seat.

After four drive-by sights on our trip, we stopped and went through an indoor and then an outdoor spot.

Alice, Giselle and I wandered in and out of our group. I noticed that Ryan and Justin would get into a pretty deep conversation from time to time.

This made me a little nervous. Were they talking about Alice? Me? The kids? Work? Someone else? Oh yes. My very feminine, girly side came out in force as I tried to read their expressions and even their lips at times.

At one point, I overheard my name as they both glanced back at me. Just like me, I was more engrossed in eavesdropping than where I was going. I kicked a low retaining wall of stone with my left foot, tripping over it. I tried to catch myself while lifting my leg over the stones, but the fake lighted tree I grabbed for balance3 tipped over, and I slammed my foot down, twisting my ankle sideways and crashing to the ground.

Alice roared in laughter as they all rushed over to my side to see if I was all right and set the decoration back upright. I flipped to a sitting position, holding my ankle to survey the pain.

I looked up to see everyone in the group standing over me plus some other sightseers. It was mortifying. To make matters worse, Alice and Giselle were still laughing, barely to get out words of concern about my condition.

I looked up at Alice. "Are you happy? I am not the winner."

"Oh, honey, you've always been the winner. Now, everyone else knows it," she joked.

I rolled my eyes and winced with pain. "Thanks. You're quite the friend."

"Oh, don't say I didn't say something to you before we left about testing fate."

"Shut up," I snapped.

Justin kneeled down beside me and took my ankle in his hands. "Do you want to go get this looked at?"

"No, I am sure it's just a silly sprain and will feel better in a couple of days." I scanned the crowd around me.

"Are you sure?" Ryan was concerned.

"Yeah. I am a klutz at times. This is nothing big. Just more wounding to my ego."

"Don't worry about it, but we should have your hands cleaned up." Justin let go of my ankle with one hand and turned over the palm of my left hand.

"Oh, I didn't even notice." I was shocked as I noticed the scrapes on my palms from landing on the gravel. "Where can I get a sink and soap?"

Ryan put his hand on Justin's shoulder. "There's some shops just a few doors down. I am sure you can take her in there and use their facilities. As a business, they might have a small first aid kit, too." He pointed down the road to the right.

"No, you guys go ahead. I'll be fine. I'll just take a cab back to the apartment and spend some time thinking about how graceful I am." I tried to laugh it off. "I don't want to hold you back from the tour. You have a schedule."

"Don't be ridiculous, Vivianne." Ryan's face was stern. "We haven't finished here. By the time you're done cleaning up, we'll be ready and can pick you up from there."

"Then go with them, Justin," I pleaded. "I don't want to take you away from everyone."

"Don't be silly, Viv," Alice jumped in. "You will need help walking from what we can tell, and I am sure he wouldn't mind one bit."

"No, I don't mind. I'd rather help to make sure there's nothing you need." He threw one of my arms around his neck, wrapped an arm around my waist and helped me up.

"Ok, but can I ask one more thing, Ryan?"

He looked at me, puzzled. "Sure?"

"Is any of the shops down there a shoe shop?" I inquired.

"Might be, why?" he asked.

"Well, I should probably get some flats, just in case," I joked at my own expense.

Everyone laughed. Ryan put a hand on my arm. "Hon, if there isn't one there, we can make a stop before the next place."

"Thanks."

Justin and I headed out of the garden and down the road. The shop keeper was very polite and quite concerned about me. She brought out a chair and some first aid items. They both looked over my ankle and assessed that it wasn't anything more than I thought.

She shuffled off to get a couple pairs of shoes for me to try on after asking my size. I settled on a pair of black ballerina flats. They were simple and comfortable. I paid for them as Justin started looking at my hands.

He went to the bathroom and brought back some wet paper towels, setting them on my hands. They were warm but stung on contact. One hand at a time, he wiped the blood off my skin, making comments that they didn't look as bad as he had thought.

He finished cleaning them up and started getting out gauze and tape. I protested, explaining that I didn't really want them bandaged, "Too many people will take notice, and I feel foolish already."

"Don't be silly. These may be just scrapes, but there's a lot of them, and you don't want them getting infected. You can take them off tonight. Just let me put some antibiotic ointment on them and wrap them for now."

"Fine, if you insist," I muttered, holding out my hands, palm up and pouting.

He laughed. "I do."

He finished bandaging me up, and we headed outside when the car pulled up. I thanked the shop keeper, and she wished me luck. I limped out to the car, hiding my hands.

Everyone was kind enough to have dropped my colossal embarrassment and were chatting about the place we had just toured and other not-me topics, to my relief. I settled in next to Alice, and Justin sat next to me as Giselle moved across the car to sit next to her newest eye candy boy.

We enjoyed most of the other stops without incident. I tried to pay more attention to where I was walking rather than what others were talking about. At the last stop, we filed out to go inside.

We were inside going from room to room. About midway through, Ryan pulled me aside and told the others I needed a break, and we'd catch up. Alice and

Justin both offered to sit with me, but Ryan assured them we were fine and to go ahead and have fun. They reluctantly did.

"You've seemed to have made quite an impression on him," Ryan said, taking my arm to lead me to a chair.

"So I keep hearing. Is that a feat or something? Maybe you two talked me up a little too much in New York," I said.

"No, actually, as excited as he was to meet you, I've never seen him like this with anyone. I am surprised. I thought you two would get along, but I didn't expect to see him this taken, especially this early. He was really worried about you back there when you fell."

"Don't remind me about my epic ways to embarrass myself. Well, we'll see, huh." I started to get up.

He grabbed my arm. "Well, at least I can see that you feel the same, right?"

I sat back down, frozen at the thought that I was more transparent than I thought I was. "Oh dear lord. Is it that obvious?"

He laughed. "Well, it's encouraging. I just want to make sure."

"Make sure of what?" I asked.

"I don't want to see either of you get hurt. If all you are interested in is shagging, then I would want to tell you not to."

"Aren't all men into that? No ties?" I snapped.

"Most men, yes, and I am sure he's had his times where that's all he's wanted. This is not the case with you," he retorted.

"What do you mean?"

"Listen, I saw something in him when we were talking about you in New York. I don't normally believe in "meant to be", but meeting Alice has changed something in me. When I saw his interest in you before you two even met, I knew there was something there," he revealed.

"Ok? What's that have to do with now?" I pried.

"Seeing him with you, that look hasn't gone away. There's something that has hit him, and it's only gotten stronger. I talked to him earlier, and he's already got strong feelings for you."

"Oh, like a movie-style, love at first sight thing?" I tried to be sarcastic, trying to hide my own feelings.

"Well, not to be clichéd, but yes," he smiled.

"Really?" I could hear the excitement in my voice.

"Yes, and I need to make sure that you're not just looking for a fling. I know you've gone through a lot in the last year, but he doesn't need to be going for one thing while you have something different in mind." He stood up for his friend. "I don't want either of you ending up hurt."

"Ryan, I don't think I have words to explain what's going on inside my head or my heart for that matter," I admitted.

He laughed. "You sound just like him. That's what he said when I asked him earlier."

"Oh? You mean? Well, I guess you already said that." I fidgeted with my necklace. "Rest assured that I am not just looking for a fling. The way he makes me feel scares the crap out of me, and I've only been afraid that he doesn't feel the same way."

He smirked. "Oh, he does. He's just nervous about how fast the feelings came on and that you don't return them."

"Well, tell him not to worry," I said.

"Will do." He started to get up.

I stopped him this time. "And what about you and Alice?"

"What about us?" He came off as if he didn't know what I was talking about.

"Oh, you know." I nodded. "You two seem to be inseparable."

"I hope so," he said coolly.

We got up and started walking to the exit to wait for the rest of the group. I looked at him and teased, "You're such a girl."

"What?" He whipped his head around to look at me.

"You are all asking 'do you like him because he likes you'," I said in a high-pitched voice.

"Oh, you're funny, Miss Can't-Watch-Where-I'm-Walking." He nudged me in the arm.

"True, but at least I'm not a gossip girl." I pulled my shoulders back, smiled a huge grin and held my head up, limping past him to the exit.

We wandered around the exit area, looking at a few decorations for just a moment before everyone caught up with us. Alice and Justin asked if I was ok. I told them that I was and said I had stepped wrong again and just wanted to sit it out. Alice looked at me like she knew something I didn't and leaned to whisper that she talked to Justin. I smiled and nodded as we walked out to the car.

As everyone else was getting in, I whispered back that the real reason Ryan and I stayed back was so we could have that conversation. I summed up what we talked about. She stood there, her eyes wide, and told me that I knew more than what she'd gotten out of him.

Suddenly, she broke her amazement and gave me a hug. I hugged back and told her that she couldn't let me down as far as her and Ryan went now. I said I was leading by example by not holding back. She needed to see that she was doing the right thing by getting closer to him.

We got in the car and took our seats that had been reserved for us between the guys. She smiled, patted my knee and wrapped her arm around Ryan's, leaning her head on his shoulder. He looked down at her with a smile and put his free hand on her hand and continued to talk to his friends.

I leaned back into my seat with a sigh. Justin was sitting next to the door to my right, staring out the window. I put my left hand on his that was resting on his leg and asked, "You ok?"

He looked over and stared for a moment; it was obvious that he had been transfixed on something he was seeing that wasn't really out that window. "Um, yeah. Sorry. I just zoned out there for a minute." He looked down at my hand on his and turned his over, entwining his fingers with mine.

My heart skipped irregularly for a moment as my breath caught. I finally took a jagged breath and looked up at his eyes that caught mine as they came up. He smiled very gently, and I returned the smile.

I laid my head on his shoulder and whispered, "Thank you for taking care of me today."

He put his right hand to my cheek and kissed the top of my head. "My pleasure."

The car pulled off towards Ryan's house to meet up with the rest of the larger group.

Chapter Eleven

Developments

At Ryan's house, most people said their goodbyes or "until laters". Mary and Henry suggested holiday shopping. We all agreed that was the perfect time. No one had plans for the afternoon anyway. That night, Tiffany was going to take the kids over to Ryan's to play with Emma's kids while Alice had dinner with Ryan and his family. Justin and I would come back later for drinks around the fire.

I told Alice that I was more than happy to find something to do. I wanted to take in some sights or do some shopping that I didn't get done with her that afternoon. She teased me about getting together with Justin, but I told her that I didn't want to push myself on him.

Ryan laughed and said I could use one of his regular cars later on, if I promised to drive on the right side of the road. I assured him that I figured I could handle that. He thanked me for being cool about the dinner, and we split up into shopping teams.

Tiffany went back to the apartment with the kids, and Emma's husband stayed at Ryan's with their kids. Most of Ryan's friends headed home or to their hotels or rented apartments. Mary and Henry went out together. Ryan took Justin. Then, Alice, Giselle, Emma and I all gathered our purses and climbed into Emma's rental car.

We had a lot of fun. There were lots of questions for me about Justin and me from all three of them. They were especially interested in what Ryan and I talked about. I wasn't sure how Ryan would feel about me telling them, so I paraphrased it.

I told them that Ryan had noticed that things were developing between us and had talked to us both. I told them how he felt, being a friend to both of us, that he wanted to make sure we were both on the same page. He didn't want to see either of us hurt if one was looking for more than the other or feeling more than the other.

That information gave rise to squeals and giggles from the three of them. I felt that schoolgirl side of me fighting to get out. Emma asked what my reply was. They wanted to know if we were, in fact, on the same page. I told them that I figured we were from what Ryan was saying. Then, Giselle asked just what that page was.

Emma pulled into a parking spot at a local shopping complex. I took the opportunity to jump out of the car, claiming to have to go to the bathroom and get something to drink. I ran off in the direction Emma pointed to for a café as Giselle called after me, telling me that I was going to have to tell her when they caught up with me.

Sure enough, as I walked out of the bathroom to the counter for a drink, they were waiting, leaned against the wall like a gang. I couldn't help but laugh as they started in on me.

"So? What is this proverbial page you and he are on?" Giselle asked sharply, tapping her foot.

"Nothing, really. We just seem to want the same thing and possibly feeling the same thing." I walked past them towards the counter.

Emma spoke up. "And how do you two feel?"

"Happy." I tried to not say too much. I ordered a strawberry smoothie from the attendant.

Alice grabbed me by the arm and whipped me around. "Listen, you. Don't make us beat it out of you. Spill it."

"Fine," I snapped as I grabbed my smoothie and headed for a table. "From what Ryan says, he talked to him earlier. I guess he's got strong feelings for me already and has been worried that I don't feel the same. I did find him in the café this morning, unable to sleep."

"Yeah. We heard about that. What about you?" Emma urged.

"Okay?" I took a deep breath, "We spent all night at the party together talking. I couldn't sleep well thinking about seeing him today. I make a fool of myself when he's around. I can't stop thinking about him. We fit perfectly together other than the fact that he's so awesome, and I'm a silly, clumsy woman that drools over him."

"Oh, so you both are falling in love?" Giselle poked me in the ribs.

"Love?" I was shocked at the notion. "No! You can't fall in love this quickly. I like him a lot. That's for sure."

"Oh, you can start falling in love right away. It's how fast will it take for you to be completely in love?" Giselle retorted.

I got up and headed for the door. "We've got shopping to do."

We headed out the door as all three chimed in song, "Vivianne and Justin, sitting in a tree K-I-S-S-I-N-G. First comes love. Then comes...."

I whipped around. "Stop, you guys!"

They burst out laughing. After a moment, I couldn't help but join in.

Alice walked up and put an arm around my shoulders. "I am happy for you. You deserve a great man, and so far? I approve."

"Wait a second." I looked up at her. "Shouldn't we be asking what's going on with you and Ryan? You two are going to have a full family dinner tonight? Isn't that something couples do?"

Giselle chimed in, "Yeah! What gives?"

"Yes. That is something couples do, and you've been insisting you two are not a couple. So?" Emma pried.

"Nothing has changed," Alice insisted. "We're great friends. I know how he feels, and he knows I feel strongly for him but I am just not ready for a relationship yet. He said he'll wait, patiently, for me."

"Aw! That's so sweet! I think I am going to get sick," I joked.

"He hasn't said anything to you guys?" Alice asked Giselle and Emma.

They both shook their heads no. "Nothing," Giselle added.

"Well, I just hope that you get ready soon. You two are perfect for each other, and I hate seeing you put off what will make you both so happy," Emma said, putting her hand on Alice's shoulder.

"I know," Alice admitted. "I don't want to draw this out any more than necessary. I just think of all the things like the distance between where we live, and me going to school. I am nowhere near as successful as he is in my endeavors. I have kids to think about. There are so many factors, and until I am sure of both of our feelings, I don't want to get head over heels into it."

"I understand that," I said. "Ok, ladies. What do you say we concentrate on shopping?"

"Sounds good to me," Alice agreed.

We spent the next three hours in and out of shops. Alice and I had brought a few things with us on the plane and had agreed that this year we were not going to do large-item gifts. Ryan said he would ship back anything we couldn't take on the plane. That was part of what he told us when he talked to us about coming out over the holidays, but we figured we'd just get them smaller gifts that would be keepsakes of the trip.

We picked up another little something for Ryan's parents. While Emma and Giselle were in a different shop, we got them each something small. Next, we wanted to get Justin something. Talking about it, we decided to go in on Justin's gift together, too. We had just met everyone, but we knew that they were going to get us something, and it would be awkward not to have something in return. Plus, I loved giving gifts. So, it catered to that side of me.

218

We put our bags in the trunk of the car and the back seat with us. It was a tight squeeze, but it wasn't too uncomfortable for the drive. They dropped us off at our apartment, telling Alice they'd see her shortly and me later tonight.

We put away our bags in our rooms and settled down to the dining room table. We hadn't gotten everything for our kids, Tiffany or Emma's husband and kids. Plus, I needed to get Alice her gift. We made a list of what I was to look for, and I headed back out, walking to Ryan's, to get his car while she prepared for her family dinner.

It was about four in the afternoon, and the shops were going to close about eight in the area that Giselle pointed me to. I also wanted to get something for dinner. I whipped through my list of things to get. Proud of my quick run through, I had finished in two and a half hours. So, I started looking for a place that sounded good for dinner.

I settled on a place that looked to have burgers and fries. I had brought my laptop so I could try to get some work done. So, I settled onto a stool at the bar and started in. I had two columns due at the end of the week, and I wasn't sure when I would find time to work for sure.

I was engrossed in my burger and about halfway through the first article when I heard a voice from behind me say, "Well, don't we just think alike?"

I turned to see who the voice belonged to, already knowing the answer. "Justin! What are you doing here?"

"I was finishing up some shopping and needed to get a bite to eat. Do you mind if I join you?" He motioned to the empty stool next to me.

"No, that would be great." I slid my drink over to give him room on the bar.

He looked at my laptop. "Work?"

"Yeah, I didn't tell my bosses I was going anywhere, figuring it wouldn't matter where I worked from as long as I wrote, right?"

"Very true." He smiled. "What are you doing wandering around by yourself?"

"Oh." I cleared my throat. "Everyone is at Ryan's for dinner, and I still had a list of gifts Alice and I needed to get. So, I thought I'd get a chance to hit London's streets on my terms. Ryan gave me a car and a map to use, and Giselle pointed me in a direction."

He laughed. "Adventurous spirit, huh?"

"So I've been told." I saved my work and closed the laptop. "I gather not unlike you?"

"No, not unlike at all." His smile was very warm, making his eyes sparkle. "So? How's your ankle?"

"Much better, thank you." I blushed.

He looked at my hands. "I see you took the bandages off."

I held my palms up. "Oh, yeah. They feel pretty good. Thanks again."

"I'm just glad you didn't hurt yourself worse. I think you scared everyone there today," he teased.

"Yeah, thanks for the reminder. I feel like a complete dork."

"Don't. Your little accidents just make you more adorable." He ordered a drink and a burger from the bartender and then changed the subject. "Ryan said something about taking a group out to his favorite dance club later in the week. Do you dance?"

"I love to dance," I replied quickly. "Not just for fun, which it is, but I also find it very therapeutic. Do you?"

"Do I dance or do I find it therapeutic?" he asked.

I laughed. "Do you dance?"

"A little, but Ryan is fun to hang out with at the clubs. So, it should be a fun night either way." He took his drink as the bartender set it on the bar in front of him. She shot him a flirty look and walked away. I don't think he even really paid attention to it even though she was being rather obvious. "You going to go?" He kept his focus on us.

"I know he has several things planned for the rest of our stay here. So, I am sure we will," I was restraining taking another bite of my burger. It was so good, but it was also so sloppy, and I didn't need that kind of embarrassment.

Just then, three younger women came up and asked Justin for his autograph. He smiled and reached out for their pens and paper and looked at me. "I am sorry about this."

He signed each one as they dished out the compliments and thanked him repeatedly. I just sat there, admiring how gracious he was with his fans. You can tell a lot about a famous person by how they treat their fans, and from what I could see, he was always grateful for his.

"No, not a problem," I said after they had gone. "It's part of the job. I understand. Heck, I'm waiting to see gossip about us in a magazine. You should have seen the outlandish things that went around about Ryan and us, especially Alice. It was insane."

"Yeah, I saw some of that, and I have to say..." He pulled a magazine out of one of his bags and slid it over to me, cover down. He looked at me with a worried look on his face. "I am sorry."

"Sorry?" I turned over the magazine to look at the cover.

Sure enough, there I was, with him, standing outside the apartments. He broke into my thoughts. "They're persistent, aren't they? I am sure it was someone at the party that tipped them off."

"Oh? Maybe that guy you scared away," I joked.

He laughed. "Maybe."

I paused for a moment, looking at the picture of us, between the doors. It was when he had just caught me and was brushing the hair out of my face, "Do I dare look at the article to see what they wrote?"

"It's not a lot. Just the unoriginal questions of rag reporters. 'Who is this woman?' 'Are they together?' 'Why is he cheating on so-and-so?' even though I'm not dating anyone." He rolled his eyes. "It's up to you, though. I spotted this while shopping and thought I'd show you. I was going to bring it later tonight. There are a few more pictures and lots of meaningless babble inside."

I turned the pages to our article, curious about the other pictures they had taken. They were all of us outside the apartments. After scanning through the article, I noted they pegged me as klutzy and some 'commoner turned famous by association'. I found myself actually a little offended by that comment, but I brushed it off.

"No big deal," I shrugged it off. "Part of my job, huh?"

"Your job?" he asked.

"Yeah." I smiled. "It's part of your job because you're the movie star. It's part of my job because I'm a friend of the movie star. Right?"

He shook his head in amusement. "I guess that's right. However, I wouldn't exactly say friend."

"No?" I was hoping to hear that, but still afraid of hearing what he *did* think of us as. "What would you say then, acquaintance?"

"No." He blushed a little with that crooked smile and looked down at his hands that were fidgeting with the end of his scarf.

Was he actually blushing? Really blushing? Don't get your hopes up. Maybe he's just nervous about letting you down. Maybe he just thinks of you in a physical way and Ryan had it wrong. Why would he think of you in that way when he... What am I doing to myself? Why wouldn't he think of me? Just wait and see what he has to say.

After a pause, he continued, "Love interest? As the reporters would say."

"And what would you say?" I searched for more of an explanation.

He looked right at me and smiled. "That you're being really cool about this whole publicity thing."

"Oh, did you want me to freak out and get all upset?" I went along with his avoidance of the question.

"No, I just didn't expect you to be so okay with it."

"Well? What choice do I have?" I looked him in the eyes. "My only other option is to not see you, right?"

"I guess so," he replied.

I shrugged my shoulders. "Is that a better option?"

"No," he whipped out his response. "That isn't better at all."

I smiled. "Then I take it with a grain of salt and brace myself for the round of interrogation I'll get when I go home and will probably start through phone tomorrow."

"You're amazing, Vivianne." He put his right hand to my cheek.

I laughed. "Watch out, this is a prime photo op for anyone watching us."

"I don't care. Let them," he said seriously.

I could feel that it was the right moment for a first kiss, but I froze and cracked a joke. "So? You're really dating her?"

He looked confused. "Who?"

"The woman you're cheating on with me. Who did they say? That singer," I teased.

"Oh. No! They have been spreading rumors about that for a while now. I think I met her at a party a while back, but we've never talked other than that," he explained.

"I'm just kidding." I patted his hand and motioned, with a nod, that his food had arrived. "I am just making sure I'm not the other woman."

Both of us sipped on our drinks and ate our burgers. I focused really hard on not making a mess while eating. I don't know what was worse, the thought of making a mess while eating or doing what I did, making myself look prissy. Well, at least he didn't have to see me with mustard running down my chin.

We chatted about shopping, the party, that day's outing and how strange it was that we kept running into each other in odd places. I always seemed to stumble when we first started talking, but I was finding it easier to talk to him as time went on.

The plates had been cleared away, and I swore I must have drunk a gallon of milk when we both realized that it was after ten. We were supposed to be at Ryan's around nine. He called over the bartender and paid both of our tabs. I argued that he didn't need to, but he insisted.

He had taken a cab. So, I asked, "Would you like to ride with me? I am not familiar with the roads anyway. Maybe you can keep me from getting lost."

He agreed with a laugh, and we loaded up the car and headed towards the apartments to drop the bags off. From there, we drove over to Ryan's. As we pulled up to park, Alice, Ryan, Emma and Giselle came out to meet me.

"Where have you been? We were starting to think you got lost!" Alice shouted as I got out of the car.

Justin opened his door, and everyone's worried expressions changed to intrigue.

"Oh!" Alice exclaimed.

Ryan walked over to Justin. "Geez, Vivianne. Picking up strays these days?" He slugged Justin in the shoulder. "You guys plan this?"

"No." Justin looked over at me, scanned the awaiting faces of the girls and back to Ryan. "I walked into the same place she went to eat, and we had dinner together."

"Well, isn't that just convenient?" Giselle teased.

We all laughed and headed inside. Justin caught up with me once through the door, and we really didn't leave each other's sides the rest of the night. After dinner, Ryan led us all to the living room where they had been sitting around the fireplace drinking cocktails and telling stories.

Mary and Henry retired about midnight, and I called Tiffany to make sure she and the kids were fine for the night just in case we didn't make it back there. She assured me that they were fine, and she knew there'd be a night or two we'd stay at Ryan's. She actually was excited. She said she was dying to make the kids her trademark Mickey Mouse pancakes.

I hung up the phone and walked back to the living room, sitting down on the ottoman in front of the overstuffed chair that Justin was sitting in. He leaned forward, wrapped his arms around me and pulled me back against him as he sat back. It was such a perfect fit.

I looked over at Alice. She smiled at me. She and Ryan were on the couch, and she leaned over and rested her head on his shoulder, mouthing the words, "It's perfect". I nodded and saw Ryan entwine his fingers with hers without skipping a beat.

About one, Giselle and Emma left the room and came back with things to make s'mores. Alice jumped up, dragging Ryan down to the floor in front of the fireplace with her.

"S'mores!" She sounded like a little kid. "Come on, Viv! You two need to get down here, too!"

I reluctantly pulled myself up from his arms as I heard him sigh. We sat down between Alice and Giselle as Emma was opening the packages on the other side of Alice. Justin sat behind me, putting a leg on either side of me, wrapping his arms back around my waist and setting his head on my shoulder. Ryan took a cue with Justin's position and curled Alice up with him.

"It's so great to see you two guys finally happy," Emma said as she passed out the utensils and ingredients.

The rest of the night was fantastic. Emma and Giselle retired about two. Alice and Ryan climbed back onto the couch and curled up. Justin and I went back to the chair and the position we were in before the s'mores.

The four of us talked for so long. I honestly don't know what time we ended up falling asleep, but it was in those seats that we did. I remember thinking I never wanted to leave that chair with him as I drifted off. Alice had already fallen asleep, and the guys were talking about going back to work in a couple of weeks.

I woke the next morning and looked around. I could hear Mary and Henry a couple rooms away, chatting over a cup of coffee at the dining room table. Emma's kids were running around upstairs. Then, there was someone in the kitchen, rustling pots and pans. I assumed it was Reggie.

Looking at Alice and Ryan, they were both stretched out on the couch. Ryan had his arm around her, holding her up from falling on the floor. I rolled over to look at Justin. He looked so peaceful. We had slumped down in the chair after falling asleep, our legs depending on the ottoman for half of our makeshift bed.

I laid there for a moment, watching him sleep and wanting so badly to reach out and run my fingers through his hair or down his arm. I restrained myself. Even though we had slept curled up with each other, there hadn't been a first kiss or anything. I didn't know where my boundaries were, and I wasn't going to be the one to open up that range in the relationship. Not until I knew that's where he wanted to go.

Feeling the pull to him, I decided I should head back to my apartment to get a shower and brush my teeth. I sat up and stretched.

Just then, Emma walked into the room, all perky. "Oh! You're up! Are you hungry?"

Everyone else started to stir and sit up. Crap! There goes brushing my teeth. "Sure," I muttered. "What's for breakfast?"

"I think Reggie is making waffles, bacon, hash browns and fresh orange juice," she said with a smile.

"Ok, if he's still making breakfast, if you don't mind, I am going to run back to the apartment and freshen up," I said, relieved I hadn't lost a chance.

"Yeah. I don't see why not." She announced breakfast to the others as they came out of their sleeping fog.

I stood up and looked at Justin. "I will be back in a few."

He smiled. "Yeah, I think I'll do the same."

"Wait up, Viv. I'm coming with you," Alice said.

"Go ahead and take the car, Vivianne," Ryan offered.

"Thanks." I pulled on my shoes, rubbing my sore ankle. "You want a ride, Justin?"

"That would be great." He leaned up and hugged me while sitting.

His hands were pressed to my lower back while the side of his face pressed on my stomach. I just wanted to pull him up and kiss him, but I pulled away.

"We'd better get going if we're going to make it back in time to have a hot breakfast." I headed for the door.

I didn't say much on the way back. I rushed into the apartment, telling Justin to knock on our door when he was done and ready to go back. Tiffany greeted me in the foyer with a wondering look on her face.

"No, nothing like that." I blushed. "We just fell asleep curled up in a chair next to the fire while Alice," I said, motioning toward her as she came through the door, "was curled up with Ryan on the couch."

"You sure that's all that happened?" She smiled.

"Yeah, she's lame," Alice joked.

"Oh, like you have a lot of room to talk." I flashed her a dirty look. "I didn't see you putting the moves on anyone last night, and I fell asleep after you."

"Well, that would be because you weren't there until after ten." She had a smug tone to her words.

"What?" I was confused. "And what, pray tell, do you mean by that?"

"We finished dinner about seven thirty. So, since you two weren't supposed to be there until nine, Ryan and I had some alone time as everyone else did their

229

own thing." Her thoughts trailed off as she sat at the dining room table. "He took me to his library, and we were talking about books. He showed me some of the first editions he has which was cool. Then, while I was skimming through a rare copy of the first run of a Dickens book, he walked up to me, pulled the book from my hands, carefully setting it on the desk, and kissed me."

"What?" I shouted.

"Yeah!" She beamed. "And I didn't pull back or anything. It was so passionate and wonderful. So, yes. There was more than you and Justin. Then, considering that the two of you were running late, he had a chance to kiss me one more time right before you showed up while we were goofing around by the bar, making a drink."

"Wow, Alice!" I was floored. "I am amazed."

"So?" Tiffany interjected. "Are you two going back to be with them soon?"

"Oh!" I jumped up. "We're supposed to be just freshening up and going back for breakfast! Justin is going to be here any minute!"

I took off for my bedroom, stopping to say good morning to the kids. They were engrossed in a movie, breaking their attention just long enough to say hello.

I threw my clothes off, grabbing a clean pair of jeans and sweater. My ankle was sore but not unbearable. Still, I decided that I had better not test it and chose a pair of supportive ankle boots.

I walked in the bathroom just as Alice did. She had changed into a green tank top with a cream colored cardigan and cream slacks. I told her that her salmon colored kitten heels would look great with her outfit. She agreed.

I washed my face, brushed my teeth, did my hair and threw on a little make-up. Alice was pretty much in time with me as we started rushing when we heard Tiffany let Justin in.

The kids jumped up to greet him. They were all telling him about the movie and begging him to sit and watch it with them. You could hear Tiffany asking the kids to leave him alone, but they were persistent.

We walked into the living room and saw Justin on the couch with Victoria on his lap, Elizabeth sitting on one side, Cameron on the other and Tina on the floor in front of him. He looked up as we stopped next to the couch.

"Aw, how cute!" Alice teased.

"You both ready?" He avoided a response to her comment with a smile.

I picked up Victoria. "Yes." I gave her a hug and a kiss, set her down and did the same to Elizabeth. "We'll be back later, kids. Ok?"

They protested our leaving as Alice and I finished our goodbyes. Tiffany picked up Victoria and assured the kids they'd have fun, and we'd be back before they knew it. They settled back into their movie, and we headed out the door.

Breakfast was great. However, the chattering about "both new couples" was embarrassing. Emma and Giselle kept telling Mary about how close we all were the night before and asking what happened after they had gone to sleep.

Emma talked about coming into the room and finding everyone curled up. "So, there must have been something more," she accused.

Ryan assured her that they were both perfect gentlemen, and we had all just gone to sleep. His assurances didn't satisfy her. They kept prying while Alice's face kept getting redder and redder. Giselle poked Alice in the ribs. "So... If they were such perfect gentlemen, why is your face so red? Huh, Alice?"

"Yeah. Your blushing isn't giving away anything, is it?" Emma said slyly.

Finally, Alice spoke up. "Okay! Before Justin and Viv got back, there was a kiss... maybe two." She turned her face down and took a bite quickly.

I don't think Ryan could have smiled any bigger.

"Just don't make a big deal of it," Alice snapped. "It doesn't change anything." She looked over at Ryan. "Your sisters should work for the FBI or something with their interrogation techniques."

"We have our talents," Giselle smirked, looking at Alice out of the corner of her eyes.

We all roared in laughter. The rest of the visit focused on Alice and Ryan and other talk about the next day, Christmas. Ryan had planned for us to gather for a formal dinner and then a gift exchange. He understood that I wanted Christmas morning to be just Alice, the kids and I.

He invited Tiffany over for breakfast so we could do our Christmas morning alone. She was more than happy to join them. A break from the kids was probably a good thing.

That evening, Tiffany went out for a while to get out of the apartment while Alice and I spent time with the kids. We played a couple of board games, watched a movie and ate dinner. Tina asked what we were going to do Christmas day.

Alice told her about our plans to have Christmas morning for ourselves and then go to Ryan's to spend the day with everyone. The kids all liked that thought, but Elizabeth looked a little concerned.

"What's wrong, sweetie?" I asked.

"What if Santa can't find us?" she asked.

"Why wouldn't he be able to find us?" I was confused why she thought that.

"We are not at home, and we didn't leave him a note to find us here. How will he know?" She was genuinely concerned.

"Well honey, Santa has a team of elves that keeps track of vacationing kids and tells Santa before he leaves the North Pole where to find them."

"Oh!" She smiled. "Ok, mama." She went back to her game.

After putting them to bed, we started wrapping gifts. I showed her what else I had gotten while she was at dinner, or "sucking face" as I teased her.

Tiffany came back about ten and helped us finish up. We put the gifts under the tree that Ryan had put up before we got there. We set all of the kids' gifts in the front and everyone else's gifts towards the back so they would be out of the way when the kids came tearing out in the morning.

Morning came too early. Elizabeth and Victoria came rushing into my room, shouting, "It's Christmas morning, Mama! Get up! Santa did find us! Get up!"

I sat up and heard similar things coming from Alice's room accompanied with laughter and Alice telling them she was going to get them back for waking her up so early.

I glanced over at the clock. It was 7 a.m. I groaned and got up, putting on my robe and slippers. I stumbled into the kitchen and found that Tiffany was already up and dressed.

"Coffee is made. Water for your tea is heating in the kettle on the stove. Ryan sent over breakfast pastries with his driver who's waiting outside for me. Have fun, and the car will be here for all of you about two?" She slid her coat on and started out the door.

"Ok. That sounds great. Have fun." I waved.

She peeked back through the door. "Merry Christmas, Ms. Cook."

"Merry Christmas, Tiffany," I said with a smile.

The kids came roaring out into the living room with Alice in tow. I poured her a cup of coffee and handed it to her with the plate of pastries. She took the plate to the living room while I made my tea and grabbed plates and napkins, taking a seat in the chair, facing the tree.

The kids started with their stockings and filtered through the stack of presents. Each of them was very happy and excited about their gifts. Alice and I exchanged our gifts for each other after the kids were engrossed in one of their new items or eating something from the plate.

I had purchased a new journal for Alice, knowing that her current one had only a couple more blank pages, and she'd have plenty more to write. Then, I found a great pair of shoes while shopping the day before. They were flats, but they were a snake skin pattern in pink with cute little leather bows on the top of the toes near the tip.

Alice had brought my gift with us. She had hinted at it before we left off and on, but I was still not sure what she had gotten me. I pulled at the bow and tore the paper off, opening the box. It was an awesome Coco Chanel dress. Alice knew how I love Coco Chanel.

It was mostly an off-white, gauze material that was sheer and came up to a high boat collar that was folded over to pronounce a three-inch wide hem. The skirt fell mid-calf length and was made up of many layers, floating away from the body with each step.

A thicker cotton material lined under the gauze and covered the bodice in a strapless top. Over the off-white material was an attached, sheer, black gauze material that was formed to look like a fitted cardigan, the length of the dress. This had embellishments that sparkled as the light hit them, and with the way they were arranged, it looked like fairy dust had been sprinkled from above it.

There was a thick black belt that sat at the natural waist and flowers made of both the off-white and black gauze material that started about three in a row at the belt and trailed down the skirt in a winding line to about eight inches above the hem.

I was choked up. "Wow, Alice. Thank you so much! It's gorgeous!"

"When I came across it, I knew it was for you." She gave me a hug. "Go try it on! You can wear it to Ryan's today if it doesn't need tailoring. This is a formal dinner after all."

I ran off to try it on. It fit perfectly, and I came out into the living room parading around like a princess. Alice laughed and said it looked perfect. I asked what she was going to wear, and she said she had brought a dress she wore to a wedding once just in case she needed something.

Nothing fancy, she said, just a cute black dress with a green and white floral pattern along the skirt hem and slight V-neck collar of the dress. Fitted, but not too tight, with short sleeves. The skirt was a stiff A-line. It was very much Alice's style.

We got ourselves and the kids ready and got in the car when it arrived at two. The kids had toys and projects strewn about, but we figured since it was Christmas, they were entitled to a day to let loose. There was always the next day to clean up.

Ryan met us at the door and took our coats. The kids ran off to find Nathaniel and Natalie who were already seated at the kids' table. We walked into the dining room where we found Mary, Henry, Emma, Reggie, Giselle, and a couple of Ryan's friends who had been on the outing the day before.

I must have been quite transparent, because Ryan leaned in and whispered, "He's in the other room."

I felt my face turn red. "Who?" I heard my voice crack.

He laughed and took Alice by the hand and led her to their seats. I felt an arm around my waist moments later and someone leaned their face in next to mine, kissing me on the cheek.

"You look gorgeous," he whispered slowly.

My pulse raced. I turned as he was coming around to face me, sliding his hand along my lower back, catching my hand in his as we came face to face. I smiled, closed my eyes and took a deep breath.

"Hi," I sighed.

He smiled and led me to our seats across the table from Alice and Ryan. We sat down as Mary and Emma started coming out with the serving dishes. It smelled so delicious, but I was distracted by the fact that he still had my hand.

He leaned in closer to me. "I missed our talks," he said.

Alice kicked me from under the table. "Ouch!" I muttered.

"So? What are you two talking about?" she smirked.

"How you are the worst friend in the world because you are abusive," I rubbed my shin.

Ryan looked over from his conversation. "What? Who's abusive?"

"I guess Alice is," Justin shrugged.

Alice and I laughed. I really wanted to have something to wad up and throw at her. In most situations, I would have. However, this was a formal dinner, and we were already showing our home roots.

"So, Alice," Justin said. "How was your Christmas morning?"

"Relaxing." She smiled. "It was nice to have a morning to spend with our kids. They had a blast." She looked at me and tilted her head. "I don't think they even noticed that there were no large gifts as far as size went."

"You know? I don't think they did." I bit the corner of my left lip and scrunched my eyebrows, contemplating that. "Cool."

Everyone conversationally mingled as the platters and bowls were passed around for us all to dish up from. I looked around at everyone and how immaculately fashionable they all were, even Mary and Henry.

After we dished up, Ryan and Alice started talking to Adam, one of the visiting friends, about some of Ryan's plans for all of us for the rest of the week. Justin was talking to Bret, another friend. I just tried to focus on not getting my dinner down the front of me.

Occasionally, someone would turn to me and say something or ask a quick question, but I would just put another bite in my mouth and nod, smiling at how at ease Ryan and Alice had become with each other.

I wasn't sure why, but I had gotten uncomfortably nervous. Maybe it was the brush of his hand on my lower back that was still giving me chills. Maybe it was the silent smiles that would light up his eyes when he would flash me a look every once in a while. Either way, schoolgirl was not how I was feeling, but I was definitely feeling something. It took everything I had to stay in my chair.

About halfway through dinner, he slid the fingers of his right hand up along the forearm of my left arm that was resting on the table and smiled at me. I jumped up from my seat and cleared my throat. "Excuse me. I'll be right back," I said, and started for the bathroom at the back of the house.

Alice looked at Justin, concerned. He just shrugged. She got up and followed me to the bathroom. "What's going on? Are you okay?"

"Um, no. I am not okay." I braced myself on the sink.

"Okay?" She sat on the side of the tub, "What's wrong?"

"Oh, just that I want to jump up and throw him down on the table and have my way with him. That's all." I took a deep breath. "I don't know why, but I can barely contain myself today."

She laughed. "Oh, is that all?"

"Is *that* all?" I snapped, "As if that's not enough? How am I going to make it through tonight?"

"Very carefully." She slapped my shoulder, "Come on, let's get back before they send the sisters for us."

"I'll be right there." I stayed braced on the sink.

The coolness of the sink top was a strong enough sensation to keep me from diving too deep into my thoughts of Justin. Alice walked out to go back to the table, checking that I was sure one last time before going. I assured her with a wave, sitting on the side of the tub once the door was shut.

I took a couple of deep breaths and headed out myself. It was going to be a trying night for self control.

I rounded the wall into the dining room and walked to my chair silently. Everyone glanced up but didn't pay too much attention other than Justin. As I sat down, he looked up at me, a bit concerned.

"Are you ok?" he asked.

Alice chimed in, "Oh, she's fine. Just having concentration issues."

I kicked her under the table as she yelped. "Ow! That's going to leave a mark." She rubbed her shin.

"I see the abuse continues," Ryan noted. "Do I need to separate you two?"

"No, I think she's got the picture to not start that again." I glared at her.

She smiled and assured Ryan that we were playing nice and joined back in their conversation.

"Concentration issues, huh?" Justin asked with one eyebrow peaked.

I laughed. "Nothing."

He nodded like he knew something but just started idle conversation back up with Bret, urging me to join them this time. We talked about the food, family and business. It was hard to just sit there and talk about nothing of great importance when I had much louder things in my head.

The rest of dinner passed by slowly. I was glad that the food was great. Otherwise, that might have been the worst meal of my life. Well, the worst and the best. I ate each bite deliberately, making sure that I was not making a mess.

Alice, Giselle and Justin each took turns pulling me into conversations. I was thankful they did. It was a nice distraction from my thoughts that made me more and more nervous. I especially needed the distraction when Justin would make an occasional brush against my arm or grab my hand and hold it for a moment to emphasize a statement.

It threw me just how much I was reacting to him that day. I wondered if he felt the same, but he couldn't. He was as calm and collected as always. He would just chat with everyone as if there wasn't a foolish woman next to him restraining herself from launching herself onto him at any moment. Occasionally, he would flash that smile and then promptly turn back to the table. During most of the brushes of his fingers, he didn't even look at me. They were probably accidental.

About four, we started getting up from the table, most of us carrying dishes to the kitchen. Emma and Mary assured everyone that they would clean up in there as long as we all helped get everything off the table. I was so ready for a release from the rush of being by his side, I pleaded to help, but Emma knew. She pushed me out of the kitchen and told me I had somewhere to be.

I scurried past him with a couple of loads for the kitchen until the table was clear. At that point, I headed out of the kitchen in search of Alice. I spotted her standing with Adam, Giselle and Ryan in the living room. I wandered over and put my arm around Alice's.

She looked at me and smiled. "Hey, what's up?"

"Nothing." I smiled. "The table is cleared."

"Yeah." She nodded her head a couple of times and turned back to the conversation.

I stood there while they chatted for a while, getting more and more anxious as I scanned the room for him.

"I'm going to go to the library," I whispered in her direction.

She nodded again without missing a beat of the conversation. I walked over to the library and started scanning the shelves that were overflowing with books, unable to concentrate on any of them.

I couldn't believe how flustered I was, even when he wasn't around. I had passed the schoolgirl phase and dived, head first, into being completely enamored. Not only could I not stop thinking about him, but I was having urges I hadn't felt in years, and never this strongly.

It was nice to get away from everyone and just clear my head for a moment. I needed to get a grip on myself before I did something rash. Not knowing where he was when I was standing with Alice a few minutes ago was torture, but I was sure that it wouldn't have been a suitable-for-all-audiences situation if he had been near me at that moment.

I pulled a book off the shelf that caught my eye. It was a compilation of Dylan Thomas poems; he was my favorite poet. I flipped through it for a moment and found "Do Not Go Gentle into That Good Night".

I read the first four verses to myself, speaking the fifth aloud. "Grave men, near death, who see with blinding sight. Blind eyes could blaze light meteors and be gay."

"Rage, rage against the dying of the light," the familiar voice finished my verse from the doorway.

"You like to sneak up on me." I kept my nose in the book.

He laughed. "Do you like Dylan Thomas?"

"Oh, he's my favorite poet," I answered.

"Honestly?" he asked.

"Yeah. Why? Don't tell me. You're one of those that don't like him."

"No," he laughed. "It's just funny how much we have in common."

"Yes, it is." I closed the book and returned it to its spot on the shelf, pausing there for a moment.

"Why are you hiding in here?" he asked.

I quietly snickered. "Hiding? No." I turned to face him. "Just taking a breather."

He smiled. "Are you ready to rejoin the party?" he asked, motioning down the hall.

"Sure." I walked past him as I went through the doorway.

As I passed him, I heard his breath catch and noticed him tuck his hands behind his back, pressing up against the door frame. I smiled, mischievously, as I reached my hand back and brushed his stomach ever so lightly with my fingertips.

He caught my hand before it had returned to my side, but I kept walking. He held my hand, walking right behind me. We got about four feet down the hall when I felt him stop. I turned around to see why.

"What?" I asked, looking at him as innocently as I could muster.

His look was a mixture of emotions that I recognized as not unlike the ones I had been feeling that led me to the library. He didn't falter in his gaze from my face as he pulled me a step closer to him.

My head was spinning. I noticed the art on the walls, the voices in the next room and the sunlight that warmed my skin from the window at the back end of the hall. However, nothing overshadowed the loud beating of my heart and the sound of my breath as it came to a sudden stop. What seemed like hours was just a moment before what I thought might never happen actually did.

He reached up with both hands, taking my face in his grasp, and leaned in, kissing me with the strongest gentle passion. I saw his eyes close and all stress of restraint vanish as my eyes closed along with his. My breath resumed but in deeper sweeps of release.

One of his hands moved to the back of my head as the other searched for the wall with mine as we backed up against it. Once I felt the wall with my hands and was securely leaning against it, I reached up and grabbed the sides of his face, and pulled him even deeper into the kiss. With his free hand, he grabbed my hip and pressed his body against mine, wrapping his arm around my waist to secure the hold.

It was all I could do to pull back as Alice stumbled upon us and yelled down the hall, "Awwww, I'm telling!"

I turned to look at her, dropping my hands from his face, his hands still in place and called after her, "Alice! Get back here!"

I could hear her laughing as she went towards the dining room. I looked up at Justin. He was smiling. He took a step back and moved his hands to my waist. I placed my palms on his chest, feeling his heart beat as quick as mine was.

"I'm sorry," I said.

He shut his eyes, smiled and shook his head. "No. We were bound to get caught."

We stood there for a long moment just looking into each other's eyes. I interrupted the moment as I reached up and held his face in my hands again, pulled him in

244

and kissed him again. His breath became jagged as he slid his hands up over my lower back, one coming to rest on the center of my upper back and one on the back of my neck.

I braced my hands on his hips and softly pushed him away, taking a deep breath. "We had better go see what she's stirring up in there."

"Yeah, before we get ourselves in more trouble." He smiled a full smile and lifted one eyebrow.

He put his hands to my cheeks this time and kissed my forehead. I took in a deep breath and sighed, wrapped my arms around his waist and leaned against his chest for a moment before turning to face the mob of gossipers. I was sure they would be plotting what sharp comments they were going to start with when we came back to the group.

We walked side by side down the hall. I had a firm grip on his hand, searching for the extra strength not to run away or say something too insulting. I wanted to avoid any prodding jokes at our expense. He flexed his fingers and adjusted our hands so my grip wasn't so tight.

"Sorry," I whispered as we walked into the foyer.

He chuckled. "Don't worry. They knew it was bound to happen. Trust me. Do you want to go to the living room to Ryan's parents, Ryan and the guys or the dining room with Emma, Giselle and Alice?"

"Can't we find the kids and hang out with them the rest of the evening?" I nervously laughed.

"I believe we'll have to face them sooner or later, and if we put it off, they'll have more time to formulate their jokes and 'it's about time' comments. So? The guys or the girls?" He pointed in each direction as he said the genders.

"Girls. Let's get it over with." I took a deep breath as we rounded the corner into the dining room.

"Well, well, well," Giselle shook her finger at us, "Nice of you two to rejoin the party."

"So, Vivianne? Get anything good for Christmas?" Emma teased.

I looked up at Justin. He was just shaking his head with a smirk. Alice was leaned against the table with her arms crossed and tapping her foot.

"Go ahead," I taunted Alice. "Get it out. I know you have something to say, too."

"Oh, you know I do," she said with a smirk. "Justin? Can you excuse us for a minute?"

He looked at me, and I nodded to tell him it was ok. He kissed me a quick kiss on the lips. "Come find me when you're done being interrogated," he whispered and left for the living room, flashing a smirk as he walked away.

All three of the girls made kissing noises and giggled. He shook his head as he went out of sight. I crossed my arms and scrunched my eyebrows together.

"What is this, high school?" I snapped.

"We're just having fun." Alice held her hands out and shrugged. "I'm sorry, but since he's not in the room, spill it!"

"What? You saw what was going on. We were kissing." I went to the bar and poured myself a glass of wine from one of the open bottles in the little fridge.

Emma cleared her throat. "No, what led up to the kiss? Alice tells us you were having trouble keeping your hands in check earlier."

"Did you attack him?" Giselle had walked up next to me and poked me in the ribs.

"No!" I gulped a large part of what I had poured. "I had actually walked down to the library to take a breather. I didn't know where he was when I headed into that room. I was starting to feel more in check and was flipping through a Dylan Thomas book, reading part of 'Do Not Go Gentle into That Good Night' aloud, when he walked in behind me and finished the part I had read aloud."

I took the last drink and set my glass on the bar. "I'll be honest and say that I did want to attack him, but I continued facing away until I could control my urges."

"Control your urges," Giselle mocked. "You're too funny."

"Yes, controlling urges, blah blah blah," I rolled my eyes.

"Anyway, We talked about Dylan Thomas for a minute. He mentioned that he noticed that we had a lot in common and asked why I was in the library. I told him that I was taking a breather. He asked if I was ready to come back."

"Yeah, yeah, yeah," Alice interrupted. "Get on with it!"

"Ok," I laughed nervously. "As I was walking past him to come back and find you guys, I couldn't help but reach out and brush my fingers across his stomach. He grabbed my hand and was just walking behind me until we got down the hall a few steps," I smiled.

"And?" Emma leaned in across the table.

"He stopped walking. When I turned and asked him why he stopped, he pulled me in and kissed me. I can't say I pulled away. Before I knew it, we were against the wall, pressed against each other and Alice was rudely ruining the moment. We kissed one more time before coming out of the hallway to find out what sort of teasing we were going to have to endure." I put my fingers to my lips, leaned my back against the wall and tilted my head back, reliving the moment for a minute in my mind.

"Wow," Emma fanned herself with her hand.

Giselle laughed. "Yeah, wow. I have to say, I wasn't lying when I told you at the Christmas party, you are making a lot of women jealous, including me."

"Way to go, Viv!" Alice patted me on the shoulder. "So? How was it?"

I didn't answer. I just stood there, half avoiding the question and half lost in the memory of the moment. I wasn't really sure what I should say. It was the best kiss of my life? I didn't want it to end? It was like the kind of kiss you only read about? I wanted more? I settled on that.

I looked up and around at all of them, settling my eyes on Alice's. "I want more."

They clamored on about how they all knew it was going to work between us and how perfect for each other we were. They were saying how happy they were for me and Justin. Emma and Giselle welcomed me to the family, explaining how they considered him family, and they saw this lasting for a long time.

I let them carry on for a while and finally walked towards the foyer. "I'm going to find the rest of the group. You ladies going to stay in here and gossip some more?"

"Maybe," Alice taunted.

I looked at Giselle. "Well, don't forget to ask Alice more about their kiss in the library the other day."

"Oh yeah!" Her eyes grew with excitement.

"I'm right behind you." Alice grabbed her glass and came up next to me as I headed for the living room.

We walked through the archway to the living room with Emma and Giselle right behind us. Ryan, Bret and Adam looked up at us. I didn't know if they knew anything. I didn't see Alice go into the living room to tell Ryan before tattling on me to the girls, but I wasn't sure if Justin would have said anything either.

I felt my face flush as Mary turned to us when we were walking in. "You ready to do the gifts?"

We all agreed, and I took it as a good excuse to leave the room for a moment. "I'll go get the kids."

I jogged out of the room, making sure no one was following me this time. The kids were in the back sitting room watching a movie with Tiffany. Once I walked into the room, the kids jumped up. Elizabeth and Victoria ran and grabbed a hold of a leg each.

"Are you kids ready for presents?" I threw my arms in the air and jumped out of the way as they tore through the doorway and down the hall towards the tree.

Tiffany laughed and turned off the TV. We both headed down the hall to join everyone. She thanked me for asking her if she wanted to get out the day before.

She told me how she went out and did some sightseeing. I was happy she was enjoying herself.

Once back in the living room, the kids were tearing open a present each from Ryan as Mary and Emma took pictures. Victoria held up her half-unwrapped gift, shook it in the air and then placed it on the floor to finish unwrapping it.

Ryan and Alice were seated on the smaller sofa with Adam and Bret sitting in a couple of dining room chairs that had been brought in. There were two more dining room chairs across the room that Mary and Henry were sitting in to be closer to the kids. Reggie, Emma and Giselle were on the larger couch, and Tiffany took a seat on the floor with the kids.

I looked at the chair, and yes, Justin was seated in it with the ottoman in the same spot from the other morning. He was looking at me. His smile was soft and warm, and there was a sparkle to his eyes that was so inviting. I couldn't help but walk right over to him and sit down on the ottoman, facing the tree to watch the kids.

As Mary handed them each another gift, Justin slid forward to sitting right behind me. He wrapped his arms around my waist and kissed my cheek. I leaned back against him and held his forearms in my hands as if I thought he was about to let go.

Alice got up and handed out the gifts we had gotten Ryan's family. We got Mary and Henry and Emma and Reggie gift cards to their favorite restaurants. We had picked a book for Nathaniel and Natalie. For Giselle, we got a gorgeous silk scarf. Everyone was very thankful, telling us that we didn't need to get them anything and all the usual courtesies.

Ryan had passed out more gifts for the kids. They were having a blast, bringing us each one of their gifts to show them off. It was obvious that Ryan and his family had gone a bit overboard, but the kids were having fun. So, Alice and I just let them enjoy it.

As the pile was dwindling, Emma took an envelope over to Alice and one to me. I watched Alice as she opened the one she was given. Her eyes got big.

"It's tickets to Hampton Court Palace where they prepare a royal feast like they did for King Henry VIII. Then to Streatham Ice Arena for ice skating," she beamed.

"Emma, Tiffany and I are going to take them on Friday," Mary said. "I hope you don't mind that we took the liberty."

"No!" I said. "That sounds like a lot of fun. Are you sure you wouldn't want us to come to help with the kids?"

"We will be just fine," Emma assured me. "Three to six is great odds. Besides, I am sure that you two are going to have other things to do."

"I am sure we can find something to do," Alice flashed me a grin. "What's in yours?"

I had almost forgotten. I sat up from leaning on Justin and carefully tore open the envelope. I pulled out a small stack of vouchers. Reading the front, I saw they were for a local spa that Giselle had mentioned.

"We all went in, and thought it would be a lot of fun for all of us girls to go have a spa day. What do you think?" Giselle gushed.

"Wow. This is a wonderful gift." I passed the tickets over to Alice for her to look at.

She took them and read the top voucher. "This is going to be so much fun!"

"I am glad that you like it," Emma said.

Alice showed Ryan the contents of the envelopes as he smiled and nodded in approval. I gathered that he had known about these plans before that day. He took both envelopes and asked for two more that were sitting under the tree, passing one to Justin.

I got up before they could hand them out and got my gift for Ryan. I held it out before him, and he looked at me, surprised by my childish excitement. He opened it and looked up at me half amused and half confused, lifting the two items out of the box, looking at them curiously.

"So," I started, but I was laughing and had to take a moment to gather myself. Alice didn't even know what I had in mind. "I had thought and thought about what I was going to get you. I mean, what do you get your best friend's love interest that has just about everything he needs?" We all laughed. "So, I got you those since I didn't get you in one while we were in Maui."

It was a grass skirt and coconut bra. He looked at me with an almost stunned look on his face. You could see the thought of having to put them on in front of us pass through his mind as he looked back and forth between me, the gift and Alice for a moment, jaw agape before he finally started laughing.

"Oh, that's hilarious!" Emma laughed.

Mary stood up, taking the coconut bra from his hands and holding it up to his chest. "That'll look nice on you, son."

This only made everyone laugh harder. She returned the top to the box as he carefully folded the skirt and laid it on top, sliding the top of the box, very slowly, back over them to close it back up.

"Nice," he laughed. "We'll have to see about that."

I smirked at him and gave a wink. "Yes. Yes, we will," I challenged him.

Alice had gotten up and returned from the tree with a gift bag and a small box of her own as others started exchanging more presents. She handed the bag to Justin to open first. He took the bag and pulled the tissue paper out of it, taking out the copy of the newest Dean Koontz book and a couple others he had mentioned that he had not read yet. She didn't know what to get him, but I remembered a conversation in the café the day after the Christmas party when he told me that he had yet to get them.

"Thank you." He flipped through them, reading over the book jackets one by one. "These will come in very handy on location in a few weeks."

"You're welcome." She handed the small box to Ryan. "Your turn."

He took the box and pulled the ribbon off, eyeing her suspiciously. Once the ribbon was tossed to the side, he opened the end of the box, and a postcard sized book fell out in his hand. He set the box down and lifted up the little book, flipping it over to read the cover.

Ryan's Coupon Book: From Alice

"I had this made for you." She reached out and flipped the book open in his hands, "It's a book of coupons from me to you for things like an evening for just you and I where I'll cook a meal. One is that I agree to go to any event with you with a smile." She flipped to a page near the back, pointing to one of the coupons. "And then, there are coupons like this one. You can ask me any question you want, and I'll tell you the truth, but you have to wait at least six months. You said you just wanted me for Christmas. Now, you can choose how and when."

He smiled so peacefully and flipped through the book another turn. She leaned back into her seat and sighed. Ryan rested the coupon book on his other gifts and grabbed her hands.

"That is the best gift so far." He wrapped an arm around her and passed me the envelope he had been hanging onto as Justin passed his to Alice.

We opened our envelopes at the same time, pulling out a single piece of paper. We both smiled and nodded at each other. I turned the piece of paper around to show Alice as she did the same. They were gift certificates for a local shoe boutique that we had fallen in love with while shopping for our Christmas party dresses.

We looked at the guys. "Thank you!"

"I take it you both can find something there you might like?" Ryan asked.

Alice laughed. "Um, yeah. I'm not sure. I think I might have enough shoes."

"No, we don't have a shoe fetish. Not at all," I joked.

"Ok, my turn again." Justin got up and walked over to the tree.

He came back with a beautifully wrapped box, handing each of the kids a gift bag along the way. They ripped out the tissue paper, pulling out a set of books each, showing them to each other with excitement.

"I know how much you stress their education and how much they love their books. I thought it was a good idea," he said.

"Books are always a good thing for my girls. They've always had a good collection and love them." I smiled. "Thank you. You really didn't have to get them anything."

"I know, but I wanted to." He smiled back.

"Yes, thank you. That was really sweet, Justin." Alice went over to check out the new books.

Alice slid me the gift under the tree from me to Justin as she was talking. I picked it up and handed it over to him. I was anxious to see if he was going to like it or not. I hadn't known him for very long, nor had I had much time to get something, but not only were my feelings growing for him, I wanted to get him something.

He took the box and opened it, lifting the top flap. I couldn't see his mouth, but I could tell he was smiling by his eyes. That's a good sign.

When I was shopping on Sunday, I stumbled upon a little shop full of antiques and vintage clothing. I was looking around more for myself when I came across a vintage fedora. It was primarily grey with blue and green pinstripes.

"Thank you, Vivianne." He lifted it out of the box and tried it on.

"You like it?" I asked.

"I love it." He set it back in the box and gave me a kiss.

I let out a breath as if I had been holding it. "Good." I could feel the goofy grin that went across my face as the pride of my gift sank in.

I went to get up and join Alice and the kids on the floor when Justin handed me the box in his hands. "What's this?" I asked.

"A gift." Alice said sarcastically, and went back to reading to the kids.

"Well, I mean, I know what it is. I just didn't expect anything." I looked at Justin.

"Good, then you don't have any expectations," he said, smiling. "Open it."

I took a breath and started carefully unwrapping the box, trying not to tear the paper. I was so nervous. A large part of me was hoping that he hadn't gotten me anything. I know that I got him something, but I liked getting people things. It was harder to be the one on the spot.

The paper fell away from the box with the splitting of the last piece of tape. I opened the flaps of the box to reveal a stack of books and an envelope. I took the top book out and looked at the cover. Star Quest by Dean Koontz.

I looked up at him in amazement. "What is this?" I asked as I started pulling out each book to see the titles. "I've never seen these before!"

"When he first started writing, he did a series of science fiction books. This is that series," he explained.

"You're kidding, right?" I was floored. "Oh my gosh! How did you? Never mind. These are so awesome!"

He reached in the box and pulled out the envelope. "There's this, too."

I took the envelope and started opening it. "There's more?"

I tossed the empty envelope back in the box as I started reading the single ticket that was inside it. It was for an event in Chicago at a smaller book store. I read on and saw that it was for a book signing for Dean Koontz's newest book. This time, I looked up at him in awe.

"I've got a ticket, too, and I'm going with you. Well, if you don't mind, that is," he said, searching my face.

I realized the look of awe was still on my face. I swallowed and started to smile. "I wouldn't want to go with anyone else!"

Before I knew it, I had set the box and the ticket on the floor and had my arms wrapped around him. I sat back, clearing my throat and calmed myself. "Thank you."

He laughed. "My pleasure."

Alice was back in her seat on the couch, and Ryan was standing behind us near the tree when Alice interjected with her usual sharp humor, "Geez, Viv, he didn't buy you a country."

I laughed. "No, but this is an awesome gift and very thoughtful. I love it."

"What did he get you?" she inquired.

I handed her the box. She knew the moment she looked inside what I meant and even more when I showed her the ticket. She was interrupted though from teasing me, suddenly. I didn't know why, but she looked up and got very nervous looking all of a sudden.

I looked over at Ryan who was still standing by the tree. I didn't realize what was making her nervous until I saw a little wrapped box in his hand. I also noticed that Mary, Emma and Giselle were all paying attention to us. They had stopped their conversations and seemed to be waiting for him to speak.

Alice jumped up from her seat and started for the dining room. "Anyone want a glass of egg nog?"

Ryan caught her hand as she tried to slip past him, stopping her from getting away, "Wait a second. You haven't opened your gift from me yet."

"You sure? I could have sworn that I did already." She looked about the room full of opened presents.

"Yes. I am sure." He handed her the box.

I sat up to the edge of the ottoman as Justin slid back up to his spot right behind me with his arms around my waist and my hands on his forearms holding him there. Everyone almost seemed to lean in like it was the pivotal part in a romantic movie.

She looked around the room getting increasingly nervous as she stalled for time. After seeing that everyone was looking at her, even the kids, she quickly ripped the paper off the small, velvet jewelry box inside. She made one last glance up at Ryan before lifting the lid. Inside was a beautiful, dangling blue sapphire and diamond necklace.

She gasped, "Oh, Ryan. It's beautiful!"

He reached over and took it out of the box. "It was my great-grandmother's. When she and my great-grandfather first started dating, she was a lot like you. She was hesitant of giving in to love considering that her two older sisters' marriages were not fairytales. My great-grandfather pursued her for almost a year before she even let him take her to dinner. On that date, he gave her this necklace to prove to her that she meant a lot to him, and he was willing to do what it took to win her heart, even wait for her," he explained. He clasped the necklace around her neck.

"This is too much." She put her hand over the pendant.

He looked her in the eyes. "No, it's just right." He took her hands in his. "This necklace was a symbol for them of his dedication to her. It means the same now. I am not going anywhere. I don't care how long it takes. I am dedicated to you."

She picked the pendant up and looked at it, pausing for a moment as he just watched her stare at it. I could have sworn I saw her eyes tear up, but I couldn't be sure. After a moment, she dropped the pendant, reached up, wrapped her arms around his neck and kissed him in one swift movement.

None of us expected that, especially not Ryan. You could see his eyes go wide and his hands shot out at his sides. Then, he started to relax, closed his eyes and carefully placed his hands on her back, pulling her in to him. Emma and Giselle started clapping.

"Yes!" Emma shouted.

"And that changes everything," I announced, pointing at them as Alice backed away from him.

"Oops," was all she said, taking a step back and glancing at Mary and Henry.

"Oops?" he asked.

She looked around the room at the fifteen pairs of eyes on her, including Ryan's. "Well? Vivianne is right. This does change everything."

Ryan smiled. "Not for me," he said, and kissed her again.

"Ok, this is enough of all the kissing today. You're all making me jealous," Giselle humorously complained.

Reggie leaned in and kissed Emma. Henry kissed Mary. I looked at Justin, and he smiled, taking the opportunity to kiss me. She huffed and crossed her arms. We laughed even harder when Bret got up and laid one right on her lips.

She pushed him away. "What are you doing?"

"You were acting like you wanted someone to kiss you. So? There you go. Quit complaining." He sat back down and took a drink from his glass, a proud look on his face.

"So? How about that egg nog?" Alice said, clearing her throat and headed for the dining room with a little stumble in her step.

This time, Ryan let her slip out of the room. Everyone laughed and started gathering their papers and bows to clean up. Tiffany took the kids back to help get out Cameron's new Lego set and some of the other toys so they could play with them.

Justin and I got up, and I headed out to find Alice. I heard Giselle calling after me to wait up for her and Emma. When I looked back, I saw Justin walk up to

Ryan, shaking his hand and giving him one of those handshake, manly hugs, patting him on the back. It was one of those moments that women get amused watching men having a bonding moment and yet remain remarkably manly.

Emma, Giselle and I walked into the kitchen. We could hear the sounds of her moving things about before we got around the corner. She had a towel in one hand and was wiping off the counter fiercely, moving each appliance as she went along.

"Hello? Where's the egg nog?" Giselle asked as she walked towards the fridge.

"Is everything ok?" There was a look of concern on Emma's face as she asked.

I walked up to her and took the towel from her hands. "Oh, she's fine. She just cleans when she gets nervous. Sometimes, I purposefully make her nervous at home when I don't feel like cleaning."

They all whipped their heads toward me. "What?" Alice snapped.

"I'm just kidding," I laughed. "I got you to snap out of it. Now, what's up? That was awesome! You should be bouncing off the walls!"

"But this is me bouncing off the walls." Her eyes were fixed on the doorway. "It's just that it did change things, and it still scares the hell out of me. I mean, I know that I meant it, and I know that I am falling for him, but it's a huge thing. Look, I'm talking about falling for him in front of his sisters. His parents saw us kiss. I'm with my kids, in his house, doing family things. That's a step I never thought I'd take again, and

I'm babbling about it. Which is a sure sign that I am...
in deep."

"I know this hasn't been something you've taken
lightly, and that's why this family has been all for you."
Emma leaned on the island counter across from Alice
and me. "Most women holding back, you can see they
would just hold back emotionally while taking him for
everything. Not you though, and we all can see that. He
can see that. So, if you are who he wants? Then, we
support him. It just also helps that we like you so
much." She reached out and placed her hand on Alice's.

"Take your time, hon." Giselle came back from the
fridge with the jug of egg nog in hand. "Like he said,
he's not going anywhere."

"Yeah." There was a distance in her eyes. "I know."

"Ok, enough with the seriousness. Let's get back.
The kids will be heading back to go to bed soon, and
everyone else is out there. Let's go have some fun." I
started taking glasses out of the cupboard, motioning to
Emma and Giselle to go ahead. I asked Alice to help
with the glasses.

"Do you see a tray anywhere? I don't want to drop
any and break them." She was searching through the
lower cabinets.

"I am not sure." I took the last couple out that we
needed and started helping her look for a tray. "Alice,
don't worry about it. Like I said before we left to come
out here, this is right. Don't go faster than you are
comfortable going, but don't hold back more than you
need to."

"I'm coming around. It's just faster than I thought I
would sometimes." She found a tray and loaded the

262

glasses on it. "Don't worry. I'll have my freak outs from time to time, but I'll be fine."

"We always are," I laughed, grabbing two glasses from the tray.

"Yes, we always are." She smiled at me as we started for the living room.

Chapter Twelve

A Night to Remember

After going back to the apartment Christmas night, Alice and I sat in the living room pretty much silent for a while. We knew we were not going to see much of the guys for the next couple days. We wanted to spend the next day with the kids, and then the plan for Thursday was ladies spa day. Yet, it made us both sad at the thought of not seeing them for over a day. We sat silent so we didn't start talking about them, emphasizing the looming couple days without them.

So when Ryan called in the morning to say good morning to Alice, I was relieved to hear her talk to him about them coming over for lunch. We all thought that was a great idea. When Justin called a few minutes later, I told him about lunch. It was even nicer to hear the excitement in his voice when he said he was glad I asked. He didn't miss me any less than I did him.

I made gnocchi and a homemade marinara sauce, which was a big hit. My girls always loved that any time I made it. They were fascinated that you could shape potato into a pasta looking shape and use it in place of pasta. So, since they loved it so much, I figured it was a safe bet. Plus, even being a homemade meal, it was fairly simple and quick.

While I was in the kitchen cooking, Alice and Ryan came into the room holding hands. I said hello and looked around them, hoping to see Justin. Ryan said he was coming over in just a minute. I blushed and finished cooking.

When Justin got there, we all sat down and ate. It was nice having them there. Plus, the meal was a big hit with everyone. We all chatted, but there was a usual quietness to the table as the kids ate more than they talked. You could feel how comfortable everyone was with each other, and that made for a great meal.

After lunch, the kids got out a few of their gifts they got Christmas day. Justin and Ryan understood that we were spending the day with the kids. So, they gathered around the games and books, interacting with the kids along with us.

I started a game of Tumbling Monkeys with Justin, Elizabeth and Victoria. Alice, Ryan, Tina and Cameron all got out Jenga. After a few minutes, everyone started getting rowdy. Before we knew it, game pieces from both of the games were strewn about the room. Victoria and Elizabeth were running around the room, being chased by Alice and Tina. Cameron and Ryan were play-wrestling. That is, until Ryan tagged Justin in, and they tag teamed him into a pin.

I sat back on the couch, enjoying everyone being so relaxed and having fun with each other. I started laughing when the guys pinned Cameron and the girls all piled on top of them, including Alice. Justin wriggled his way out from under the pileup and dragged me off the couch into the heap of laughing faux-wrestlers.

I grabbed both of my girls, one in each arm, and started scooting backwards, telling everyone that if they came for me again, I would tickle the girls. Everyone laughed and played like they were giving up their guns at a stand-off and surrendered to me. We all collapsed on the floor, laughing and trying to catch our breaths. The kids ran off to find something more to play with as we picked up the game pieces.

Ryan left about two. He had promised his brother-in-law they'd go out and play some billiards before dinner. Justin stayed a little longer, per my request. I wasn't ready to have him go, but I knew I wasn't going to be ready no matter when it was. It just seemed like a reasonable excuse at the time for me. I told him it was because we needed another adult to make even partners for Trivial Pursuit Disney edition. He gladly stayed, saying he would just catch up with the guys later.

Thursday came before I knew it. By the time Mary, Emma and Giselle arrived Thursday morning to pick Alice and I up to go to the spa, we were looking forward to the whole day. A spa day was just the thing to release some stress and occupy us until that evening's group dinner. The feeling of missing Ryan and Justin had settled back over us, and as much fun as we were having with the girls, it's hard to not think of the person that's on your mind all of the time.

Giselle jumped out of Emma's van when we came out of the front door, giving us both a hug. It seemed that we had been missed, and from what we heard, it wasn't just the women that missed us. Of course, that made us both very happy.

"Oh my god, Alice. You have got to come back to the house. Please tell me that you're coming to dinner tonight, both of you," Giselle begged.

266

"As far as I know." Alice looked at Emma and Mary, wondering why the urgency. "What's up?"

Giselle interrupted Emma before she could speak. "He won't stop talking about you. We will be talking about something, and somehow, he ends up bringing the conversation back to you and your kids. It's really getting annoying. I am just glad that I don't live all that close to him. When you go back to the States, I will feel bad for his friends around here." She giggled.

"I am sure he hasn't talked that much about us," Alice laughed.

"You have no clue," Emma said. "If I didn't like you, I am sure I would have taped his mouth shut or something by now. I don't know what you've done to him, but wow. He's a goner."

"I think it's sweet," Mary spoke up. "My son finally has someone worth ogling, and he's letting himself fall into it. Just don't break his heart, honey. I've never seen him like this before."

"I don't plan on it," Alice assured her. "My hesitance isn't me thinking it over. It's me taking my time to be absolutely sure because of what I've had to deal with in the past. I know he's a great catch. I just need to ease my way in so I don't jump back out in fear."

"I commend you for knowing yourself as much as you do." Mary leaned out her window and patted her on the shoulder.

We climbed in and started out for the spa, "And what about Justin?" Giselle brought up.

Crap! I knew they were going to bring this up at some point.

"Oh, yeah." Emma looked at me with a smirk. "Speaking of guys that have gone head over heels."

"What?" I blinked like I didn't know what they were talking about. "So, he likes me. It's nothing like Ryan and Alice are." I pointed at Alice, hoping they'd return to that topic.

"No, no," Emma said. "Don't give me that. I wasn't kidding when I said he's never had this look before. He is our brother's best friend, and like we've said, we've known him for years. He's never had great luck with women. With his family being who they are, and him being who he is, he attracts women that have other agendas. He's usually very nonchalant with his dates, and you can see that he's just not having fun dating anymore. I think he's been afraid of getting close in fear that they're just with him for fame or money... or both."

Giselle sat forward. "That's so not the case with you, honey. When he looks at you, he lights up. He lights up even when he talks about you. Ryan told us how something came over him when Alice and Ryan were talking about you in New York. Justin hadn't even met you, but Ryan said it was like he was drawn to you even then. He also said that since seeing the two of you react to each other the way you have, there's no other explanation than 'meant to be'."

"And I understand that you were a fan?" Emma teased.

I was fidgeting with my coat zipper. "Yeah?"

They laughed. "And you didn't recognize him at the party but was enthralled with him despite that?"

"True." I continued to look down.

"That's rich," Giselle blurted out. "I agree with Ryan. You two are meant to be."

Mary leaned forward. "Vivianne, I have seen young men fall in love with the wrong women. I have seen young men run from women that are good for them. It is a different thing to watch a man fall for the right woman. There's a sense of magic about it. It's like that with Ryan and Alice, but it's different with you and Justin. He feels this pull towards you, and he's just letting it take him wherever it leads him. It's very rare that anyone, let alone a man, will give in to something so powerful. Ryan is letting himself fall, too, but Alice is, understandably, easing into it. It's a natural thing. However, there's no hesitation with either of you, and that's what fairytales are made of." She had a certain wisdom about her.

"Not that what Ryan and Alice have isn't just as right." She smiled at Alice. "It's just different to watch their love blossom slowly and your relationship come about so powerfully. They are both a joy to watch."

"Wow, Mary." I blinked. "I hadn't even thought about it."

"I am sure." She smiled. "That's the beauty of it. Neither of you are thinking about it. It just is, and you're both ok with that."

"Wow, mom," Giselle exclaimed.

"Yeah," I said. "Now that I am thinking about it, what do I do?"

"Nothing," Alice interjected. "Just keep doing what you've been doing. Mary is right. It's only been a few days, but I don't think anyone here would argue with

269

that after seeing you two together. You two are just right together. Don't do anything to mess it up."

"Oh, great. This is where I do something stupid now that I'm thinking about it." I put my hands to my head and laughed.

"I doubt that," Emma assured me.

"Viv, I've been your best friend for how long? Fifteen years? I know you, and you do not change the way you act for anything. Knowing this might make you more aware when you're with him, but it won't change the way you are." She slapped my leg with the back of her hand. "You are an extremely spontaneous person that's very set in her spontaneous ways, as confusing as that sounds."

"I'll take your word for it." I couldn't help but worry.

At the spa, we all pretty much got to stay together. It was a large facility, and we had reservations. So, getting in at the same time for each treatment wasn't a problem. That was really nice.

Alice did crack a joke at one time about Maui. She made mention that she was glad Ryan wasn't there. They all looked at her, curious as to why. She simply said that she would hate to lose out on one of our spots there, at the spa, because of him. They were still confused, so we explained how her spot at the spa in Maui had been given to him.

As it turns out, he hadn't told them about that, the hotel or the restaurant. He just said that he had met a woman in Maui, and he was head over heels for her. Alice and I laughed so hard about that, the masseuse had to stop until we gathered ourselves.

This conversation spurred a longer conversation about what had transpired between Alice and Ryan in Maui, including the bit about Alice falling into the ocean. I loved telling that story, especially since it embarrassed her so much, and they loved hearing it. Then, they shared stories of Ryan and Justin from over the years.

We finished up the treatments after about seven hours. I thought I was going to have to be carried out, I was so relaxed. There were plans to go right from the spa to dinner at a local pub where Ryan knew the owners, the whole group minus the kids. However each of us at the spa wasn't sure if we would be able to stay awake.

Alice mentioned what we all were thinking about as far as being so relaxed and ready to go find a quiet place and take a nap, but Emma was quick to remind us who was waiting for us at the restaurant. Needless to say, we both had a renewed sense of energy... and a case of the jitters, in my case.

We pulled up to the restaurant, and everyone else was already there having a beer. Part of me wanted to run in and jump on Justin, hugging and kissing him. Then there was the part of me that wanted to run to the nearest cab and go back to the apartment. I wasn't sure why the second part of me surfaced. It must be because everyone else now knew, and it was up front in my face.

I mentally slapped myself across the face, telling myself that I needed to get a grip. Nothing had changed. The man that I was falling for was sitting inside that pub, waiting for me to arrive, just as anxious to see me as I was to see him. I was sure he also knew that everyone else knew, but he probably wasn't freaking out about it like I was.

I gathered all the maturity I could and followed the others inside.

"The women are here!" Reggie shouted.

"Ok, maybe they've been here for more than one beer." Emma shook her head.

I stayed towards the back of the group as we walked in. The scared part of me wanted to see what he did when he saw me. It actually bothered me a lot how insecure I was feeling, but if I decided that I needed to escape, I didn't want to have people behind me to stop me. I also kept reminding myself that as long as I didn't run from love, it would help encourage Alice.

Reggie, Henry, Adam, Bret, Ryan and Justin were all sitting at a table in the back. Some girls were asking for Ryan and Justin's autographs, as usual. So, they were preoccupied when the others stood to greet us. Emma was right, they had been there long enough to have more than one beer, and Reggie displayed this by coming around the table to pick Emma up, twirling her around. She laughed and told him to put her down.

They all took their seats around the table except for Alice and me. We stated that we'd be right back and headed for the bathroom. I knew she felt my apprehension as we walked in. She always knew when something shifted in me. She was right when she said that I didn't normally let things effect my actions even when I was nervous, but I think she was worried this was different.

I looked over at Ryan and Justin signing autographs. They both were being so polite, as usual, talking to the girls and thanking them for their compliments. As we walked by, Justin did a double take and stood up.

"Vivianne!" You could see a mixture of excitement and relief on his face.

I stopped for a moment. "Hi."

Alice grabbed a hold of my arm, "We'll be back," she said to Justin.

I didn't break my gaze on him, not even when I stumbled over a chair leg. I don't know if it was him looking concerned and how he started after me to help in case I fell or the look of excitement and relief from a moment earlier, but I was feeling a bit more settled.

Alice didn't stop. She yanked me forward with her. Luckily, I didn't fall down. He must have noticed that I was fine and that Alice wasn't stopping. He stopped and stood there for a moment, half paying attention to the girls, who were obviously jealous of his attention to me, and half watching me as I was being pulled across the room.

"What's up with you?" Alice demanded as we got inside the bathroom.

"Nothing. Why?" I was startled by her abruptness.

She rolled her eyes. "Whatever. You've been acting all strange since the spa. I know something is up. What's up?"

"I know. I'm fine," I insisted.

"I know your 'I'm fines'." She stared at me as if she was searching my mind for what she was looking for. "There's something in your head that's bothering you."

273

"Yes, I am bothered by your badgering," I laughed. "But if you must know, I was just unnerved by the conversation about Justin and me earlier. It's just different hearing what everyone else said about us, and it just sparks some of the fears I know you've been feeling. That's it."

"Why are you so worried? What we were saying is right. You two are great together, and he's as much into you as you are into him. You can see that. You could see that just now, when he saw you on our way in here." She pointed towards the door.

"Has feeling all of this and hearing it from others helped you with Ryan?" I asked, feeling that she'd understand.

"Good point." She shook her head. "But you're the one that has her head on straight a lot more than I do when it comes to emotions."

"Ok, also a valid point, but it doesn't mean that it's any easier. Nor does it mean that I'm not entitled to a breakdown here and there." I washed my hands, taking a slip of the paper towel to dry them. "It's just very surreal. Then, I saw him, and things came back into focus. I am fine. No, I am fabulous."

"Ok?" She started for the door.

I grabbed her arm. "Alice, I am fine. You freak out in your way, I freak out in mine. I'm not going to do anything stupid. I just need an occasional extra deep breath or extra bathroom break. That's all."

"Good." She walked out of the bathroom.

I took a moment to make a mental check. I told her I was fine, and I thought I was. However, I had been known to make a fool of myself. The last thing I needed was to go back out there and freak out. You know, run into a waiter with a tray full of food. Blurt out something personal to Justin about how I feel, loudly. Then, just the possibility of the usual tripping on something. That was something that seemed to be a regular event when I was around him. I also decided that alcohol was out of the question. Like I needed any help being clumsy.

Once I was sure that I was collected, I casually walked to the table. There wasn't an embarrassing moment when everyone looks up at you, and you just know they know what you are thinking, thankfully. I sighed with relief and went to take the seat reserved for me between Alice and Justin. They were all engrossed in conversations.

As I got to the chair, Justin stood up and wrapped his arms around me, kissing me softly on the lips, then leaning in for a hug. "I missed you," he whispered in my ear, kissing my cheek.

I looked at his eyes, warmed by the sincerity in them; I reached up and pulled his face to mine, giving him another kiss. "Exactly." I sat down.

Dinner was great. Yeah, the food tasted great, but I felt the same ease of conversation I had with him before with the addition of holding hands under the table and occasional silent gazes in each other's eyes.

After dinner was over, we all stayed for a while just talking and spending time together. We played pool and mingled. I stuck with my decision to not drink in fear I'd again freak out about my feelings.

Around ten, we rearranged the seating arrangements for rides home. Ryan brought Alice, Justin and me back to our places. There hadn't been concrete plans for the next day other than the kids were going on their outing. So, we were talking about what we were all going to do.

Alice brought up how Emma was hinting at us all spending the day together. Ryan jumped right in on that idea, saying that he hoped that we would want to. We all started throwing out suggestions. Movie, lunch, a tour of sorts and maybe even some combination of those.

I suggested just spending time at Ryan's house, "He has a rec room, a large screen TV and a large kitchen to cook in. Why go out? We can just hang out there and spend time with each other rather than distractions of the public."

They looked at each other. "Sounds good to me," Alice shrugged.

"If that's all right to invade your house, that is," I said, suddenly realizing I just offered up his place.

"Yeah, that's fine." Ryan smiled. "I like the idea."

"Then it's settled," I announced. "Wait, you haven't said anything, Justin. Do you have other plans, or are you game, too?"

He almost looked startled that I asked. "Yeah. That sounds like a good idea. What time?"

"The kids will be leaving about eleven," Alice said. "Vivianne and I can be ready about then?"

"I'll come pick all three of you up then." Ryan gave Alice a hug and said goodbye.

Alice walked into the apartment, waving good night to Justin, leaving us alone. I felt a little of the nervous feeling from earlier creep back in. It was almost instantly interrupted by him taking a couple of steps towards me and taking my hands in his.

"I'm glad I got to see you tonight," he said softly.

The usual shade of red that occupied my cheeks when he was around was coming back. "I'm not sure I could have held out much longer before I would have come to find you."

He laughed. "Yeah, I thought about that, too. I almost came to ask you to breakfast before you left for the spa."

"I would have gone." Thoughts of what Alice would have said to that ran through my head. I giggled, "That would have made for even more gossip for them today. You should have heard them."

"Oh really?" He lifted one eyebrow. "What did they have to say?"

"Just talk. You know. Things like how happy they are to see us getting along." I sounded very nonchalant and played girly for a moment, wondering what he would say to such a bland description.

"To see us getting along?" He cocked his head and looked at me out of the corner of his eyes.

I laughed. "Yeah. Pretty much."

He huffed.

"What?" I asked.

"Are you sure that's all they had to say about it?" He smiled.

I knew they must have grilled him, maybe even offering some information up from things I've said. At that moment, I wanted to fade away. What did they say? What did he know? How did he feel? What should I say?

I stood there, frozen for a moment, before I grabbed at something to say. "Well, no, but it sums it up."

"Huh," he huffed again. "I would think they would have described it differently knowing what they've told me and what they've gotten out of me." He dropped my hands and smiled his melting crooked smile as he walked over to stand in front of his door.

I took a deep breath. "What they've said?" I walked over to stand a couple steps from him.

"Sure. They've been talking to you and Alice, right? Didn't you think they'd offer me something in order to get me to talk?" He leaned against the door frame, arms crossed.

"Oh no," I gasped.

"Oh no? Did you say something that wasn't true?" He laughed.

"No, that's the 'oh no'. I've told the truth. They know. With what they were saying this morning, I can only imagine what they would have told you considering how close you all are. I never even considered that." I put my hands to my face.

I heard him laughing as he ran his hand over my arm. "If it helps, I like what they told me," he whispered gently.

I looked up. He was looking me in the eyes right away. I could feel my body melting and stiffening at the same time. My breath caught in my throat, and I had to close my eyes to keep from falling over.

I grasped his wrist in my hand as he was running his fingers up and down my left arm. "Ok, what did they say?" I lowered his hand and tucked my hands into my pockets.

He looked up. "Well? They told me that you get really nervous, especially when you're about to see me." He ran his fingers through his hair and leaned back against the door jamb as his dark, wavy locks fell back into place. "They said they asked you what you thought after our first kiss, and your reply was that you wanted more. Plus, you are falling for me?"

I was truly embarrassed at that moment. I didn't know how to react. I could only think about strangling them for this. I tossed my head back, shaking it, trying to regain my composure so I didn't take off running. Resting one hand on the short fence that surrounded the small sidewalk garden in front of our apartments, putting the other hand on my hip, I just looked up at him and bit my lower lip, shaking my head again with eyebrows raised.

"I take it they haven't told me anything untrue?" He searched my eyes.

"Nope." I tried to not say anything more so I didn't give any more away.

"What did they tell you?" He searched my eyes again.

I wished I had more to tell him, but I didn't. I just told him what I knew. "Basically, that they are glad that we are getting along so well, and that they have never seen you with this look in your eyes. They don't say what look. They just say they've seen you with other girls, but you've 'never had this look before'."

"Huh." He leaned back against his doorframe.

I waited a moment for him to say something more. After a moment, I scoffed, "*Huh*? That's it? That's all you have to say? You can't do that! You can't tell me what you've been told and leave it like that." My voice grew louder and went to a higher pitch. I stomped like a child.

He laughed. "Sure, I can. However, as it seems that my information is more revealing than yours, I might be able to let you in a little more."

"Ok?" I urged him on, motioning for him to keep going.

He stood up straight, reaching his hands out toward my waist. As his fingers wrapped around the tops of my hips, he pulled me in toward him, about a step away. He looked down at his hands as he slid them, slowly, around my waist to my lower back, stopping one above the other.

His eyes scanned over me as they came up and stopped at my lips. He bit his lower lip which made my breath catch again. Then, he tilted his head slightly and touched the side of his face against mine, slowly moving his cheek so his lips were barely brushing against my ear.

I could feel his breath and hear every quiver in his breathing. He stepped forward so I could feel the heat from his body reach mine through my winter coat. I was shaking and hoping that he wouldn't notice. I heard him draw in a slow and steady breath.

I closed my eyes as he whispered, "But, not tonight."

My eyes shot open, and I tried to jerk back so I could look at him, but I was caught by surprise at the control he had where his hands were positioned. He kept one hand on my lower back yet quickly moved the other to my upper back at my movement, holding me in the embrace. I could feel a smile form on his face through his cheek that was still pressed to mine.

I huffed and relaxed in his grip. Was he still thinking about how he felt? Was that why he didn't want to say something? Was he amused at my feelings and knew he didn't feel the same but wasn't sure how to say it? Did he feel the same but was afraid to tell me? I couldn't read him since he wouldn't let me see his face.

"I will say this, though." He pulled his head back so I could see the look in his eyes. He was sincere in saying, "What I know, among other things, put my mind at ease."

"What do you mean?" I whispered.

"I mean, it doesn't change how I feel, but it makes me more assured in my feelings." A look of shyness came over his face.

I am sure he could see the surprise all over me. "Oh!"

He laughed. "Oh?"

"Um," I cleared my throat. "Yeah, that's all I got."

"That's all you got?" he teased.

I really didn't know what to say. I looked into his eyes and smiled. "Not tonight," I said, laying my head on his chest and curling my arms around him to clasp my hands on his back. A feeling of being anchored to the world came over me, like I had felt like I was going to float away before that simple action.

We stayed there for a few minutes until I could feel the cold biting at my lungs. I didn't want to go, but I knew that tonight was not the night for either of us to go into the other's apartment. Things were going fast enough. Even if it was just supposed to be to talk and spend more time together, there was such a strong pull that I knew I would be risking a step I wasn't entirely sure I was ready for.

The cold was getting to me as I started to shiver. He rubbed my arms to help warm me, but I could feel him shivering, too. I pulled myself tighter to him for a moment before I let go and stepped back.

"I should go in." The words seemed dreadful as I spoke them.

His eyes were still closed when I looked at him. He took in a deep breath. "Yeah. That's probably a good idea." He cleared his throat. "I'll see you tomorrow?"

"Yes," I blurted out. "We have plans, right? A double date?" I giggled.

"Why yes, we do," he said with a knowing smile.

He took one of my hands and bowed to me, kissing my hand as he came back up. As he held his lips to my hand, he turned his eyes up to look at me. The melting, the blushing, the feeling faint. Yup, I knew it was more than just attraction or some fan girl crush. I was falling, and fast.

I pulled my hand from his hands before his lips parted from my skin and stood straight up, trying to gather myself. He stood up and looked at me with a puzzled and almost hurt look on his beautiful face.

"Are you ok?" He reached out.

I took a step back to avoid his touch. "Yes. I just know that if I don't go in my apartment and direct you to yours now, I don't know what I might do. However, I am pretty sure it would be along the lines of my getting into trouble."

"Oh really?" He got that look on his face and took a step closer to me. "Trouble, huh?"

I stepped back again and found myself against the railing to the little garden. I held my hand out and put it on his chest. "Stop right there. I still don't know what page you're on, but I do know what page I'm on. So, to reiterate, I'll say to you, 'Not tonight'."

He tossed his hands in the air. "Nope, I agree. I was just messing with you. I had no idea that you were so… bothered. I am flattered."

"Flattered?" I scoffed. "Great. That's like a woman telling a guy that they're such a nice guy."

"What? No!" He scrambled for a way to reword it. "Listen, I just mean this to be along the lines of what I said earlier. It seems the more I learn about how you feel, I get more assured in how I feel."

"I still don't quite know what you mean by this," I pried.

"Not tonight." His smile looked deep as he ran a finger along my lips. "Just know that I will be thinking of you when you leave me tonight. I will dream about you when I sleep tonight. What little sleep I will get while I am anxious to see you tomorrow. Then, I will think about you all day until I do get to see you. I will have to fight the urge to make up an excuse to see you just so I can."

I opened my mouth, but nothing came out. I wanted him to say more, to clarify why he wanted to see me so bad. Just to hear the words. Yet, I did know what he meant, and my heart jumped from that knowledge. So, I froze there, just looking at him, unable to speak.

He reached out again, and this time, he was able to connect. He set both hands on my cheeks and tilted my face up to meet his. I tried to divert my eyes, but I couldn't help but look up, knowing the inevitable. I swooned. I could see the sincerity in his eyes. I could feel the assurance in his steady breath. I melted.

His hands slid down to my shoulders. As they did, I could see the loss of control of his emotions on his face yet feel the control of his actions in his fingers. They were slightly stiff as they glided over me, however soft his touch was. His eyes had fallen from mine and were following the trail of his hand.

"You're cold," he said after a long moment.

My teeth chattered as I said, "Yes. I am."

"Then you had better go inside." He was very quiet in his words, very controlled.

"Ok." I turned and started for my door. "Good night."

"Vivianne?" His voice let a small bit of desperation out with my name.

I stopped and looked down at the ground. "Yeah?"

He walked up right behind me and wrapped his arms around me. "Have sweet dreams." He kissed my cheek, holding his lips there for a moment.

As he let me go, I turned to him. "You too."

I leaned up and gave him a quick but forceful kiss on the lips and ran off through my door. I couldn't say that I was happy to be in my apartment and away from him by any means, but I was glad I didn't have to control myself for a moment.

I leaned my back against the door and slid myself down, sitting in a slump, on the floor. Putting my hands on my face, I let out a frustrated growl. I was not aware that Alice was leaned against the wall just a few feet away.

"Well then," she taunted me. "That looked intense."

"I don't want to talk about it," I scoffed.

She roared with laughter. "This is so funny, watching you with him. In all the years I've known you, I've never seen you so... so... how do I put this? Oh! I know!" She looked right into my eyes. "In love."

"What?" I snapped up from the floor. "I'm not *in love*. There's no way. I barely know him."

"That's funny. That's exactly what he said to Ryan when Ryan confronted him about his feelings for you," she snickered.

"Ok? So? We both recognize that it's too soon to be falling in love. Good." My heart sank just a little. "I'm glad that we're both being realistic about this," I said, even though a part of me wanted to hear that he said he was in love with me.

"No, it's good that you both haven't given in to it yet. I'll give you that. However, it's not that it's not happening. It just means that neither of you are getting completely lost in it, thank god." She wiped her forehead with the back of her hand as if there was sweat there.

"I don't know what's happening." I walked into the kitchen. "I know there's something there, and maybe it's what you say it is, but no matter what, I just don't think that I am ready to know what it is."

"What do you mean? I mean, aren't you Little Miss Can't Stand Not Knowing?" She pulled down my tea for me as I turned the burner on under the kettle.

"Thank you," I said for the tea. "Yes, normally I am. If I really think about it." And I was. I normally couldn't be in a situation that I didn't have a grasp on. I stood for a moment thinking about this.

"And?" She pried.

"I am sure it's got something to do with the feelings that I am having versus not knowing what feelings he is having. That's why I don't want to think about what we were just talking about."

"Wait." She whipped around to look at me. "You did come in kind of flustered. What were you two talking about?"

"I just said that I don't want to think about it." The kettle started to whistle.

She yanked the kettle off the burner before I could get to it. "No, no, no. You don't get any water until you tell me everything." She snatched up my mug, too.

"Fine," I huffed. "Emma and Giselle apparently were trying to get info out of him, but they had to exchange some info about things I've said to get anything out of him. So, they told him about me saying that I am falling for him."

"Oh, man!" she laughed. "Did they get info from him?"

"I didn't think they had talked to him about us at all before learning about this." I threw my hands in the air. "However, he claims that his information is more revealing, but he wasn't going to tell me anything tonight."

"I'd be so mad!" she said, still laughing.

"Oh, don't think I wasn't. I told him that he couldn't leave it like that." I grabbed my mug and the kettle from her hands and mixed my tea. I took a sip, burning my lips. I winced. "He did tell me that knowing what I said about how I feel doesn't change how he feels, but it does make him more assured in his feelings. Whatever that means." You could hear the disdain dripping from my words.

"That says a lot." She slapped her palm to my forehead. "You really must be trying to ignore the feelings in this."

"Whatever," I scoffed.

She rolled her eyes. "Whatever? You do realize that he basically just told you that he's either on the same page and is falling for you, too. OR! He's already in love with you and 'assured' that you are going to be in love with him soon enough."

I sat on one of the dining room chairs and leaned back, thinking about that for a moment. Alice just stared at me, waiting for a response. A million thoughts ran through my mind. She was right, and I knew it. I just wasn't really ready to be faced with it. I mean, I had just met him a mere week ago! That's it!

"Does this really happen outside of the movies?" I had been asking myself this a lot lately.

She slumped in the chair next to me. "Apparently it does."

"I wanted to go into his place with him," I said into my mug.

She pulled the mug down from my face. "Why didn't you?"

"Don't you think it's all going fast enough?"

"Fair enough, but could you imagine waking up next to him?" She smiled.

"It would be nice to even just have him hold me all night. No sex. Just have his arms wrapped around me." My thoughts trailed off.

"Why are you still sitting here then?" She pointed towards the door. "Go get a few toiletries and get your behind over there!"

"No. It just doesn't feel right tonight." I suddenly felt a strange sense of giddiness about the impending right moment, which brought back the schoolgirl feelings. "I think I am just going to go to sleep. I'll see him tomorrow."

"True," she shrugged.

I got up from my seat, took my mug to the kitchen, rinsed it out and headed to bed. "Good night, Alice."

"Good night, Viv," she replied.

I went into my room and got ready for bed. The whole time, I couldn't get him off my mind. In fact, I couldn't get settled into bed, he was so much on my mind. I got up after about an hour of tossing and turning and sat on the bench in front of my window, staring out at the night sky.

I wondered if I would have been as bothered as I was if it wasn't for him being right next door. At one point, I found myself wondering if he was still up. Was he just as bothered by me? Was he tossing and turning or pacing the apartment?

I am sure not. He is probably sound asleep, clear of the thought of me. I'm probably the only one so preoccupied by this.

Finally, about two-thirty, I crawled back into bed and fell asleep. However, it didn't last long. I woke up about seven. At first, I had every intention of trying to go back to sleep. Then, I had a thought.

I jumped up out of bed and rushed into the bathroom. Brushing my teeth and arranging my hair to look presentable without really doing it, I picked out my cutest sweats and long-sleeved T-shirt. I threw on a pull-over hoodie and tennis shoes and headed out the door, grabbing a blanket on my way out.

Once outside, I shivered. I wasn't sure if it was from the cold or the thought of doing what I was about to do. I took a deep breath, which bit into my lungs, and walked over to his door, pausing for a moment before I started to knock.

I waited for a moment, but he didn't come to the door. I was about to go back to my place and just go back to sleep when the door started to open. He opened it just enough to see who the mad-person was that was waking him up at such an ungodly hour.

He was so cute half-awake and mildly scruffy. His hair was disheveled. He wasn't cleanly shaven. Then, the groggy look on his face had an alluring quality all on its own. I couldn't do anything but smile.

"Vivianne?" He sounded concerned.

"Um, yeah. I'm sorry to wake you," I apologized.

He opened the door a little wider. "Is everything ok?" He looked down at the blanket in my arms.

"Oh! Yeah. I just couldn't sleep, and I was just wondering if you would be interested in... well? You know, it's silly. I'm sorry to wake you. I'll let you go back to sleep." I started to turn to go back to my place again.

He gently grabbed my arm as I turned. "Vivianne? I'm interested. Whatever it is."

I stopped and turned back to face him. "Well? There's a park down the road, and I was wondering if you would walk down there with me and watch the sunrise. I'm sorry. Like I said, it's silly. I shouldn't have woken you."

He let go of my arm and opened the door as far as his arm could reach. "Vivianne, I'd love to. Come on inside and warm up while I get ready."

I smiled. "Ok."

He held the door for me as I walked in. "Cold?" he asked from behind me.

"A little," I lied. "But I brought a blanket for the walk."

He rubbed my arms to warm me up a little and then walked past me, motioning to the living room. "Make yourself at home. I'll be right back."

I sat down on the couch and watched him as he walked into his bedroom. He was wearing a simple white T-shirt and black boxers with a white design on one of the legs. I couldn't help but think about how sexy he looked all barefoot and half asleep.

While he was getting changed, I looked about the room from the view of the couch. It was decorated fairly similarly to ours, just not as many rooms. It was very clean. Even the dishes were all done. I have to say, I was impressed for a single man.

He didn't take long, maybe ten minutes. When he came back into the room, he was wearing a pair of black sweatpants, a black zip-up sweatshirt over the white T-shirt, with a red dragon design on the back and a pair of black and white Adidas shoes.

His hair was a bit less disheveled, yet it was still his usual tussled look. He hadn't shaved, which I was happy about. I noticed that he was cute a little scruffy. However, all in all? He looked fairly refreshed.

"Are you sure I'm not bothering you?" I asked.

"No! Not at all. Actually, I love the idea." He held up a thicker blanket than the one I held in my arms. "I'll bring another just in case. Shall we?"

I got up and walked to the door. "It's cold out. I'm just warning you."

"Good. Then maybe we'll need the blankets." He smiled. "Oh, by the way..." He stopped talking, so I turned to see why. Before I knew it, he wrapped his arms around me and kissed me. "Good morning."

I curled my lips in and found myself coming down from my tiptoes, "Mmmm... good morning."

He smiled and took me by the hand, leading me down the street. We got to the park before I knew it. I looked around to see where would be the best place to sit comfortably and see the sunrise. I spotted the swings and led the way. He shook out his blanket and draped it over one of the swings, sitting on it and wrapping it around his shoulders.

I started for the swing next to him when he spoke up. "Where are you going?"

"To sit down." I pointed at the other swing.

He held his arms out. "Again, where are you going? Get over here."

I blushed and looked down at the ground as I walked over in front of him. "Ok?"

He grabbed my hips, turned me around and pulled me onto his lap. I laid my blanket across my lap as he wrapped his blanket and his arms around me. I rested my head back on his shoulder as he kissed my cheek.

"Thank you for asking me to come out here with you," he whispered.

I leaned into him, closed my eyes and pulled his arms tighter around me. As I opened my eyes, I noticed the horizon was just starting to get brighter. We sat there quietly as the sun came up. It's amazing how relaxing and yet extremely romantic it is sitting in silence, curled up in a blanket, on a swing, with someone you're falling for while watching the sun come up.

The sun had fully come up when I felt him start to shiver. I pulled his arms from around me and stood up. "You want to go get some coffee? I am sure our café is open."

"That sounds perfect. Let's just drop off the blankets at my place on our way." He got up and folded his blanket, taking mine from me.

As we approached the café, he went to take the blankets to his place, saying he'd be right there. I went in and took a seat at the same table we had when we were there before. I waited to order until he got back.

When he came back, he sat down across from me, just looking at me. "You are so adorable in the morning."

I giggled. "Thanks, I guess."

"Hot chocolate?" he asked as he stood back up.

"Oh, I can get it. I was just waiting until you got here to order." I started to get up.

He shook his head. "No, I got it."

He kissed me on my forehead and headed up to the counter where three younger women were giggling and gossiping. I couldn't help but think about his comment about me being adorable in the morning? Me? Had he not looked in the mirror?

I overheard one of the girls telling him that they heard he was in town. She added in that the soundtrack to his latest film was her favorite CD since he does a few of the songs. Plus, the trailer for his newest movie was just released. He looked a little embarrassed but did his usual polite thank you response, took our drinks and returned to the table as the girls all pulled out their cell phones and started texting. It wasn't long before a few girls came in that were obvious friends of the employees. We were quickly pointed out.

Justin stiffened in his seat. "I am sorry."

"I'm getting used to it," I smiled.

The girls came over timidly and asked for his autograph and started asking questions. He gladly signed the pictures and papers and answered a few of the questions that pertained to his movies and his music.

It wasn't long before a few more girls came in. His smile turned into a work face when pictures started getting snapped. I could see that he was starting to get a little irritated as they started to get a little pushy. I stood up and went around to the back of his chair. A couple of the girls flashed me dirty looks.

I slid my hand down his arm. "We should get going."

He finished signing the picture in his hand and handed it back. "Yes. We should." He fluidly lifted his hand with my movement and took my hand as he stood.

He thanked the girls as we walked out. We were a couple steps away when the door finished closing. Both of us laughed at the sounds of squeals and "oh my gods!" that came radiating through the doors.

"So?" He looked at me. "What now?"

"Well," I shrugged. "I am getting hungry. I can cook breakfast."

"It's about eight-thirty. Are we going to wake anyone at your place?" he asked.

"No, it's hard to wake them up," I said, hoping that they would still be asleep so I could get some more alone time with him before they did get up.

He put his arms around me as we walked across the street. "Sounds good."

As we walked through the door, I heard the kids up and playing. I knew we were caught when I heard a little "Mama!" coming at me from down the hall. I looked at him and shrugged.

As we went into the living room, we were both bombarded with hugs from the kids as they ran back off to the dining room. Alice and Tiffany both crossed their arms and started teasing us.

"And where have you two been?" Alice tapped her foot.

"Yeah, you were supposed to be in bed, missy," Tiffany said with a laugh.

"I couldn't sleep, so I woke him up to go watch the sunrise with me," I said very matter-of-factly.

Tiffany lowered her arms. "Oh! That's so romantic!"

Justin laughed. "It was a beautiful sunrise."

"So, you want me to believe that you were here all night and just went over there this morning after what you said last night before I went to bed?" Alice flipped her hair.

"Alice!" I grunted.

"What she said?" Justin started walking over to Alice. "What did she say?"

"Nothing!" I snapped and grabbed his arm. "Tiffany, I think Justin and I are going to have breakfast at his place this morning."

He looked at me with a huge, mischievous smile. "Wait, I'm curious about what you had to say last night."

Alice cleared her throat. "Oh, let's just say that I would just be surprised if she waited to come over until this morning."

"Alice!" I shouted. "Shush!"

"Really?" He looked at me.

"Fine," I scoffed. "I was a bit… bothered last night after our talk out front, and I told her. She tried to get me to go find you right then, but I didn't. I am sure that's why I couldn't sleep well last night. Can we drop it?"

"Drop it?" he smirked. "Ok. However, forget it? Probably not."

"Great. Thanks, Alice." I picked up a towel off the counter and threw it at her. "Can we go have a quiet breakfast at your place without Alice's wonderful ability to keep things to herself?" I glared at her.

He hadn't taken his eyes off me. "Sure."

I kissed the kids goodbye and headed out the door with him very close behind. Outside, I stopped and asked him. "Do you have stuff to make breakfast, or do I need to go back and get it?"

"I've got it, and I get to cook for you this time." He gently pulled me in through his door.

"Are you sure? I mean, I can cook. It's the least I can do for waking you up so early," I said as we walked to the kitchen.

He started pulling out eggs and bacon from the refrigerator. "No, it's the least I can do to show you that I appreciate you coming and waking me up. I really enjoyed that." He walked over and sat me down on one of the stools at the breakfast bar. "Now, sit down, relax and let me do this for you."

I was a little shocked. "Ok?"

He cooked bacon, cheese, mushroom and bell pepper frittatas with sides of fresh fruit. I was impressed that he had this sort of food in his fridge. To me, that said a lot about him.

We chatted as he cooked. I got to help cut the fruit. So, I didn't end up feeling totally useless. As he finished up, he set my plate in front of me and took his place on the next stool.

I turned my stool towards him to chat while we ate. The meal was delicious, and the idle chattering continued. Before I knew it, we were facing each other, more engrossed in conversation than the food.

"Ok, we've talked about a lot of things like favorite foods and colors, authors, movies and so on. You also know a lot about me and where I come from, but I want to know more about you." I set my fork down and leaned in towards him. "Sure, I've read about you in magazines, but you never know what's true and what's not. I want to know the real Justin. The Justin you don't get in magazines and Internet sites. You said you've spent a lot of time in southwest Texas but have been to a lot of places. Where? Where is your favorite? What's your family like? Do you have siblings? Do you have any animals? I would like to get to know more about you that you can't find on a fan page."

He laughed. "Fair enough considering I've asked you a lot over the last week. Ok." He looked up out of the corner of his eyes, smiled and looked back at me. "All right, yes, I've spent a lot of time in southwest Texas, and I miss it terribly. Especially since my parents and both sets of grandparents are there. However, my favorite place to be? I guess I don't have one. Anywhere that I am enjoying myself."

"I have three sisters," he continued. "Two are still in Texas. One is younger and one older. Both married with two kids. One is out in LA, close to where I live. She's single without kids, trying to make it as a singer. She's not bad. Yes, I live in LA. Yet, I have a close relationship with my entire family, not unlike Ryan and his family."

"Then why didn't you go to Texas with them for the holidays?" I asked.

"Well? Ryan invited me out here, and I couldn't say no. It was like something was telling me that I had to." He looked happily deep in thought.

"What do you think it is? Do you miss London?" I was completely naive to what he meant.

He shook his head and laughed. "Well, I do love London. However, it wasn't that."

"Then what?" It dawned on me as I spoke the words. I could feel my eyes widen.

He must have noticed, because he smiled. "Yeah," he laughed. "I wasn't kidding when I told you that I was drawn to knowing more when they were talking about you at the benefit in New York. So, when he called me up to tell me that you both were coming out for this and asked if I was interested in coming out, too. I couldn't just walk away with out knowing why I felt so pulled."

"Ok? And?" I searched for more information.

We sat there for a moment as I watched him look over my face. I could see a kind of look like he was taking it all in. Strangely, I was not self-conscious. I smiled slightly and bit my lower lip.

He reached out and took the glass I was holding and set it on the counter. He then set his hands on my face; his fingertips reached the back of my head, pulling me in. Our foreheads were touching as we both closed our eyes. I could hear his voice was a little jagged.

"I understand now," he whispered.

I took a slow, deep breath. "What?"

"That I am supposed to have met you." He turned his face up until our lips connected.

It was one of those slow, gentle and restrained kisses. One of those moments where you can't not kiss, but you know that if you do not have control over every movement, you would be in danger of taking it farther than you intended. I could feel a quiver in his lips and the muscles in his hands stiffen.

Before I knew it, he was off his stool and standing, pressed against me. Both of us had our arms wrapped around the other. Our breathing had grown faster, and the kiss wasn't as soft. There was a growing fierceness to it.

I raised my hands to his chest, noticing for a moment the strength it held, and pushed him back. There was a look of rejection for a moment in his eyes until he saw the look in my eyes that told of my longing and restraint from that longing.

He cleared his throat. "I have a cat. His name is Traverse." He sat back down on his stool.

I looked at him and shook my head. "Really?"

We both started laughing so hard that I had tears streaming down my cheeks. The conversation resumed, and I got a bit more insight on him, his family, places he had been. I learned a lot about him that morning while we exchanged little brushes of our fingers and looks that had a secondary conversation all of their own.

About 10:45, my cell phone rang. It was Alice telling me that the kids were getting ready to go. I wasn't ready to go, but I knew I didn't want the kids to leave without saying goodbye. Plus, Ryan was going to be over soon to pick us up. So, I said I'd see him soon and raced over to my place to see them off and get cleaned up.

The kids left just as Ryan pulled up. I hadn't showered or anything. There was no way I was going to spend the day with them looking like that. Justin could easily pull off his adorable just-woke-up look. I just looked like a hobo.

"I've got to take a shower!" I ran down the hall as Alice let Ryan in.

I heard Alice explaining, "Well, the two of them decided that they wanted to get up early and watch the sunrise together at the park. Then, they went to his place for breakfast. So, neither of them is ready to go."

"I'll go check on Justin then. I'll be right back." I heard him go out the front door.

I started the shower and got in, knowing that Alice would be right in to find out what happened. I was wetting my hair down as she came in.

"All right, what happened?" she demanded.

"Nothing! I woke him up, we walked to the park. I sat on his lap on a swing, curled up in a blanket watching the sun come up. We went to our café, but he got bombarded by fans. We were going to come here and have breakfast, but you were all up. So, we went to his place. He cooked me breakfast, and we talked. That's it!" I glared at her around the curtain.

"Are you sure?" she pried.

"Yes!" I snapped. "Now go listen for them to get here. The longer you talk to me, the longer I'm going to take."

I finished my shower and got ready to go. Going through my clothes, I tried to keep in mind that we were just going to be hanging out at Ryan's, just the four of us. So, I could keep it casual. I settled on jeans, a red tank top with a black cardigan and my little, black Converse low tops with red trim. I kept my jewelry and make-up simple.

When I walked into the living room, Justin was there with Alice and Ryan. He had changed, and his hair was wet from obviously having taken a shower. He was wearing a jersey style T-shirt, jeans and black Doc Martens.

Every one of us had dressed casually. This was a relief to me. I was wondering if I had dressed down at all, but obviously not. However, even dressed down, he was still so sexy. I had a hard time taking my eyes off of him.

They got up as I walked into the room. "Are you all ready?" I asked.

"Yup. We're just waiting for you." Alice came over and took my arm.

Alice led me to Justin's side as she flitted off to Ryan's. She took his hand as they walked to the door. I stepped in front of Justin and looked up at him. He looked down at me and smiled.

"Good morning, again." He kissed me.

Once at Ryan's house, we all went straight for the rec room. It was very nice to see Ryan and Alice together. She was finally giving in, even if it wasn't diving in. Her feet were in the pool, so to speak.

A couple hours of playing pool went by before anyone mentioned having lunch. So, about one-thirty, Ryan and Justin headed in to the kitchen to make up some paninis while Alice and I got the cards out to start up a game of euchre.

I sat down in the seat next to Alice. "Is this really happening to us?"

She looked at me a little puzzled. "What? Playing cards?"

"No, Captain Oblivious," I joked. "Are we really in Ryan Perry's house, in London? Are you really dating

301

Ryan Perry? Am I really dating Justin Ronin? Is this really happening?"

She laughed. "I try to not think about it."

"What do you mean? How can you not? I mean, I don't think about it all of the time, but you have to have it cross your mind from time to time." I shrugged.

"I think about it, but yeah, it's a lot to take in. So, I try not to think about who he is when I'm with him." She kept shuffling. "If I just keep him an everyday man in my mind when we're together, it helps."

"I guess I can see that." I took a stack to help shuffle. "It only dawns on me every once in a while, but when it does, I sort of freak out a little. It's intimidating."

"Yeah, I know what you mean," she smiled. "It's very cool."

We started giggling as the guys walked in.

Justin looked at us curiously. "What are you two gossiping about?"

"Oh," Alice jumped on that and pointed at me. "She was just telling me how fantastic she thinks you are."

"Alice!" I scolded. "Thanks."

He walked over to me as Ryan stood in the doorway laughing. "Good," he said as he kissed me on the head and put an arm around my shoulders. "We were just coming in to see what you ladies would like on your paninis."

The rest of the day was relaxing. There was an exciting and intimidating aspect to being with them, for sure. However, part of the intimidating factor was just how easy it was being with them. Alice agreed with me on this point. There was no questioning it. Justin was right, we were meant to meet, just as Ryan and Alice were.

Saturday morning started with a bang. A real bang. I was woken up by Emma and Giselle banging on my and Alice's doors. Tiffany had let them in, letting them know that we must be catching up on the lack of sleep from the prior nights considering that we had all gotten home about seven. The kids were in bed by eight, they were so tired from the day. Then, Alice and I had gone to sleep about ten.

It was nine in the morning, and we were still not awake.

"Get up! It's time to go shopping!" Emma hollered.

"Yeah, ladies. Let's go! We have a lot to do today!" Giselle added in.

I rolled over and put my pillow over my head. The next thing I knew, Elizabeth and Victoria were both climbing on top of me. I tossed myself onto my back and play growled at them. They both jumped back, screeching and laughing.

"Come on, Momma!" Elizabeth begged. "Emma and Giselle said they are taking you and Aunt Alice out to get pretty outfits. Don't you want to go get pretty outfits?"

"Do you think I need more pretty outfits?" I asked as I sat up.

She plopped down next to me and put her finger to her mouth, scrunched her eyebrows and looked very deep in thought for a moment. "Yes. I don't think you can have too many pretty outfits."

She jumped up, and they both grabbed one of my hands and started pulling me off the bed. I couldn't help but laugh at how cute they were as they tried to pull me up, yelling that they had gotten me up to the instigators on the other side of the door.

Alice came out of her room just as I did. We stopped to look at each other, nodding as we both had the same thought. *Man, I'm getting too old for this.* We laughed and headed for the kitchen. Me, for my tea. Her, for her coffee. Once there, we were handed what we were going for as Tiffany was already five steps ahead of us.

"You are the best." Alice patted Tiffany on the shoulder.

I took a sip of my tea. "Can we keep you?"

"Ok, ladies. We have to shop for the New Year's Eve party and for tonight," Giselle announced.

"Tonight?" I asked.

"Yup," Emma replied as they each held up a credit card. "The boys want to go to the club tonight. Soooo..." She drew the word out. "They would like to treat you both to a new outfit, in addition to the one Ryan already told you that you would need for the New Year's Eve party."

"No, this is too much." I waved my hand to motion her to put the cards away.

Alice crossed her arms. "Yeah. This is way too much."

Giselle handed Alice the card in her hand as Emma handed me the card in her hand, saying, "This one is from Justin. He wanted to be the one to treat you to your outfits."

304

I took the card and looked it over. "I can't do this. I can just buy my own. They've been too generous." I held the card out for her to take back.

"I don't think it'll go over well if you don't let them treat you." Emma pushed the card back towards me.

"What are they going to do if we just buy our own?" Alice asked.

Giselle started laughing. "Honey, you wouldn't want to hurt their feelings, would you?"

"I doubt they'd be too crushed," I said.

Emma shrugged and picked up my cell phone, handing it to me. "Ok? Give him a call. I told them that you'd be like this, but they insisted. So? Call then."

I dialed his number and hit send. It only rang once before I heard his voice. "Just take it," is all he said.

"But," I tried to argue.

He cut me off. "No buts. Just take the card. Go get both outfits. Go all out. I want to do this. Please let me."

"Are you sure? At least let me buy one outfit." I was hoping he'd give in.

"Nope. You'll hurt my feelings if you don't let me do this for you. I'll see you tonight, outside your door, all dressed and ready to go at nine. Ok?"

"Ok." I reluctantly gave in. "Justin?"

"Yeah?"

"Thank you."

"My pleasure. I'll see you tonight, beautiful." He hung up.

I looked at Alice and shrugged. She shrugged back. "I know better than to argue with Ryan if Justin is determined." She threw her hands in the air.

"All right, then." Giselle started pushing us towards our rooms again. "Go get dressed. Let's hit the stores. You're not the only ones that need new outfits!"

Alice and I got dressed and cleaned up. I didn't go all out with my outfit considering Emma and Giselle were in jeans and decorative tops. I followed suit. We were going shopping with Emma and Giselle. So, I should expect a long day and needed to be comfortable.

We breezed through shop after shop, trying on outfit after outfit. About one, we stopped at a café for lunch. I wasn't all that hungry. So, I just ordered a soup bread bowl. We then went right back to more shopping.

About five, the last outfit had been picked out, and the last accessory had been paired. Also, the last question from the sisters had been asked. They were so funny all day asking us questions about things that have happened, how we were feeling and what we were thinking. They were so excited for us. At times, I thought they were more excited than we were. However, their excitement brought out Alice's, and that made me happy. She needed to be more outwardly excited.

Back at our apartment, we each took turns showing off our new outfits. Emma got her usual pretty and classic designs while Giselle went more towards the hip and chic styles. With her figure, she could pull off the latest runway styles without a hitch.

Alice had chosen a green halter dress with a gold trim for the club. Her accessories were all simple and gold. Her shoes were a similar green with gold trim around the soles. It looked great with her red hair and complexion.

306

Her New Year's Eve party dress was gorgeous. It was a simple, mid-thigh length, fitted tank top style dress all in a shimmering gold. She had a long, black beaded necklace that hit at waist length. She also got a matching black beaded bangle bracelet and large, black hoop earrings. Her shoes were a simple patent leather 80s-style three-inch heel. It was a flattering outfit for her.

My club outfit was a pair of black, wide leg slacks that had wide cuffs with a burgundy shirt. The shirt was a satin tuxedo vest style. The waistband was fitted. The main part of the shirt connected around the waist but came up and gathered around the neck. It left the back exposed, and in the front, created a deep V that came down to about the navel. On the back, there were ten strands of tiny, silver beads that hung down from the center of the back of the neck and fell down to about the top of my lower back.

I paired it with a black satin choker that had a silver amulet and a garnet in the center that matched my silver bracelet, also with garnets. My shoes were dancer style in matte black with rounded toes and two-and-a-half-inch heels. They were simple yet added a lot of character to the outfit.

Giselle's favorite outfit of the day was the one I picked for the New Year's Eve party. I had picked black leggings that were capri length. My top was a crayon red cotton altered tunic. The waistband was fitted, but this one was designed to be fitted around the hips. It billowed slightly and had flowing short sleeves and a boat-neck collar. The neck tied in back to create a large opening.

The shoes were my favorite. They had a four-inch skinny heel in black. The main part of the shoes were the same red as my top but were a black lace-up style with a bow halfway between the toes and the ankle. As for accessories? I chose a silver, spiral-design cuff bracelet, a silver slide necklace that carried a matching spiral pendant and a simple silver band ring on my right hand.

Off we went to get ready. Emma and Giselle headed back to Ryan's. They told us the plan was that Justin and Ryan would be picking us up at nine, just as Justin said earlier, and they'd be meeting us at the club. Giselle wanted to come pick us up so we had more girl time, but the guys insisted they be the ones to come get us.

So, at nine, our doorbell rang. We had said good night to the kids and put them to bed and were sitting at the dining room table having a late snack before going out. Alice got up and got the door.

"Hi," she said as she opened the door.

"Wow, Alice. You look beautiful." Ryan stepped through the door, took her in his arms and passionately kissed her.

After she regained her footing, she laughed. "Thank you, but if you do that again, I'll have to reapply my lipstick."

We all laughed as Ryan looked around the corner at me. "Hey, Vivianne. How are you tonight?"

"I am fantastic." I got up to put our dishes in the sink. "Where's Justin?"

Justin walked into the apartment as I asked. I saw a glimpse of him from around the corner as I finished rinsing the dishes. He was his usual dapper self in a pinstripe suit, untucked, white, button-up dress shirt and his black and white Converse All-Stars.

"Didn't I say I'd meet you outside your door at nine?" His hands were clasped behind his back, and he had a confident swagger in his step as he hollered back to me.

"I'm sorry," I said as I walked around the corner into view.

He stopped as he saw me. I saw his eyebrows lift, his eyes got wider and his jaw fell open slightly. I tried to remain casual, but I knew that I was anything but casual in that outfit, and I can't say it didn't make me feel just that much more awkward.

"What do you think?" I did a little spin.

He shook his head slightly, blinking his eyes and pulled his jaw up. "Wow, Vivianne. To be honest, I'm a little concerned."

"Concerned?" I asked. I couldn't imagine why he would be concerned. That is, unless he didn't like the outfit.

He walked over to me. "Yeah. I'm concerned that every man in that place is going to be captivated by you, and you're going to find some big, London bloke to run off with."

I pushed him back a step and laughed. "Oh, yeah. You know, because there's so many other men out there more fitting for me. I'm just looking for a reason to trade up." I started to walk past him towards Alice and Ryan, who were locked together in the doorway, talking.

"So I get to be the proud man with you on his arm tonight while the others drool, wishing they were me?" He started to follow me.

I stopped and turned towards him. "Not as proud as I am to be on your arm. Look at you. You're gorgeous." I smirked and started for the door again.

He stepped quickly right up behind me, gently grabbed me by my shoulders, pulled me to a stop and put his lips to my ear, whispering, "Vivianne, you don't know what you do to me, do you?" He let go of my shoulders and walked past me.

His words sent shivers down my spine. *Tonight is going to be very interesting*, I thought to myself. I just smiled and headed for the car.

We met up with everyone else outside the club. Emma, Reggie, Giselle, Adam and Bret were all there waiting for us. Emma and Giselle looked hot, and I remember thinking that I couldn't compare with them. However, to my surprise, they raved about Alice and me as we got out of the car. It was borderline embarrassing, but it was nice at the same time.

We all sauntered up to the club. No one was surprised when people started calling out to Ryan and Justin and reaching out for their attention. Then there were the camera flashes from both the fans and the tabloid reporters that were waiting outside the club for anyone interesting.

Ryan took Alice by the hand and pulled her towards the club doors. Justin threw his arm around me protectively as we all started to walk a little faster. You could hear several of the women moan in disapproval. He didn't look up once but did look over at me a couple of times with a look of concern on his face. I could only assume he was wondering if I was ok with all the attention.

Of course, despite the rather long line out front, we were let right in. It was a beautiful club, a remodeled eighteenth century ballroom. There were ornate carving in the woodwork throughout and a balcony floor that surrounded the main dance floor, overlooking the whole thing. Also, there was a separate bar room and two separate lounges on the main floor.

We were greeted by one of the workers who showed us to a private area on the balcony floor. It was a great little area where you could watch the dance floor. Plus, it had very limited access. So, that was nice to have a place to go away from the fans and the crowd.

We all ordered our first drinks of the night and settled into the area. I walked over to the edge and leaned on the railing, looking down at the people dancing. Justin walked up next to me and watched me as I watched the people below.

"What are you thinking?" he asked.

I smiled slightly. "Analyzing the crowd."

He looked around the room below and back to me. "And?"

"I think I will enjoy dancing tonight." I nodded.

"Oh, that's right. I heard you used to be a dancer?" He leaned towards me a little.

I kept looking at the crowd. "Yes. I used to freelance for clubs. I'd get paid a little to come and dance from open to close to get others on the dance floor. It was fun."

"I take it dancing is a passion of yours?" He sounded truly curious.

I stood up straight and blinked. "Yeah. I guess you can say that." I looked at him. "Some people have sitting in a quiet room. Some people have hiking in the mountains. My meditation? Dancing. It's more than a passion. I'd have to say it's more of a therapy."

"Huh." He scrunched his eyebrows. "I learn something more about you every day."

"Do you dance?" I asked.

He smiled. "A little."

"Are you going to dance with me tonight?" I wrapped my arm around his and turned back towards the crowded room.

He sighed, "Maybe."

We stood there for a moment, quietly watching the crowd. It was nice to have someone that could appreciate people-watching as much as I do. Finally, Giselle came over and grabbed my free arm.

"Alice says you're a dancer?" Giselle sounded excited.

I blinked, not expecting that. "Um, yeah?"

She pulled me from Justin. "Let's go then!"

I looked back and waved to everyone, almost as excited as she seemed to be. We took off down the hall as I heard Alice say, "And it begins." She got up and grabbed Emma, looking at Justin. "We'll be back, but I'm not sure you'll see Vivianne the rest of the night," she laughed as they caught up with us.

We found our place on the dance floor. At first, as usual, I swayed a little as I read the surrounding dancers and got into the music. It was a mix of top forties, nineties and eighties dance, some light goth/ industrial and rave music. I was glad since it was music I could get into. It wasn't often that I could find a club with such diversity and be able to mix it well.

Alice started right off. She and Giselle got into a groove right away as Emma more or less watched them with a half-attempt at dancing. She was having fun, but she didn't get into dancing like we did.

Before I knew it, another song came on. First, "So What" by Pink, "Stronger" by Kanye West, "Gett Off" by Prince, "Drilled a Wire through My Cheek" by Blue October, "If You Seek Amy" by Brittany Spears and finally the music slowed down with "Protection" by Massive Attack.

I was lost in the music. Halfway through "Protection," I looked around and noticed the others had left the dance floor. I then noticed that there were few other people on the dance floor with me. I kept on dancing, but it dawned on me that I felt eyes on me.

I looked up. Just as my feelings told me, there were several pairs of eyes on me from our little area on the balcony, Justin included. My heart skipped a beat. I wasn't sure why they were all watching me. I hadn't been dancing a lot for a while. Maybe I looked as out of practice as I suddenly found myself feeling.

The song changed, and I thought about getting off the dance floor. However, it was "Eye" by Smashing Pumpkins. I couldn't walk off. I was actually surprised at how dancing still had such a hold on me. The music picked back up in tempo from there, and it was another five songs after that before I took a break.

I stopped dancing, realizing I was in need of a glass of water, desperately. I looked up to our balcony area to see Justin still watching me. He was casually leaned on the railing in the same manner I'd left him. I couldn't help but wonder if he'd left that railing since I left the balcony.

I headed for the bar, got myself a glass of water and walked upstairs. I was about halfway to our area when Alice came towards me. She had that look of 'I've got to tell you' on her face.

"Yes?" I spoke first.

She placed her hands on my arms. "I'm not sure you want to go in there."

"Why not?" I thought that was a silly notion. Why wouldn't I?

"Well?" She smirked. "Let's just say you haven't lost your... talent?"

"What are you talking about?" I was getting frustrated.

She let go of me and crossed her arms. "Ok. You've been watched, and pretty much everyone has been taken by your dancing. You know, like what used to happen to you? Justin hasn't left the railing the whole time."

"Whatever," I scoffed. "I'm sure you're exaggerating."

"Ok?" She shrugged. "Go ahead and see for yourself." She motioned down the hall.

I couldn't imagine that people as talented as they were could see my club dancing as anything special. It was just club dancing. Plus, I didn't really dance like the others there. I knew I stood out, but I just never saw my dancing as special, just different. Not even when I did it for a living, did I think I was special. I just thought I wasn't bad. I would dance a night away. I was always surprised when people complimented me.

However, when I walked into the area, I was shown I was wrong. Everyone started clapping as I came in. I turned red. I had always been told I was good, but for some reason, this group of people made the compliment different.

Adam looked around as I walked up. "Wow, Vivianne. You didn't tell us that you could dance."

"Ok? I can dance. So can Alice." I pointed at her.

Alice laughed. "Sure, I can move to the beat, but Viv? You can dance. Can't she, Justin?"

The song changed to a slower tune, "A Woman's Worth" by Alicia Keys. Justin had turned away from the dance floor and was leaning his side on the railing. He held his hand out and motioned with a nod for me to come to him.

He was like a magnet for me. I couldn't ever seem to deny him. I don't think I ever even hesitated. I took his hand as I walked up to him. He took my empty glass, set it down and he pulled me in tight. He threw my arms around his neck and wrapped his arms around my waist as we started to sway to the music.

He never looked away from my eyes. As the music picked up, so did his lead. I heard Alice at one point telling us to go to the dance floor, but we just kept our focus on each other. I was locked on his gaze as I was shown that I wasn't the only one of us that could dance.

After the song was over, he handed me a fresh glass of water and said, "I thought you might need this."

"Thank you." I drank down half the glass.

"You know, you are so beautiful." He brushed my hair from my face.

I looked up at him. "Even all sweaty?" I cleared my throat. "Thank you."

"I couldn't help but watch you dance. Where did you learn to dance like that?" he asked.

I shrugged. "I've always danced like that. I mean, I worked clubs and all, but my style hasn't really changed much from when I first started going."

"Huh." He smiled. "I think I might go stand with the guys before we get asked to go somewhere besides the dance floor."

He kissed me on the forehead and joined the guys on the other side of the room before I could reply. I watched him walk away, a bit stunned by his comment, then worked on the rest of my water while leaning over the railing and watching the crowd below. I wanted to go back down to dance more, but I was in need of a break, and another glass of water.

It wasn't long before several in the group were ready to go back to dancing, and of course, I was pulled along. Justin waved us on, deciding to stay behind with Emma, Reggie and Adam. I grabbed water on the way.

As we danced, I would look up and see Justin looking down. He actually encouraged me when he watched me. Normally, someone watching me would have made me uncomfortable, but not him. I could feel that he wasn't judging me. He just wanted to watch me dance.

The guys decided they were done after a couple songs, but Giselle and Alice stayed out with me. Of course, we were approached every once in a while by persistent, drunken guys. However, it wasn't difficult to get rid of them for the most part.

Later on, Ryan and Alice paired off and Justin came and joined me. The night flew by even though we had moments that someone would recognize Ryan or Justin, but we'd just all head up to the private area, and the attention would subside.

Up at the tables at the end of the night, we were sitting around just chatting. Alice was sitting at the table next to mine. We kept exchanging mischievous looks. Finally, I wadded up my drink napkin and threw it at her. It went right down the front of her dress.

She glared at me for a moment before cracking up and shouting, "Yeah, thanks for growing up."

I almost fell off my chair laughing. The rest of the group looked at us, wondering what we were laughing about. We both held up our hands and shook our heads.

"I don't know what you're talking about," I lied.

Alice threw it back at me, starting a momentary napkin war.

Shortly after, we headed out to walk to a nearby diner for a late night meal. Everyone was laughing and joking around as we were walking down the sidewalk. Giselle, Alice and I were dancing as we walked.

Not far away, I realized I had left my cell phone inside. I asked everyone to wait while I ran back. I walked up to where we were hanging out and found it on the table. I was relieved and hurried back outside. I noticed a man followed me out, but I didn't think anything of it until he grabbed my arm just outside the club.

317

He was rough in his actions and was slurring his words. "Hey baby, I saw you dancing tonight, and I'd like to take you home with me."

"Forward, aren't we?" I pulled away. "Thanks but no thanks. I am with my boyfriend."

"I'm sure your boyfriend doesn't do the things I'd do to you." He got even more explicit.

I looked him in the eyes. "I said no, thank you. I'm going to go now."

He tried to grab my arm again as I started walking away. "Hey, come on, you know you want this." He pushed me up against the wall.

"I really don't. Get off me!" I tried to shove him off.

He was pressing harder against me and trying to kiss me. I kept turning my head to avoid contact, but my pushing was getting nowhere. There was a part of me that started to panic. I looked around but couldn't see anyone--everyone was too far down the road to really see anything. I wasn't sure they could even hear what was going on.

I screamed, "Get off me!" and shoved.

It only encouraged him more. He grabbed my shoulders and pulled me around the corner into the alley and threw me against the dumpster. The back of my head slammed into it as I fell to the ground.

He stumbled over top of me and started to fumble with his belt. I tried to scramble to my feet but the pain in my head was intense, and I hadn't had time to gather my wits. I closed my eyes, shook my head and blindly kicked at his legs.

He dropped down on top of my legs. I couldn't move them. Then, he started trying to go for my zipper.

I heard myself screaming for him to get off me again and yelling for someone to help me. I was hitting him, but he didn't even seem to notice.

I didn't know if anyone knew where I was. Had anyone heard me scream? Could they hear my screams now?

My eyes were tightly closed when I felt the weight of the man disappear. I opened my eyes to see Justin pulling him off of me. Then, I noticed everyone else coming around the corner. Alice, Emma and Giselle came running over to me to help me get up and check to see if I was ok.

I looked at Justin. There was a rage in his eyes that was exacerbated by his protectiveness over me. He threw the man against the wall on the other side of the alley and threw a solid punch against his jaw. The man crumpled to the ground as Justin reached for him.

Ryan and the others went to Justin and held him back. The man fell back to the ground as they pulled Justin back. We could all see he was not going to stop there without someone calming him down. Adam and Bret picked the man up and shoved him back against the wall to keep him from getting away.

Alice went and put a hand on Justin's shoulder. "Justin?"

He didn't answer.

"Justin," she tried again. "You should really go and see if Vivianne needs you."

He just looked at her for a moment. Then his face changed from rage to worry and panic. He searched frantically around the alley for me until he saw me sitting against the wall with my knees pulled up to my chest and my arms wrapped around them.

He rushed over and knelt next to me. "Are you all right?" There was still a strong tone of ferocity in his voice.

"I think so." I tried to keep it together.

I felt his hands on mine, but I didn't move. I wanted to reach out and throw myself into him, but I was still so full of emotion. I didn't know if I was full of rage, full of fear or what. I just told myself that if I stayed sitting just like I was, I wouldn't have to react considering I didn't know if I was going to go over to that guy and hurt him or start crying and not be able to stop.

He stood up and looked over at Ryan and the guys who were still holding the man against the wall. Reggie had called the police. Justin looked back at me and then to Alice. I could see he couldn't decide what to do either. I know he wasn't done with the man when Ryan pulled them apart, but he didn't seem to want to leave me either.

Ryan walked over to Justin and put a hand on his shoulder. "Listen, I know you want to take this asshole out, but we've got this. Alice is right, Vivianne needs you. Let us take care of him. He's not getting away."

Justin nodded. "I know. I just want one more good hit."

Alice chimed in. "I'm pretty sure, by the look of him, you did a good enough job with the first one. However, I didn't get a chance. So, how about my turn? I'd like to lay him out."

"Oh, that slut deserved it," the man coughed out. "And you, Miss Thing, I'd like a chance at you, too."

Ryan turned towards the man, bewildered at his audacity. Justin started after him, but Ryan stuck his arm out to hold him back. He stepped up to the man and looked at him for a moment.

"Really, sir?" he asked.

The man scoffed at Ryan. "What? You guys with these sluts?"

Ryan looked back at us and back at the man. Without saying anything, he landed a blow to the man's chin that sent his head back into the wall. He started falling to the ground, but the guys held him up.

Ryan turned back to Justin. "Was that a good alternative?"

Justin laughed. "You know... it was." He patted Ryan on the back and returned to my side.

"Are you sure you're ok?" he asked as he kneeled back down next to me. "We heard a lot of banging, and he's not a small guy. Are you sure he didn't hurt you?"

"I don't think I'm hurt," I said, trying to evaluate my head and body. Then it dawned on me that my head hurt. I raised my hand to the back of my head. "Oh, he slammed my head pretty hard against the something."

Justin leaned in quickly to look at my head, feeling for a lump. "There's no lump, but we had better tell them when they get here to have the paramedics look at you." His eyes grew more serious. "Wow, and that," he said, pulling my right shoulder around to get a better look.

That's when I noticed the blood. I had managed to cut my shoulder pretty bad during the struggle. Then, I noticed all the little cuts on my hands. The new ones on top of the ones I got during the outing several days prior. I got embarrassed. I wasn't sure why, but I was. I slid my hands out of sight and pressed my shoulder against the wall.

"I am sure it's nothing. I had a couple of drinks tonight. I'm probably just bleeding more because of that." I tried to make it seem less than it was.

"Still, you should get looked at." He stood back up.

"Sure," I conceded.

Justin started pacing while we waited. At one point, one of the bouncers came down to make sure things were under control. Justin didn't get very far away from me as he paced. It was a very protective gesture, and as I came out of shock, I appreciated that gesture.

He kept looking up and down the street, watching for the police and the paramedics. Then he'd look back to me as he paced back by us, making sure I was ok and Alice or one of the others were still with me. After a few minutes, we heard sirens coming down the road.

The man struggled to get away harder, but the guys kept their hold on him. Adam threw an elbow into the man's face, getting the point across that he wasn't getting away. Bret rushed out to the curb to flag them in as Justin came right to my side.

"Let's get you out of here." He reached for my hands.

I really didn't think I was ready to move, but I reached out for him anyway. He bent down, put one of my arms around his shoulder and pulled me up by my waist. I wasn't stable on my feet, to my surprise. He helped brace me as we headed out to the sidewalk.

The police got there quickly. A couple of the officers went over to the man and took over for the guys. Soon after, the paramedics pulled up. They came rushing out with their medical bags. I couldn't help but feel like the whole thing was being overdone, but I went along with it to make them feel better.

I started to notice flashes from down the sidewalk. I looked at Justin who was firmly stationed next to me. "You and Ryan should get out of here."

"Not a chance. I'm not leaving you here alone," he insisted.

"I'm not alone. The rest of the group can stay here, but there's people taking pictures. This is going to get plastered all over the papers, and you don't need that," I tried to convince him.

"Vivianne, I really don't think it matters. I just want to make sure you're all right," he replied.

"Ryan." I waved him over. "You need to take Justin and get you both out of here. People are taking pictures. Just go to your place, and we'll come there when we take care of this."

"All right. The police want to ask Justin some questions, but we'll get out of here as soon as we can," he nodded.

Justin looked at me pleadingly, but I just leaned up and kissed him. "I'm fine. I'll see you soon. Get out of here before this becomes a media circus." I realized what to say to convince him. "I don't need that."

He leaned back over and kissed me on the forehead. "Ok. Just promise you'll call my cell if you need anything."

"I'll be there soon," I promised.

Ryan came back over. "The police said they'd come by the house to ask their questions. Let's go." He kissed Alice and started back for the cars. She whispered something in Ryan's ear. He looked over at me for a moment and back at Alice, nodding like he understood. "I'll tell him."

Justin looked at me to make sure I was sure I wanted him to go.

"Yes. I'll be there before you know it," I insisted before he could say anything.

He got up and followed Ryan. I waited for a moment to make sure he was far enough down the sidewalk. The paramedics were cleaning up my shoulder, and the police were asking everyone questions about what happened.

Once he was far enough away, I grabbed Alice's arm. "What did you whisper to Ryan?"

"Nothing. Don't worry about it." She tried to blow it off.

I tightened my grip on her arm. "No, I won't forget about it. He looked at me funny. What did you say to him?"

She shrugged. "I just told him that you used to have run-ins like this when you used to dance all the time. Not this bad, but that you would be fine."

"Oh, great." I shook my head. "I can only imagine how that's going to go when he tells Justin."

Alice just shrugged again. "I was aiming for setting his mind at ease."

I looked down. "For some reason, I think it's going to make him see me as more of a victim and worry him more."

The paramedics finished looking me over, cleaning the wounds and bandaging me up. Then, I answered all of the questions the police asked. The officer asking the questions told me we could go, and they would be at the house shortly after they transported the man to the station.

We all headed over to the cars. People were gathered in a crowd outside the club, watching the chaos. Some were still taking pictures and asking what happened. Some were shouting questions about the guys and our relationships with them as we walked by. We just ignored everyone and tried to hurry past them. Part of me wished Justin was there with me, but I knew he didn't need any of this, and neither of us needed any more of it landing in the papers than it already was.

Back at Ryan's, Justin came out to the car as we pulled up, almost running as he approached. His look was serious yet focused. He opened my door, threw a coat over me, rushing me in from the cold.

"I stopped by your apartment and had Tiffany get me some things for you. I hope you don't mind," he said as we closed the door behind us.

"The police should be here soon. Are you ok?" I asked him.

"Am I ok?" He looked stunned.

"Yeah." I chuckled. "You seem more worked up than I am."

He guided me to our chair in the living room. "Well? To be honest, I don't know what I would have done if Ryan and the guys hadn't come up. I have never had so much anger before. I just reacted when I heard you screaming." He took a deep breath to calm himself.

"I'm just glad that you were not hurt any more than you were."

I curled up on his chest. "Thank you. I'm not sure what I would have done if you hadn't showed up."

The police were not far behind me. Alice and Ryan walked them into the living room. They asked us all a barrage of questions. We were exhausted by the time they were finished, but were pretty sure they had a clear picture of what happened. They assured us he'd be taken care of, took our information and said they'd call us if they needed any more information.

As soon as they left, Justin looked at Alice. "Are you staying here then?"

"Yeah. I called Tiffany to fill her in. She was pretty confused about what happened. I told her we wouldn't be coming there tonight. I didn't think the kids needed to see us like this."

"Ok? Where are we staying then?" I asked.

"Ryan said you could stay in his spare room," Alice replied.

"Or," Justin added, "You can come to my place. Call me protective, but I kind of don't want to let you out of my sight."

"Ok?" I looked at Alice.

"You know," she said. "That's not a bad idea. I'll stay here, and you can go to Justin's apartment. That way, I know you're not alone. He can check on you through the night."

"I really am fine, guys," I insisted.

"Still," Alice said. "You hit your head, and I don't think it's a good idea for the kids to see you right now with your bandages and all. Just wait. Tiffany said she's got the kids, and Justin got you everything you need to stay. So, pick. Here with us or with Justin?"

"With Justin," I looked at him.

"Thank you," he whispered. "I'd like to get going then. We could all use a good night's sleep."

"I agree," Ryan said. "I'm going to go make something to eat and go to sleep. Is that ok with you, Alice?"

"Yes. Food sounds good." She stood up. "I'll see you in the morning?"

"Yeah. Brunch." I hugged her.

Ryan gave the keys to the car to Justin. We said our goodbyes and headed out. He held my arm all the way out to the car and helped me in, doing the same into his apartment. He ran outside for my bag after making sure I was comfortable on the couch.

"Are there pajamas in there?" I asked when he came back in.

"I believe so." He handed me the bag.

"Good." I headed towards the bathroom. "I'll be right back."

I went into the bathroom and looked through the items Tiffany had packed. There was the usual toiletries, a pair of jeans, sweater, long-sleeved shirt, a casual dress, undergarments, casual shoes and a pair of dress shoes. Also, a note and two pairs of pajamas.

Vivianne,

I didn't know what all you needed, nor do I know what's going on. So, I tried to pack light but have a variety. As far as pajamas, I packed two. One is just

your regular lounging pants and matching shirt. The
other is a cute nighty I found in your drawer. I hope
you don't mind, but I thought you might want it. I hope
everything is ok. Justin seems a little upset
I'll see you tomorrow. Have a good night.

--Tiffany

I chose the nighty. I held it up to take one last look at it before putting it on. It was a dark blue baby doll style nightgown with thin straps and had a small, white and green floral print all over. The material was lightweight cotton. So, it wasn't too sexy, but it wasn't frumpy. It was also very comfortable.

When I came back into the living room, he had changed into sweats and a T-shirt. He sat up and looked at me, trying to assess if I was still all right, and then smiled. I walked over and sat next to him on the couch.

He slid a leg behind me and pulled me into him, wrapped his arms around me and laid his head against mine. I curled up on my side and moved my head onto his chest. I could hear his heart slow and his breathing become less jagged. I took a couple deep breaths, and he tightened his hold in response. That's when I fell apart.

I started crying. He just let me cry for a few minutes, rubbing my arms to comfort me and brushing my hair from my face. When my sobs came slower, he pulled me up and wiped my tears.

"You're not ok," he said softly.

I drew a rough, deep breath. "Yes, I am. I just have never had anyone there for me like this before."

"Ryan said that Alice had told him you've had to go through things like this before." He sounded apprehensive to bring it up.

I looked down. "Yeah. Close clubs most nights, and you run into a few unsavory types from time to time, but nothing quite this bad. I've usually been able to convince them to leave me alone or someone walks by and scares them off."

"I am so sorry I didn't walk back with you. I should have…"

I cut him off. "Don't even go there. You were there, and I can't think of the words to thank you enough." I sat up.

"Vivianne, I…"

I grabbed his shirt and pulled him in to me, kissing him deeply. "You came, and that's what matters. I am fine, and you are the one that I have to thank for that. I know what you're saying, but nothing more happened. I just want to relax and try to salvage the rest of the night."

He smiled and kissed my cheek. "You are truly amazing, Vivianne."

I stood up. "Can I get something to drink?"

"Yeah, what would you like?" he asked.

"Just a soda." I headed to the kitchen.

He followed me in and took a Pepsi from the fridge. "Pepsi ok?"

"Perfect, thank you." I took a drink.

We stood there, talking for a while. I could tell he was worried about me, but he was doing as I asked and avoiding the topic. After a while, we wandered back into the living room and sat on the couch.

"Ok. I know you want to talk about it, and I think I am calmed down enough to do that." I changed the subject.

"Do you want to?" he asked.

I smiled. "I should. I know I feel fine, but I know I was pretty shook up, and if nothing else, I know you have questions. So, ask me what you want to, and I'll answer."

"I really don't know what to ask. I mean, it's more that I want to make sure you're ok physically and emotionally and apologize for not being with you so he wouldn't have even thought to approach you." He scrunched his eyebrows as he talked.

"How could any of us have known? Do you think if I could have known that I would have gone back into the club alone?" I pointed out.

He nodded. "Ok. Fair enough. Yet I just can't help but think that I could have stopped him sooner if not altogether."

I put my hand on his cheek. "I know, but you can't dwell on that. Just know that you were the reason he didn't get farther. If it wasn't for you… I don't want to think about what could have happened." I shuddered.

He turned so his body was turned towards me. "How's your shoulder?" He looked at the bandage.

I felt around the tape holding the gauze down as I turned towards him. "I think it's ok. It's a little tender but not bad."

He pulled my hands in front of him and turned my palms up. "And your hands?"

"Oh, they're fine. Just small scrapes from the cement." I flexed my fingers.

He reached up with both hands and brushed my hair back. "And your head?"

"My head?" My breath caught.

He smiled. "Yeah, where you hit it.

"Oh, yeah." I blinked. "I'm fine, really."

We sat there for a moment just staring at each other. The rest of the world seemed to just disappear and take the stress of the night with it. I felt a sense of safety with him, and in moments like this, I had never felt so alive. He ignited something in me that I hadn't ever truly felt before, and I couldn't pull myself away from it… or him.

"Vivianne." He didn't break his gaze.

"Yes?" I answered.

He finally blinked and took my hands. "I know that we haven't known each other long by any standards, but…" he paused. "Well?"

"Yeah?" I tilted my head to catch his view.

He looked up at me. "I knew that I was pulled to knowing you in New York. When I saw you last weekend at Ryan's Christmas party, it took everything I had to stop myself from walking up to you, even before Alice pointed you out to me. Plus, this whole week has been amazing."

I smiled. "Yes. This week has been… more than I expected, to say the least."

"Well, tonight made me realize something." His eyes refused to hide his hesitation.

"What?" I felt my smile turn to a look of concern. I sat up and scooted back a bit. "I'm sorry. That ruined it, didn't it? It's too real for you. I'm too much trouble." I was babbling.

He scooted closer to me and took my hands back in his. "No. nothing like that. Actually, just the opposite."

"What do you mean?" I couldn't believe what he was saying.

"When I heard you scream, I didn't hesitate. I ran back toward the club, looking for you. Once I saw him over you, I just wanted to kill him. I was so afraid he had hurt you, more than he already had, that I was willing to do anything to get him away from you." He put one of my hands to his chest. "At one point, a thought that I could have lost you ran through my mind. I don't want to ever think that again."

"Well? If what you are trying to tell me is to not walk alone like that again, I'll make sure not to if it'll make you feel better." I searched his eyes.

"No." He swallowed hard, taking in a deep breath. He looked me in the eyes. "Vivianne, I am falling in love with you."

I couldn't say anything. I couldn't believe that was what he said, then he spoke again. "No. that's wrong. I *am* in love with you. I've never been so sure in my entire life of anything, but I am sure that I love you, and I don't want anything to take you away from me."

I sat straight up and took my turn at a deep breath. "Justin, are you sure the intensity of the situation hasn't made your feelings feel like more than they are?"

"That wasn't the response I expected." He laughed. "No. I was thinking that was where my emotions were going before. Tonight just put it in the spotlight. You don't have to say it back if you don't feel that way. I just want you to know how I feel."

I put my forehead to his, our noses were touching. "I love you, too."

"Are you sure?" His eyes were closed.

I flashed back to the conversation I had with the others about this very thing. "Without a doubt." I closed my eyes and kissed him.

I felt his hands touch my hips and run up my sides, sliding back to brace me as he laid me back on the couch. His body pressed down on mine. I could feel his body heat getting higher as he followed the curves of my figure with his hands. The kiss grew more passionate and more intense.

He broke from my lips and lifted himself back away from me. Staring at me for a moment, he gave me a gentle kiss and got up from the couch, picking me up and carrying me into the bedroom. He laid me down on the bed and took off his shirt.

I sat up on my knees and pulled him to the edge of the bed. He lifted my chin and brushed his lips over mine, returning to the kiss just as passionately and intensely as before. He climbed onto the bed and guided me over to the pillows.

His fingers traced my curves, his caress more detailed and far more sensual than before. I was having trouble finding a stride in my breathing. I caught my breath as he moved his lips to my neck. I tilted my head back and moaned.

His hands found their way to my shoulders. He wrapped his fingers around the straps to my nightgown and slid them down. He kissed my skin as he pulled the material down, exposing more and more until he stopped at my waist. I felt each kiss on his way back to my lips like they were small electrical shocks.

He wrapped his arms around me as I wrapped mine around him. The skin-on-skin contact was enough to send my heart into fluttering. I calmed my breathing and concentrated on his. I could hear the longing and an almost animalistic quality to it.

I scooted up to gain a little footing. I wasn't ready to give in yet. I wasn't sure this was really happening. Had he really told me that he loves me? Was he really there with me in his bed?

I was trying to process it when I felt his grip get stronger and a moan escaped his lips. I melted and gave in. Before I knew it, neither of us had any clothes left on, and we were locked together in more passion than I could have imagined possible.

My moans grew stronger and louder. They only seemed to encourage him as he moved over me. He seemed to know exactly where to touch me and how to move with a surgeon's precision. By the sounds of his moans and how his eyes would close with every pause of his breath, I wasn't far off the mark with him.

As he slid his hands over me, I felt how soft his hands were and how gentle his touch was even with the fierce hunger showing in his eyes. He was attentive to every part of me and every need I had while delving deeper and deeper into the passion that was taking over both of us.

The intensity grew with each passing moment. Our hands memorized each line and dip in each other's frames as our lips sent shocks through the other's body with every brush of our lips on the other's skin.

My body was shaking almost violently as I felt his muscles contract. I heard my moans get louder and a purely animalistic growl in his throat. He grabbed the headboard with one hand and pulled me into him with the other arm. Our breathing was coming faster and faster.

I opened my eyes and looked at him. His eyes slowly opened, and he saw me looking at him. He smiled. I pulled his face to mine, kissed him deeply just before I was thrown back against the pillows in an overwhelming wave of ecstasy. I wasn't sure which was louder, my screams or the moans I heard coming from him as he gripped the headboard and the pillow as hard as he could.

He collapsed on top of me, still breathing fast. We were both completely sweaty, out of breath and still allowing little moans of exhaustion and ecstasy to escape us. He pulled himself up enough to move back so he could look at me again.

I smiled and started kissing him repeatedly. I wasn't sure where the energy came from, but I just wanted more. I gave into the exhaustion and fell back into the pillows again. He carefully climbed over next to me and lay down, curling me into him with his arms around me.

He pulled the blanket up over us and relaxed around me. Every once in a while, he would brush his lips over my neck and kiss me gently. After a few minutes, he leaned over and picked up a remote off the nightstand.

"I have a song that I'd like to play for you." He skipped through the tracks of a CD.

The song started with a piano chord. He paused it and leaned up on one arm, "This is Blue October's '18th

Floor Balcony'. It has hit home for me over the last few days, and I want you to hear it."

I nodded, lifting myself up on my elbows.

He hit play again, and the piano chords rang out. He sat up and sang along with the lyrics.

I close my eyes and I smile
Knowing that everything is all right
To the core
So close that door. Is this happening?

I closed my eyes and took a deep breath, taking in the lyrics. He continued to sing along, his emotions coming through in his voice.

And I'll try to sleep to keep you in my dreams 'til I can bring you home with me

My heart faltered at the sentiment expressed. I giggled at myself and almost had to shake myself into reality. I looked up at him; we smiled a soft smile at each other. The final chorus rang out as he ran his fingers along my arm.

So here we are on this 18th floor balcony, yeah
I knew it from the start. My arms are open wide
Your head is on my stomach. No, we're not going to sleep
Here we are on this 18th floor balcony... we're both...
Flying away

His voice went perfectly with the lyrics. Or maybe it was that I was listening more to him than the singer despite the singer being great on his own accord. But seeing that emotion stirred something in me. Knowing he was singing it was because of me? Well, you know. It was romantic. It was… just like him and why I loved him so much.

"I didn't know you could sing," I said.

He let out a quiet laugh. "I dabble a little with a band."

"You have a great voice," I complimented him.

"I'd like for you to hear us play some time." He pulled me in tighter.

I sighed. "I would like that."

We lay down and cuddled up to each other. I was just about asleep when I felt his arms tighten very slightly, and I heard him sigh.

"What?" I asked.

"Nothing." He kissed my cheek. "I'm just happy."

"Good." I smiled and squeezed his arms.

"Vivianne?" he whispered.

"Yeah?"

"I love you."

My heart skipped a beat again. My breath caught in my chest. My head felt like the world was spinning. I could hardly believe that I could be this fortunate. A surge of emotions hit me that made tears well up in my eyes in response. I really did love this man, even if it came on so quickly.

I buried my face in his chest and smiled even more. "I love you, too."

I laid there in his arms, pressed up against him with my head on his chest, and fell asleep. We stayed like that all night, content to be with each other. I hadn't remembered ever sleeping that soundly in my life, and I never wanted it to end.

Chapter Thirteen

Revelations and Declarations

The next morning, I woke up to him running his fingers through my hair. "Did I wake you?" he asked.

"No," I replied.

"How are you this morning?" He leaned back to look at me.

I smiled, not knowing exactly what to say. The swirl of emotions came back with force. My eyes welled up again so I turned my face away, hoping he wouldn't notice.

"I'm great," I sniffled.

He leaned back more and pulled my face up to look at him again. "What's wrong?" He was worried.

I shook my head. "Nothing. That's just it. I just can't believe last night with you."

"What can't you believe?" He sounded concerned. "Do you regret anything?"

"No!" I sat up. He followed suit as I continued, "That's not it at all. I mean, you are amazing and talented and gorgeous. You came to my rescue last night. You took care of me afterward. Then, how passionate and amazing you were after? As if that's not enough, you said what you said."

"And you said it back." He smiled. "I consider myself the fortunate one here. It amazes me that you think of me the way that you do when you're you. I've never met anyone like you in my life, and you seem to feel the same way about me that I do about you. I can't believe it, especially that you told me that you love me, too." He kissed me.

I pulled back. "Are you sure you don't want to take anything back? I mean, you can. I know that last night was very traumatic, and we've only known each other for a really short time. I don't want you to have said something that you might rethink later. Emotions were high, and all," I rambled.

He put a finger to my lips. "Shhh... I don't want to take anything back. I've never been one to get lost in my emotions. Nor have I ever been this deep in them before. I know this is right, and I know I meant what I said. I love you, and I want to be with you. I'm not going to rethink anything later. I am positive about this."

I felt a tear fall down my cheek. He leaned in and kissed the tear away before it fell from my chin. I closed my eyes and took a slow, deep breath as he continued to softly kiss a trail to my collarbone.

I tilted my head back and felt a hand on the center of my back, fingers spread, holding me up. His lips traced further down, along my breastbone and back up, straight up to my mouth. His kiss was forceful as he lowered me down, not losing the connection, until he pressed against me like the night before. I could taste the salt from my tear on his lips as we dove into the passion again.

I rested there, afterward, my mind reliving the recent events, a smile plastered across my face. My head was on his shoulder, and he had an arm around me. Our breathing had regained a normal pace. You could feel the mixture of peace, giddiness and exhaustion radiating from both of us.

My phone rang. He reached over and picked in up off of the nightstand. "It's Alice." "Great." I smiled and shook my head. "Hello?"

"Are you two about ready?" She sounded bouncy.

I looked at the alarm clock. "Oh crap! I didn't realize what time it was!" I sat up.

"Are you even up?" she asked.

I laughed. "Um..."

She gasped, "What?"

I avoided her obvious realization. "Ok, how long do we have?"

She cleared her throat. "It's 10:30 now. We're supposed to be at brunch at eleven. Ryan and I were going to come pick you two up in a minute, but can we?"

"All right, wait fifteen minutes and then head over. We'll rush around."

"Will do. See you in a few." She hung up.

Justin was already up and pulling on his sweats. "I take it we're running late?" He leaned back in and gave me a kiss. "I'm going to go start the shower. Would you care to join me?"

"For more than one reason." I smirked.

I got up and walked into the bathroom behind him, neglecting to put on my nightgown. I stepped right up to him and kissed him back. He moaned as I rubbed his back and pulled myself into him.

"Mmmm... You're going to make us even later than we already are." He held me close.

341

"Nope. I'm just going to make you think about last night and this morning all day," I said as I turned to get my toiletries.

"Oh, don't think I would have had a problem doing that." He walked around to my back and wrapped his arms around me, kissing my neck. He took off the bandage on my shoulder. "It looks pretty good today. You're lucky you didn't need stitches. I've got the bandages and antibacterial cream the paramedics left for you. I'll recover it after the shower."

"Thank you." I smiled.

It took everything we both had to keep our hands off each other during the shower. Of course, we slipped up here and there, but all in all, we finished up and got out pretty quick. We dried off, and he reapplied my bandage. We then got dressed in time to hear the doorbell ring.

The clock read 10:55. Justin went to the door as I returned to the bathroom to dry my hair and throw on some make-up. I heard Ryan and Justin in the living room. Alice made a bee-line right for me when Justin told her I was in there.

"So?" She burst through the door.

"So what?" I stayed focused on the mirror, putting on my eye liner.

She leaned over into view. "Oh, whatever. You both have wet hair, and you were both still in bed when I called this morning. Plus, I don't believe there's more than one bed in this apartment. So...are you really going to play me like I'm stupid?"

"We don't have time right now. We're late." I tried to stall the conversation.

Alice stepped to the doorway. "Ryan?" she shouted. He came to the hall. "Yes?"

"You might need to call your mom and tell her we're running behind and have her tell Tiffany to order for the kids. They might get restless if they don't eat." She sneered at me.

I looked at Ryan. He looked a little puzzled until he saw Justin smiling and put his hand to his head. "Oh. You ladies need to talk?"

Alice nodded. "Yup."

He shook his head. "Well, don't be too long. I'll call them and let them know."

Alice turned back around to look at me, shutting the door, firmly, behind her. "What's going on?"

I set down the eyeliner brush and smiled at her.

She gasped again. "No! Tell me! Tell me, please! What happened?!"

"Ok, but you have to promise to not judge or anything!" I pleaded.

She grabbed my hand and shook it. "Promise," she said, and sat on the side of the tub, picking up my make-up bag to rummage through.

"Well? We made love... twice." I couldn't help but smile even bigger.

"What?" She dropped the bag.

We heard a knock on the door and Justin's voice. "Are you ok in there?"

She dismissively waved at the door. "Yeah, yeah. We're fine. We'll be out in a minute." She looked back at me. "Twice?" She helped me pick up the make-up that was scattered over the floor.

343

I set the bag on the counter and went back to applying my eyeliner. "Yup. Once last night and once this morning."

"There's something more." She pointed at me, waving her finger up and down. "I can see it in your face."

I turned around and braced my back to the counter. "Ok..." I took a deep breath. "He told me he loves me."

She shot up from her seat. "What?! Already? How? When? Last night? This morning? What did you say? How could he know so soon? What are you going to do? What did you say?"

I couldn't get a word in to answer her questions, she was speaking so fast. I put my finger to my lips. "Shhhhh! They're right out there! Lower your voice."

Just then, we heard Ryan's voice, saying, "What are you thinking? How do you know this soon?"

I don't know what Justin's response was. That was the only thing we heard. However, we both giggled at the fact they seemed to be having the same conversation as we were. Then, Alice started back in on me. I was hoping they would have distracted her, but no such luck.

"Ok. Let me get this straight. You not only slept with him, but you also said the "I love you' thing?" She folded her arms.

"Yup." I finished my make-up and set the bag towards the back of the counter.

"Huh." She bit her lower lip.

I looked at her. "Oh, no, you don't. What? Now it's my turn to ask you what you're hiding. Spill it, missy."

She smiled and raised one eyebrow. "Well, I was going to tell you about my night with Ryan, but you trumped me."

"What?" I shouted, "Tell me!"

She sat back down. "Yup. After everyone left or went up to bed, he and I cleaned up the kitchen. He was telling me that I could choose where I wanted him to sleep. He said he would behave himself if I wanted to share his bed, or there was a fold-out couch in his study that he could take."

"What did you say?" I asked.

"I didn't say anything. Well, not with my voice." She had a knowing smile. "I attacked him. Thank god no one came out of their rooms. We barely made it to his room before clothes were flying off."

"Oh wow! I should have known that when you'd cave, you'd explode." I laughed. "So?"

"Well, I didn't hear any 'I love you's, but it was amazing. I'm pretty sure he's hooked." She shrugged. "What about you? You haven't said anything about how he was."

"Um. Yeah," I cleared my throat. "Wow!" A small shudder ran down my body, remembering how intense it was.

"Really?' she asked. "That good, huh?"

I curled my lips in and nodded my head. "Yup."

We walked out in time to hear Ryan saying to Justin, "Well, I trust you know what you're doing, and I'm happy for you. She seems perfect for you."

"We're ready to go," Alice announced.

345

Justin sprang to his feet and was next to me before I knew it. "Hey there, beautiful." His crooked smile had a hint of a smirk to it.

"Hi," I said softly and took hold of his arm.

We headed out to the car Ryan and Alice brought over. The ride to the restaurant was pretty quiet. Each of us was lost in thought. I leaned my head onto Justin's shoulder and almost fell back asleep. He kissed my head as we parked.

As we walked in, we noticed that everyone was there waiting for us. Emma looked at Justin. "You're late. I was getting worried after what happened last night."

"We're fine." He looked at me, smiled and put his arm around my shoulders. "We just slept in."

Mary looked up, asking, "How are you doing this morning, dear?"

"I am doing fine. Thank you for asking." I took my seat.

"That must have been rather frightening for you," she commented.

I took a drink of my water. "It was, but I was very lucky." I took Justin's hand and looked at him.

Mary looked at him. "Yes, I hear you were the hero of the day. I'm glad you were there. I'd hate to think about what might have happened if there was no one there to help her."

"Yes." He looked at me and squeezed my hand. "It makes you realize just how much you care about someone when you're faced with something happening to them." He looked back at her.

She smiled her all-knowing smile. "Yes, it does indeed. I'm glad you're all right, dear."

Adam started telling about Justin's heroics as they came around the corner and saw how he had reacted so fast when he heard me scream. We were sharing our own sides of it and leaving out the worst parts of before Justin showed up. I guess they were all floored at how he truly took off like a "superhero", as they put it, down the sidewalk to "save" me. I was amused at the animation they put in their descriptions.

Alice threw in her opinion on what she wanted to do to the man. "I would have dragged him further down the alley and left him for the rats."

"Really?" Ryan found her temper funny.

Alice laughed. "Yeah. He hurt my best friend. All bets are off. If it wasn't for there being several of you guys there, if I would have been the one to have to take care of it? There wouldn't have been anything left for the cops to deal with. No body, no crime. I've heard stories of London rats. I would have played Myth Busters."

"I adore you," Ryan said, smiling.

Alice didn't skip a beat and replied, "I love you, too."

Everyone's jaw dropped, including Ryan's. I threw my hand over my mouth to keep myself from bursting out in laughter.

Alice tried to recover. "Wait! Pause! Rewind! I adore you, too, Ryan."

Emma coughed. "Wait, wait, wait just one second."

I looked at Mary. She had the biggest grin on her face. It was as if she had been waiting for this moment.

Alice threw her hands in the air, interrupting Emma. "No, no, no. I paused and rewound that moment. There was no record button on. We're moving on."

We all looked at Ryan. I don't know if it was shock or happiness on his face, but it was a priceless look, whatever it was. He blinked and went to say something, but Alice started back up, trying to deflect from her slip-up.

"So? Anyone ready for a drink?" She looked around the table.

I laughed. "I think you might already have had one."

Everyone burst out in laughter as Alice shushed me. She kicked me under the table and gave me the look of death. "This is all your fault."

Justin saw me wince. "Really? How have you two stayed friends this long?" He glanced under the table.

"Oh, don't pretend you guys don't play rough," Alice retorted. "Besides, she gets lippy. Someone's got to put her in her place."

"So," Ryan said, changing the subject. "Vivianne, I hear you make a mean pizza."

"What?" It took a moment and a sly look from him before I realized what he was insinuating. "Oh!"

He was referring back to our pick-up line conversation. I snapped my head around to look at Justin. He quickly looked away. Alice and Ryan were laughing as Justin tried to avert his eyes. I huffed and shook my head.

Henry looked over. "I love pizza. You can come to our house and make us pizza anytime, Vivianne."

I didn't know what to say, but Alice said it all. She had been taking a drink as Henry spoke. That drink was sprayed all over the table in front of her. Ryan patted her on the back as they tried to regain their composure, laughing at me in hysterics.

"Oh, Henry," she choked out. "I am sure she'd love to come make a pizza for you. Vivianne loves to cook, and from what I know, she's an excellent chef. Isn't that right, Justin?" She sneered at him.

Justin sat up straight, swallowed hard, looked at Alice very confidently and said, "I've never had better pizza in my life. So, yeah, she's an excellent chef, if you must know."

Alice smiled and nodded at him. "Good boy."

I was pretty sure all the adults had caught on to the conversation by that point. I was also pretty sure that I had reached a new shade of red. Thankfully, the server showed up at the point with our food.

I requested a bib for Alice and quickly moved my legs out of range for her. She threw me a dirty look and went to work on her food. We all calmed down and started eating.

Emma looked down the table at us. "Guys?" She addressed Ryan and Justin, "I'm glad you both finally learned what good taste in women is. I'm also glad they're so funny. I'd hate to not get along with the ones we're going to have sticking around."

I looked at her and smiled. "Thank you. We're glad that we're welcome."

Giselle wiped her mouth with her napkin, "Welcome?" she laughed, "You both are more than welcome. If they don't keep you around, we might trade them in for you."

"I'm pretty sure none of us are going anywhere." Ryan smiled at Justin.

"Nope," Justin simply replied.

After brunch, we all split up. Alice, Tiffany and I took the kids back to our apartment to spend some time with just us. We got out the board games and shared more stories of things that happened over the last few days. As much as we missed the guys, it was nice to have some play time with the kids again.

Tina asked about the story from the Saturday night she overheard at brunch that day. I simply told her that I was not thinking and walked down a city street by myself at night. That a man tried to hurt me, but I was very lucky, and Justin saved me from him. She was so mature. She understood without me having to go into detail.

Around five, Ryan and Justin came over for dinner. I made pot roast, gravy, vegetables and rolls with brownies for dessert. Everyone cleaned their plates, to the credit of my ego. I cleaned up the dishes with Tiffany's help. She had gotten curious about what was going on.

"I don't mean to pry, but what's going on?" She smiled and nudged me as we wrapped up the leftovers.

I looked at her and smiled back. "Well? I'm assuming you mean with the guys?"

She nodded.

"Obviously, Ryan and Alice are a lot closer than they were when we first came. I have to say it's about time."

"What about you and Justin?" she pried more.

"Well?" I searched for the words to describe it. "It's a whirlwind thing. He told me he loves me last night."

She bounced and clapped, cheering for me. "What did you say?"

"I told him I love him, too, of course," I answered.

"Oh!" Her look changed. "I am so jealous! You two are so lucky! Not only do you have movie stars that like you, but you belong with them. This is definitely a fairytale. I hope you are cherishing every moment."

"Oh, don't worry about that. I'm having trouble believing it's true, but there's no doubt about that." I finished rinsing the last pan and set it in the dishwasher.

It was hard letting him go that night. We all got along so well that I had almost forgotten that he wasn't staying. It was just so natural. However, when the kids started getting ready for bed, the guys said their good nights to them and then to us.

Justin was going over to play some pool with Ryan and the guys. Alice and I had a bottle of wine planned. We walked them to the front door and were kissing them goodbye when I felt a tug on my pants.

I turned and saw Victoria standing there, looking up at us. Her little voice was so endearing as she spoke. "Mommy? Is he going to be our new Daddy?"

I had no clue what to say. That was a question I wasn't prepared to answer. I looked around at Alice, Ryan and Justin, searching for an answer.

"Why would you think that?" I asked.

She answered innocently, "Because I've only seen Daddy kiss you like that, and you don't kiss Daddy like that anymore. So, is he my new Daddy?"

My heart sank. I was at a loss for words. My eyes filled with tears, and my hand went right for my heart. My mouth was open, but no words came out.

Justin knelt down next to Victoria and answered for me, "My love for you, your sister and your Mommy is growing every day. I hope to be a large part of your lives, but your Daddy is and always will be your Daddy. Just because he and your Mommy do not love each other the same, it doesn't change how much he loves you and your sister or how much you two love him. Okay?"

She looked up at me and back at him, threw her arms around him, gave him a huge three-year-old hug and kissed his cheek. "I love you, too."

She ran off as he stood up. He looked up at me to see if I approved of his response. I was still in shock that she asked, let alone made that observation. Then, there was the fact that he handled the situation perfectly.

"Was that ok?" he asked.

"That was more than ok," I replied. "I couldn't have explained it better. Thank you."

"Well? Kids love the truth. So, that's what I told her. I do hope to be a large part of your lives. I feel like I belong in your life, and they'll have to choose what role they'll have me take on in theirs. However, I could never step between them and their father. It just wouldn't be right," he explained.

"I don't think you could have handled that better," Alice said as she took Ryan outside to give us a moment of privacy.

"I'm just surprised that you would have thought about this," I said to Justin.

He put his arms around me and gave me a hug. "I didn't say those words lightly. I thought about the weight of what they meant. I also know that your kids are a package deal with you. It's not that I'd deal with them to have you, though. I've been around them quite a bit. They're amazing kids. I see so much of you in them. That makes them easy to love, too."

I blushed. "So, I'm easy to love?"

He smiled. "Very. At least for me, I fell in love with you right away. However," he leaned in and whispered in my ear, "Pretty much everyone around you loves you." He kissed my forehead.

I smiled and kissed him good night. Neither of us wanted to let go, but Alice came back in and pried us apart.

"She's mine tonight," she laughed as she pushed him out the door.

I threw my hands in the air like I couldn't do anything about it. Ryan waved goodbye as Alice closed the door. We heard them getting into the car and drive away. We broke out more board games and that bottle of wine.

Monday morning, I woke up and laid in my bed thinking about so many things. It was difficult waking up and not having him there. One morning of waking up next to him, and I was hooked. However, we knew we'd see them soon enough.

I was lost in thought about the night before when Alice started banging on my door. "Get up, lazy butt. Emma and Giselle are waiting in the dining room for you to join us. We need to get our hair and nails done for tonight. Come on!" She walked in. "Just giving you warning in case you snuck him back in last night."

I threw a pillow at her and groaned. "What time is it?"

"It's nine." She plopped down on the bed next to me and hit me with the pillow. "Now get up."

"Ok, let me get this straight," I argued from under the pillow. "We stayed up until four in the morning last night. The party doesn't start until eight tonight. Yet, you still want me to get up at nine? What's wrong with you?"

She tore the covers off of me. "Yes. That's exactly what I am telling you. We are going to get some breakfast. Our appointments start at eleven, and there are four of us. Plus, we'll need time to come back and finish getting ready. If you get up now, I'll let you call him this afternoon. If you don't, I'm going to keep this with me all day." She held up my cell phone.

I reached for my cell, but she stood up and ran over by the doorway. "I'm going out to finish my coffee. I'll see you in five?"

"Fine," I snapped.

I got up and got myself together. We all left and had breakfast at the café on the corner. We arrived at the salon on time. I really didn't need anything done with my hair, so I just enjoyed getting a manicure and pedicure.

While the others went from hair to nails, I snuck off to call Justin. Alice had given me back my phone when we left the apartment. I walked over to the lobby and took a seat in the back corner. He and the guys were picking the last few things up for the bartender.

"Hey, love," he said as he answered his phone.

I giggled. "London is rubbing off on you... love."

"Yeah. I guess so. So, how you are ladies doing?" he asked.

"We're good. They had to drag me out of bed this morning. Alice and I stayed up until about four so when Emma and Giselle showed up to get us about nine, I was not ready to get up," I complained.

He laughed. "I bet you're tired."

"You have no idea," I sighed. "But I had to call."

"Ok? Was there something you need?" he asked.

"Yes. I needed to hear your voice." I ignored feeling silly.

"Good. I have been thinking about calling you all day," he admitted. "I'm glad you called. I woke up early and almost came to your place this morning."

"I would have loved that." I smiled.

"Next time I get the urge to, I will. Oh, I'll be at Ryan's pretty much the rest of the day to help set up. Have you and Alice figured out how you are going to get there?" he asked.

"Not yet." I hadn't thought about that. "That is, unless Alice has already talked to Ryan about it."

"Ok. Well, I left the keys to the car I've been using with Tiffany. You can take that, or I can come pick you up. It's up to you," he offered.

I thought about it for a moment. "Well? As much as I'd love to have you come and get me so I can see you before we're in a crowd, I'm sure we can just take the car."

"Are you sure?"

"Yeah. I'm sure Ryan will need your help anyway." I tried to be responsible about it. "I'd better get back in there before they realize I'm gone. I'll have them all out here in the lobby dragging me back in by my feet."

He laughed harder. "You don't need that kind of a scene. I'll let you go. Thanks for calling."

"I'll see you in a few hours."

"See you soon." I was about to hang up when I heard him again. "Vivianne?"

"Yeah?" I brought the phone back up to my ear.

"I love you," he said.

I felt a lot better hearing that, a lot less restless. "I love you, too."

"Bye." We hung up.

I walked back to where the others were getting their manicures and pedicures. Alice looked up at me and shook her head. She knew where I'd been. If for no other reason, she knew by the look on my face. She resisted the urge to tease me.

I sat and talked with everyone as they finished up. Emma and Giselle were telling us about the little they had seen as far as decorations for the party. The general consensus was that the place was going to look awesome.

Giselle was saying that their annual New Year's Eve parties were something she looked forward to every year. Their parents had always had the holiday parties when they were growing up, but when they grew up, the kids took over. Then, when Ryan had enough room in his house, he started having them and did ever since.

With his spare rooms, it made it convenient for everyone to stay together.

They dropped us back at the apartment at six to get dressed. Alice went right to her bedroom to start getting her clothes. I sat on the couch for a while first to rest. She came out a few minutes later and saw me still sitting on the couch.

"Are you going to get ready?" she asked.

I nodded. "Yeah?"

"Well?" She looked at me, puzzled. "Tonight?"

I scoffed, "Yes."

"Ok. I was thinking we might get there a little before eight," she said, hoping I was ok with that.

"All right." I reluctantly got up.

As excited as I was to see Justin, something told me I was going to need that rest. It was New Year's Eve, and I was sure we were going to be out late. However, Alice was very giddy and ready to go find her Ryan. She was getting ready in record time for her. So I figured I had better step it up.

While I was getting dressed, I started feeling the same giddiness Alice was. I found myself checking and rechecking the mirror to see how I looked. Part of me found it silly that I was back to feeling like a schoolgirl, but I did. I couldn't wait to see Justin and his reaction to seeing me.

So, as we pulled up to Ryan's about 7:30, I hardly waited until Alice put the car in park before I bounded out and up to the front door. Alice called after me to wait up, but I couldn't.

I knocked on the door, and Giselle answered. "He's in the kitchen," she said with a huge grin on her face.

357

"Thanks." I bounced past her.

The DJ was just starting for the night. The bartender was setting up the last of the bar, and the caterer was bringing out the cold dishes. The ambiance and decorations were that of a 1930s bandstand. It was classy and yet cheeky at the same time.

I was swiftly walking through the rooms and winding around busy workers on my way to the kitchen when I heard his voice. "Well hello there, gorgeous."

I spun around. "Hi." I let out a sigh and ran into his arms.

"Oof." he grunted as I crashed into his chest and hugged him. He laughed. "You ok?"

"I am now," I quickly responded, then noticed Ryan was right next to him. "Hi Ryan." I said, not lifting my head.

"Hello Vivianne." he replied.

"Wait until you see Alice." I picked my head up and nodded in her direction as she entered the room.

"Wow." His eyes grew wide. "You are..."

She sauntered up to him. "I know, but thank you for noticing." She smirked at me as she walked past to go hang her coat up.

"Would you like me to take your coat, Vivianne?" Justin asked.

"I'm not sure." I looked at him through my eyelashes and playfully batted my eyes.

He smiled. "I'm sure you look beautiful."

I let out a quick sigh and slid my coat off. He reached out to help me and kissed my shoulder. I stepped back as I let go of my coat. He threw it over his arm and looked at me. His smile turned to a sly smirk as he shook his head.

"You must be determined to make this a long night." He took a step back.

"A long night?" I asked.

He stepped back, placed a hand on my cheek and kissed me. "Yes. For two reasons. One, having to fend off the guys that'll be flirting with you all night and two, trying to keep my hands off of you in the process." He walked past me to go hang up my coat, almost with a strut.

People started showing up right at eight. The food was in place, the DJ was playing and the bartender was handing out drinks. I wandered away from the group to look around. For whatever reason, it always makes me feel better to occasionally roam through a party on my own and take it all in.

It was a really good crowd. Many of the people from the Christmas party were there. There were also quite a few others. Again, a general mix of everyday people, celebrities and artists from all walks of life. I mingled with everyone, occasionally touching base with Justin and Alice.

About two hours into the party, Justin and I were talking with Tom Scalova when Alice came up and grabbed my arm, yanking me a couple feet away. She looked like she was not happy.

"I'm going to kill the slut," she snapped.

I couldn't help but laugh, which I normally did when she got irritated, it seemed. "Who?"

"There's some skank all over Ryan." She motioned to the foyer.

"Ok? Tell her he's with you," I suggested.

She shook her head. "I did. She acts all nice to me when I'm around, but the moment she thinks I'm not watching, she's rubbing all over him and flirting."

"What does he do?" I asked, trying to catch a glimpse of him.

"Well, of course, he tries to pull away and keeps telling her he's taken, it's not the point," she huffed. "She's not getting the picture, and I'm not getting any more understanding."

"Where is she?" I started for the other room.

Alice led me into the foyer and pointed towards the woman who was trying to keep hold of Ryan's arm. He would shrug from time to time to get her off, but she would just laugh and pat his shoulder, then try again after a moment. She was butting into the conversation and trying to touch his face. It was actually embarrassing to watch.

I watched as Alice walked up to them. The woman spotted her and took a step away from Ryan, smiled wide at her and acted like she was her friend. Alice shot a glance back to me. I nodded and walked over.

I walked up to the woman and whispered, "You know, you're just embarrassing yourself."

"What do you mean?" She tried to act innocent.

I laughed. "Oh honey, you don't think you're being coy or anything, do you? Besides, you've been asked to leave him alone. He obviously doesn't want anything to do with you. So, go find someone else to rub all over."

"Listen. I don't know who you are, but mind your own business," she said with a scowl.

"Ok. You can act like that, but I'm going to warn you this once. Don't mess with my friend." I motioned to Alice, and continued, "and don't upset me. This is a fun party, but we have no problem with taking out the trash right now. So... scoot." I waved, dismissively, in the air for her to go away.

"Whatever." She flipped her hair at me and shot Alice a dirty look as she walked past us.

Justin walked up as the woman was walking away. She stuck her hand out and ran her fingers across his stomach as they passed. Alice was on the other side and caught her by the arm before she was too far away.

"Do you not know how to keep your dirty mitts to yourself?" she snarled at the woman.

"Like you two own every hot man in this place?" she snapped.

Alice shook her head. "No, but there's no reason you need to touch everything. Don't you know how to keep your hands to yourself? Or do you like coming off as a skank?"

The woman whipped around and got right up in Alice's face. I heard Ryan and Justin talking about breaking them up. I held my hand up at the guys and went towards the two irritated women.

I grabbed the woman by the skin under her bicep, pinched and pulled her away. "Why don't you come with me?"

She winced and came along reluctantly. "Ouch, ouch, ouch! Let me go, you psycho!"

I heard several people chattering behind me, but I didn't look back. I just kept dragging her towards the

361

closest door. "Oh. Do you really think this is psycho? You are as naïve as you are tactless, aren't you?"

I heard Giselle comment, "Oh, slam!" and several others laughing.

The woman looked at me. "So what? Are you their mini bodyguard?"

"No, I just care a lot about my friend's comfort, and you were making her uncomfortable by being all over her boyfriend. Who, incidentally, had already told you to leave him alone. You were being a nuisance. Then, you proved yourself to be even less classy by reaching out to another man right after. As if that wasn't disgusting enough, it was coupled by the fact that he was my boyfriend, and that just plain pissed me off. So, now you get to leave."

"You can't kick me out," she taunted.

I let her go just outside the back door and stood, leaning on the open doorway, "No? And why is that?"

"What? You're four feet tall? Like you can stop me from touching anyone I want." She waved her finger in the air.

I laughed. "Darling, I just dragged you through the house by an inch of skin and oh yeah... there's this..." I slammed the door shut in her face and locked it.

She yelled through the door. "There are other doors. Are you going to lock them all?"

"No, but just know that a lot of people just watched and heard all of that. So, if you really like humility, go ahead and come back in." I unlocked the door. "But don't think for one minute you'll be a welcome guest. Just go home and sleep it off."

I heard her huff as she stomped off. Suddenly, there was an outburst of applause from behind me. I turned around and was surprised by the decent-sized crowd standing in the kitchen.

Emma walked up and handed me a glass of wine. "Nice job Vivianne."

"Yeah, I am pretty sure she won't be coming back in tonight," Giselle laughed.

"Well, she was making things uncomfortable for a few people and had to be dealt with. I was trying to be quiet about it though." I looked around.

Alice walked up. "Oh, barely anyone noticed, but I grabbed a few people and the rest followed."

"Thanks." I wrinkled my nose at her.

Justin and Ryan came through the crowd. Ryan took Alice by the hand, nodded at me and went back to the other room. Most everyone followed after commenting to me, expressing their approval.

Justin came up, leaned in and said in a low voice, "Boyfriend, huh?"

It dawned on me that I had said that, and that he had heard the whole thing. "Oh. Um, yeah. You heard that, huh?"

"Yes, I did," he smirked.

"Well, is that a problem?" I asked, leaning back a little.

His smirk turned into a smile. "Not at all." He leaned further in and whispered, "We have said that we love each other." I heard him chuckle as he backed up to look at me. "I just liked hearing it. It was the first time you've said anything like that."

"Oh." He was right, and the realization that I hadn't said that shocked me. "Does that make me your girlfriend then?"

"To say the least." He hugged me. "To say the least."

We walked back into the living room where the DJ was set up. There was a section of the room that was changed over for a dance floor. Alice and Ryan were dancing to "To Make You Feel My Love" by Garth Brooks.

We took our place on the dance floor near them. Justin brushed my hair back and pulled me in. We swayed back and forth as I thought how easy it would be to get used to having him for these moments all the time.

I looked over at Alice when I heard her and Ryan talking. She said, "Thank you for all of this. We have been having so much fun."

He smiled. "I'm glad. I hope that you can come back soon."

"I am sure we will, but are you sure after that whole thing with your stalker?" She looked up at him through her eyelashes.

"You're so cute when you're jealous." He smiled.

Alice shook her head, "I wasn't jealous. I was annoyed. It was Viv that got jealous when the stupid woman put her hands on Justin. That's when I saw all hell break loose in her mind."

"No, I'm pretty sure I saw a glimpse of jealousy in you." He raised an eyebrow.

She jokingly snarled, "Fine. Maybe I was, but she was all over you despite my warnings. I don't share well with others."

"You had no reason to be jealous. You have nothing to worry about when it comes to me. I'm not going anywhere." He ran his fingers along her chin.

"I know. It's just been a long road to get to this far. I don't want to lose you now. Besides, aside from losing you, it was the fact that she had no respect for either of us. We both told her to back off. She's lucky I held my temper." she pointed out.

"Alice?" He looked at her.

"Yes?"

He took a deep breath. "I love you."

She stopped dancing and looked up at him. "Ryan…"

"No." he interrupted her. "You don't have to say it back. I know yesterday wasn't on purpose, but it got me thinking. I knew I felt this way, but I had refrained from saying anything to you. I just don't want you to leave without being able to tell you."

"Ryan," she started again.

Again, he interrupted her. "I know you haven't settled into anything one way or another yet. Just let me tell you I love you and be happy I got to say it."

"Stop." She shook him slightly. "I love you, too."

He blinked at her. "Don't say it if you're not ready. I didn't say it to get you to say it back to me."

"No. I mean it. I love you, too, Ryan." She leaned up, kissed him and laid her head on his chest.

He closed his eyes and rested his head on hers, pulling her up to him. I wanted to grab her and start squealing like school girls, but it was such a romantic moment. I didn't want to ruin it for her.

She opened her eyes as she swayed past me. I smiled as she smiled back. She closed her eyes again and melted into Ryan's arms. I looked up at Justin. His eyes were soft, and by his look, he heard the exchange, too.

"Awesome," I exclaimed.

"It's about time." He looked over at them and back at me.

I nodded into his chest. "Yes it is."

Another slow song came on next. We all stayed on the dance floor, barely noticing that all but two other couples had left. When the next song came on, a faster dance song. Alice snagged my arm and pulled me into the kitchen. I saw the guys shaking their heads and laughing as I stumbled through the crowd, reaching back for Justin.

"All right. I know you heard that. Say what you want to say and get it over with." She pointed at me as we got away from the crowd.

Emma and Giselle had seen her dragging me through the dining room and followed us, knowing something was up. Emma pried, "This looks like something we might need to hear."

"Alice told Ryan she loves him." I yanked away from her grip.

"Again?" Emma laughed.

"This time, it was from both of them and for real." I stepped back, expecting her to hit me.

"Why don't you just tell everyone?" Alice crossed her arms.

"Ok." I shrugged and started to turn towards the doorway.

"No!" she shouted. "This is why I pulled you in here. I didn't want everyone hearing about it."

"I know, but you know they would have found out, and if anyone else deserved to know, it's them. Oh, and Mary," I explained.

She picked up a glass and filled it with water. "Ok. I see your point, but please don't just go and tell everyone."

I tilted my head. "Do you seriously think that's something I would do?"

She shot me a very accusatory look. "Viv?"

"I mean about something like this." I slapped her shoulder.

"Ok, fair enough," she said.

Emma and Giselle started in on what and how it was said. As she told the story, they both said "oooh" and "aaah" a lot. She actually started smiling when she said the words. I was surprised. She really meant it.

As she finished explaining, I chimed in with "You had me at hello."

They laughed. Emma came back with, "I'd miss you even if we had never met."

"You have bewitched me, body and soul," Alice added.

"No! No! No!" Giselle laughed. "I've crossed oceans of time to find you."

"Ooo... that's good," I complimented. "How about, I'm just a girl, standing in front of a boy, asking him to love her. Or!"

I waved my hands.

"I hate the way you talk to me, and the way you cut your hair. I hate the way you drive my car. I hate it when you stare. I hate your big dumb combat boots, and the way you read my mind. I hate you so much it makes me sick; it even makes me rhyme. I hate it, I hate the way you're always right. I hate it when you lie. I hate it when you make me laugh, even worse when you make me cry. I hate it that you're not around, and the fact that you didn't call. But mostly I hate the way I don't hate you. Not even close, not even a little bit, not even at all," I bowed.

Emma threw her hands up. "That was... grand, but what about, Take love, multiply it by infinity and take it to the depths of forever, and you still have only a glimpse of how I feel for you."

Alice retorted with, "I came here tonight because when you realize you want to spend the rest of your life with somebody, you want the rest of your life to start as soon as possible."

"That's kind of perfect for you, huh?" I said.

She wrinkled her nose at me. "Oh, like you have room to speak."

"Oh, I don't, but I'll shout mine from the rooftops." I sounded snotty.

"Would you really?" I heard Justin from the doorway.

I gasped as everyone laughed. "Why is it that every time we're having a moment, one or both of you guys are always listening in?"

"I guess we're good like that." He took a bow, mocking my earlier one.

"Nice. Thank you." I sneered.

He walked over next to Alice and put an arm around her shoulders. "So, we're curious about this shouting something from the rooftops thing."

"Oh, no you don't." I pointed as I walked away.

They followed me, badgering me about it and taunting me to make a big display. I kept trying to ignore them or come back with a quick and snippy remark. I spotted Ryan in the foyer, chatting with some guests. I thought if I could get over by him, they'd stop.

As I approached, I tried one last snip to brush them off. "At least I can tell people I love you; Alice is too scared to tell her man just how in love she is with him." The music paused for the next song as I said those last sixteen words.

I stopped in my tracks and felt the shock run through my body. I took a deep breath, my eyes grew wide, and I started to turn around slowly. Alice's look was indescribable. I couldn't tell if she was embarrassed, furious or what. She just took off.

Emma, Giselle and I walked into the dining room. We couldn't help but laugh at the scene going on in there. Alice was behind the bar, bent over, rustling with things. She stood up with a bottle of tequila in one hand and a shot glass in the other. We just stood there and watched as she poured herself a shot, slamming the glass down on the bar top after downing it. She looked up at us as she poured another one and quickly downed it, too.

"You all right there, punchie?" I asked, walking slowly to the bar.

"Yup. I am now." She smiled.

"You might want to put that away." I pointed at the bottle. "We don't need another high school graduation incident."

Emma and Giselle looked at each other and back at us with very curious looks.

"I don't believe it was my idea to jump off the roof of the pool house into the pool. That was you, little missy." She pointed at me, shaking her finger as she did another shot. "I just added the trampoline, and if you do remember correctly, you went first."

"Yeah? What was up with you and that kick? Watch a little too much David Lee Roth before going?" I grabbed the bottle from her hands.

"Maybe." She reached for the bottle as I pulled it back. "At least when I did it, I was wearing something under my cap and gown."

"Ok, maybe. But I didn't tell the cops, 'It was all her idea! Take the valedictorian. She's brainwashed us all' while you pointed at me."

At that moment, we realized we had an audience aside from the sisters. Ryan, Justin and some of the guys had walked into the room. I placed the bottle back on the bar and took a step back. "Hey, nobody got hurt, and we did talk our way out of jail," I said, raising my hands in the air. We were laughing so hard we had to lean on the bar so as not to fall on the floor.

They just looked at each other, joining in laughing. Ryan said to Justin, "I have a feeling there are a lot more stories where that came from."

Justin shook his head. "I truly do not know how you two have stayed friends."

I laughed at Justin. "Once again, always there."

"How could I miss this? The more I walk into these conversations, the more I learn about you," he said.

"This is true. We might have thought you both innocent if not for these little insights," Ryan joked.

Alice grabbed the bottle and put it back with the others. "Oh come on, Ryan. Don't make me ask your sisters what you were like when you were eighteen."

"I was a very proper prep school boy," he said with a joking properness to his demeanor.

Even Justin didn't believe it. "Oh, sure," he laughed.

"No, don't believe it," Emma assured us. "He knew how to work the system not to get caught, that's for sure, but innocent? Absolutely not."

We all laughed even more and started sharing stories about things we had gotten into when we were younger. Some had more recent stories. It was not only amusing but entertaining and interesting to hear about some of the things some of the others had done. It was definitely enlightening.

Ryan's apartment was pretty full by eleven, and Alice was glued to Ryan's side. I wasn't surprised by that. It was actually nice to see them so close. This trip was exactly what they needed for them.

I had wandered off with Giselle. We were hanging out in the kitchen, sipping our drinks and munching on the toppings before the food was taken out. It was nice considering that Giselle was a bit of a party drinker, and she kept refilling my glass. So, the food was a good buffer.

I love a good party, but the crowd had grown so much that it was difficult to move, let alone find anyone. It was nice to have some place to stand that wasn't too crowded and with someone that was worth spending any period of time to chat with.

She was telling me how Justin came to be a part of their family and more about him and his family. Ryan and Justin had met on the set of a little known movie when they were twelve. They spent a lot of time hanging out and getting together at the arcades when they weren't on set.

So, after filming stopped, both families made a point to keep in touch. She said Ryan is as much a member of Justin's family as Justin is a part of Ryan's. She said they've all met each other, and she loves them.

I wanted to ask more about what kind of people they were and everything, and she offered a little, but I didn't want to pry. I didn't want to know too much. I just listened as she raved about how funny and warm his mother is and how his sisters are like her and her sister.

She then flipped suddenly to telling me about a guy she'd been flirting with earlier as she spotted him walking through the crowd. She grabbed my hands and asked if I minded if she went to find him for her midnight kiss. I giggled and told her she'd better hurry before she lost him to someone else. She ran off.

It was 11:45, and I was trying to decide if I was going to brave the crowd to find my midnight kiss or just hide where I was when he walked up. "Are you going to hide in here all night or come with me to ring in the New Year?"

"I was just wondering that myself," I admitted.

He walked up and took my hand. "Would you rather stay in here?"

"No. Giselle and I were just talking. She just ran off after some guy." I pointed toward the crowd. "I just didn't know if I'd find you through the mass of people in time. So, I was thinking about just staying put."

"Ah," he said. "Then I solved your dilemma. Let's go." He squeezed my hand.

He led me through the crowd, saying hello to people as we kept moving, over near the bar where Alice, Ryan, Emma and Reggie were standing. They were waiting for us to get there, holding champagne glasses for us.

Alice wrapped her arms around me and laid a huge kiss on my cheek. She held her glass in the air. "To having the best friends and the best families."

We held our glasses up and toasted with her. The countdown began.

We all called out, "Ten! Nine! Eight! Seven! Six! Five! Four! Three! Two! One!"

Justin slid a hand onto the back of my neck and pulled me in. We both fumbled to find the nearby bar top to set our glasses on. Setting the glasses down, our free hands were not free for long, finding a place on the other's back and holding tight.

I don't' know how long we were locked in that embrace, but I heard Emma speak up, "Wow, Reggie, remember when our love was that new?"

Reggie laughed. "I still feel that way for you, love."

I felt a hand on my shoulder and heard Alice say, "And I thought Ryan and I had passion. You need me to call you a cab for you two to head out to Justin's?"

I kept my eyes closed and pulled away from his lips, resting my forehead on them. "Can't a girl get lost in a moment?"

Before Alice could respond, Emma scoffed, "Oh no. Here they come."

We all looked in the direction she was. Giselle was dragging her new man towards us. She looked so excited. She was always a vibrant woman, but she beamed at that moment.

"What?" I asked, "She just met him tonight. I think it's awesome that she's interested in someone."

"Oh, but Giselle gets carried away." Emma shook her head.

Ryan added, "Yup. She'll be in love in no time. He'll be infatuated with her for a while and get bored. She'll be broken-hearted. We'll be picking up the pieces. That's what always happens."

"I don't know. Look at what's happened for us," I shrugged. "Maybe she'll be as fortunate."

"I would love to see that, Vivianne. I just see her pattern, and this is how things usually go," Emma said as Giselle approached.

"Hey guys!" Giselle beamed. "This is Roland."

We exchanged greetings. Emma and Ryan stayed very polite and hid their concern for their sister. He was very well-mannered and seemed genuinely taken by Giselle. He was a painter and owned a small graphics company in Glasgow.

Maybe this isn't like the others that they're talking about. Maybe this one is well suited for her, and she's found someone worth it. Why not? I found Justin at one of Ryan's parties, I thought.

374

We all chatted for a while and talked about the evening. Giselle was firmly attached to Roland's arm. Whenever a friend of hers would walk by, she would smile and point at him in a 'look at what I have' manner. After a few minutes, they excused themselves to go to a different party at a friend of his' house on the other side of town. I told her to be careful and have fun.

The crowd started filtering out after one, which was nice. I was able to walk around and find people. By two, I was starting to get tired. I found Alice, Ryan and Justin sitting on the sofa in the living room.

I walked over and sat down next to Justin and leaned my head on his shoulder. He put his arm around me, and I snuggled into him, pulling my feet up and closing my eyes.

"I take it you're ready to leave?" he asked.

I looked up at him. "I don't want to take you away just to take me back to where I'm staying. You're having fun. I'll call a cab in a few."

"Cab?" Ryan sounded shocked. "You won't need a cab. I am sure any one of us will be happy to take you back. You're also more than welcome to take the couch in the study, as usual."

Justin looked at me seriously. "I guess I took this for granted, and I shouldn't have. I would love it if you would stay with me tonight."

"Are you sure?" I asked. "I mean, I would love to, but I don't want to smother you with being around too much."

He sat me up and turned toward me. "Vivianne, you're going back to Michigan in two days, and I've got to go back to filming next week. I want every moment with you before we can't see each other for a few weeks."

"We'll see each other for the Dean Koontz book signing on January 20th, right?" It dawned on me at that moment just how long away that date felt.

"Yes, but I still want every spare moment I can get with you. So? What do you say?" He worked at convincing me.

I looked over at Alice as she spoke up. "Tiffany doesn't expect us back tonight."

"Then, yes." I grinned and leaned back into him.

He whispered, "Good."

I wanted to explain that I really did want to come over and yet I didn't want to just expect that I could. However, something told me that he knew. He seemed to always know what I was feeling and thinking. I guess that's what happens when you find that someone you click with, perfectly, right?

As we started for the door, Alice asked if we wanted to meet for coffee at the café in the morning. We all figured it would be a good idea since she and I would be spending a lot of that day packing. So, we agreed to meet at ten.

We said our good nights and headed over to his place. He started a fire and then went into the kitchen as I settled onto the couch. A few minutes later, he came back with a couple of bottles of water. He handed one to me as he sat down, putting a leg behind me so I could lay right against his chest.

We sat there like that for a long time, just holding each other. I couldn't say how long, but I can say that I might have been able to stay there like that forever and be happy. It was nice to be with someone and not have to talk... and not have it be an uncomfortable or angry silence.

Finally, he spoke. "Are you happy?"

I sighed. "I was just thinking about that."

"You were thinking about that?" he asked. "And what were you thinking?"

"Well?" I paused, trying to figure out how to put it without going on a long babbling journey into my thoughts.

He chuckled. "Really?"

I sat up and playfully slapped his shoulder. "Smartass. I was trying to figure out how to say what I was thinking."

"Oh." he laughed as he rubbed his shoulder, making a bigger deal of it than it was.

"I was thinking how wonderful it was just sitting here with you and not having to talk. Most people don't have that. If there's silence, it's usually uncomfortable or angry silence. Then again, we seem to be able to talk for hours and not run out of things to say. I just like how we fit together intellectually and physically." I stood up and started pacing. "I guess a lot is running through my head, and mostly you."

"Me?" He sat up and watched me pace.

"Yeah, I love the sound of your voice, your sense of humor and how you get me, how my hands fit in yours just right, how you walk into a room just when you should... or shouldn't." I glanced at him out of the corner of my eye with a slight grin. "Oh, and I love the way it feels to have your arms around me. I just don't want to do anything to mess it up. That's why I didn't want to just assume I could stay with you tonight." I stopped and set my hands on my hips.

He got up and walked over to me. "Vivianne, you would have to do something incredibly horrid to mess things up, and you're always welcome to stay with me any time. Remember that song I played for you Saturday night?"

I started to fidget with the hem of my shirt. "Yeah?"

"That line in the song, 'And I'll try to sleep to keep you in my dreams 'til I can bring you home with me' said it. When you're not with me, I'm thinking of you constantly. I can't wait until I can take you home with me." He reached and took my hands to stop me from fidgeting. "And as far as your list of things about me and us goes? I have one just as long if not longer. I love your smile. I love to hear you say you love me. I love that you can keep up in conversations about things I'm into. I love that you can take care of yourself but let me do the job here and there. And yes, I love the way you feel in my arms, too."

He wrapped his arms around my body and stepped up to me. There it was. I melted, as usual. We spent the rest of the night making love. We started in the living room and moved through the apartment until finally ending up in the bedroom. It was passion like I had never known with him or anyone else.

Around eight, we both collapsed back onto the bed. As exhausted as I was, I was even thirstier. I pulled on one of his button-down shirts, rolled up the sleeves and walked into the living room where we had left our water bottles. He leaned over as I was passing by him on my way back in and pulled me back onto the bed.

"You are incredibly sexy with my shirt on." He smiled.

"You should see me in your pajama pants." I laughed. "I will be confiscating those at some point."

"You think so, do you?" He flipped me into my back and knelt over me.

"You going to stop me?" I taunted him.

"We'll see."

That bantering started a new round of passion. At some point, I wondered how people could ever go through life without this kind of connection. How did we ever stay with anyone we didn't have this with? We were connecting on so many levels. It wasn't just physical or emotional. We were compatible in so many ways, and I was hopelessly in love with him.

We had to pry ourselves apart at 9:30 to get ready to meet Alice and Ryan. As tired as I was, I was still full of energy from just being with him. He had that effect on me, but I knew I would need a nap if I was going to make it through the day once I went back to the apartment to pack.

He went into the bathroom to get ready. Once the door was closed, I started to get dressed. I slid on my leggings and was about to put on my shirt when I changed my mind. I tossed my shirt onto the chair and put his shirt back on.

I walked over to the mirror and looked at how it looked on me. I liked how it hung on my shoulders. Funny how his clothes even complement me, I thought. It was true. It was obviously a man's shirt, but with the leggings, it hung just right to show that I had curves yet didn't cling and didn't billow in the wrong places. I smiled and went back to freshening up to leave.

Alice and Ryan were already there when we walked through the door, sipping their coffees. They had obviously slept and were cleaned up from the night before. Alice shook her head when we walked in. She knew me well enough to know when I looked like I had been up all night, and I was sure I looked like I had been up all night.

We ordered our drinks at the counter. The girls were in rare gossip form since both Ryan and Justin were there. I over heard one girl saying that Ryan had requested they not tell their friends until after we left. I guess she agreed once he offered autographs. So, one of the girls had gone to get magazines for them to sign.

I took my seat next to Alice while Justin was adding the sugar and cream to his coffee. She elbowed me and gave me the 'I know what you've been up to' look. I just smiled back and sipped my hot chocolate.

Alice greeted Justin as he came to the table. "Hello there, stud."

He blushed. "Good morning, Alice."

"So, I take it you both had a good time last night?" Ryan asked.

We looked at each other before Justin replied. "You can say that."

"Well, I am glad. I wanted to ask something before I don't get a chance. This is for both you and Vivianne." He looked at Alice. "I was wondering if you would all stay a few more days."

She shook her head. "I don't know, Ryan."

He reached across the table and took her hand in his. "You have the time off work since you and the kids don't start back to school until next week. We don't go back to filming until next week. I will pay to extend the tickets. I am just not ready for you to go home yet," he pleaded.

"I agree." Justin stepped in. "I'm not ready either. Just stay until Friday, and you'll have all weekend to get settled in back at home."

"There's a lot to do before I go back to work and school. Plus, the kids need to get back on our time zone schedule. We just can't. We need the time to get back on track. I would love to, but we just shouldn't." You could see how much she wanted to, but she made sense.

I didn't know what to say. She did make sense, and I couldn't argue with that. No one said anything for a few moments. We were all trying to come up with an alternative or a more convincing argument one way or the other.

Justin sat straight up. "I've got an idea. What if we go with you?" He looked at Ryan. "That is, if you don't mind us intruding, and you, Ryan, wouldn't mind going to filming from there. Then, instead of having to part tomorrow or Friday, we don't have to leave until Sunday. What do you think?"

"I love the idea." I searched Alice's face for her response.

She raised her eyebrows at Ryan. "What do you think?"

"I love the idea." He squeezed her hand.

"Then I'm ok with it, and I'm sure the kids will love to have you two there. They're not really excited to leave." She smiled.

"Ok then, I'll call today and make arrangement for a hotel," Justin announced.

"Hotel?" Alice asked. "I am pretty sure you both can stay with us if you want to. That is, if you want to." She looked at Ryan.

"That would work for me." Ryan looked at Justin.

Justin looked at me. "I would love to, if you don't mind."

"I would love that." I looked him in the eyes.

"Then it's settled. Now who's going to call for the additional airline tickets?" Alice asked.

"I got it." Justin got up and walked into the bathroom hallway to make the call in silence.

He came back after a few minutes and announced that they had two tickets on our flight for the next day. I couldn't believe how nervous I was. Justin was going to come to our house. That thought brought on a mixture of excitement and embarrassment. I tried to focus on the excitement.

I was a little surprised considering how many times Ryan had been there. So, I knew it wasn't the star status. It had to be what he meant to me. It was going to be on my turf, so to speak, and I wasn't sure I had everything up to par. I knew this by the fact that my line of thinking was suddenly very sports-oriented.

We started to head out about noon after eating a light lunch at the café and the guys signed the magazines for the baristas. They walked us back to our place. We made plans to all go over to Ryan's for an early dinner. His family was leaving on a late train that evening to head back to their homes. Alice and I wanted to make sure to see them before they left, and Ryan reminded us to pack up the boxes that would need to be mailed out and bring them with us.

Alice and I packed up all the extras and the boxes to be shipped in just a couple hours. There was a lot more than we thought. We made sure we had everything we needed for our last night and the flight the next day.

The flight didn't feel as much of a looming sadness as before. Now, we were all excited. The kids were especially ecstatic about them going with us. They loved to have Ryan there, and to be able to show Justin around made it sound that much more fun.

We got over to Ryan's at four. Ryan, Justin, Emma and Giselle all greeted us at the door. The kids started right in, jumping around and asking if it was true if they were coming with us. The guys laughed and confirmed that they were. You could see the bonds between the guys and the kids in that moment. We were just onlookers in the excitement.

Emma and Giselle stepped in to start the hugs with us. It was starting to feel like a last day, and that almost made me cry right then. We were all babbling and starting to tear up when Mary came into the room.

"All right kids, dinner is on the table." She waved us in.

Everyone was there, and we were all chatting more than usual during dinner that evening. I could tell that we were all ready to be back at our own homes, but no one was ready to leave each other. People were making plans to get together in the next few months, contact information was exchanged, and there was talk started about the next year's holiday parties.

We all moved into the living room after dinner for drinks and to hang out longer. Alice and I went out and brought in the boxes for Ryan to have shipped the next day. Since they were going to be on the early flight with us, he was having a good friend of his come to pick them up and take them to the post office.

At eight, Mary started rounding everyone up, with her usual grace and class, to head out to the train station. Their train was leaving at 9:30, and she wanted to make sure they had plenty of time to get there. So, she brought them their coats and gave the kids kisses and hugs. The rest took the cue.

The group all meandered to the front door to say our goodbyes. More hugs were exchanged and tears fell. Emma and Giselle made Alice and I promise to keep in touch any way we could, phone, Internet or snail mail. Something told me that we would have been more than happy to do so even without the forced promise.

Once we were back into the living room, Ryan said, "Considering the flight is so early in the morning, I was thinking we should all maybe stay at the same place. Would you be all right if Justin and I came and stayed with all of you tonight?"

I looked at Alice as she shrugged, "Sure. I don't see a problem with that. Do you, kids?"

The kids cheered at the idea of having the guys stay. Tina took this as a cue to ask Ryan a question, "Um. I was wondering something, Ryan." Her voice was meek.

"Yes, my dear?" Ryan replied.

"Well, are you really going to be around a while? I mean, I know you're going to be traveling and all, but I mean dating my mom." She looked up at him.

Ryan looked over at Alice just as Alice looked at Tina in awe. He took a breath. "Yes. As long as your mom will let me."

I hadn't seen Tina smile that big in a long time. She threw her arms around Ryan. "Good. I like you, and I think you're good for my mom." She looked over at Justin. "And you too, Justin. I am glad you're both around."

No one knew quite what to say; the honesty of a child, and the approval of a daughter. Alice hugged Tina as she stepped away from Ryan. "Well? I'm glad you approve."

Ryan loaded his bags into one of the cars. He locked up as he went through the house and left a note for his cleaning person. He had called her earlier after we made the decision for them to come with us, and she agreed to start this week instead of next. She always took care of his place while he was away for his films.

Alice had taken a moment to look around before she stepped through the door to leave his place for the last time, this trip. We headed out to our apartment. Elizabeth and Victoria had fallen asleep on the couch at Ryan's and stayed asleep for the drive back.

We got the kids changed and into bed and packed up the last of the things we didn't need in the morning. All bags were set by the front door. Justin needed to go back to his place to finish cleaning and packing. He asked if I would come with him so we could let them have some alone time and be alone ourselves for a little while, and of course, I was more than happy to have alone time with him.

He held the door for me as we went in but then went ahead of me to start bringing his things out of the bedroom. He, too, had done most of his packing earlier that day. He gathered the last of his things, keeping out what he would need, as I wandered around.

As I walked through the living room, I felt what Alice must have felt leaving Ryan's that day. Justin and I may have met at Ryan's, but we had spent several moments in that apartment together, intimate moments. It was hard to think that we'd probably never get back to this spot.

As I wandered, I reached out and passed my fingers along the furniture and over the knickknacks. The contrast of the wood and the fabric on the couch ignited the memories of laying with him there. I stopped and looked down the hallway.

I could hear him rustling things around in the bathroom. So, I walked into the bedroom while he wasn't looking and lay on the bed, waiting for him to come in. As he walked in, putting his things in his carry-on, he froze when he saw me.

It took him a moment before he said, "Could you be more beautiful?"

I blushed and looked down at the comforter. "I don't know how to respond to that."

"You don't have to. Just know that you are the most beautiful woman I've ever seen... and the sexiest." He walked over to the bed.

I sat up on my knees in front of where he was standing and put my hands on his chest. "You make me feel like the most beautiful woman in the world."

"Good," is all he replied with in words as he laid me back to show me in his actions.

We made those last few hours very memorable before locking the doors to his apartment and heading back. Part of us was reluctant to leave, but both of us were excited to walk into our future together.

The memories made in London that trip would stay with us forever, and I would never be able to thank Ryan enough for having us out there.

That night, I was surprised how comfortable it was having him there. The kids were just down the hall, and they knew he was staying over. I was sure it would be awkward, but it wasn't. We changed into comfortable clothes to sleep in just in case the kids came in to wake us in the morning before our alarm went off.

I curled up on his chest, and he put his arms around me. He started singing the Blue October song he played for me the first night we made love. I struggled to stay awake, even for a few moments. I wasn't ready for the trip to end, but I drifted off to sleep, very happy.

Chapter Fourteen

On Home Turf

The process of getting ready in the morning and the flight both went relatively smoothly. Since it was such an exciting adventure for us all, the kids were very tired. Despite the departure being mid-afternoon, they slept through the waiting period in the terminal. I was very happy for this, though, considering how tired I was.

Ryan had put the cars in London in long term parking while Justin arranged cars for us back in Michigan. They got one for Tiffany so she could go straight home and get settled in. As sad as it was to part ways, she was ready to get home and have her own things in a familiar atmosphere.

He got two cars for the rest of us so we were not squeezed into a SUV with the luggage. Alice and Ryan took one with her kids, and my kids rode with Justin and me. Alice kept texting me about being happy they were coming with us, and how great it felt to be driving somewhere as a family.

I was pretty sure the conversation was only meant for me, but since I was driving, I had Justin reading them to me and responding for me. Despite the things she'd text me being personal, he would just smile at me and nod; he figured saying something would embarrass her more than me. However, when we got home, Justin knew exactly what to say.

"So, were those meant for Vivianne, or did I do a good enough job answering?" he said, straight-faced.

Her eyes grew big. "What?!"

"I thought you might have wanted me to show her when you were talking about me, but I thought I could field that one ok." He put an arm around her.

"You read those? What were you doing with her phone?" She threw his arm off her shoulder and shot a glare at him.

I stepped in and grinned. "I was driving. Don't you think that would have been unsafe to drive and text?" I asked sarcastically.

"Yeah, she was busy driving, so I took her calls and texts." He just smiled a huge grin as she started walking back towards the car.

Alice slapped his shoulder as she walked past him. He laughed and smiled again. She just glared at me and mumbled something not loud enough for me to hear as she started unloading the luggage. I took him by the hand and headed for the house as we smirked at each other.

We set down the bags in the living room before making the rounds to turn on some lights, check the rooms and turn on the furnace. Once satisfied, we carried the kids in and put them to bed. I was pretty sure they were happy to be in their own beds considering they both cuddled into their blankets and smiled the moment their heads hit the pillow. With that and having Justin helping me put them to bed, I was happy, too.

We joined Alice and Ryan in the living room. All of the children were asleep in their own beds, and we were all talking about getting some dinner and heading to bed early when I looked up at the clock.

I did a mental check of the time; we had left the airport at about 3 p.m., and the flight was about six hours. Why does the clock say 5:56 p.m.?

I checked the math again. It was a six hour flight, and an hour and a half drive to home from the airport and time to unload and get the kids in bed. Then I realized the time difference. I also realized that everyone else was as tired and I was and having the same confusion.

I started laughing. "So, I now understand true jet-lag."

Alice looked at me, completely confused, "What do you mean? Being tired?"

"No, being exhausted from a trip is expected. Being ready for bed because your body thinks it's 11 p.m. is another." Everyone looked at the clock and joined me in laughing.

"Should we get the kids back up?" Ryan asked.

Alice and I chimed in at the same time and sharply said, "No."

I continued, "Let them sleep. If we're lucky, they'll sleep through the night."

"True," he smiled.

We decided to call ahead and order dinner from a local restaurant, and I went out for it. Once full, we sat back, turned on a movie and just relaxed. It was definitely a fun trip, but it was an understatement to say that it was exhausting.

Alice and I flashed each other smiles periodically. Even though we were too tired to be up and around, we both still were very happy to have the guys at our place. I was, especially, considering Justin had never been there before. What made it even better was how comfortable he seemed being there.

When it came time to head into bed, we grabbed our bags and started down the hallway. Suddenly, it dawned on me that I had not cleaned up before leaving. With being too tired to unpack, I hadn't gone into my room to remind myself that I had clothes, shoes and jewelry all over. I suddenly became embarrassed.

I turned towards Justin and pointed at his bag. "Why don't you go into the bathroom and do what you need to get ready for bed. I've got to..." I paused, cleared my throat and smiled. "...make sure everything is presentable. I don't think I cleaned up before leaving for London from packing."

He smiled at me, understanding of my little quirks and kissed my head. "Sure, hon. I'll be over in just a moment."

I whipped through my room putting clothes away, hanging necklaces back in the jewelry armoire and tossing a few items in drawers just so they were not lying out. I was pulling my night shirt on over my head as Justin came through the door. He stopped as he shut the door and looked at me for a moment before speaking.

"I have always loved my life. I have always been blessed in so many aspects. Family, friends, work, hobbies. I never thought something was missing from my life or that I was searching for something." He walked over and sat on the edge on the bed and took my hands in his. "Yet now, I can't imagine how I ever thought my life was complete before you. I am looking forward to knowing what a truly fulfilling and blessed life is like."

He pulled me in for a deep and passionate kiss. I pulled away and just looked at him for a moment. I understood exactly what he meant. I may not have been as blessed as he was, but I have always loved my life. Yet, I felt the same way. I don't know how I ever didn't miss him.

We curled up in bed and just held each other that night. It was a nice wind-down from the fast-paced couple of weeks we just had. I was a breath away from being sound asleep when I felt him tighten his grip, and right before dozing off, I heard him whisper, "You are what I didn't know I needed in my life."

For the first time in a long time, I was not only excited about life again, but I was looking forward to the future.

Chapter Fifteen

Looking Forward

We tried to keep the time we had with the guys at home as tame and relaxing as possible while they were there. We had to deal with a few 'sightings', but Alice, the kids and I were all getting used to that by now. So, it wasn't too terrible for Alice.

We spent a lot of time just hanging out at the house. We watched movies, played cards, finally had some down time to just chat and get to know even more about each other. We also took turns cooking meals. Occasionally, we would venture out for groceries and to show Justin around town.

The kids said goodbye to Ryan and Justin before they headed over to their respective fathers' houses Saturday. I am sure the kids would have loved to have been able to go with us to take the guys to the airport, Sunday, but Alice and I wanted to have our girly moments without the distraction of keeping tabs on the kids. Plus they hadn't seen their fathers in a while. So it was nice for them to go.

Alice and I went together to drop the kids off so we would have a few minutes to chat on the way back. Our exes were their usual oh-so-pleasant selves with Tim as the leader in the 'who can be the biggest dick' contest. Neither of us made any sudden moves so as not to make the situation turn hostile. We kissed the kids and headed out quickly.

On the drive home, Alice turned down the radio and said, "And let the games begin."

"Let what games begin?" I was confused.

"Really?" She pushed my shoulder. "At home? Hot guys? No kids? Do I need to break out the color crayons?"

"Nice." I shook my head. "However, a good point... about the games thing, not the color crayon thing."

"Uh huh," she laughed.

"It does feel right to be going home and knowing they will be there."

"Well? I was more talking about what I, at least, plan on doing when I get there, not that I was being all mushy." She turned the radio back on and started flipping through the stations.

"But it does, though." I hit the power button, turning it back off. "You have to admit it. We've finally got good men."

She cut me off. "Whoa there. They both are great guys, but you're the only one that's in a serious relationship here. I'm just slightly seeing Ryan."

I huffed, "Don't tell me you're reconsidering."

"Not reconsidering. I'm just still really cautious. I don't want to get hurt, and I don't want to hurt him or my kids. There are a lot of factors, and personally, I think I need more time to get settled into everything and see where it goes over time. There's no reason I need to rush into this."

"So, are you saying that you think I'm making a mistake?" I asked.

"No." She paused for a moment. "I think you know what you want much faster than most people, and Justin is a great man and great with your girls. You both just fit together, and I'm glad that you're finally happy. You deserve someone like him."

I went to say something, but she continued, "Yeah, yeah. Ryan is a great man and great with my kids, too. Just give me time. I'm not pulling away, and it does feel great having him at the house to come home to. I just don't rush into things, I do the exact opposite. I take my sweet old time. We will get there."

"What? When you're on your death bed when there's no risk?" I taunted.

"Very funny." She scowled as we pulled in the driveway. She put her hand on my shoulder. "Listen, the first one was a complete jerk. There's no denying that, and he almost killed me, it hurt so bad when things fell apart. Ryan is virtually perfect. Can you imagine what it would do to me if he cheated or just decided that he didn't want me anymore? I don't think I am ready to risk it yet."

"If you let this guy pass you by because you're just afraid of the chance it won't work out, then you might as well bank on staying single the rest of your life."

"I'm not going to let him pass me by. I just need time to brace myself in case it doesn't work out. Just give me time." She got out of the van before I could respond.

We got out of the van, both eager to get inside to the guys. As we approached the door, Alice leered. "Not to change the subject, but... 'Let's Get It On'." She sang that last part as if she was a female Marvin Gaye. I laughed and shoved her through the door, telling Ryan she needed to control his woman.

They laughed as Alice grabbed Ryan by the arm and pulled him down the hallway. I sat down on the couch next to Justin. We talked for quite a while before retiring down the hall ourselves to have one last night together before they had to leave for filming.

After what felt like a very short weekend, come Sunday evening, we were on our way back to the airport. As we loaded into the car to go, we confirmed plans for the next few weeks. Visits, trips and looking forward to seeing each other again. It was going to be hard to be without them for even a day, let alone a week or two.

At the airport, you would have thought our hands were super glued to theirs. I couldn't believe Justin was leaving. It hadn't seemed real up until the point where he had his carry-on in hand and was kissing me goodbye.

"I love you, and I'll see you very soon," he said as he wiped a tear from my cheek.

"I love you, too, and I am going to miss you so much."

He pulled me into his chest and wrapped his arms around me. "I know, and I am going to miss you, too. I'll call you when we land and as often as I can around filming. Things can get pretty hectic, but I will be sure to call and email as much as possible."

"I'll see you in a couple weeks?" I asked.

He kissed my cheek. "If not sooner, my love."

"I love you."

I looked at Alice and Ryan. Alice had her face buried in Ryan's chest. Knowing her, it was her way of being affectionate without letting anyone know that she was fighting back tears. She looked over at me and rolled her eyes.

Ryan placed his hand under her chin and tilted her face up until her eyes met his. She sighed, "Miss me."

"Always," he replied and kissed her, holding her tightly.

Ryan and Justin got into the security line. We watched until we couldn't see them anymore. It was bittersweet when they both turned back to wave. We then watched out the large windows as the plane took off.

Both of us were quietly crying as the plane left the ground. We just walked back to the parking lot. The terminal was fairly full, but I don't think either of us even noticed the other people, nor did we even pay much attention to each other. We walked slowly, stifling quiet sobs and focusing on getting to the car to head home as others whizzed past us in the normal hustle and bustle of an airport terminal.

Alice and I spent the drive home quietly, aside from the occasional sniffle. Finally, almost an hour into the drive, Alice turned to me and said, "I'm scared."

"Scared?" I was confused. "Of what?"

She stared out the window. "The 'R' word."

"You've always been afraid of relationships." I laughed at her reference to relationships as 'the 'R' word'.

She snapped a glare at me. "It's just like you to make fun of me when I actually need you as a friend."

"Alice, you're my best friend." I stifled my laugh. "I love you to death, but there's no reason to be so afraid of this. You know it in your heart that this is right, and you'll go at your pace to make it happen when you're comfortable. He's a great guy. He loves you to death, and he's great for your kids. You just have to work on getting past this thought that he's going to hurt you. Ryan is nothing like the others."

"I know this." She turned back to stare out the window. "I know life is handing us what most women only dream of, but you know me. I don't take gifts confidently. I keep waiting for the catch."

"The catch?" I thought for a moment about that. "I am sure it's just to accept it, treat them well and take care of each other. Just like our friendship."

She punched me in the shoulder. "Seriously? That cheese is your great advice?"

We both laughed.

Nothing about our future was certain except that there was a future, and I for one was looking forward to it. I leaned back into my seat and drove home to wait for the call that they had landed. Even though we were not happy that we wouldn't be able to see them for a while, I was pretty sure that we would have fun in the excitement of each call, each email and the eventual knock on the door.

Dear Reader,

When in Maui came to me in a time of my life when I needed a fantasy. When I needed a completely unattainable love story. When I normally would have curled up in a book or lost myself in a movie. But this story swooped in and carried me away, holding off all other pieces I had been working on and falling out of my brain and onto paper before I even knew what happened... all with the help of my best friends encouraging me and my closest friend giving me bits to feed it along.

I realized that we all go through those times... when we need a fantasy to swallow us up and help us through times we are not sure how we will make it through. And... we will all handle it differently... just as Alice and Vivianne do.

I hope you fell in love with these characters as I did and that it brought some escape when you needed it... or at least made you laugh. Because we all need to laugh no matter where we are in life.

Colleen Nye

About the Author

Colleen Nye was a budding writer at an early age with her love of books and her adoration of jotting down her vast imaginative stories in her journals. This was coupled by her longing to travel and go on adventures.

Through her school days, she won awards for her poetry and short stories including a Sarah Endres Award for Young Writers. She was also published in a few smaller magazines and newspapers. In high school, Colleen started a Poetry Club to be able to share writing styles and projects with her fellow students, which she loved, and drew inspiration from learning the versatility of creative outlooks from others.

As an adult, Colleen branched out and worked as a freelance writer for corporations and non-profit organizations, writing press releases for newspapers, magazines and online blogs and web sites. She also worked with politicians to create campaign and promotional fliers, bios and web site blurbs. Other works she has done have been research and photography for a few Mid-Michigan sites highlighted in the book Paranormal Lansing by Nicole Bray and Robert DuShane. She's also worked with several companies, creating their how-to articles and product descriptions.

Through her years of writing and experiencing different styles of the art, her heart lies in creative writing and sharing the imaginative stories that run through her mind with others. She is a member of a local writers group, Writing at the Ledges. She has been in two of their three self-published anthologies, providing short stories to the compilations of other short stories, essays and poetry.

She now lives in Mid-Michigan with her two daughters, both budding creative thinkers. Together, they share their very different views of the world and inspire each other to see the world through each other's eyes and create many, many fun and imaginative adventures to share.

...and yes, she's working on her next book...
always.

Follow and contact Colleen at:
Email: author.colleennye@gmail.com
Twitter: Colleen_Nye
http://www.writingattheledges.com/members-pages/colleen-nye
Facebook: http://www.facebook.com/pages/Colleen-Nye

When In Maui:
Email: wheninmaui@gmail.com
Facebook: http://www.facebook.com/WhenInMaui